For the first time since he boarded her in Naples, Redding became aware of the scent of *Constitution*, a blend of cotton canvas, oak, Douglas fir, and tar-impregnated hemp rope. It was a penetrating therapeutic aroma with a calming effect that, together with the only sounds he could hear—the creaking of the ship, the churning of the bow wake, and the wind playing an unfamiliar rhapsody on the cordage of her rigging—seemed to transport Redding's spirit to a different dimension in time and space.

He was at peace for the first time since that day in the Gulf. Hours passed like minutes, but the scene remained the same until the figure of a man appeared in front of him, near the main mast. The officer's uniform on the figure was period early-nineteenth century. A dim but glowing corona surrounded the figure. He was turned sideways but appeared to be looking at Redding. The moonlight glinted off a gilt-braided epaulet on his shoulder, and one hand rested on the butt of the sword strapped to his side.

Praise for David Tunno

Finalist in the Adventure Writers and Chanticleer Global Thriller awards.

"Intrepid Spirit is a swashbuckling tale on the high seas that will put saltwater in your veins as the crew of *Constitution* battle international terrorists using only their wits and the canvas sails and black powder guns of the historic warship."

~ Dirk Cussler

"The plot is impressively inventive and briskly paced. The action sequences offer moments of vivid, cinematically explosive violence. A refreshingly original and immersive seagoing thriller."

~ Kirkus Reviews

"Tunno does a terrific job of reflecting the real-life political situation that the US faces in dealing with global terrorism…a thrilling action-adventure at sea that will appeal to anyone who has a taste for action thrillers."

~ Readers Favorite

"Readers will enjoy this story that returns a haunted historic naval vessel to combat. The premise is entertaining, unusual, and high-energy from cover to cover."

~ BookLife Prize

Intrepid Spirit

by

David Tunno

Intrepid Spirit

COPYRIGHT © 2022 by David Tunno
Based on the screenplay, *Constitution*, by David Tunno, copyright © 2006
David Tunno - Water, Wind and Fire, 2019 TXu-156-2

Contact Information: info@thewildrosepress.com

Cover Art by *Kim Mendoza*

The Wild Rose Press, Inc.
PO Box 708
Adams Basin, NY 14410-0708
Visit us at www.thewildrosepress.com

Publishing History
First Edition, 2022
Trade Paperback ISBN 978-1-5092-4290-0
Digital ISBN 978-1-5092-4291-7
Hardback ISBN 978-1-5092-4292-4
Published in the United States of America

Dedication

To all those, past and present, who have served on the front lines to found and protect America.

Prologue

Off the coast of Libya, 1805

The sea boiled off the bow of USS *Constitution* as she cut an angry gash through the waters near Tripoli, eager for her first taste of battle against the enemy she was built to fight, the Barbary Coast pirates.

Lookouts strained for a glimpse of the enemy through breaks in the heavy fog cloaking Tripoli harbor dead ahead. Commodore Edward Preble didn't wait for them to call down from the fighting platforms aloft. "Battle stations!" he ordered. "Run out the guns!"

The boatswain's fife signaled the command, and the pulsating beat of the drummer added an ominous rhythm to the chorus of clamoring boots over the ship's fir decks. Gunports flew open along the ship's oak hull. Once as sleek as a racing yacht, it now bristled with the iron barrels of forty-four heavy guns. Their crews huddled behind them, awaiting orders to hurl their massive ordinance into enemy ships and fortifications. Sharpshooting marines, their muskets slung over their shoulders, climbed the heavy net-like rope shrouds to the fighting platforms on the masts.

Preble assessed the performance of his officers and crew as they prepared for battle and relished the chance to visit destruction on the North African marauders. With their eighteenth-century felucca galleys, powered by both sails and oarsmen, the pirates had enjoyed the profits from unfettered pillaging of small coastal villages in nations surrounding the Mediterranean and as far north as Iceland. The inhabitants they didn't enslave, they murdered. They raided helpless merchant vessels and extracted great wealth, in the form of tribute, not only from European countries, but from an ill-equipped America as well. Now, they were about to encounter a state-of-the-art warship ordered built by President Thomas Jefferson when he had had enough of what he called the "Musselmen."

"Harbor lights five points off starboard bow!" came the call from the lookout above, peering over the blanket of fog that enveloped the ship's hull below.

From his position near the helm, just forward of the mizzenmast, Preble nudged the helmsman and pointed to a new heading to starboard while his second in command, the untested Lieutenant Andrew Blair, issued orders to the junior officers.

The fog had created a hazard for the ship entering the harbor, but Preble used it to advantage. Without it, a surprise attack by the 1,900-ton, 200-foot-long vessel with a mainmast that scraped the sky at over 200 feet would have been impossible. Her oil lamps extinguished and with reduced sail, *Constitution* now cut silently through the fog like a ghost ship.

As the sun peeked over a distant rise, *Constitution* punched through the fogbank into Tripoli harbor and into full view of the enemy. Horns blasted their alarm from the fortifications on a hill on the ship's port side and trumpets on the enemy vessels, anchored in the harbor, stirred their crews to action.

Moments later, the fort batteries fired on

Constitution, nipping at her web of rigging and puncturing her sails, but otherwise causing little damage.

With his hands clasped behind his back and his braided cocked hat and double shoulder epaulets standing out from every other uniform on the ship, Preble calmly approached an ensign in charge of the carronades on the spar deck, the upper or "weather" deck, of *Constitution*. "The fort is the main threat, but it's out of range for your carronades. Get the order to the gun deck to target the shore batteries with the port long guns."

The ensign ran to a companionway staircase and shouted Preble's orders to the long-gun crews below, who elevated the barrels of their guns to target the Libyan fort ramparts where enemy cannon fired on *Constitution* with increasing accuracy.

Sporadic fire from the Libyan fort was answered by a decisive broadside from *Constitution*'s port guns. Twenty-four-pound balls from the long guns reduced the walls of the fort to rubble while the US ship's starboard batteries took aim at the nearest of three enemy ships now underway and closing the distance.

"Steer ten points to port," Preble commanded the helmsman. The captain waited as her starboard guns came into alignment with the oncoming enemy, then called out to his officers, "Fire as your guns bear." One by one, the cannon on both decks unloaded on the felucca, tearing the pirate ship to bits and sending its surviving crew overboard, but the onshore wind that had pushed them into the harbor now was dying, and with it, *Constitution*'s ability to maneuver her guns to bear on the two remaining feluccas.

Unaffected by the fading wind, the rowers on the enemy ships bent their oars as they strained to take advantage of *Constitution's* predicament. The rising sun threw threatening glints of light off the enemy's scimitars waving in the air as they bore down on *Constitution*.

Lt. Blair pointed aloft to *Constitution's* slackening sails and called out to Preble, "We're losing the wind, sir."

Preble drew his cutlass and pointed it at the approaching felucca galleys, now plowing through the floating wreckage of the first enemy victim. "Prepare to be boarded. Helm hard to port."

Confused, Blair replied, "Port, sir? We'll stop moving. We'll be in irons."

Preble's eyes squinted against the rising sun, throwing a warm glow over what was already a battle scene marked by fires and smoke. "The offshore wind is coming, Lieutenant. I'm gambling it gets here in time and the ship has just enough momentum left to bring the starboard guns to bear."

Ensigns and midshipmen repeated Blair's orders throughout the ship. Crewmen dipped into buckets of pistols and drew from a pile of cutlasses brought to the deck. Marines with muskets took up positions on the rails. Sharpshooters on the fighting platforms above drew down on crewmen in the approaching galleys. Crews on the heavy guns prayed for a chance to use them against the approaching enemy, eliminating the need to fight them on their own terms and spill blood on *Constitution's* deck.

Preble gazed aloft. He read the wind in the sails and the remaining speed of the hull. *Constitution's* great weight gave her the needed momentum for another maneuver. "Helmsman, hard aport," he ordered. "Starboard batteries, fire as your guns bear."

Constitution proved surprisingly nimble and would soon show the enemy her starboard side. The enemy galleys' only chance was to get closer—fast—so close that *Constitution*'s guns couldn't tilt low enough to hit their smaller ships. The enemy crews strained harder on their oars, and the effort was paying off. *Constitution* turned into position to fire, but her gun crews couldn't aim low enough to hit the two galleys. Neither could she sail out of harm's way. Her crew could hear cheers ringing out from the Barbary crews. Waving scimitars, they fired their muskets wildly at *Constitution*, exchanging fire with the marksmen aloft and the marines on deck.

The people of the Mediterranean countries know the sirocco wind by many names, but all know its ferocity. Created by the vast Sahara Desert to the south, it makes its presence known across the sea from Portugal and Spain to Greece and beyond—and it is predictable. This was the offshore wind Preble was counting on.

The first gust of hot dry wind slammed into the uppermost of *Constitution*'s sails, filling them and bending the masts until it seemed they would snap. She rolled hard to port, every fiber in her wooden structure and rope rigging filling the air with painful moans from the strain on her masts and hull.

"Starboard batteries, pick your targets," Preble ordered with confidence.

"But, sir—" an ensign responded, seeing the starboard batteries aiming at the sky.

"Patience, Ensign," Preble replied, holding up his hand and looking into the rigging.

The junior officers spread the captain's orders across all the starboard battery groups. The blast of wind disappeared as quickly as it arrived, and *Constitution* responded, rapidly rocking back to starboard. Long-gun crews on the gun deck and carronade crews on the spar deck looked through the gun ports at the two approaching galleys as their guns began tilting down to their targets.

Now at point-blank range, the enemy looked at the muzzles of two dozen huge guns tilting down on them. Some of them froze. The smart ones dove off their boats and into the harbor.

"Fire!" shouted Preble.

The recoil from the full broadside shook *Constitution* and sent a shock wave over the harbor, soon covered in splinters of wood and wreckage barely recognizable as tools of the pirate trade.

"Well done, Mr. Blair," said Preble. "Set a course due north." Then he walked to the bow to shouts from the crew on deck and in the rigging. "Huzzah! Huzzah! Huzzah!"

Preble spotted a young sailor not joining in the revelry, but instead looking into the rigging with a wrinkled brow and shaking his head. Preble approached him. "What is it, sailor?"

The sailor snapped to attention; his smooth cheeks blushed. "I don't know, sir. I can't put it into words. It's just a queer feeling."

"Queer?"

"It seems to me there's just something strange about this ship."

Preble smiled and held the boy's shoulder. "I have also felt it and can't describe it either."

The offshore wind returned as a steady, warm hand urging their departure from Tripoli. *Constitution* obliged, her bow slicing through the calm sea and her stern wake stirring a sea stained red with blood that faded to blue and white.

Chapter One

Lieutenant Moses Redding leaned against the instrument panel on the bridge of *Minerva*, a fast US gunboat. Binoculars hung from his neck, but he didn't use them, nor did he pay attention to the actions of his second in command, Lieutenant Junior Grade Brad Carter. Redding stared out to sea.

"Something on your mind, Skipper?"

Redding awoke from his thoughts. "Yeah, Brad. Our mission and the rules of engagement."

"To protect US shipping, unless I missed something in the briefing with Admiral Towne."

"Uh-huh, but how? Did you ever hear a more convoluted set of engagement instructions?"

"I guess not, but I haven't heard that many to start with. Anyway, I don't think you scored any points with Towne by speaking up about it," Carter added, alternating his attention between the radar screen and the horizon.

"Oh, we're cool. He loves me like a son—a cheating wife's *bastard* son."

The air rushed from Carter's lungs as he held his ribs and tried to catch his breath, but he was laughing so hard all he could manage was to wave off any attempt at a response.

"No, you're right. I'm my own worst enemy when it comes to that—as my record will clearly show. If I'm going anywhere in this man's navy, I need to dog down my mouth. I'm working on it."

Sobered by Redding's comments, Carter stared at him for a moment, then returned his attention to the radar screen.

"Sir, radar contact bearing 280 degrees," Carter said as he pointed in the direction of the contact without taking his eyes off the screen. "A large vessel, probably steel, maybe corvette sized, and a smaller, slower one, fishing vessel size, probably wood."

Redding trained his binoculars in the direction of the bearing. "Wood, due to a low radar signature?"

"Affirmative."

"Are they on the same course?"

"Affirmative."

"Which one is leading?" asked Redding, still scanning the horizon.

"The smaller vessel, but the larger one is closing fast."

"Now, why would a corvette be so interested in a fishing vessel?" Redding said half to himself. "Whose side of the line are they on?"

"Our side," Carter answered, then turned to Redding. "International waters."

"Set an intercept course. Flank speed."

"Steer 280 degrees. Full throttle," Carter ordered the helmsman, who spun the wheel as he watched the compass needle point to 280 degrees. The bow wave of *Minerva* kicked up, and stern water churned as the engines responded to the wide-open throttles.

"Battle stations, Mr. Carter," commanded Redding,

peering dead ahead through his binoculars.

Alarmed, Carter turned to Redding. "Sir?" he asked, raising his brow, but Redding only locked his eyes on him until he went into action.

Over the loudspeakers on deck came the order from Carter. "All hands—battle stations!"

Wide-eyed crewmen shot surprised looks at one another and to the bridge as they scurried to the gun lockers for small arms and helmets. Gunners on the .50-caliber machine guns port and starboard pulled off the covers, fed the belt ammunition, and chambered the first rounds. The crewman on the 25 mm Mark 38 chain gun cannon mounted on the foredeck turned on its multi-function display and checked the action of the mount, swiveling the gun side to side.

Seaman Jimmy Bauer gripped the handles on his .50 caliber and turned to Chief Petty Officer Virgil Jeffries.

"Relax, kid," came the reassuring voice from Jeffries. "You know how the skipper likes to hear these things go off. I've seen it before. Some guys just like the smell of cordite. Probably another drill."

"Yeah, sure, Chief. No big deal," Bauer responded as he loosened his grip and turned away from Jeffries.

Carter pointed to the horizon and called to Redding. "There they are, sir!"

"I see them, Brad," Redding responded. "What do you see on the deck of that old boat?"

Carter peered through his binoculars. "It's a crowd, sir, and they're not fishing."

"Right. Could be refugees. We'll know soon enough." Redding aimed his binoculars at the trailing corvette and focused on her ensign. "The corvette is

Iranian. They're at battle stations!" He pulled down his binoculars and addressed a nervous Carter: "Get Fleet Command on the emergency frequency."

Redding refocused his lenses for a sharper image. "The people on the small boat are waving at us. Looks like they want our attention."

Carter looked at the Iranian corvette, then at Redding. "Captain, you do understand they have the greater firepower."

"I know. Get the chain gun to target their main battery."

Carter hesitated.

"Just in case!" Redding continued, impatiently.

"Right," Carter responded, nodding rapidly, then opened his mic. "Chain gun, target the main battery."

The gunner on the 25 mm cannon swiveled the weapon into position and trained its sights on the heavy gun mounted on the foredeck of the corvette.

Aboard the wooden vessel, a man pulled a large red, white, and blue cloth from inside his jacket. He and another unfolded it, and the crowd yelled, waved at the crew of *Minerva*, and pointed to the American flag stretched out on the lifelines.

Redding lowered his binoculars. "Nice people. Reduce speed to—"

Automatic weapons fire from the corvette at long range raked the water in front of the bow of the wooden vessel.

"What the hell?" Carter gasped, let go of his binoculars, and turned to Redding.

Redding grabbed the radio microphone. "Iranian vessel, this is US Navy ship *Minerva*. Cease fire and alter course. You are in international waters."

Redding pointed to Carter. Carter looked at the radar screen and gave him a thumbs-up.

The speakers on the bridge crackled with the incoming message. *"US Navy ship, we are in Iranian waters and intercepting terrorist vessel en route to Saudi Arabia. Go back, American captain."*

"Negative, Iranian vessel!" Redding shouted into the microphone while he looked through his binoculars. "You are in international waters! Cease fire!"

"I've got Fleet on the radio, sir," Carter said, sweat now streaming from his forehead. "Admiral Towne is on the speaker. Your mic is hot."

Over the speakers on the bridge came the bulldog voice of Admiral Towne. *"Lieutenant Redding, this is Admiral Towne. I'm hearing your communications. What is your status? Are you under fire?"*

"Negative, sir," Redding shouted into the mic over the engine noise of the *Minerva*, never taking his eyes off the scene on the water. "An Iranian warship is threatening a boatload of what appear to be refugees. Sir, they'll be wiped out! Permission to intervene!"

"I heard the Iranians. Do not engage!" bellowed Towne. *"I repeat, do not engage!"*

The Iranian corvette closed the gap on the wooden vessel, which rolled with the weight of the human cargo clinging to the life lines encircling its deck. The corvette fired a second burst across its bow. Redding focused his binoculars on the fishing boat. Passengers screamed, waved at him, and pointed to the corvette. He took up the mic again. "Sir, you're not seeing what I'm seeing! If I don't act now—"

Admiral Towne cut him off. *"You have my orders, Redding! Towne out!"*

Carter and the helmsman looked to Redding.

"Damn!" Redding shouted as he clenched his fist hard around the microphone.

Carter pleaded, "Sir, we can't just let—"

"You heard the orders as well as I did!" yelled Redding. He cursed under his breath. "Secure from battle stations."

Redding focused his binoculars again on the wooden vessel just when the Iranian corvette opened up on it with light and heavy automatic weapons fire. The carnage was instantaneous. Rounds ripped through the boat and people alike. The riddled bodies of the men holding the American flag reached out to the *Minerva* before they went limp and fell into the sea, taking the flag with them. Then the small boat burst into flames.

The blood rushed to Redding's eyes as he exploded, "Shit! Belay that order! Open fire!"

In what seemed like a millisecond, the *thump, thump, thump* of *Minerva*'s 25 mm cannon blew the corvette's deck cannon off its mount and proceeded to rake the ship's superstructure. Simultaneously, it was joined by the faster-firing .50 calibers and the small-arms fire from her crew targeting gun positions on the Iranian ship fore and aft.

Almost immediately, the corvette returned fire, ripping through the glass of *Minerva*'s bridge and sending a rain of shrapnel throughout the cockpit, striking down the helmsman.

"Carter!" Redding yelled, pulling the injured helmsman to the floor. "Take the wheel and get a medic to the bridge!"

Every gun on *Minerva* zeroed in on the Iranian corvette. The cannon found the range, ripping across the superstructure, sending steel and men into the air. Its exploding rounds set fire to the ship. The preemptive strike on the corvette knocked out most of their heavy firepower. The remaining fire from the enemy ship withered to a halt as the penetrating rounds from Minerva's cannon exploded ammunition on the enemy vessel, nearly cutting it in half.

"Oops," said Chief Jeffries with a twisted smile in Redding's direction, prompting a disapproving glare in return.

Redding ran out onto the foredeck and called to CPO Jeffries, "Cease fire!"

Jeffries repeated it across Minerva's deck. The words still hung in the air when a massive explosion from the superstructure of the corvette that had yet to sink sent a shock wave that rocked Minerva and broke the burning wooden vessel into pieces, scattering smoldering wreckage on the surface as the remnants of the hull began to sink beneath the waves. All aboard Minerva grabbed onto their fixed weapons or railings to keep from being tossed overboard.

Jimmy Bauer, breathing heavily, drenched with sweat, and still shaking as he secured his weapon, leaned over to Jeffries. "Some drill."

Carter came down from the bridge to the foredeck, staring at the flaming debris of the refugee vessel on the water. Redding redirected Carter's attention. "Get the wounded below," he ordered. He scanned the scene of the wooden boat, now a flaming coffin, cremating all aboard, the dead and the still living. A motion on the water caught his eye, and he raised his binoculars for a closer look. An arm rose from a prone figure precariously gripping a piece of wreckage.

Redding threw off his binoculars, ran the length of the foredeck, and dove over the lifelines into the sea. Swimming under a slick of burning oil, he reached the wreckage; a portion of the curved transom of the vessel was barely afloat. A woman, bloodied, burned, and with her lower body submerged, clung to it with one arm. Her other arm held an infant on top of the wooden structure. Blood streamed from Redding's forehead as he held on to the wreckage with one hand and motioned to *Minerva*. The woman raised her head from the surface of the transom and pushed the child into Redding's chest. He struggled to hold the child out of the water with one free arm. The transom rocked. The motion released a bubble of air from beneath the wreckage. The woman slid off and looked straight at Redding as she descended to her death below the waves.

Redding treaded water with one free arm and held the crying child above the chop with the other as a Zodiac inflatable boat from *Minerva* sped toward him, zigzagging around patches of flaming fuel and wreckage.

The Zodiac reversed its engine as it neared Redding. He lifted the infant into Chief Jeffries' arms. Crewmen helped the exhausted Redding over the inflated outer hull and into the boat.

Back aboard *Minerva*, Redding took the screaming child from Jeffries. It calmed as he rocked it in his arms while he stared back at the flaming debris field. A cloud of black smoke curled high into the clear skies of the gulf and marked the watery graves of the refugees. He motioned to Seaman Bauer to approach and handed him the infant. Redding was solemn and still glassy eyed from the crisis. "Get the medic to check this child out for injuries and shock, and see if the cook has any ideas about what and how to feed it."

Redding toured the deck of *Minerva*, supporting his exhausted body by grabbing whatever was within reach. Carter supervised seamen patching up a half-dozen wounded men. No wounds were so great they couldn't wait for professional care when they returned to port. The helmsman struck by the opening volley from the corvette was the lone fatality. Redding returned to the cockpit and stood by as seamen put the dead man in a body bag.

Carter entered the cockpit and turned Redding's shoulders so he could see his face.

"Sir, you've got a shrapnel wound. Your forehead."

Redding dabbed the wound with his sleeve, smearing blood across his cheek. "Set a course for port, Mr. Carter," said Redding, gazing for a last time at the empty patch of sea that was the burial site for the refugees.

Carter checked his navigation screen, directing his attention to the seaman who had assumed the helm. "Helm, your course is 252 degrees, ahead full." The helmsman spun the wheel and opened the throttles.

Redding's eyes stayed fixed on the site where the refugee boat sank as *Minerva* sped away.

Carter approached him, keeping his voice low. "My report will back you up, Skipper, but I don't envy you the meeting you're going to have."

"Thank you, Mr. Carter, but that's my problem." He paused, held Carter's shoulder, and looked him straight in his eyes. "Careful how far you stick your neck out for me. I've learned the truth won't always set you free."

Redding turned his focus to the horizon and his mind to the unknown destination. Would it be just a way point on a long voyage, or his final port of call?

Chapter Two

The white letters on the black-faced desk sign read US Naval Forces Central Command—Vice Admiral Chester Towne. The American flag and obligatory photos of the president and the secretary of the navy adorned the wall behind Towne's desk. Next to a black and white photo of himself as a linebacker for a much earlier edition of the Naval Academy's Midshipmen football team was a photo of the USS *Missouri*—the Mighty Mo—during her appearance in Operation Desert Storm, the last time a battleship of any nation saw active duty, an appropriate distinction for the ship that hosted the signing of documents ending World War II.

Towne's black complexion and leathered skin, the effect of many years at sea in tropical regions, contrasted with his dress-white uniform and gave the impression that his image would be more appropriately adorned by salt-stiffened sweaty khakis. He was a man of few words—most of them loud. His once-athletic physique, now a memory as retired as *Missouri* herself, filled his swivel armchair. Disorderly mounds of paper covered his desk. Dirty windows looked out over a base that included a harbor for navy vessels and an airstrip for navy F-18 Hornets, SEAL Team Black Hawk helicopters, and Marine Corps Harrier fighter jets.

The admiral brushed away ashes from the stub of a

thick cigar as they fell on his lap, staining his white trousers and the pages of Redding's file, open before him. As he read it, his forehead alternated between a furrowed frown of disapproval and a raised brow of admiration. He was in no hurry to meet Redding or for Redding to meet his fate; he wondered what he would have done that day at sea, facing down the Iranians. Over the radio, Redding had said that Towne wasn't seeing what Redding was seeing. He couldn't forget those words or the tone in which they were spoken.

The roar of an F-18 taking off interrupted his concentration. He stood and walked to the window. Redding's file didn't show him anything that would lead him to believe his story wasn't true—nothing to indicate he would have taken such an action without just cause. He viewed the transgressions in Redding's file as being of a nature consistent with a superior officer taking exception to Redding disagreeing with an order, but not outright disobedience. Such reports were always one-sided explanations from the commanders themselves, sometimes without an entry from the accused. Such was the case with Redding's file; there was never a comment from him in his defense.

That was curious. Towne had been in the navy all of his adult life and was pretty good at reading between the lines in personnel files. He had also witnessed superior officers using criticism of their subordinates to cover their own mistakes.

Redding was smart, no question about it. Could it be he was just too smart at the wrong times and under the wrong commanders? On paper, Redding reminded Towne of himself, many years ago—before he got wise, as he put it, to the need to toe the line if he wanted a navy career. Now, with orders from his own superior officers and one year from retirement, he wasn't about to go to bat for a case he didn't have the facts to make. He would carry out the orders from those who also hadn't seen what Redding saw and were basing their decisions on knowledge and positions even more remote than his—positions that had more to do with politics than judgment of a commander at sea. He would put this episode, and his feelings about it, behind him. Before he called for Redding, he would get into character and be ready to act the part.

****

Redding sat expressionless in an uncomfortable straight-backed wooden chair in a pale-institutional-green anteroom at the navy base in Manama, Bahrain, headquarters for NAVCENT. Nothing broke the silence but grumbles, like distant thunder, of Admiral Towne clearing his throat in the adjacent office, the occasional takeoff thrust from the engines of an F-18, and the clicking of a computer keyboard on the neatly arrayed gray steel desk of the admiral's aide, Seaman Ben Holcomb. Holcomb wore a headset dwarfed by his outsized ears. He squinted through the thick lenses of his horn-rimmed glasses at the screen in front of him.

The long wait had given Redding too much time to think. From a young age, he had considered nothing but a navy career. It struck him that the morgue-like surroundings he found himself in would be an appropriate setting for it to end.

On his trip to NAVCENT, he had already racked his memory of superior officers under whom he had served, searching for a voice that might intervene on his behalf. But there weren't many advocates from their ranks, nor, for that matter, was it his habit to ask for favors—or leniency. He had always taken his medicine stoically, but then it had never yet been medicine for a diagnosis this severe.

A buzzer sounding on the desk jolted Holcomb and roused Redding from his thoughts.

"Sir?" Holcomb replied into his headset mic while pressing a button. Then to Redding, "The admiral will see you now."

Redding rose, straightened his uniform, and looked at Holcomb for any read he could get on the mood at the other end of the intercom.

Holcomb avoided eye contact. Redding took that as an answer.

Entering the admiral's office, Redding's height put his face at smog altitude. A thick layer of cigar smoke hung in the air with no escape. From the multiple chewed butts in an ashtray made from the base of a brass casing from a five-inch deck gun, Redding could tell the smoke in the air hadn't come from just the one cigar jutting from the side of Towne's mouth as he glared at newspapers on his desk.

Redding fidgeted while watching Towne stew. Then he tried to break the uncomfortable silence. "Sir, I—"

"Stand at attention," growled the admiral without a glance in Redding's direction.

Towne set the newspapers aside, picked up an inch-thick file folder, and pretended to judge its weight with his hand. "I've been doing a little light reading lately." He showed Redding the file cover with Redding's name on it, then set it on his desk, opened it, and picked up the first few pages. "These are from the

Naval Academy. Reading between the lines, it tells me a lot." He flipped through some of the pages. "Scholastically nothing to crow about—particularly your marks in political science. No shit. Good in athletics, particularly combat-related stuff, like fencing." He looked up at Redding. "Not much call for that these days." He returned his gaze to the pages. "Excellent in strategic thinking. Good in history, as long as it was ancient naval history—John Paul Jones, Admiral Farragut, 'damn the torpedoes, full speed ahead' type stuff. Captain Oliver Perry, can't forget about him. No, I'm getting that you were something of an anachronism at the Academy—and you still are.

"So now, let's have a seminar about current events and your favorite subject, political science. You may have been a little out of touch recently," Towne said in a low, emotionless voice, "so let me catch you up. The vice president's peace conference is about two weeks away—the peace conference you put in jeopardy." His lower jaw jutted forward, and the furrows in his brow grew deeper. "Do you have any idea what a big deal that is? Do you have a clue how long it took to get the Iranians to the table? Have a look."

Redding relaxed his posture only slightly, prompting a bullet glare from Towne, stiffening Redding back to attention.

Towne clicked a remote control aimed at a TV/VCR set up on a credenza. A video flickered to life showing a dark-eyed middle-aged man with a pock-marked complexion in a uniform adorned with more medals and fruit salad than Audie Murphy. The chyron text at the bottom of the screen read *Colonel Hakeem Farzad, Iranian Deputy Minister of Foreign Affairs*, a nonmilitary administrative role. Farzad spoke in English from a podium with an Iranian flag at his side.

"*In a good faith effort in support of the cooperative relationship that was to be the subject of our diplomatic initiative with the West—*" Farzad was terse and reading from a teleprompter. "*Our brave seamen were engaging a terrorist force within Iranian waters and were attacked by US Navy forces.*" Pausing for dramatic effect, he locked his eyes on the camera lens. "*We do not export terrorism. Those forces were on their way to infiltrate Saudi Arabia.*" Farzad turned up the intensity in his voice, and his gestures became more animated. "*To cover itself, and to further its design to create tensions between Iran and our neighbors, the US Navy vessel destroyed our patrol boat, killing all the witnesses to its crime.*" He held up an eight-by-ten of Redding's Annapolis graduation picture.

Redding's jaw dropped, then clenched as his eyes bored in on the image of Farzad with his photo.

Farzad continued. "*From interceptions of radio transmissions during the battle, we were able to learn the identity of the US pirate.*" He shook the photo at the camera. "*This is the real face of terrorism in this region: Lieutenant Moses Redding.*" Now holding up a picture of Admiral Towne, and with a much calmer voice, he added, "*We have not forgotten you, Admiral Chester Towne.*"

Redding's eyes went to the ceiling as Towne fired a furious look his way.

Farzad's voice rang out: "*Your commands to Lieutenant Redding don't fool us, Admiral. We know he was acting under your orders, and you, for that matter, under orders from the highest levels of your corrupt government."*

Farzad wound himself up for the big finale. *"All the nations of our people, we, the people of the religion of peace, can only interpret this act as a true indication of what we should expect from the US in the future: subterfuge and ulterior motives. Under those conditions, peace talks are impossible."*

Towne clicked off the video.

"Sir—"

Redding's attempt at an explanation produced a broadside from Towne.

"Stow it! Jesus jumping Christ!" Towne unexpectedly rose up and paced back and forth in front of Redding, chomping his cigar. Inches shorter than Redding, the top of his head just brushed the bottom of the layer of pollution. Then Towne pulled a binder from a bookshelf, leafed through pages of ship profiles, stopped at one, and showed it to Redding.

"Is this the type of vessel you encountered?"

Redding looked at the black profile of an Iranian corvette. "Yes, sir."

"Then you were outgunned, which means the only way you could have tilted the odds in your favor was to surprise them by firing first and decisively."

Redding set his jaw. "Yes, sir. I'm sure the Iranians *were* surprised that a US Navy warship would actually fire first—or *ever.*"

"Watch it, Lieutenant! Don't act like a guy walking a tightrope over Niagara Falls while downing a fifth of bourbon."

"No, sir," Redding replied, regretting the violation of his self-admonition to dog down his mouth.

"Who must have fired first is a fact not lost on the

Iranian navy, nor the navies of any of the participants in the peace talks. But, in one sense, you lucked out. That baby girl you rescued—"

"Girl?"

"Yeah, it's a girl." He pointed to the TV. "They don't know about her, and her very existence puts the lie to that jerk's 'terrorist' claim. You saved her, and she saved you."

Redding shrugged. "Then why—"

"Because while internally that works for you, the Iranians can simply say we're lying about her to cover our—your ass. It's not as if a video exists of the incident. The only recorded evidence is the radio transmissions."

Redding looked hopelessly at the ceiling.

"Has it occurred to you why, after all these years, you're still stuck at lieutenant grade? Has it occurred to you that you yourself might have something to do with that? Christ, when trouble comes looking, it doesn't seem to have a hard time finding you. You are some kind of magnet for this crap. You mine your own waters, then set a course straight through them."

"Sir, I take full responsibility—"

"*Negative!* You're under *my* command, and you are *my* responsibility! Let me draw you a picture." He leaned over the desk. His dark eyes bored in on Redding's. "I've got the State Department so far up my ass they're chewing my tonsils, and there's enough Pentagon brass up there with them to make a chandelier." Towne resumed pacing. "That's a lot of souls I'm unaccustomed to entertaining in that manner. The eyes of the entire world are watching what's happening in this part of the world—meaning *my* part of the world, if you get my drift."

Redding caught himself considering a response but bit his lip in restraint.

Towne pointed to the TV. "This character Farzad popped up out of nowhere. All we know about him is that he was placed in a high position in Iran by their president. Some buddy of his or something. Apparently, Farzad helped save his ass during the Arab Spring uprising and was instrumental in putting down the revolt. They made him a colonel and decorated him up. They do that kind of thing there. The State Department and the CIA are trying to learn more about this guy. He's something of a mystery to them and us—but *you* aren't."

Redding took a deep breath and twisted the stiffness out of his neck. "Sir, permission to speak freely."

Towne stared at Redding. "Why not?" Then he sat down and leaned back in his chair. "Go ahead and hang yourself."

Redding resigned himself to going down fighting. "Sir, I was about to say that I take full responsibility *for not acting sooner*!"

"You forget yourself, Lieutenant!" Towne said as he leaned forward and pointed at Redding. Then he paused and sat down. The tension seemed to drain from Towne. He swiveled in his chair and looked out the window. "At ease. Sit down."

Redding hesitated, then settled into a chair.

Towne rubbed his forehead with his hand. "The reality is this: Whether the Iranians are lying or not doesn't matter. Whether those poor bastards were refugees or not doesn't matter."

Redding shifted in his chair, looked at the ceiling, and bit his lip.

"Hell, if terrorists were sent to Saudi Arabia," Towne continued, "it would be Iran who sent them there. Your AIS system will prove where you were. That matters to you, and it matters to me. But *we* don't matter. We are dealing with a situation where the truth doesn't matter, with a people, an enemy, who don't give a damn about it. They'll just say we're lying and the physical evidence that we aren't is at the bottom of the Persian Gulf. And don't forget, the Saudis heard those transmissions too. They heard terrorists were on their way to their shores. Maybe we convince them otherwise, maybe we don't. In this part of the world, the only thing you can count on is chaos. No one trusts anyone, and allies one day are enemies the next. Welcome to *my* world."

Towne stared out the window. "Unfortunately, that goes for a lot of Americans. It's ugly, but there's a lot of anti-American sentiment within the States. To them, America can do no right, and they're just looking for a reason to point fingers. That includes many in the media. In Russia, China, and Cuba, you get thrown into prison for those kinds of lies, but we have to live with it," he added with disgust.

"Naturally, election-year politicians, not all of whom think before they speak, are getting into the act. Anything they can use as ammunition against the current administration they use, and all this right before these critical peace talks." The admiral crushed out his cigar. "Now, if that's not enough, there's a lot of people in the media and the general public that see you as a hero and they don't even know about the kid."

"How could they not—"

"Because the navy is keeping it under wraps. The State Department is in a tough spot, because if they expect to get anywhere, they have to play nice with those Iranian bastards. They don't want to get into a fight about who did what. They need to get that incident off the front page and keep the peace talks on track. To do that, they'll eat shit if they have to and they'll throw you under a bus if they have to. Now you know why bureaucrats and diplomats are *not* my favorite life forms."

Redding stared blankly at the photo of the *Missouri* over Towne's shoulder.

Towne positioned himself in Redding's view. "You think you've got it rough? The brass knows about the kid, of course, but doesn't know whether to go to bat for you or not. They look at the balance sheet. They're in a tough spot. The timing is such that we can't buck the State Department. Speaking of which, the buck has been passed to me to deal with you."

Redding braced himself.

Towne pulled out a large envelope from a desk drawer. "Before I get to this, I thought you'd like to know that little girl you saved is okay. She's at the base hospital, but the chief of staff there says she's fine. He said the nurses are crazy about her, and they hate having to turn her over to some outside authority in a few weeks. Don't know who that's going to be, probably the Saudis. The hospital staff is faking her medical condition for now, just to buy time."

"Thank you, sir."

Towne opened the envelope and pulled a one-page document. "Your new orders," he said through a thin smile.

"Like most commanders, you all want a bigger ship. Well, here it is."

Redding squinted and cocked his head to the side.

"Your new crew is about five times bigger than your last command." He paused and looked at Redding. "The hull is two feet thick at the waterline. Yeah, they don't build them like that anymore. She's one of our older models so she's a little slow, only about thirteen knots flat out."

What? Redding mouthed.

"But she packs a hell of a punch—forty-four of the heaviest guns in this man's navy, and they've all been fired in anger. Yes sir, you're getting a real proud, distinguished war veteran." Towne looked wistfully at the papers in front of him. "If I were only younger..." He handed the envelope to Redding. "Navy regs require commanders in this position, so congratulations on the promotion."

Redding stood, took the envelope, took a step back, and was about to salute, when Towne showed him the palm of his hand.

"Oh, there is one last order, *Commander* Redding. Everything you heard in here today and everything that happened on the Gulf is classified, off limits for discussion. Your XO, Carter, and the rest of the crew have been given the same orders."

Redding glared at Towne and clenched his jaw, then managed an unenthusiastic salute and made for the door. When he opened it, Holcomb nearly fell into Towne's office.

With Redding gone, Holcomb asked, "Admiral, sir, did I hear he's getting a warship?"

"Relax. Even Moses Redding can't cause me any more trouble where's he's going."

****

Hours later, at the base officer's club, several empty beer bottles and the unopened envelope adorned the bar in front of Redding. How many bottles could be accounted for by his visit to the infant girl in the base hospital and how many by his meeting with Admiral Towne, he didn't know.

Hanging from the walls of the club were photos and paintings of navy ships, new and old, likewise of famous naval commanders, including Chester Nimitz and William Halsey. Models of ships lined shelves, and navy aircraft hung on fishing line from the ceiling. Redding stared at the photo of Halsey and remembered from his academy class the monumental mistake Halsey had made during the battle of Leyte Gulf during World War II, chasing off after a decoy Japanese task force and leaving the landing force on Leyte defended by a much smaller force against two enemy battle fleets bearing down on them. Redding considered that was a much bigger screwup than anything he had done—yet Halsey was forever enshrined as one of the great heroes of the war.

Laughter erupted from a table in the club where three young male officers vied for the attention of a very attractive female ensign. She didn't appear to mind. Redding sat down at the end of the bar, as far from them as possible, but their gaiety occasionally pulled his attention away from himself and his now empty bottle.

With a noticeable wobble, he motioned to the enlisted man tending the bar. "Another one."

"Sorry, sir, I have to cut you off," the bartender responded politely.

Redding glared at him for a moment, then waved him off. He scanned the row of beer bottles in front of him for one that might contain one last swallow. Finding none, he stared at the envelope, then looked at the bartender, who was cleaning a glass but glancing at Redding out of the corner of his eye.

"What the hell," Redding said through a sigh. He grabbed the envelope and ripped it open. "All right, Admiral, I know you were playing with me."

He took a deep breath and began reading. His eyes widened as he worked his way down the page.

"Admiral, you son of a *bitch*!"

Chapter Three

Off the coast of southern Italy, the bow of USS *Constitution* sliced easily through the calm waters of the Mediterranean, past the Isle of Capri, where white stucco buildings clung to steep shoreline hillsides above the beautiful, clear, blue-green waters of the Amalfi Coast. Smoke hung over the summit of Mount Vesuvius as a reminder of its past and inevitable future. Off the starboard bow was the Port of Naples, waiting to provide respite for a voyage that didn't require it.

As with the entire crew, Seaman Charles Tebic's modern navy uniform was packed away. The full-time uniform for *Constitution*'s crew was the circa 1800s design: a blue jacket and cap, white waistcoat, and knee-length white trousers over long white stockings. Tebic sat on a wooden stool in a makeshift radio room, ignoring a partially disassembled radio next to him in favor of gaming on his smartphone.

Whereas a modern warship requires a full-time communications technician on all watches, *Constitution*'s needs were relatively simple, not unlike a large pleasure yacht. While Tebic liked to think of himself as the ship's communications specialist, in reality his primary duty was as the ship's cook, one assigned to him when it was learned he had worked through his teen years as an assistant in his father's southern barbecue catering business, Tebic's

Tantalizing Tri-Tips.

But cooking wasn't for Tebic. As the kid in high school who lived in the AV closet, he was the go-to guy for all things high tech, the only power position available to a diminutive bespectacled geek. He took full advantage of it—until an acrid smoke cloud emanating from the physics lab caused the fire department to show up and evacuate the school.

With the ship close enough to Naples for Tebic's smartphone to receive a signal, a tone signaled a waiting text. As with most of his fellow millennials, being out of touch, or even feeling as though he was out of touch for a brief period of time, generated anxiety and withdrawal symptoms. Tebic eagerly opened the new text message from Seaman Holcomb.

—*Met your new captain: Moses Redding. That's right, Moses! He's going to lead you to the promised land. LOL! Admiral chewed him a new one. Have fun on that pile of firewood you call a ship.*—

"Holcomb, that dweeb," Tebic muttered as he pounded out his reply, grinning with delight.

—*At least I'm ON a ship, you geek.*—

Then it struck him that what the crew had assumed about the change in command of *Constitution* was wrong. "Who's Redding?" he said to himself.

His smartphone announced the arrival of another text. He and Holcomb had been through basic together and being two of a kind—an odd kind—had found it helpful to form a protective alliance against the jocks that more commonly populated their ranks. But they didn't let the bond interfere with a war of words, lame though it was.

—*Look who's talking. Winner of the Geek Douche*

of the Universe contest.—

"That asshole," Tebic muttered as he left to spread the news of the new captain and to dream up an appropriate retort to Holcomb.

After preparing meals for the crew, Tebic was used to eating his own meal cold, a sacrifice he remembered hearing about from his mother on countless occasions. He entered the mess room where most of the crew were nearly finished with lunch, still thumbing his smartphone, but he wasn't expecting another message from Holcomb. In their battle, victory was achieved by getting in the last word, and he was not yet willing to concede defeat.

In her war years, *Constitution* had carried a complement of over four hundred sailors and marines. On this tour, sailing duties were light, and the marines were there mostly for show. Tebic and a helper had to prepare chow for less than a hundred.

The crewmen ate in shifts, sitting at hanging tables, taking precautions not to spill soup on their period uniforms. The dark blue blouses weren't so bad, but the white shirts and trousers were a bitch to clean, and any sloppiness created more than just embarrassment with the tourists and dignitaries who toured the ship. It was one of the few issues that the officers could find to enforce discipline on the oldest commissioned warship in the world—seen now as more museum than ship. For that reason, the crew complained whenever Tebic served soup, especially tomato soup, but soup was the easiest and fastest meal for him to make for a large group, giving him more time in front of an LCD screen.

****

Museum or not, the Boston Naval Shipyard had

done a remarkable job with *Constitution*'s recent refit, some twenty years after her previous overhaul. The work was done in the same dry dock originally built in 1833, just in time for *Constitution* to be its first customer.

It had taken a forest of oak to build her at the turn of the nineteenth century, and many more American oak trees gave their lives to replace her planking and ribs. Every strand of hemp rope in her complex rigging was replaced with new, as was the copper sheathing below the waterline, making her as strong and fast as the day she was launched.

There was plenty for the tourists to ogle. A couple of her big guns were converted to salute guns that fired blank cartridges—small but still loud enough to impress civilians and infinitely safer than the real thing. Racks of cannonballs, muskets, pistols, cutlasses, and all the weaponry of the ship's heyday were on display. The navy wanted the public to feel as if they were transported back in time to the decks of a ship that was ready for action.

The refit was just in time to celebrate her bicentennial birthday in style. Starting with a gala celebration in Boston Harbor, she sailed the eastern seaboard, visiting ports along the way, invariably greeted by hordes of pleasure boats blasting air horns and harbor fireboats spouting fountains of water in her path. The navy didn't want its history forgotten and reasoned it would be more difficult to ignore the past when "Old Ironsides" sailed into a hometown harbor and equally difficult for parents and teachers to ignore the question from kids, "What's that?"

Constitution was in such good shape that the navy,

and specifically Secretary of the Navy Admiral William "Bucky" Buckholter, wanted to show her off to the world, and he wanted it done on his watch. It would probably be the last time it could ever be pulled off. The idea bounced around the Washington, DC, Beltway for years until it hit the desk of Dr. Miriam Hannah, an aide to Vice President Virginia Mitchell.

Dr. Hannah was a navy history buff, and her boss was picked to lead the US delegation to yet another attempt at Mideast peace talks. Miriam took the bit in her teeth and ran with the idea, pestering everyone in DC who could make it happen until she got her way. In consultation with the State Department, the Pentagon, and the White House, it was determined that, in connection with the subject of the Middle East, a little reminder of relevant history might not be a bad idea for that region of the world either. The joke flying around was, "Who gets to answer the question, 'What's *that*?' "

The results were mixed. If you liked America, you liked the gesture. Detractors, on the other hand, tried to warp *Constitution*'s tour into a campaign of American imperialism and military might. Generations had come and gone since 1941, the last time the United States seemed unified to any great degree and galvanized into acting accordingly. In the ensuing period, it became fractionalized, seemingly more so with each passing year.

****

Tebic filled his plate at the chow line in the crew's dining room and squeezed in at a table. Knowing something no one else in the crew knew was, for him, a power play. Power also came from his knowledge of the crew. He studied them and picked up all the information he could, often on the sly. It was more than a curiosity with him; it was a survival tactic. Not being one who could defend himself physically, he needed to know who an ally might be and who to watch out for.

"We're getting a new captain, and it isn't Lieutenant James," he announced puckishly as he commenced chowing down, delighted with his knowledge but acting indifferent in spite of the sounds of tableware being dropped by the surprised crewmen around him. "Uh-huh, a Moses Redding. Anyone heard of him?"

Tim McAvoy—"Mac," as he was called—a tall, broad-shouldered, tight-end type, mouth full of dinner roll, gestured to Tebic with his bread knife. "Refugee Redding? Yeah, it was all over the news a few days ago. Oh, my bad. Computer games don't show the news."

The crew laughed, and a few string beans from dinner plates flew in the direction of Tebic's head. Mac was delighted in the rare occurrence when he got his shipmates to laugh. The son of a Montana rancher, he and his language skills were out of place away from Big Sky Country, cattle, horses, pickup trucks, and country girls, but as gentle as he was, he was also an imposing figure and crewmen knew better than to challenge him.

"That sucks," spouted Robert Basker. "Where does that leave James?"

"Second in command—still." Jorge Guzman chuckled, still chewing his food. "Never dug him much anyway. Stuck up. Always got a broomstick up his ass, strutting around like he's pretending to be an officer in 1800 or something, picking on little shit, like your hat's not on straight, crap like that. And when he thinks no one is watching, those lame hits on Dr. Hannah—like, *sure*, he's got a shot with her."

At a safe distance from Guzman, Basker countered, "He's all right. You just hate officers." Then he muttered under his breath to the crewmen next to him, "And just about every*one* and every*thing* else."

Basker liked to get a rise out of his crewmates, most of whom ignored him, knowing he was just a goof—a tall, lanky goof. Guzman wasn't one of them, but like most, Basker knew where the line was with Guzman and not to cross it, a skill he learned from an inner-city childhood not unlike Guzman's, but one his parents did their best to insulate him from.

Guzman had a chip on his shoulder that contributed to the crew's impression of him as a young Latino with a checkered past. It didn't help him any that he looked and acted the part. Before serious trouble found him, his mother and the juvenile justice authorities found the solution, Tall Ships Youth Adventure, the largest sail-training operation in the world and the only nonmilitary source for tall ship sail training. With grants from the Department of Justice and the Office of Juvenile Justice and Delinquency Prevention, they offered character-building programs to teens with problems.

Lieutenant Paul James, second in command of *Constitution,* had gone through the program, but under different circumstances.

In Guzman's case, the jury was still out on the program's effect on his character, but it did teach him how to sail tall ships and hooked him on life at sea. The navy and an assignment to *Constitution* took it from there.

****

Constitution tugged restlessly at the lines confining her to the slip in the Naples harbor, the tide and freshening breeze seeming to beckon her out to sea. Even a languid pleasure cruise for the benefit of tourists and the politically connected was preferable to being tied up.

Seamen scurried about her deck, continuing to secure her lines and reef her sails under the direction of Ensign Roberta Cooper, the current Officer of the Deck. A slightly built woman of twenty-one, she was "Bobbi" to the few she allowed close to her.

Normally, a female on board would get longing looks from the men, be cast in a daydream or two, or even be the target of advances, but Bobbi Cooper was something of a tomboy. She fit in—or at least blended in—in some ways but not in others. Her sexual inclinations, or more to the point, questions about them, were only the subject of quiet talk. They were never an open issue.

As a junior officer, she gave orders to the seamen on her watch. For the more seasoned sailors, serving under female officers wasn't unusual. Most had no problem with it. Guzman was not among them.

Tourists on deck craned their necks and pointed to the men high in the rigging, like aerialists risking their lives performing for a circus audience. The Naples tourists snapped pictures of one another standing next to a big gun or straining to lift one of the thirty-two-pound cannonballs.

"We like to have those cannonballs in their place, sir. Just in case we have to go into battle on a moment's notice," came a voice from over the shoulder of a tourist. The plus-size middle-aged man put the cannonball back in the rack as his wife and all the tourists nearby laughed at the order from Ensign Matt Gunderson, their tour guide.

Gunderson, a fresh-faced recent graduate of Jacksonville University in Florida and its Navy ROTC program, loved the navy and his job as the tour guide of choice on board *Constitution*. The other ensigns—Cooper, Justin Kobach, and Brandon Bates—knew as much about the ship, but none had his singular personality for this role. His warmth, charm, and Southern drawl delighted audiences. He liked people and people liked him. If he wasn't doing it for the navy, he could have had the job with anyone. All day long he could deliver the same spiel over and over and with just as much enthusiasm at the end of the day as at the start.

The gangway was lowered. Gunderson's job wasn't over until he made sure the tourists and special invitees got off the boat without falling into the harbor. As they migrated toward the gangway, Gunderson was often their photographer for commemorative photos.

A seaman in a modern uniform rushed up the gangway against the flow of disembarking tourists, meeting Cooper at the top.

"Permission to come aboard, ma'am."

Cooper returned the seaman's salute. "State your business."

The seaman produced an envelope. "Correspondence for Captain Lawrence."

"I'll take that, sailor," she replied, returned the sailor's salute, then approached Captain Lawrence but stood away from his conversation with Lieutenant James.

"The crew is going to miss you, sir, and, I think, the ship too," said James respectfully.

"That goes both ways, Paul, but I'm looking forward to retirement." Looking the boat over, Lawrence was both nostalgic and pleased. "I was one of those who pushed hard to get *Constitution* back to sea for this cruise. Maybe that's enough to be remembered for. Besides, I'm confident she's going to be left in good hands—someone who worked his way up from the ranks. You make the navy proud."

"I would do my best, sir."

Noticing Cooper waiting for his attention, Lawrence waved her over and continued with James while opening the envelope she'd handed to him. "I know you would, and I hope my recommendation still means something with the big brass."

As the captain read the letter, his optimism disappeared. He handed the letter to James, whose shoulders slumped as he read down the page.

After a long, uncomfortable pause, Lawrence put his hand on James' shoulder. "It was my fondest desire that my last command, this ship, would be handed over to you, Paul. You know that. I'm sorry." He could no longer look at James, whose downcast eyes stared at the deck.

Chapter Four

It was standing room only in the massive lecture hall. Its ornate design, reminiscent of a palace ballroom, trumped function as the marble-covered walls made for horrible acoustics. That and the unique ambiance created by the blended scents from countless thousands of humans and ancient fabrics over the centuries, absorbed into the porous stone, made the presence of a projector, screen, and loudspeakers seem out of place.

Americans from the western states marvel at two-hundred-year-old buildings on the East Coast. In Italy, that's the new stuff. The oldest university in America is Harvard, founded in 1636. By then, the oldest nonsectarian university in the world, the University of Naples Federico II, had been in the education business for more than four hundred years. The venue for many prominent confabs and speeches over the centuries, it was a natural for a PR presentation by the United States during the preface to peace talks soon to be held across the Mediterranean Sea, in Egypt.

At the speaker's podium stood Dr. Miriam Hannah. The program identified her as the top aide to Vice President Virginia Mitchell. She wore a charcoal-gray Ann Taylor suit, bought off the rack, but perfect for her size six figure. The shine in her shoulder-length black hair picked up the light directed at the lectern. Her white-collared blouse, open at the neckline, contrasted with her dark complexion. But for an inexpensive watch, she wore no jewelry.

The adopted daughter of a Jewish-American naval officer turned diplomat and a Lebanese Christian mother, Dr. Miriam Hannah was everything her parents could have hoped for. By the time she came of age, it appeared to those ignorant of her adopted status that she had inherited her good looks from her mother. With her raven hair, chocolate-colored eyes, and olive complexion, she could blend easily in the ethnic soup of the Mediterranean and Middle East.

When Mitchell was stuck in closed-door meetings—as she was now as the point of the spear in the Middle East peace talks—in the public eye Miriam became her alter ego. She was most definitely a talent put to good use by Vice President Mitchell, especially when the need arose for someone who could argue in several languages.

The audience was a mix of academics and diplomats too low-level to attend the upcoming talks and others on assignment to hear what VP Mitchell wanted the world to hear through her surrogate. Also present were members of the media. It was an impressive speech—urging peace but painting a picture of a dark cloud in its absence—and, to a great extent, a history lesson. By the end, Miriam had put to rest any question from the audience as to why she was the VP's spokesperson, but that didn't mean there were no other questions.

With the last of her slides on the screen, a map of the Middle East, she wrapped up her presentation. "Historically, we've run through the continuum of foreign policy options in the region: from what we would call state-sponsored terrorism—starting with the Barbary Coast corsairs of two hundred years ago but also including more recent examples. Now a different model is about to be put to the test, when even the Iranians are sitting down at the table for peace talks in a couple of weeks. That process, of course, led by Egypt's President Aziz."

Hands flew up in the audience as fast as the lights came up in the lecture hall. The heels of Miriam's black pumps helped elevate her well above the top of the podium and able to survey the number of waving hands seeking her attention. "Wow! I see the press found out about the free buffet," joked Miriam, attempting to get the Q&A started with a light mood. "Let's see." She pointed to one of the most eager representatives from the press corps, Bashir Safar, a reporter from the Al Jazeera news network.

"Dr. Hannah, it has been suggested that your role is to spin Middle East history to make US ally countries like Egypt, Oman, and Kuwait look good and Iran look bad by means of a veiled comparison to the ancient Barbary Coast history, a key component in your doctoral thesis on US Navy history. What is your response?"

"That's your question? Am I in the spin business?" she responded flatly, but with a wry smile for the benefit of the audience.

Safar's eyes narrowed as he stared at Miriam during the seconds it took the audience to stop reacting to her jab, then attempted to take back the stage. "Are we to believe the timing of the presence of USS *Constitution* in the Naples harbor, an icon of your references to historic lawlessness in the region, in conjunction with the peace talks—*and* virtually on the heels of the Taliban's victory in Afghanistan—is just a *coincidence*?"

Safar stood proudly, waiting for Miriam's response.

"First of all, thanks for buying the book." The murmurs turned back into laughter, and the reporter sat down. "Secondly, if the Iranians look bad in comparison to the other countries you mentioned, it's because of their own policies. As for Afghanistan, for all practical purposes they are a new nation and are not a party to the talks. That may change. You can appreciate the lingering effects of wounds—on *both* sides—made deeper over many years, but I would remind you, where blood was first drawn on US soil. If you come to the States, I'll give you a tour of that site. In the meantime, if you have information that conflates Iran with that nation, I'm sure our state department would love to talk to you."

Like spectators at a tennis match between two skilled ground-stroking professionals on the clay courts of Roland Garros stadium, the audiences' eyes bounced back and forth between the two opponents.

Safar was quick with a follow-up question, jumping ahead of others. "Can't it be said that 'looking bad'—in light of the recent bloody incident in the Persian Gulf—is a problem for the US, not Iran, as Colonel Farzad has recently detailed in a broadcast? We all heard his accusations, I'm sure. How can that incident not affect your upcoming peace talks?" Pleased with himself, he sat down, but on the front edge of his seat.

This was the question Miriam had dreaded. She

had been briefed on the incident, but brief it had been. Anyone who knew the facts had put a lock on the subject that even her security clearance couldn't penetrate, leaving her only with Farzad's version of the story. She would have to dodge the question without appearing to do so, while trying not to blush at the aggravation the subject had caused her, Vice President Mitchell, and the entire delegation team.

"Accusations from Iran are something all too common in recent years—along with chants of 'Death to America' and 'Death to Israel,' I would add. We don't yet know all the facts. That is a military matter, and the Navy Department is looking into it. As for the peace talks, all the parties involved have a history of animosity to overcome. That's no small task, but these upcoming talks are about the future, not the past."

Safar crossed his arms and took no notes on Miriam's answer.

She took a drink of water and continued. "Egypt, as well as other countries, has proven that with or without oil and without nuclear arms ambitions, they can provide a peaceful and prosperous existence for their people—in large part by their positive and peaceful relationships with the rest of the world."

Miriam turned her attention to the rest of the audience, pointedly making eye contact with as many as possible. "Yet that doesn't mean those nations are uninvolved. Oman, for example, is playing a key role in brokering the current talks." Then she pointed to an elderly man from the academic section of the audience. "Professor Cereghino."

"Nevertheless, Dr. Hannah, labeled a goodwill tour or not, don't you think there's a danger *Constitution* might stir up two-hundred-year-old memories in a region where memories last a long time?"

Without hesitation, Miriam adroitly turned the question onto itself. "As a history professor, Dr. Cereghino, I'm sure you would agree that what is truly dangerous is to forget the past. That goes for nations with histories much longer than that of the US."

Cereghino raised an eyebrow in amusement. "That could almost be interpreted as suggesting the ship was, indeed, sent as a not-so-subtle reminder of America's attitude toward negotiations, especially given the reason for her existence in the first place—and, I would add, the fact that her itinerary includes a stop in Tripoli."

Miriam had prepared herself for the topic and was quick to respond. "Hmm, just what part of history would we be reminding the world of, Professor? *Constitution* was built as a response to the attacks by the corsairs from Tripoli, Tunis, Morocco, and Algiers and their demands for tribute. When asked by Thomas Jefferson and John Adams why those nations were hostile to the US, a country that had never threatened them, according to Jefferson, Tripoli's ambassador to Great Britain replied that the reason"—Miriam flipped to a page of her notes and read—"was founded on the laws of their Prophet, that it was written in their Qur'an, that all nations who should not have acknowledged their authority were sinners, that it was their right and duty to make war upon them wherever they could be found, and to make slaves of all they could take as prisoners, and that every Muslim who should be slain in battle was sure to go to Paradise." She cocked her head to the side. "Surely you're not suggesting a comparison to the behavior of any nation involved in the upcoming

47

talks."

A French journalist, with an accent so thick Miriam strained to understand him, jumped in. "Since we're on the subject of history, it would not be unprecedented for the US to engage in showings of strength, masked as so-called 'courtesy visits.' I remind you of the world tour of the Great White Fleet, as it was called, ordered by President Theodore Roosevelt after the turn of the twentieth century."

Trying to trip up Dr. Miriam Hannah on a point of US Naval history was futile. "Those warships were state of the art for their time, and, yes, you could say they implied a 'don't mess with the US' message," she answered, delivering her setup. "But as for *Constitution*, give her a break. She's more than two hundred years old. I'm pretty sure no one feels threatened. Instead, they're getting to see something they'll never see again. As to your question, I'm more of a historian than a diplomat, but I think everyone in this room with any knowledge of history would have to agree that the history of American cooperation in the Middle East is much longer than any conflicts." Pausing again for effect, she adopted a more sober tone. "Nevertheless, if the world needs a reminder that history tends to repeat itself, then so be it." She pointed to another reporter in the front row.

"Dr. Hannah, you seem to be suggesting two possible outcomes. Are you at liberty to suggest which is the more probable one?"

Miriam paused for a moment, then answered slowly and deliberately. "The Iranians are a difficult customer. Clearly, they want to engage fully as a respected world power, yet they continue to sponsor terrorist groups as a back-channel way to move certain of their policies forward." She swallowed, carefully composing the rest of her answer. "We can only conclude that, to a degree, they are interested in instability in the region—so as not to be left behind, as a Shiite state in a Sunni region. Their hope seems to be to create other Shiite states—a kind of midwifery effort to produce natural allies."

"What's wrong with that?" the reporter countered.

"It doesn't work," she answered with a shrug. "The Iranians' efforts would be just as likely to produce an ungrateful offspring—as the US did when it backed the Taliban against the Russians. The irony is that Iran could achieve the leadership role it wants in the world by following the lead of President Aziz." She checked for a response from the reporter but, seeing him struggle, continued. "For example, would Egypt like to be a nuclear power? Maybe, but Aziz gets it. He knows that leadership is about sacrifice and compromise. By abandoning their nuclear weapons ambitions and recognizing Israel, Egypt has gained the respect of the world. That has been to the benefit of their people and the rest of us. Unfortunately, there haven't been enough examples of peaceful solutions in that region."

Bashir Safar, the Al Jazeera reporter, jumped up aggressively. "Your Vice President Mitchell is well known for her outspoken views on Christianity and so-called Christian values," he said derisively. "With that history, do you think she is the person to best represent your country in talks with Islamic nations?" He sat down, self-satisfied.

Miriam stared at Safar and counted to herself to control her temper. "The purpose of the talks is to create a lasting peace between Islamic nations and nations from around the world—many of which are predominantly Christian, including America. I'm sure you wouldn't suggest a non-Muslim would be best to represent those Islamic nations in the talks."

She pointed to a young woman at the back of the room who had been waving her hand throughout the Q&A period.

"Dr. Hannah, what's your read on the Iranian involvement in the talks?"

"Well, as I alluded to earlier, the Iranian leadership is the puzzle. The world is right to be skeptical—"

Her response was cut short by Safar, producing critical grumbles from the audience. "But they're talking as though they want peace," he insisted.

"Historically," Miriam continued, glancing at her watch, "that's another matter. Their direction has been otherwise, and I'm sure that very subject will be on the agenda at the peace talks. President Aziz has welcomed Iran's involvement and given them a prominent role, so we will see. With that, I thank you."

She acknowledged the enthusiastic response, collected her papers, waved goodbye, and left the hall.

****

Applause spilled out of the radio speaker in a limousine that pulled to a stop in front of Cairo's Nile Ritz-Carlton. In the distance across the Nile River stood the Great Pyramids.

Colonel Farzad sat in the back seat, contemplating Dr. Hannah's speech. Seated on either side of him were two members of the Amazonian Guard. A third drove the limo.

The Guard was an elite band of female bodyguards

created by Muammar al-Qaddafi as his personal shield. The ultra-fit women were highly trained in firearms and martial arts, required to take an oath of chastity, and screened for their fervent dedication to the cause of jihad.

Ultimately, the death of the Libyan dictator proved the mission of the Amazonian Guards was unsuccessful, but all in all not a terrible concept if you are the "Great Socialist People's Libyan Arab Jamahiriya" or any other less-than-popular dictator and especially if you love beautiful women, another Guard requirement.

In addition to leaving the Guard scattered and hunted by Qaddafi's foes, his death resulted in a highly skilled, dedicated, ready-made, unemployed security force looking for a powerful leader to guard. That suited Farzad.

Farzad looked to his right at Batul, leader of the Guard. She was beautiful, athletic, and mechanically cold. She looked back at him momentarily with her deep-set black eyes; then just as the BBC News host was wrapping up the program, she turned off the radio.

Chapter Five

"As you heard, reporters were eager to question Dr. Hannah, as she is to join US Vice President Virginia Mitchell's delegation, making her the highest-ranking participant in the peace talks available to the media. Our next broadcast will be from Cairo after the talks begin. This is Nigel Phillips for BBC News."

"Damn, woman, you're almost as bad as me, but you don't know a damn thing about that Gulf action," Redding mumbled to himself as he shifted his posture sideways, trying to find room for his six-foot-two frame in the back seat of the Fiat taxi.

The driver looked over his shoulder. *"Scusami, signore."*

"Oh—nothing. You can turn that off now."

Americans admire things that are big, preferably the biggest. Sometimes big means tall, like skyscrapers. It can mean wide, like the Mississippi River. It can mean long, like a bridge or a roadway—and when it comes to roads, Americans give them *one* name. All this occurred to Redding during that depressing cab ride through Naples on his way to his new command.

Coming from Southern California, he was used to long streets like the one the cab was on. He remembered Sepulveda Boulevard, over forty-two miles long. Giving directions to someone in LA might be "Drive down Sepulveda for thirty-eight miles, then turn right." The difference Redding noted was the name of the street didn't change. It struck him that sometime over the many centuries of the country's existence, Italians must have decided, regardless of how long or short a street was, it was better to change its name every block or so.

Redding arrived at that conclusion on the long boulevard tracing the arc of the harbor after about four name changes in a mile. Frustrated with not being able to track where he was, he tossed his map of Naples on the floor of the cab and looked out at the harbor, a hub of shipping activity—from supertankers unloading oil from the Middle East to cruise ships unloading tourists from just about everywhere. There were also US Navy vessels, whose crews wandered the streets of Naples and nearly equaled the local men in their boorishness toward women.

Ancient buildings are the norm in Italy, but this one stood out: a tall castle-like structure built, for Italy at least, in relatively modern times—the Middle Ages. The cab driver looked at Redding through his rearview mirror and pointed to the building.

"*Signore, è Civico di Castel Nuovo.*"

While the driver stumbled, struggling to think of the word in English, Redding picked up his map, judged the location of the building by other landmarks, and scanned for it on his map with notations in English. Finding it, he answered for the cabbie. "Museum. Thanks for pointing that out."

"*Si, signore. Prego.*"

The street was jammed with tour buses loading and unloading people wearing Bermuda shorts and baseball caps, so Redding's cab left him at the curb and a long walk to his new command. He stopped for a moment to admire a sleek destroyer at anchor in the harbor. Another hundred yards of weaving his way through the swarm of tourists and there she was, *Constitution*. Her two-hundred-foot masts towered over every other vessel in the harbor, and for that matter, the harbor itself. She was impossible to ignore.

Still moving against the tide of tourists, Redding arrived at her bow. Stopping there, he was struck by the intricate carvings on her billethead. *Ships' bows had character then, almost like a face. Like the Oldsmobile his granddad had when he was a kid.*

It had been an old car even then, but Granddad wouldn't give it up. Couldn't stand modern cars. Could never figure out how to work all the new gadgets. "Don't give a crap about that stuff," he'd said over and over, even more so the older he got. And without all that "crap," the Olds was still running when Granddad was gone.

Constitution seemed to be watching Redding like an old portrait in a murder mystery—as if it had eyes that would follow him if he moved. Redding stood on the dock in his modern navy uniform as he stared back at the design, a face with an uplifted curve like a woman's come-hither half smile, a face nearly two hundred years his senior that would still be looking out to sea when he was no longer a memory.

The Naval Academy curriculum didn't include many courses in art, and when they did teach it, it was in connection with history and sociology. "Symbols in Art Through the Ages." The only reason Redding could remember the name of the class was that he remembered the teacher, Dominique DuBoise. Her name rolled smoothly off the tongue, which when it came to the male cadets was usually, if not literally, hanging out. She was hot. So hot, the female cadets could never find a seat in the front rows at her lectures.

Professor DuBoise, he remembered, taught the iconic use of the acanthus leaf in art and architecture, an image the ancients viewed as symbolic of immortality, rebirth, longevity, and healing. The ancient columns with their carvings of acanthus leaves, Redding remembered on his cab ride through Naples, reminded him of DuBoise's lecture. She explained that once you know what they were, you would see them everywhere. She was right. He was seeing them again here, carved in relief and painted white against the black of the bow of *Constitution*. Not a warlike image. Not war paint designed to instill fear in the enemy, like the shark mouths on the World War II P-40 Tomahawk fighters of the Flying Tigers, but like the acanthus flourishes on the Roman columns, meant to be both beautiful and timeless.

No need for a wooden carving of a naked woman below the ship's bowsprit, and she didn't need tradition or a feminine name to give her gender. She was clearly female—but not in the warm, soft sense of that word. "Warrior goddess" was more like it, as if she had been evoking gender equality since long before that term became enshrined in the modern lexicon. She seemed to be able to speak and to say all she needed him to hear from her in one sentence: "Am I going to have trouble with you?"

Redding found himself uncomfortably examining his uniform, as if reacting to a critical glare from a superior officer at a formal occasion, and glanced over his shoulders for anyone who might be watching.

The ship's bell signaled 1600 hours, stirring Redding from his thoughts. He had completely lost track of time. He looked down the length of her black hull, highlighted by a wide white stripe along her gun deck, which announced to friend and foe alike, "I'm no feather merchant."

The gun ports were closed on both the spar deck and the gun deck below it. Only the salute cannons had been fired to announce the ship's arrival in port, giving passengers a thrill and advertising her presence, the way a circus arriving in a new town in a bygone era would parade down Main Street to stir up business.

It was a long walk to the gangway. As much as he hadn't looked forward to getting this far, the next few steps would be especially depressing.

Chapter Six

Lieutenant Paul James sat in the captain's quarters, staring out the window, the orders received by courier still in his hand. Until this moment, he had been an eager navy officer looking forward to the future, never doubting his choice of careers.

Lacking a degree of imagination, he'd gravitated to his father's job in law enforcement. A career beat cop, his dad encouraged him to aim higher. He pointed out that the police brass often came from the military and with some higher education.

James earned a two-year degree in criminal justice and joined the Navy Reserve. That's when his career choice took a different tack.

He fell in love with the navy and naval history. Tall Ships America—not far away in Newport, Rhode Island—provided James with a connection to the navy of the past and, as he discovered, a family history. He had finally excelled at something, even becoming an instructor until he transferred to the regular navy and was admitted to Officer Candidate School. When he learned the navy was looking for an experienced crew for *Constitution*, he went after the assignment with a vengeance.

The sound of the fife on deck signaled the arrival of Redding. James tapped the document on his knee, composed himself, grabbed his cocked hat, and left the quarters for the spar deck.

Gunderson was in full docent mode as he guided a group of tourists about the deck. As the Officer of the Deck, Cooper stood at her post near the gangway. By the time Redding arrived, all on board had the news of their new commander and knew it wouldn't sit well with James. When James appeared on deck, both Gunderson and Cooper looked away uncomfortably.

James slowly approached the gangway from the companionway to the captain's cabin on the deck below, attempting to achieve an attitude that would belie his feelings and hold it for as long as it took to get through the coming awkward moment.

Ensign Roberta Cooper, the officer of the deck, snapped to attention as Redding arrived. He faced and saluted the ensign flying from a halyard at the stern, then saluted Cooper.

"Permission to come aboard."

"Permission granted." Cooper returned the salute as Redding looked at *Constitution* from bow to stern.

"Excited about your new command, sir?" Cooper said with a broad smile.

Stone faced, Redding only nodded and replied without answering. "Thank you, Ensign."

James closed the distance and signaled Cooper to make the introduction.

"Sir, may I present Commander Redding." After a quick salute, Cooper turned smartly and walked away.

James mustered as much enthusiasm as he could. "Welcome aboard, Captain. Lieutenant Paul James, your XO. Sorry I didn't have the crew assembled. We didn't know when you would arrive."

Redding barely acknowledged James. "Thank you,

Lieutenant. I'd like to go to my quarters."

James attempted pleasantries while trying to get a read on Redding. "I thought perhaps the captain would like to meet the officers."

Redding deflected the attempt. "Not just yet."

"This way then," said James, as he pointed to the opening of a companionway leading below.

They passed a group of tourists who had just boarded, one of whom called out to Redding, "Say, you're out of uniform, aren't you?"

Redding glared at the laughing tourist.

James masked his amusement. "Sorry about that, sir."

Gunderson approached the group. "Ladies and gentlemen, if you'll follow me." Leading the group to the far side of the ship, he continued: "*Constitution* is the oldest commissioned warship in the world. Launched in 1797, long ago, she earned the designation as America's Ship of State." Gunderson motioned the group toward the bow. "This way, please. Her first mission was to fight the Barbary Coast pirates, also called corsairs, not that far from where we are now. Just across the Mediterranean in North Africa."

Redding stopped, held up his hand, and turned toward Gunderson.

"Her record in combat is a stunning 33 and 0, the same as the longest win streak in NBA history by the Los Angeles Lakers. The difference is, *Constitution* never *did* lose."

James followed Redding's eyes. They were focused on Gunderson as he ushered the group across the spar deck.

"She really earned her stripes in the War of 1812

against the British." Looking the crowd over, Gunderson added, "With apologies to our friends from across the pond. It was during her first battle in that war that *Constitution* got her nickname, 'Old Ironsides.' Cannonballs from the British frigate *Guerriere* bounced off her hull.

"The ship has been refitted a number of times. That means rebuilt or repaired extensively. Back in the 1800s, the navy was looking ahead. Knowing it took a long time to grow white oak trees, the navy planted a forest of them in Indiana for the future needs of this ship alone. They were used for *Constitution*'s refit in the late 1920s."

"That's Ensign Gunderson," James noted. "He's good at that, don't you think?"

"He's the man for that job, all right," Redding replied, looking the ship over as if in response to Gunderson's tutorial.

"He wrote the speech himself," James added, keeping an eye on Redding for a reaction, "from one of the books in my—your cabin." Then James forced a chuckle. "Of course, all except for that Laker reference."

Gunderson smiled mischievously as he looked over the group of tourists. "Her famous battles aren't the only stories that are legendary about this ship. Plenty of sailors, even in modern times, have witnessed what they claimed was evidence of ghosts." He looked over the crowd, whose eyes widened and jaws dropped. "One of them even has a name, Neil Harvey. Poor Neil fell asleep on his watch in the 1800s. His punishment, ordered by the commodore, was to be stabbed to death, then to have his body draped over the end of one of those huge guns over there and blown to bits." The audience gasped. "Thank God the navy isn't *quite* that strict today, but trust me, no one falls asleep on their watch just the same.

"Others, and recently at that, have claimed to have the feeling they were being watched and someone blowing on the back of their neck. You've all seen that the decks on *Constitution* are arched higher in the middle. That's to the make water run off. Just a few years ago, when the ship was still and stable, a crewmember saw one of those cannon balls roll across the deck from one side to the other, going downhill and *uphill* all by itself and ended up where it came from.

"But it gets better. In 1955, a lieutenant commander set up a camera aimed at the wheel. According to one report, around midnight, a figure in a nineteenth-century captain's uniform appeared and was caught on film, complete with the gold epaulets on his shoulder, and—get this—he was reaching for his sword." Tourists covered their mouths and looked around the ship. "Sometimes I tell those stories when I need to get the tour group off the ship in a hurry." Gunderson laughed along with his audience.

Redding turned to James. "Ghosts?"

"Uh-huh. To this day there are sailors that are afraid to stand watch, and the subject is kind of taboo among the crew, that is, until a new guy shows up, then it's part of the hazing process. This way, sir. Over time, you'll be hearing that spiel often enough."

As James led Redding below decks, Gunderson didn't miss a beat. "You're going to hear some strange-sounding words from me, folks. Centuries ago, nautical terminology became like a language of its own, and we still use the same words and pronunciations that were used by the sailors on this deck more than two hundred years ago. For example," he said, pointing to the short wall-like structure surrounding the upper deck, "that's not a wall, that's a bulwark, or more usually called a gunwale, g-u-n-w-a-l-e, but it's pronounced 'gun'l.' The sails are all reefed now, meaning gathered up and tied to their spars—those horizontal wood beams, also called booms. That huge sail on the bottom of the mainmast there is the mainsail, but pronounced 'mains'l.' Above that are top sails, pronounced 'tops'ls.' Above them are top gallants, pronounced 't'gallants.' Way up at the front are tall triangular sails called jibs that look like slices of pizza, and there are so many more names of sails we can't get to them all. Everywhere you look, there is a name for something that doesn't sound anything like what you're looking at.

"All around you see what *you* call ropes, but that word is only used to describe one use of cordage on this ship. That's the thick rope you see attached to the big guns. Otherwise, there are no ropes on a sailing ship. If it's for trimming a sail, it's a sheet. If it's for tying up the ship to the dock, it's a line. If it supports a mast from side to side, it's a shroud. If it supports a mast fore and aft, it's a stay. And we have no windows on a ship, only portlights."

Gunderson pointed to the back of the ship. "We're standing on the spar deck, but that part of it back there is called the quarterdeck. You see the US flag flying above the quarterdeck, only we call it the ensign, just like my rank."

Ensigns Kobach and Bates on the fighting platform of the mizzenmast teased him with salutes. He shook his head and turned back to his group

"And those long wooden beams protruding back from that mast in the rear, behind the ship's wheel, called the mizzenmast, are the spars, or booms, for that huge sail called the spanker. It's what we call a gaff-rigged sail, because it has a spar at both the top and the bottom." Gunderson looked at his audience. "I know, weird name for it, huh, but please don't ask me how it got its name. I've never been able to find out, but I will tell you this, when that sail sweeps back and forth across the quarterdeck with a change in the wind direction relative to the ship's heading, you'd better be out of the way, or you'll get more than spanked. You'll get knocked for a loop, swept overboard, or killed outright—just one of the many threats to life and limb for tall-ship sailors."

****

James and Redding arrived at the captain's cabin, on the gun deck, one level below the spar deck. Redding bashed his forehead on the beam over the door.

"Damn!" he groaned, touching the bandage on his forehead and picking his cap off the floor. "It knew right where to get me."

"Sorry about that. I should have warned you."

"It reminds me why I didn't pick submarine duty," Redding muttered, still rubbing his head.

"That wound on your forehead. You want me to get it looked at?"

"No, it's all right."

"That's from the Gulf incident?"

"Incident," Redding replied. "Good name for it. Nice and sterile."

James chewed his lip. "Sorry to say, your cabin is normally part of the tour. You can change that if you like. If not, a seaman is assigned to keep it—"

Redding waved his hand. "Consider it changed."

"Very well. Your new uniform is in the closet. Let me know if it doesn't fit," James added on his way out.

Redding walked to the interior of the cabin, lightly touching the wound on his forehead and muttered, "I can tell you *now* it doesn't fit."

He surveyed the cabin, adorned with artifacts of the ship's storied history, and had to admit it was better than his cabin on the *Minerva*. Except for the low ceiling, it could pass for a drawing room in a modest home at the turn of the nineteenth century. Modest in that day would be considered elaborate today. Woodworking skills were something to marvel at back then, a lost art long since. But the question struck him as to why naval architects of the period found it necessary to include such ornate trim in a warship. Looking at the extensive array of portlights in the captain's stern quarters, he envisioned the shipwright's work destroyed by just one well-aimed cannonball.

His question about the motives for the ornateness of the cabin's construction was answered when he spotted his period uniform hanging on the wall, complete with a fringed epaulet on the right shoulder signifying a lieutenant commander, gilt buttons, embroidery, and metallic braiding. And the hat! It was a masterpiece of showmanship. *Those guys were into style. Did they used to fight in this stuff or just pose for paintings?*

Next to a mirror was the portrait of Commodore Preble wearing the cocked hat, appearing to look straight at Redding. He tried on the hat in the manner shown in the Preble painting with the crown running fore and aft, then turned it sideways, like Napoleon. "Hell, no," he muttered. "And I don't care if it's you that's supposedly haunting the ship." He replaced it with his modern officer's billed cap, then looked again at the Preble portrait, staring at him. "*What?*"

A tourist suddenly opened his cabin door. Redding spun in his direction.

"Sorry, I was looking for the restroom."

"It's called a *head*." The glower from Redding shrank the man by a suit size as he sheepishly closed the door.

Redding examined the artifacts in his cabin and fixed on a large antique pewter pot on a low cabinet and read the inscription on the plaque: Chamber Pot, circa 1800. He looked inside and said, "What, no contents? I can fix that."

He pulled a book off the shelf, *A History of USS Constitution*, took it with him to the starboard portlights, then tossed the book on a chair and stared out at the harbor. The sun was setting on a long day. His thoughts raced through the events that started with the Persian Gulf battle and ended with him standing in the cabin of a ship he had only read about at the academy. He picked the book up and sat down to read.

Chapter Seven

The following morning marked the beginning of a day off for *Constitution* from entertaining tourists, but not for her crew. The ones who weren't returning from shore leave, still wearing their period uniforms and waving goodbye to local girls on the dock, were consumed with the never-ending chores required of a historic tall ship. They swabbed the deck, varnished the brightwork, polished the brass, and spread hot tar on the hemp rope, all under the watchful eye of Ensign Cooper, the officer on watch, who paced near the gangway with her arms clasped behind her.

In her role as a junior officer, Cooper was all business and always in character. But when she was alone, especially in the silence of a watch at night, she indulged herself in the pride in her accomplishment. She was walking the same decks as some of the most famous captains in US naval history. There wasn't much darkness in Roberta Cooper, but what there was could imagine the bloodstains on deck, long since scrubbed clean or replaced in a refit.

A wallflower through her school years, she had bloomed in the navy. It was home to her, more than Wichita ever was, something worth dedicating herself to, and she did, with a work ethic far above the norm.

Crushed that her high school GPA was just below the Naval Academy's minimum, she rerouted her desire for a navy career through the U. of Kansas' ROTC program. That included a class trip to east coast navy bases, so Kansas students accustomed to a sea of wheat could smell the salt air of the real thing and walk the steel decks of their future homes, but it was on a side trip to USS *Constitution* in Boston that she found herself. All the lingering questions as to who she was and where she was meant to be were swept away.

The clicking of high heels on the gangway turned Cooper to Miriam, her arms wrapped carefully around a stack of books as she walked up the ramp. It was a warm day. Miriam wore the suit from the lecture the day before but carried her jacket, revealing her figure and the lacey white undergarment visible through her blouse. Neither went unnoticed by the crewmen nearby.

Cooper had admired Miriam from the first day she'd come aboard. She was smart, accomplished, and confident, but also down to earth. She could mix it up with the crew but command the attention and admiration of dignitaries, statesmen—and the navy. She bonded with the crew, but she and Cooper had a genuine bond. They shared a berth, and Miriam was the only one allowed to use the nickname Bobbi.

Cooper beamed as Miriam walked up the gangway, and Miriam smiled in return.

"Ensign, permission to come aboard."

"Permission granted, Dr. Hannah. Welcome back. Cool speech."

"You heard it?"

Cooper pointed to other crew members, who waved at Miriam. "We all did, on Tebic's radio. We missed you last night."

Miriam rearranged the unwieldy books in her arms.

"I stayed in town with Professor Cereghino and his wife."

"That guy?" Cooper replied with a frown. "It sounded like he didn't like you."

"Some friends like to play chess." Miriam chuckled. "We like to argue. Did the new captain show up?"

Cooper hesitated. "Yes, ma'am, but he's been below since he got here."

"Is that him?" Miriam asked as she looked at Redding, who had just emerged on deck, wearing his modern uniform.

"Yup. I mean, yes, ma'am."

A faint grin curled Miriam's lips.

James finished with orders for Gunderson, spotted Redding, approached him, and stared for a moment at his uniform. "Shall I muster the men, sir?"

"Negative. I'm just stretching," answered Redding.

"Did you sleep well?" James asked, but did not receive a reply.

Miriam waved goodbye to Cooper and turned toward James and Redding but paused as she examined Redding from a distance. His tan was deep and his jaw wide, sharp, and strong with a chin to match. Not pretty, nothing soft about him, more of a better-looking and much taller version of Humphrey Bogart and with the same troubled look in his gray eyes. He didn't need the naval officer's uniform to complete the picture—but it helped.

Redding's eyes were fixed on her as she crossed the deck toward him. He shot a questioning look at James, but Miriam was there before James could answer.

"Hello, Lieutenant James," she said, then turned to Redding.

James gestured toward Redding. "Dr. Miriam Hannah, Commander Moses Redding."

"Ma'am," Redding answered tersely as Miriam stared at him. Redding's brow rose as he cocked his head. "Do we know each other?"

Miriam glanced at the bandage on Redding's forehead, then looked him straight in the eye without smiling. "I saw you on television—in the form of a photo shown by that Iranian colonel."

"Hmmm," Redding responded without changing his expression.

Miriam looked away briefly, then resumed with a polite smile. "Congratulations on your new command."

Redding just nodded but glanced downward a couple of times at an angle even lower than the one produced by the nine-inch difference in their heights.

Discreetly feeling for the buttons on her blouse, Miriam discovered the top two had come loose. She hid her amusement and continued the conversation while she refastened her buttons. "Moses—that's an unusual name." Again, she got nothing. Still trying to fill the awkward pause, Miriam pressed on. "I look forward to my last couple of weeks on board."

Redding's eyes widened as he turned to James.

Annoyed, Miriam managed a less than cordial "Nice talking to you. Please excuse me."

Redding's gaze followed her as she walked toward a group of sailors. When she was out of earshot, he turned to James who launched into an explanation.

"Miriam, uh, Dr. Hannah has been on board for the last month by special arrangement from the navy and at the request of Vice President Mitchell."

Redding stared back at James vacantly.

"She works for Mitchell—her top aide, I hear—some kind of history expert. I understand she was a big part of getting this cruise put together."

Redding remained stone-faced.

"She's writing a new history book on the ship. The crew likes her a lot!" James offered in an upbeat tone, but Redding's expressionless stare didn't budge.

"Okay. She rejoins the vice president's party after we cross the Med."

"Not soon enough," said Redding as he looked across the deck at Miriam admiring the work of crewmen varnishing the brightwork. "A civilian woman on board a navy ship? Nice of the admiral to leave out that little detail."

"Uh, yes, sir." James looked away for a moment, then back at Redding. "Changing the subject, does the academy still teach the tall ships?"

"Coast Guard, yes. Navy, no. Guess we're a little behind the times."

James scratched the back of his neck. "Uh, any experience with sail yourself?"

"Lots of racing off Southern California and a couple of Transpacs," Redding replied, looking up at the ship's rigging.

"Transpac. That's Long Beach to Diamond Head, right?"

"Uh-huh. But look, Lieutenant, what are we really talking about here—keeping the VIPs and schoolkids from falling overboard? That kind of thing?"

James bristled. "Maybe a little more than that, sir. We're on an ambassadorial mission—" He interrupted himself as Redding squinted, shielded his eyes, and focused down the deck toward a marine sergeant and a corporal who was standing at attention.

Redding studied the sergeant, a tough-looking man in his late sixties. A battle-scarred version of the actor Robert Duvall who paced with a limp back and forth in front of the youth and appeared as much out of place on *Constitution* as Redding.

Redding started toward the two and looked to James to follow. "Who's the fossil with the bad wheel?"

"Master Gunnery Sergeant Jack Buckley, sir. He has a pile of Purple Hearts and the Medal of Honor."

"Damn! Gulf War?"

"*And* Vietnam," answered James.

They walked toward Buckley, but Redding stopped before they were within earshot of him. He turned and pointed to James. "Did I read about him in *Stars and Stripes?*"

"That's him."

"What the hell is he doing here?"

James lowered his voice. "As I understand it, the brass figured they owed him, so they offered him a choice of retirement or this. Word is, they didn't think he'd take it."

"The Corps' mandatory retirement age is sixty-two for enlisted men and non-coms," Redding added. "He's got to be older than that."

"Yes, sir, he's sixty-seven, turns sixty-eight next month. That's the limit. Someone got him classified under 'specialized personnel' to give him the maximum years until retirement."

"Specialized personnel?" questioned Redding.

"I'm sure it was a gift, sir. Do you want me to put in a request for his transfer?"

"No," Redding insisted. "I notice millennials are well represented on this ship. There's room for some gray hair. Let's see what he's got."

"Dismissed!" barked Buckley.

As the young marine made his hasty departure, Redding and James approached. Buckley grimaced slightly as he straightened his figure and brought himself to attention. He saluted.

"At ease, Sergeant." Then he motioned to the departed marine. "Trouble?"

"Not at all, sir." Buckley's matter-of-fact tone produced a faint wry smile from Redding.

"That marine, what's his name?"

"Corporal Joshua Aarons, sir."

"He's a problem?"

"No, sir," Buckley replied emphatically. "He's my best man."

The reply amused Redding, who nodded his understanding. "Carry on, Sergeant."

Buckley saluted and limped off in the direction of a group of young crewmen who were admiring Miriam from a distance, but when the men saw Buckley walking in their direction, they were galvanized into looking as busy as possible.

James excused himself. "With your permission, sir, I'll carry on."

"Of course, Lieutenant," Redding replied, then turned to see what the crewmen were staring at. Miriam was going through a martial arts workout routine wearing a loose, thin cotton dress that the sun shone through.

Redding stared at her and sighed. "Oh—my—Lord."

Chapter Eight

Air Force Two sat on the tarmac at Rome-Fiumicino International Airport. Inside was its usual passenger, Vice President Virginia Mitchell. During a whirlwind schedule of meetings with NATO allies in advance of the Cairo peace talks, she used the plane as her office. Her phone calls were so sensitive the State Department didn't want her taking any chances with insecure communications from a hotel.

Secret service men relaxed in the jet's dining area, while in the forward section of the plane, Mitchell spoke on the phone with Egyptian president Hasan Aziz.

"Yes, Mr. President, I'm looking forward to it too. My aide Sandra Phillips has us visiting the museum the afternoon before the talks begin."

****

Egyptian President Abdul Hakim Aziz leaned closer to the speaker phone in his office in the presidential palace at Heliopolis, adjacent to Cairo. He spoke haltingly, seemingly having to catch his breath to gather energy for even one more sentence. He cupped his ear. "You mentioned Sandra Phillips. I was looking forward to meeting your assistant, Dr. Miriam Hannah. I heard her speech on the radio. I wanted to compliment her and also to thank her for *her* compliments."

"Sorry, Mr. President. She won't be at the museum.

I gave her some time off for a special project of hers, but you will see her at the talks, and she is looking forward to meeting you as well. So, I'll see you soon, and a good day to you."

"And to you as well."

Aziz turned off the speaker phone.

Colonel Hakeem Farzad sat in a high-backed conference chair across the desk from Aziz, along with Egyptian Minister of Foreign Affairs Hamid Rahal and General Hadi al-Husseini.

Aziz turned to Rahal and pointed with a shaky hand. "Everything is ready? You are satisfied with the security arrangements, both ours and the Americans?"

"Yes, Mr. President. The museum is a relatively easy venue to secure. It will be no problem. General Husseini's staff have taken the lead on those preparations and have been in close communications with the aide to Vice President Mitchell, the one named Sandra Phillips that you just heard mention of, and the US Secret Service."

"We cannot afford any mistakes," insisted Aziz before nodding at Farzad. "With our Iranian friends coming to the talks, this is our best chance for a lasting peace."

"Mr. President, *everything* is ready," General Husseini said brusquely. "My security detail will work side by side with the Americans, and the army is in charge of the escort to and from the museum."

"Colonel Farzad, is the Iranian delegation content?" asked Aziz.

Farzad nodded. "We trust General Husseini completely and are honored by your hospitality."

Aziz studied Farzad a moment, then slowly walked

to a window overlooking the city and the great pyramids in the distance. With his back to the window, the frail Egyptian president marshaled as much energy as he could. "We are indeed encouraged by the participation of Iran in these historic negotiations." He paused, then turned to Farzad. "But I question your judgment in the speech you gave last week on television. How, may I ask, did your hostility serve the greater purpose for which we are now engaged? And if you and your Iranian superiors think the takeover of Afghanistan by the Taliban changes the complexion of these talks—if you intend to use that issue to advance a position contrary to the long-term peace of this region, then you will find yourself alone with your dreams and ostracized by the rest of us."

Farzad smirked, leaned back in his chair, and crossed his legs. "The Americans have a saying that we believe applies to these negotiations. 'Good cop, bad cop' they call it, indicating a role-playing arrangement designed to extract a better result from a third party than if, in this case our side, appears completely unified. We are satisfied that Egypt should take the 'good cop' role. Iran, on the other hand, believes it must enter these talks from a position of strength. That will serve to keep the Americans off balance, giving us an advantage. You heard the speech from Dr. Hannah in which she was critical of Iran and, frankly, vague as to the impact of the Afghanistan victory. We feel more than justified in taking this stance. We have also observed that America has become timid. It is easy to get them to back up. You cannot deny observing that yourself. Even the American media is a useful tool. With their help, and irrespective of Afghanistan, our reaction to the incident in the Gulf *did* serve our 'greater purpose.' That is," he added assuredly, "the greater purpose of our *combined* interests."

Aziz pursed his lips and shook his head. "Nevertheless, it would be best if you were not present tomorrow at the museum. The media will be there, and the event could be unduly focused on your comments to the discomfort of Vice President Mitchell. Your provocative speech has already tasked her with the difficulty of entering these peace talks on a positive note. I will be there tomorrow as her host. It would be discourteous of me to allow her to endure any discomfort. Any 'good cop, bad cop' dynamic, as you put it, would be better suited to meetings behind closed doors. Even then, I am skeptical of that tactic. It is a game—and I don't wish to be playing games."

Farzad crossed his arms and held his chin high. "I have no wish to cause anyone discomfort—least of all you, Mr. President. I will not attend the museum event. I hope that satisfies you, sir, and best wishes for a successful meeting with the Americans."

"It does satisfy me, and I will so notify Vice President Mitchell." Aziz pressed a button on his desk. The office door opened, revealing an aide standing just outside. With a wary eye on Farzad, Aziz dismissed the group. "Good day, gentlemen."

Husseini glanced over his shoulder as he and Farzad walked down the steps outside the palace toward a limousine parked at the curb. "I thought you handled that well," said Husseini, "but I don't think he trusts you."

"I'm *sure* he doesn't, but neither does it matter. He is weak, and he won't have time to act on his instincts anyway."

"Any problems at your end?" Husseini asked.

"No," replied Farzad. "You sound like that old fool. And your army, they will follow you?"

"I *am* the army." Husseini waited for passersby to walk clear of them. "And your plan to seed it with our supporters over the years has worked perfectly. I have gradually worked those officers into positions of power, and Aziz's friendship with the US has supplied us with all the best weaponry we will need. It will be ironic to engage them with their own weapons." They both smiled. "But I must congratulate you on your success at acquiring a deep operative within the US administration. That was brilliant."

Farzad nodded his thanks. "It was the result of years of work, and a lot of others share the credit. When we started, we actually had no idea we would be using the asset in this way. Allah had a hand in that."

"In the near future, I will be calling you at your presidential palace from mine," Husseini added, looking back over his shoulder at the presidential palace.

"Tomorrow's transmission setup is critical," Farzad warned Husseini. "That is your responsibility?"

"Yes. The final preparations are being made as we speak. The wartime British military phone lines we found buried in the Libyan Desert were like another gift from Allah."

Husseini reached into his pocket and pulled out a piece of paper. "Here are the instructions for our next and final meeting before the museum event. We must maintain our practice of no phone or internet communications between the two of us, not even in code. The Americans can pick them up."

Stopping on the sidewalk beside Farzad's limousine, Husseini faced him. "Your father would be proud. It is fitting that you should fire the first shot of the holy war."

"It is gracious of you to remember. We will show them an Arab Spring they could never have imagined."

Farzad signaled the limousine. The beautiful leader of Farzad's Amazonian Guards, Batul, jumped out of the vehicle, followed by a second bodyguard who scanned the area while Batul held the door for Farzad. They wore their dress uniforms—gold fringe on the epaulets of their jackets, gold braid sashes, and gold-trimmed folding garrison hats. Batul carried a dagger in a sheath on her belt.

"Amazonian Guards?" Husseini asked. "Where did you get them?"

"Craigslist," Farzad replied with a smile.

Husseini frowned, shook his head, and looked around. "You're not afraid of calling attention to yourself? For all his faults, Aziz may have made a good point."

Farzad looked Husseini straight in the eye. "I can either fear or be feared. I choose the latter."

Farzad climbed into the luxury car followed by the second guard member and Batul, whose shapely figure was accentuated when her slacks pulled tight against her backside.

Catching Farzad admiring her, Batul quickly sat, frowned, slammed the door, and motioned to the driver, the third Amazonian Guard.

On the drive away from the Egyptian presidential palace, Farzad contemplated the plot he had spent so many years devising. It was bold and on a grand scale but also relatively simple. Farzad's version of an Arab Spring was to ignite Shiite uprisings in countries with sizable Shiite populations governed by Sunni autocrats or kings. That might be the easy part, as many such countries were ripe for revolt and needed, Farzad believed, only the impetus and the right leader to light the match. They would then join existing Shiite nations—dominated by Iran—to form an overpowering presence in the region.

The years that saw the US trusting Iran to abide by the nuclear deal had paid off for the Iranians. Its funds were freed up; pallets of money were paid by the US. With the time it bought, Iran continued its nuclear weapons and missile programs unconstrained—albeit underground. Iran also continued efforts to infiltrate neighboring countries and fund terrorist organizations that would soon emerge from the shadows as brigades of a new order in the Middle East.

No longer would Arabs be fighting Arabs, or Persians. No longer would oil-rich nations have cozy relations with the West. Most importantly, there would no longer be a reliance on a factionalized resistance. There would no longer be an al-Qaeda or ISIS or Hamas, Hezbollah, Taliban, Boko Haram, Muslim Brotherhood, Palestine Liberation Front, al-Shabaab, Sipah-e-Sahaba, Abdullah Azzam Brigades, or the scores of other terrorist organizations operating around the world, including in the US. Farzad would merge them into one army. The present-day utter and ongoing chaos gripping the region was his ally. His would be no small caliphate. Instead, it would occupy an entire subcontinent and grow from there.

America's attribution of acts of terror to individual lone wolves and small cells operating within its borders had served the cause well. Nearly one hundred Islamic terrorist groups had been established in Europe and America alone. Those groups that lacked skilled leaders were seeded with leaders trained by Farzad. Mass emigration had spread great numbers of people from the region to the European continent, England, America, Canada, and around the globe. Farzad had sent leaders mixed in their ranks, creating a large underground army of Islamic terrorists. They too would be organized, ready to strike with orders from his central command center in Iran. Any differences between the various groups were minor and mostly a matter of tactics. Overpowering those petty differences were shared values: an abiding hatred for anything Western, any religion not Islam, and any rule of law not Sharia.

As fanatical as he was, Farzad was also a realist. The plan was ambitious beyond all measure. But if in the end all they accomplished was a campaign of worldwide arson, that would be a victory in itself.

****

The antique but venerable Douglas DC-3, a relic of World War II that had never left North Africa after service with the U.S. Army, sat near a warped corrugated-steel hangar on a remote dirt landing strip twenty miles outside the oasis settlement of Siwa in western Egypt, three hundred and fifty miles from Cairo. Built by the German Luftwaffe to support General Erwin Rommel's ground forces, the airstrip hadn't been improved since the war. It was far from the gaze of the Sphinx near Cairo and, more importantly, far from the airspace of Egyptian air traffic control.

The robust construction of the DC-3 had kept the type in continuous service for decades since the war, flying people and cargo in and out of remote locations all over the world. In the Sahara, it had replaced most, but not all, previous modes of transporting goods— including camel caravans. The model had long since been surpassed by others in technological capabilities, but nothing compared with its bang for the buck. For many of the settlements in the poor region, air travel meant flying in the "Gooney Bird."

The pilot sat in the cockpit blowing cigar smoke out the open window. Thumping on the fuselage below his window grabbed his attention.

Outside, a ground crewman in an Egyptian army uniform pointed to a cloud of dust rising in the distance on the long dirt road to the airstrip. He twirled his finger.

The pilot tossed his cigar, switched on the magnetos to his starboard engine, and hit the starter button. The engine starter whined, the prop labored into motion, and the engine fired with a characteristic belch of smoke.

Both engines were running and warm by the time Farzad's limousine pulled into the hangar. Batul and the other two guards retrieved duffel bags from the trunk before escorting Farzad out of the hangar and closing the hangar doors behind them.

The prop wash buffeted the women as they climbed the aluminum ladder into the plane. The ground crewman got close to Batul and tried to help her up the ladder, but she slapped his hand away a millisecond after it touched her lower back. Momentarily stunned, the crewman followed them into the plane and latched the door. With a grin still on his face, he offered to help the women buckle the threadbare canvas seat belts on the crude bench seats occupied long ago by US and British paratroopers but was stopped in his tracks by a "halt" hand signal from Batul.

He turned to Farzad who shook his head and waved him off.

With a gesture from Farzad, the pilot pushed the throttles forward. Kicking up a dust storm, the plane taxied to the end of the runway. The pilot checked the tattered windsock for direction and speed of the wind, then rammed the throttles home for the takeoff. The antique but bullet-proof World War II-vintage Pratt and Whitney radial engines roared in response.

Inside the cabin, the deafening noise throughout the flight precluded conversation. The three Amazonian Guards, Farzad, and the crewman could only kill time on the long flight by looking out the small dirty windows of the DC-3, viewing the vast Sahara Desert until at last the Mediterranean coastline appeared, indigo blue against a lifeless landscape washed in carrot orange by the sun setting through dusty clouds.

As the plane neared its destination on the Gulf of Sidra in Libya, a row of lights appeared on a plateau near a craggy promontory that separated a small harbor from an adjacent cove. On the cape lay the ruins of an ancient fort, its mud-brick walls eroded from hundreds of years of exposure to salty Mediterranean fog and sirocco winds. Mounds of sand near the ruins signaled the site's recent excavation. The pilot throttled back and dropped his flaps as he banked into a turn toward the landing strip marked by headlights from a line of trucks.

Taxiing back from the end of the makeshift runway, the plane's landing lights illuminated a contingent of over fifty armed soldiers lined up in front of the trucks. When the plane stopped and the crewman opened its door from the inside, one of the armed men helped him attach the steps and moved to help the Amazonian Guards off the plane until he caught the crewman frantically waving him off.

The soldiers rushed to form a review line for Farzad and straightened to attention as he approached. He looked deep into their eyes as he passed each man, then stood back from the line so all could see him.

"We are defenders of the faith. We will not let the Americans and their European dogs dictate to us any longer." He continued like a football coach in a pregame locker-room speech. "We will strike at their heart and tear it out! A dog respects only strength, and his obedience comes from fear. They will fear us!"

While the men cheered, Batul and the two guards under her command stood silently in the background.

"Our nation will be born, and our fallen brethren will be avenged!" shouted Farzad. "Go now. Pray and let Allah know the purity of our purpose. Let him know we will be sending him the souls of many infidels."

The men raised their weapons above their heads and cheered, then loaded themselves into the trucks and drove toward the fort ruins.

Chapter Nine

Constitution sailed on a leisurely heading south through the Tyrrhenian Sea from Naples. With favorable winds from the north, the two-hundred-mile voyage to Messina would be, for a square-rigged sailing ship, an easy downwind run. As with her cruises out of Naples, she again passed close to the Isle of Capri, near enough to shore to keep in sight the mountains of Calabria in southern Italy.

On the spar deck, James took a noon sighting of the sun with his sextant, checked his watch and looked up the corresponding latitude and longitude on a declination table, then marked the ship's position on a chart. The click of Miriam's camera shutter caught his attention. He smiled and posed with the sextant.

Not smiling was Seaman Rachel Dover as she appeared to be carrying out her tasks while keeping one eye on the two of them.

When Guzman had once accused James of having "a broomstick up his ass," he may have had a point. For reasons known only to her, that stiffness and allegiance to formality acted like a sexual pheromone on Rachel. Blessed with rare amber eyes that were larger than normal, she had taken needle and thread to her period uniform, making it fit more snugly to her shapely figure. Like Miriam, she turned men's heads and was frequently the topic of conversation among the male crewmen on *Constitution*, any one of whom would have been delighted to be the target of her affections. In spite of James' apparent indifference, she persisted with her efforts to attract his attention. Where he was concerned, she embodied the words of Emily Dickinson, "The heart wants what it wants."

"Are we on course?" Miriam asked, walking toward James as he marked his chart.

"Within a couple of miles or so."

Miriam raised her brow. "A couple of *miles*?"

"Uh-huh." James held up his sextant. "That's about as close as you can get with a noon sighting on a moving deck."

Miriam wrinkled her face.

James shrugged. "This isn't a jet. At these speeds, that's close enough until we get close to land; then we use visual references."

"Are we going to make Messina on schedule?"

"Let's find out," James replied as he motioned her to follow him to the bow.

He pointed to a lump of sea foam approaching the bow and looked at his watch, then followed the foam the length of the boat and checked his watch again as it reached the stern and jotted down the time on his chart. Miriam followed him to the helm where he took pencil to paper.

"That looked so primitive," she said while James did his math.

"I suppose, but it works." He continued as he did the math with pencil and paper. "The time an object takes to go from one end of the ship to the other, calculated together with the length of the ship gives us the speed. We're doing about ten knots; that's about eleven-and-a-half miles an hour."

"That's all?"

"That's pretty good. Top speed is only about thirteen knots, uh, fifteen miles per hour and that's with the full acre of canvas up and a brisk wind. We don't push the old girl that hard these days, but she loves to sail downwind."

Miriam wrinkled her brow.

"That means the wind is coming from behind," James added. "It's like a car rolling downhill. It's easy on the car."

James used his dividers to check the distance on his chart. "At this rate, we'll make Messina on time."

"Good. Let me see that chart."

James handed Miriam the chart, then walked to the helm position, looked at the sails, then at the compass. "Fall off three points," he ordered the seaman at the helm, then waited for the course correction to check the effect on the sails.

Redding emerged from his cabin, clipboard in hand, and motioned to James to approach. "The itinerary shows we're headed for Tripoli. Bit of irony for this ship, don't you think?"

"Yes, sir. Sounds like you've been reading the history book in your cabin?"

"The academy doesn't teach the tall ships, Mr. James, but it does teach history," Redding responded dryly, not looking up from his paperwork.

"Of course, sir," James responded.

"But what's this stopover in Messina involving NATO? It doesn't say much about it on the itinerary."

"Yes, sir, that's a joint operation with a NATO squadron. Should be a lot of fun. We sail into the harbor with them, show the flags, meet each other, and there's a dinner aboard *Constitution* that evening."

"You mean a boat parade," Redding replied dryly.

"Well, I guess you could put it that way," James replied, looking away. "And, um, I'm not supposed to know this, but the junior officers have something special planned for you at the dinner."

"Huh?"

James looked around them. "I'm only telling you in case you catch wind of it in the meantime. You can act like you don't know and be surprised."

"I can handle being surprised," Redding replied, half muttering to himself. "I've had practice lately."

James pointed to Redding's clipboard. "I think you'll also find reference to a stop on the Libyan coast before we get to Tripoli."

"Yes, actually I was more interested in that. It just says 'Dr. Hannah research.' It's in pencil in the margin. What's that about?"

"It's not on the official itinerary. It was a last-minute thing. We're supposed to take Dr. Hannah ashore to check out some historic ruins. It fits in somehow with the book she's writing."

"Ruins. I'm the perfect guy for that mission," Redding replied under his breath, then Buckley and a group of marines caught his eye and he approached them.

A full complement of sailors was busy with the rigging aloft, trimming sails to the freshening wind on commands from Ensign Gunderson below, the Officer of the Deck.

Miriam took a position on a hatch cover, away from the scrambling seamen. Sprawled out on a mat in shorts, T-shirt, and sandals, with notes, books, camera, and a notebook computer in front of her, she typed on the keypad and occasionally snapped a picture of the crew in action.

As Redding passed by Miriam, he caught her glancing in his direction, but she quickly turned away. *Great. I've already pissed her off without even trying. Must be a gift.*

He strolled the deck, watched the sailors at work, and occasionally leaned over the gunwale to stare out to sea, but his thoughts were on Miriam. There had been a distance between them, a subtle friction he attributed to his own lousy attitude from day one, which he had feebly tried to smooth over. But there was something else, something from her side of the ledger that had yet to reveal itself.

Navigating the female psyche was so far out of his wheelhouse that, until he understood what was underneath the surface with her, he wasn't going to confess his attraction, nor create any gossip, a common problem on board a ship. If just one crewman saw him admiring her, the rest of the crew would know about it by that night, before they fell asleep in their hammocks.

He stole a quick glance in Miriam's direction, but she didn't notice. Then raised voices on the after deck pulled his attention away.

Buckley instructed his marines on the ins and outs of muzzle-loading pistols and muskets and didn't see Redding standing just behind him. When his class came to attention, he turned and saluted.

"As you were, men," Redding said. "What have you got there?"

"A pistol from our display, sir," he said, offering

Redding the muzzle-loader.

Examining the gun, Redding fingered the firing mechanism. "This is caplock. I was expecting flintlock. Didn't they have them on board this ship?"

"Caplock came along after the War of 1812," Buckley answered. "So, these are still period correct."

"What are your men learning today?" Redding asked.

Pointing to components on the pistol, Buckley explained, "Well, sir, some of these guns are in need of cleaning, and the salt air is causing rusting, so we're learning how to get them all back into operational shape."

"The muskets too?" Redding asked.

"Aye, sir."

"May I ask why?"

Buckley hesitated, then shrugged. The truth of that unspoken response struck a chord with Redding. He handed the pistol back to Buckley. "I see. Carry on."

****

The gentle rocking of the ship, the sounds of water slipping over her hull, and even the creaking of the timbers helped put Redding to sleep that night, but it wasn't a restful sleep. Dreams alternated between the nightmarish battle on *Minerva*, the crackling of automatic weapons fire reverberating in his head, and his upbraiding by Admiral Towne. When he wasn't tossing and dreaming, he got up and paced. He had never imagined himself in a career other than the navy, but what now? Was this assignment to be his last? Would he retire like Captain Lawrence, in command of a floating museum, a warrior no more?

When the morning light was at last pouring

through the aft windows of his cabin, Redding lay asleep in his bunk, still in his uniform.

A loud boom that didn't fit with the nightmare of the battle scene jarred him awake. He looked at the long guns in his cabin that had been quiet for two centuries. They stared off silently and cold behind their closed gun ports. Another boom and Redding jumped to his feet. He slapped on his cap and rushed out in his stocking feet.

Still groggy and now cranky, he reached the top deck to the thunder of another blast, throwing fire and smoke into the morning air.

"What the hell is going on up here?" Redding fumed as he stomped over to James.

"Firing the salute gun, Captain. It's a safety requirement for when we operate it with tourists on board."

"I don't know how much safer a navy ship could possibly be, Lieutenant. Let's knock it—" Another boom interrupted him.

James yelled to Gunderson, who was directing the gun crew. "Secure from the drill, Mr. Gunderson!"

The thick cloud of smoke from the last blast drifted to Redding, and he muffled a choke.

"Sorry about that, sir. That can be pretty nasty."

But to Redding's surprise, it wasn't. The smell of black powder smoke wasn't like cordite. It was better. He didn't wave it off. He let it drift over him and remembered a song about it: "The Last Gunfighter," the Johnny Cash version. A thin crease of a smile curled his lips.

Miriam appeared on deck with her camera and out of breath. Redding ginned up the nerve to start a conversation with her, tipped his hat, and launched into a question he had prepared for the occasion. "Dr. Hannah, I've been looking forward to discussing your research—"

"Sorry, I just ran up to watch the gun drills. I just love that."

Sailors secured the gun. James shrugged.

She looked at Redding, who could only muster a "Ma'am" as he returned to his cabin.

****

Rachel Dover went about her duties serving dinner to the officers, but more quietly than ever. There was a chill in the air of the wardroom that the dim lighting from the oil lamps could not overpower. Redding ate quietly, seemingly unaware of the silence but using his peripheral vision and quick glances to view the faces at the table. Gunderson wasn't his usual affable self, occasionally stealing a glance himself at Ensigns Bates and Kobach. James did not show any interest or emotion, other than what could be ascertained by his stabbing at his plate. Miriam paused occasionally, as though about to say something, then seemed to shake it off. By the time eight bells rang out from the spar deck above, the room was empty, save Redding, who sat alone staring at the flame of an oil lamp at the center of the table.

****

The white inner walls of the hull, including the massive timbers of her frames and knee braces, as well as the ceiling and bulkheads in the crew's mess room, helped the kerosene lanterns spread their light on the evening's meal—spaghetti and meatballs—the result of a rare extra effort on the part of Tebic and a recipe he

92

got from a chef in Naples. Conversations between small groups of sailors occupied the three dozen of them at that dinner shift, and the downwind run of *Constitution* made for a level deck and tables. Still, cloth napkins were tucked into the necks of shirts to keep them from being stained with spaghetti sauce in advance of their hosting duties for the NATO gathering in the following day.

Tebic looked around at the faces silently chowing down on his dinner. "*Area 51* was canceled, which sucks. I have the whole series on my drive if you guys want to watch." His offer was greeted by eye rolls and groans.

Basker chimed in. "Screw that, Trebek. How's the Yankees doin'?"

"It's 'Tebic'—I told you guys like a hundred times. It's Hungarian. And why would I waste my time downloading baseball?"

Basker looked around at the crew but got only a shrug from Mac.

He pointed to Tebic. "I'll take 'Sci-Fi Losers' for five hundred, Alex."

"Talk about losers. You think the Yankees are just waiting for your hitch to end?" Tebic countered and checked for reactions.

"Robert Basker's gettin' off this ship next year and walkin' on them Yankees. Them Bronx Bombers will be lucky to have me."

"Basker, you'll be lucky if they sell you a ticket," said Mac through a mouthful of spaghetti.

Laughter broke out among the crew.

"That's A-Rob—what they called me in Double-A. I was starting. Woulda made the show too, if anyone up there had any brains."

"Brains?" Mac responded. "Couldn't have been your 7.5 ERA, could it?"

The mess room erupted with whistles, laughter, and groans. Basker buried his face in his dish.

Tebic nudged Mac and whispered. "7.5 ERA. Is that bad?"

Guzman held up his hand to the crew and confronted Basker. "We got a captain with an attitude, and you're worried about bullshit."

The mess room went silent.

Chapter Ten

The sun was high and bright as *Constitution* entered the harbor at Messina with flags flying.

Blasts from the ship's salute guns brought cheers from crowds of people waving from shore. Cars honked their horns on the Viale della Libertà, the Avenue of Freedom. Air horns sounded from boats in the yacht basin and from the foghorn of a massive cruise ship tied to the seawall where it dwarfed the nearby multistory residential buildings with their street-level cafés and shops.

The harbor was created by a long fishhook-shaped cape that was tightly pinched at its opening—great for protecting the harbor from invading Peloponnesians or Carthaginians but a squeeze for a square-rigged ship the size of *Constitution* that did not have an auxiliary engine. A tugboat soon pulled alongside to nudge the 2,000-ton *Constitution* to the place reserved for her along the seawall.

The tip of the cape was the perfect place for a defensive fort—not lost on the Sicilians. The rounded walls of the ancient fort San Salvatore traced the semicircular tip of the cape and supported a 200-foot-tall octagonal stone pedestal. On it, a 23-foot-tall gold statue of a woman faced the inlet, her arm raised, as if to hail homebound sailors.

Miriam and James waved at the crowds onshore

from over the starboard gunwale. Redding stood alone at the stern, admiring the modern NATO warships, including a US Navy frigate that trailed *Constitution* into the harbor.

James engaged Miriam in conversation whenever possible, and Miriam wasn't blind to the reason why. The vast difference in education was apparent in their conversations, a source of discomfort to James that Miriam tried to minimize, but she couldn't lessen James' disappointment when, seeing Redding standing alone, she broke off their conversation and approached the captain.

Standing right beside him wasn't enough to jar Redding loose from his thoughts or his attention to the NATO ships.

"Vos et ipsam civitatem benedicimus."

Redding turned to Miriam. "Huh?"

She pointed to the fort. "That's the inscription you see under the statue."

"Something tells me you know what that means," Redding said, returning his gaze to the NATO warships.

She tugged his sleeve and pointed to the statue. "That's the Virgin Mary and the words are, 'We bless you and your city.' "

"That's what the Sicilians think the Virgin Mary said?" asked Redding, now giving in to her persistence.

"That's what she *did* say, or so goes the legend."

"I sense a history lesson coming on."

Miriam squinted her eyes at him but pushed on. "In the year 42 AD, Saint Paul—who wasn't a saint at the time—"

"That I get," he quipped.

"Paul came to Messina to convert its people to

Christianity," she continued. "He was successful enough that some of the locals returned with him to Palestine to meet Mary. They persuaded her to send a letter back with them to the people of Messina, and so she did, tying it up with a lock of her hair." Miriam pointed to the inscription on the fort. "Allegedly, those words right there are how she closed that letter—which is why she is known here as *Madonna della lettera*—Madonna of the letter."

Redding nodded his head, then pointed at Miriam. "But you don't have the tooth—um—the letter," he said, laughing at his own joke.

Miriam furrowed her brow. "Tooth?"

"*Jaws*? The scene where the mayor...sorry, dumb movie reference. Never mind."

Miriam tapped the rail of the gunwale, trying to think of a way to keep the conversation going and looked to Redding for help.

"You really dig old stuff," he said.

Miriam couldn't contain her laugh but collected herself to make a point. "Not *old* stuff so much as things that last. Things that are important enough to preserve. Things that stand the test of time, to be pedestrian."

Redding shook his head emphatically. "You may be a lot of things, but pedestrian isn't one of them."

Miriam smiled briefly at the compliment. "What I mean is, lessons from history that have withstood the passing of centuries: values, principles, concepts, beliefs that remain relevant. Human desires, ambitions, ideologies haven't changed. Governments haven't changed too much: there are good and bad." Pointing to the statue, she asked, "Are the people who put that up, who believed in the legend, so different from the people on those streets over there, or anywhere? History offers the answer: not much."

"Well, now," Redding answered, "if you're going to talk over my head, you don't have to aim so high."

Miriam cocked her head, pursed her lips, and squinted at him. "Over your head? My foot. I know about you."

Redding leaned back and stared at her with a wrinkled brow.

She turned to walk away with a delighted look on her face, but he stopped her.

"Someday maybe you'll tell me what you meant by that—but for now I'm wondering how we happen to be having this conversation in light of what I earlier detected as an air of disapproval."

Miriam stared at him for a moment, then looked out at the harbor.

"Don't tell me you don't know what I'm talking about," Redding insisted.

"Yes, I know. I figured since I won't be on the ship much longer, I would just forget about it."

"But since I brought it up…"

She hesitated, chewed on her lip, then turned to him. "But since you brought it up—you must know what my job is." Miriam's breathing became heavy, and she brushed the hair from her face. "It's important, what we're about to do—of course, I mean the peace talks."

Redding screwed up his face and looked away.

"It's going to be difficult enough," she continued, "and anything that makes it even more difficult—well, like your actions in the Gulf…"

"*My* actions!" Redding jumped in indignantly. "You mean you bought that load of crap from that guy on TV—Colonel what's-his-name?"

"I'm not naïve! I'm sure he was dramatizing it for his own purposes, but the State Department and the Vice President's staff heard nothing to the contrary from the navy."

Redding walked a few steps away from her, fuming, then spun around. "Who the hell do you think you are? You think the navy tells you *everything*?"

Miriam crossed her arms in front of her. "It's not important what I think. It's not about me. We have a job to do. There's a greater purpose here. These talks represent—"

Redding clenched his jaw and cut her off. "So, the success or failure of the peace talks rests on me. World peace is on me. Fine, let's swap places. Put me across the table from those Iranian bastards, because I know who the enemy is."

Miriam put her finger to her lips and looked around the deck.

Redding lowered his voice but not the intensity. "I'm not a politician. I don't get my information from filtered briefings on pieces of paper. I don't have the luxury of discussing a course of action with team members over lattes or asking subordinates to get back to me with reports before I take action on a crisis that's right in front of me!" He held his gaze into Miriam's eyes.

Her mouth slightly agape, she managed a reply. "Maybe I *don't* know about you." She turned and walked away.

Chapter Eleven

Constitution's spar deck was outfitted as a large outdoor dining hall. Tivoli lighting hanging from the rigging crisscrossed the width of the hull. Redding, James, Gunderson, Kobach, Bates, Cooper, and Dr. Hannah were seated with officers from the NATO vessels in dress uniforms. Other local dignitaries joined them for a feast of local seafood favorites from one of the gourmet restaurants near the harbor.

Redding, still troubled by the afternoon's conversation with Miriam, avoided eye contact with her, but he spotted Buckley headed for the enlisted personnel's table and waved him over. "Sergeant, over here."

"Sir, I don't—"

"I insist." Redding spotted Rachel Dover nearby. "Seaman Dover, would you please add a chair to this table?"

"Aye, sir," Rachel replied, grabbed the nearest chair, and carried it to the officers' table.

"Thank you," Redding continued, "and please set another place for Sergeant Buckley."

A look of disapproval showed on James' face as Buckley graciously took his place at the table.

Redding rose to make the introduction. "Everyone, this is Master Gunnery Sergeant Jack Buckley. He wouldn't mention it, so I will. He's a recipient of the

Medal of Honor, among a slew of other hardware. We're lucky to have him aboard."

James applauded just enough not to stand out from the enthusiastic applause from everyone else at the table that caused Buckley to blush and nod his appreciation.

The captain of the US Navy frigate reached across the table to shake Buckley's hand. "Sergeant Buckley, I'd sure like to hear your story, if you're willing."

"Me too," Redding chimed in while starting in on his meal. "If you can pry it out of him."

Buckley shrugged off the invitation and took the dinner plate from Rachel.

Gunderson stared at his dish and nudged Cooper. "What *is* that?"

"Calamari," she responded in a hushed voice.

"*What?*" he whispered.

Cooper leaned close to Gunderson's ear. "Squid. Just eat it."

Sailors from *Constitution* and those selected for the privilege from the other ships sat at additional tables arranged around the deck, but most of the guests were too interested in the array of antique military hardware to be content sitting at their tables.

Basker showed off the carronades to a group of curious sailors from several nations. No one seemed to care that few of them understood a word he was saying.

Mac was on the fighting platform of the mainmast with another group of NATO sailors enjoying themselves while looking down on everyone else. Many clung to the shrouds below the platform, awaiting their turn on its limited space.

Tebic displayed his skill with computer games on his smartphone to the amusement of some of the foreigners crowded over his shoulders to see the screen. Tebic's eyes widened, he raised his fist in the air, and cheers went up from the group.

Rachel had attracted her own fan club amidship at the pinrail of the mainmast near the officers' table. The club was exclusively male. From a distance, no one could tell what they were talking about, but it didn't appear to have anything to do with the ship. She periodically looked over her shoulder at the officers' table, and specifically at James.

The local wine was good—perhaps too good. Miriam kept an eye on Redding, who rarely looked up from his plate except to signal the waiter for more wine.

Kobach caught the attention of Cooper and pointed at his watch.

She nudged Gunderson. "It's time," she whispered. Then to Redding, "May we be excused, sir?"

Redding nodded his approval and continued his dinner.

Miriam sneaked a look and a smile at Cooper.

The Greek captain put his fork down on his empty plate, looked around at the American sailors and marines. He turned to Buckley sitting next to him and examined his period uniform, then addressed Redding in Greek.

Redding looked at the captain, shrugged, and looked around the table.

"He asked why you're not wearing the old uniform," said Miriam.

Redding wiped his mouth with his napkin. "Tell him it didn't fit," he said in a monotone, then returned to his dinner.

Miriam held her eyes on Redding for a moment,

then addressed the Greek captain in his language.

James whispered to Miriam, "What did you say?"

She poked at a morsel of calamari and replied matter-of-factly, "I told him it didn't fit."

The captain of the British destroyer in the squadron pushed his plate away with satisfaction, then turned to Redding. "I was just thinking, Captain, how being on the very ship that caused our navy such grief more than two hundred years ago makes me feel eerily out of place."

Redding downed the last swallow of wine from his glass, then hoisted it toward the British captain and answered brusquely, "I can relate."

The British captain stared uncomfortably at Redding for a moment, then looked around the table.

James and Miriam quickly looked away.

The captain of the US frigate intervened. "I could get used to this. It sure beats where we're headed— patrol duty in the Gulf."

The British captain chimed in, "Us too. It seems the phrase 'international waters' is one unknown to the Iranians." Then to Redding, "You want to swap?"

Miriam laughed nervously, then tried to change the subject. "Where do you hail from?"

Redding jumped in, his speech now somewhat slurred. "Swap? No way. I love it here, especially since I know what *you're* sailing into. Don't believe for a second your mission is to protect the innocent, because if you do, you might find *yourself* in command of a wooden doghouse." He turned to the British captain. "Or maybe your navy isn't as forward thinking as ours. See, that's our edge. First, our navy is in step with the green movement. No oil burning here. No carbon footprint. And keep this under your hat: *Constitution* barely shows up on radar—she's mostly wood, rope, and canvas. The wood absorbs radar waves. She's a stealth ship. This is what you should aspire to. Everyone even gets to wear cute costumes. Swap? Wouldn't think of it."

Redding wasn't so inebriated that he couldn't recognize the range of reactions from surprise to embarrassment. He hung his head and played with the fork on his plate.

Cooper and Gunderson walked carefully toward the table with a cake too large for one person to carry. It was decorated with two toy ships, one sinking into the top layer, with words that read "Huzzah! Redding 1— Bad Guys 0." Beaming, they placed it on the table in front of Redding. Sailors and marines gathered around from all over the spar deck. Cheers rang out from the sailors in the rigging.

Redding stared at the cake, fought back a choke, then managed a smile and a nod at Gunderson and Cooper. He could only look briefly across the table at the blank faces staring back at him.

James looked at Miriam, but her jaw was tight, and she looked away.

Redding rose. "Everyone, enjoy. Please excuse me. It seems the wine has caught up to me." He picked up his cap and headed for his cabin.

The sailors and marines who had gathered near the table looked at one another. Some shook their heads. All backed away and dispersed back into their groupings.

Redding disappeared belowdecks.

The US frigate captain looked at the faces around

the table, forced a smile, and picked up the carving knife near the cake. "I, for one, am going to enjoy a piece of this victory cake." He turned to James. "May I do the honors?"

"Of course, sir," James responded. The rest of the guests smiled uncomfortably. Some looked at their watches.

Miriam played along, but her mind was fast at work on the issue of how she would deal with Redding in the encounter she knew was coming. She took on the role of hostess and did her best to help the US captain rescue the event—while privately working up a head of steam. For their part, the guests made her feel as though it worked, but they soon thanked her, made their excuses, and disembarked. The cake remained largely untouched.

****

The sounds of foot traffic on the spar deck above faded as Redding sat at the desk in his cabin, massaging his head with his hands.

He ignored the knock at the door, but it opened anyway. Miriam entered and stood in the half-opened doorway.

Redding turned briefly to her, then away. "Lady, where I come from you wait for a response. If you don't get one, you go away. Here, let me show you." He rose and approached her, but she closed the door behind her.

"What made you such a bastard, Redding?"

"Is that a response to a *Jeopardy* cue? What was the dollar value on that one?"

"All right, I'll answer my own question. After I met you that first time—you remember, right? When I got the cold shoulder?"

"As I recall," Redding interjected, "there was a chill coming from your general direction as well."

"And I explained why earlier this afternoon," she answered, pointing to the quarterdeck above Redding's cabin. "I don't want to revisit that, but it does seem to fit with some research I did on you."

Redding's eyes widened.

Miriam pointed to herself and answered his questioning look. "Security clearance." She paced in front of him, alternately looking him straight in the eye, at the deck, and out the portlights. "You've built yourself quite a reputation in the navy. You've been stuck at lieutenant for how long? Why's that? Your score on the admissions test was off the charts, yet your academic achievement at the academy was mediocre. You were all about individual achievement in sports and anything having to do with combat: fencing, boxing, sailing the one-man skiffs, almost made the Olympics—but a team guy? Not so much."

"Oh, so you have a double major in psychology?"

"I can connect dots. Recognition in one-on-one competition is what you've always been about. You don't like taking orders. You'd rather trust your instincts."

Redding turned his back. "Are you still here?"

"The one time you had control of a team was on the *Minerva*. That didn't work out too well. You didn't get the recognition from the navy you thought you deserved. Others were in control of that, not you."

"I wasn't looking for recognition. I was too busy trying to win a battle. Look, *Doctor*, I've been scolded by the best. You need to up your game."

Miriam ignored him. "You want to be a navy man

but only on your terms. In letting you down, the navy confirmed your view of people and organizations that you can't control."

Redding whipped around. "Then maybe I don't belong on this ship either."

"If you have the feeling you were born in the wrong century, this would have been the perfect command for you. In her fighting days, the captains of this ship didn't receive orders over a radio from someone at a desk hundreds of miles away. But now this ship represents something you don't seem to appreciate. She represents the birth of our navy, and for more than two hundred years, it has been an honor for navy men and women to be associated with *Constitution*, to carry on traditions. You asked me earlier who the hell I think I am, well, who the hell are you to dishonor them?"

Redding's jaw was set. He faced Miriam, but his eyes wandered as he searched for a response.

She approached him slowly. "You need someone or something to shake you up, Commander. You need, uh, an epiphany, or something, something I don't think anyone can give you." She turned to leave, opened the door, and paused a moment. "I wish I could. Personally, I think you *may* be worth it."

"Wait a minute!" Redding paced with his head down as Miriam stood at the door. "Close the door."

She hesitated.

"Close the *God damned door*!"

Miriam's jaw dropped. She closed the door but stood leaning against it.

Redding kept pacing and chewing on his lip. Then he halted in his tracks. "Screw it! Okay, Dr. Hannah, you like epiphanies, you're going to get one. You describe me as a loner who acts on his own, who doesn't like following orders, not a team player. Maybe some of that is true, and it certainly will be in a minute. You think I need something to shake me up? I've had that, thank you. Here's what you don't know about that day in the Gulf and where your *security clearance* wouldn't have done you any good, because it was buried beyond your reach."

Redding proceeded to tell Miriam every detail of every high-resolution image of the Gulf event that had plagued him since and refused to leave him in peace. By the time he got to the meeting with Admiral Towne, her head was down, her hands covered her face and she sobbed, but he didn't let up.

"There, now I've just lived up to your image. I've acted on my own and in the process violated a direct order. I'm not sure I give a damn anymore, and I'll tell you why. Because I had a close-up look at the faces of those poor people screaming at me, looking straight at me, expecting me to save them—and I *could* have, but for a few precious seconds when I hesitated. I thought of something else, about my orders. Maybe I was thinking of my screwups in the past and didn't want any more of that. My career, you know. Whatever it was, those seconds were all the difference to those people— and I have to live with that. My bonus prize, my medal to commemorate the event, to emblazon it forever in my memory, as if I could ever forget, is knowing there's a little girl in a hospital with no one—*no one*— and a mother who considered nothing but saving that child before she died."

Redding resumed pacing, trying to cool himself

off. It didn't work. He stopped, stared out the window and delivered his conclusion to Miriam precisely and deliberately. "Everything I've told you would have been verified by my XO on the *Minerva* and the entire crew—but in consideration of *your job, your mission*, the navy put a lid on it! They stuck me here, and they put a lid on it!" Redding looked down at the cold, dark waters of the harbor. He was spent, and the heated exchange had propelled the wine straight to his head.

Miriam looked up, her cheeks soaked with tears and her voice cracking. "Why did you tell me this?"

Redding wasn't sure himself. Maybe it was part relief from having to hold it in. Or maybe he didn't want Miriam to hold onto the image of him she'd had just moments earlier. "A minute ago, you wanted to leave. You are now excused."

Miriam, stunned and unsteady on her feet, choked back her sobbing as she quietly left.

****

Miriam couldn't bear going to the quarters she shared with Cooper. She didn't want to explain her puffy eyes and the redness in her face. She would need a lot of time to force them from view. On deck, she made her way aft, avoiding eye contact with anyone who came near. She leaned against the gunwale just over the port side of the captain's cabin. Below her, light from the cabin reflected on the water below. The shadow of Redding standing near the window was animated by the gentle rocking of *Constitution* responding to the incoming tide. An hour later, the scene had not changed, but the need for sleep overtook her and she went below.

Chapter Twelve

Constitution sailed with the outgoing tide the next morning. A brisk wind and a white-tipped chop on the sea presaged a change in the weather. In the bow wake beneath the ship's ornate billethead, dolphins played and chirped as though conversing with the ship, to the great amusement of members of the crew leaning over the gunwale.

Miriam stared at the bow wake but stood off from the others. Even the gaiety of the dolphins could not distract her from her thoughts of the previous night. She was still shaken by the images Redding had burned into her mind, by the understanding of what they would mean to the rest of his life, and by the distance that conversation had put between them, realizing only then how much that distance now meant to her.

But for the occasional greeting and brief conversations that she tried to avoid, Miriam spent the day alone, mostly on *Constitution*'s bow, looking forward, avoiding the ship's stern and its view of the past. The ship spoke to her with creaks and groans and the whistling of the wind through her rigging—but it was an unfamiliar language. She did not respond.

In a few days she would be leaving the ship and, hopefully, those thoughts, those memories. She would be in Libya examining the ruins of the ancient fort, but now with less interest than she'd had days ago. If it weren't for the possible connection the ruins had with her history research, she would have asked to skip the stop and head straight to Tripoli—anything to get off the ship and start the process of forgetting. Rejoining Vice President Mitchell's staff and being preoccupied once again in her work was looking more attractive.

****

That evening, Tebic didn't dine with his crewmates. He stayed in his radio room, his dinner in front of him. Keeping him company was an elaborate array of electronic devices, among them the ship's radio, his smartphone, and a notebook computer, interconnected by a tangle of wires. Beaming with pride at his creation, he got a little too excited and knocked over his can of soda.

"Ahhh!" he yelled, grabbing for a rag and frantically mopping up the mess.

Satisfied that he had avoided a catastrophe, he flipped a switch to turn on the electronic menagerie. Lights flickered on the devices and screens displayed the booting process. He heaved a sigh of relief, but then caught his breath when smoke curled from the radio.

Tebic panicked, turned off the power, and gripped his lower lip as he looked pleadingly to heaven for divine intervention.

****

It was well after midnight. Redding resigned himself to another sleepless night as he lay in his berth, fully dressed, turning his cap in his hands, unable to forget the scolding Miriam had given him. Not knowing the facts of the Gulf encounter, she had nevertheless touched a nerve with the truth about him. The portrait of Captain Preble seemed to be staring at him. He surrendered to his sleeplessness, donned his cap, and went topside.

Mac was at the helm getting directions from ensign Justin Kobach, the Officer of the Deck. Both saluted Redding as he appeared on the spar deck, but he walked toward the bow without acknowledging them.

Redding strolled without purpose or direction. He stopped to feel the cold of the iron carronades, asleep for more than two centuries. He looked out to sea and imagined their targets of that era. As bloody as the fight had been on *Minerva*, he thought, it was sterile compared to what must have been the savagery of those historic battles—men standing on this blood-covered deck staring down the barrels of the enemy's guns at point-blank range.

On deck and in the rigging above, seamen chatted in small groups, awaiting commands from Kobach to trim sails according to changes in the wind. Redding ignored their stares as he came near them. He walked to the bow, perched himself as far forward as he could, wrapped one arm around the massive bowsprit and looked down at the wake churned by *Constitution*'s bow. The algae, excited to a state of phosphorescence, and the full moon illuminated her ornamental billethead.

Kobach and Mac glanced at one another as Redding approached their positions at the helm, then he stood silently for a full minute before he motioned Mac away from the wheel. Redding fitted his hands to the rounded handles protruding from a ring of oak on the huge varnished spoke wheel as Mac and Kobach stood by. He tested the tension as he gently applied left, then right rudder while looking into the rigging and the sails.

"She favors starboard, doesn't she?"

"That she does, sir," replied Mac, glancing at Kobach.

Redding looked aloft. "That's a sail trim issue. Probably costing us a half a knot. We'll let that go for tonight. I'll take her. You're relieved."

"Aye, sir."

"That goes for you too, Mr. Kobach," added Redding. "You can both get some chow, turn in, and tell your relievers the same thing."

Both men saluted Redding and walked away. Kobach looking at him warily, but Redding ignored it and kept his attention on the sails and the feel of the ship through the helm.

From the moment he took the wheel, the mood of the night acquired a surreal quality. One by one, the two-dozen remaining crew on duty became silent motionless silhouettes against the bright moonlight.

For the first time since he boarded her in Naples, Redding became aware of the scent of *Constitution*, a blend of cotton canvas, oak, Douglas fir, and tar-impregnated hemp rope. It was a penetrating therapeutic aroma with a calming effect that, together with the only sounds he could hear—the creaking of the ship, the churning of the bow wake, and the wind playing an unfamiliar rhapsody on the cordage of her rigging—seemed to transport Redding's spirit to a different dimension in time and space.

The weight of the Gulf incident and the tensions of the last few days melted away. He was at peace for the first time since that day in the Gulf. Time was paralyzed. The scene remained the same until the figure of a man appeared in front of him, near the main mast.

113

The officer's uniform on the figure was period early-nineteenth century. A dim but glowing corona surrounded the figure. He was turned sideways but appeared to be looking at Redding. The moonlight glinted off a gilt-braided epaulet on his shoulder, and one hand rested on the butt of the sword strapped to his side.

"Lieutenant James? Is that you?"

The figure turned, walked away into the shadow of the mainmast, and disappeared from view. Redding took a step in its direction, but didn't let go of the helm. He looked around at the other crewmen—dark, two-dimensional frozen figures. He started to call out to them but froze as well and a chill went up his spine. After a brief moment, he repositioned himself behind the wheel and relaxed his hold on it. He ignored the compass, letting *Constitution* balance herself and seek her own heading.

The sails were full and quiet, not luffing. The spanker, the huge parking-lot-size sail over the quarterdeck, mounted to the mizzenmast in back of the helm, was stretched taut between its spars. It angled sharply to starboard and strained at its sheets as it drove the ship forward. Then, inexplicably, the wind in the spanker alone went slack. He looked quickly at the other sails. They had not changed. The wind was still brisk and bulging the square sails on all three masts. He looked back at the spanker. The boom swept aft, like a baseball player pulling his bat back, waiting to swing, the sheets lay loose on the deck under the boom.

"That impossible," he said to himself.

Then, as he was still looking at the sail, it slammed back to starboard flat against the wind with a thunderous clap, tight against the sheets, sending forward a shock blast of wind.

Redding's officer's cap blew off and sailed over the rail, spinning in the air until it landed in the sea. He had no reflexive reaction to reach for it but walked to the gunwale and looked overboard as it floated away, enveloped in the phosphorescent glow of the stern wake as if consumed by fire.

He scanned the crew's shadowy figures as he returned to the helm. They were frozen as before, but there was no fright or anxiety in him. The reflection of the moon on the sea ahead blazed a pathway south. He allowed *Constitution* to follow that path unassisted, as he sailed on unaware of the wind, sounds, the crew, or the passage of time until the night was adjourned by a soft glow from the east. The mysteries of that night faded with the light.

The dawn was just bright enough for Tebic to study Redding's face as he timidly approached from below.

"I was told I could find you here, sir," Tebic said, uneasily.

"And so you have, Seaman Tebic," Redding answered without a look in Tebic's direction.

"Aye, sir," Tebic responded. "It's—it's like this," he continued, looking up briefly, as if the right words might be written across the sky. "I believe we may have a communications problem."

It took only a glance from Redding to see the fear in Tebic's eyes, but the captain masked his reaction, looked away, and stared off in the distance. "Oh, I don't know, Seaman Tebic. I think we've been communicating all right."

"Uh, n-n-n-no, sir, I mean the, uh, the radio. It

seems to be out of order."

"Then I guess Fleet Command won't be able to bother us," Redding responded with a shrug.

Tebic finally exhaled.

Redding hid his smile from Tebic. "That is, until you fix—what—you—broke."

"Y-y-y-yes, sir."

Redding stepped to the side of the wheel. "Now—take the wheel."

The panicky expression Tebic showing to that point only worsened as his eyes widened. "Me, sir? I've never…no one ever."

Redding pointed to the compass. "Put her on course 185 degrees."

Tebic took the wheel and locked his focus on the compass in front of him. Using both hands to grip one spoke handle, he turned the wheel to the right.

"No, the other way," said Redding, "turn to port until the compass needle points to 185 degrees."

Tebic wiped his brow. "Oh—sorry, right, I mean *left*, turn *left*."

Tebic turned the wheel as he focused on the compass, then Redding pried Tebic's fingers loose from the spoke handle. "Spread your arms out wider. Gives you more leverage."

Redding helped Tebic find the right spread of spoke handles for his limited reach, lingering a minute until the young sailor calmed down.

"Relax," he said. "The ship knows more about sailing than any of us."

He took a last look around and caught the dawn sending a wave of golden light that first illuminated the topsails, then urged the darkness away as it pressed downward to the deck, the hull, and the wake curling away from the bow. He headed belowdecks.

As he entered the companionway, he spotted Ensign Bates coming out of the head.

"Mr. Bates, I need an Officer of the Deck. You're it. Sorry if it's not your watch."

"No problem, sir. Just need to get changed."

Redding passed by Buckley's quarters. A light shone under the door. He hesitated, then knocked.

"Yes, who is it?"

Redding called through the door. "I saw your light. Got a minute?"

"Of course, sir."

Buckley opened the door and drew to attention, but Redding waved it off as he entered and looked around the tight quarters. The room was nearly devoid of personal touches but for a number of books on a shelf and a couple of Marine Corps flags—the official one with the globe and anchor and the original Gadsden flag with the coiled snake and motto, Don't Tread on Me.

Near the flag was a framed copy of an oil painting of a marine officer in an early 1800s uniform. Redding picked it up and read the inscription. "First Lieutenant William Sharp Bush. Cool name."

"I...borrowed that from the museum display," Buckley replied, showing some embarrassment.

"Who was this guy, and why does he rate a place of honor in your quarters? Distant relative?"

"In a way. He was a marine who served aboard this ship in the war of 1812."

Redding grinned. "Hah! Knew I saw a resemblance."

Buckley smiled briefly. "Yes, sir. He was the first

US Marine to die in that war. It was in the battle with the British frigate *Guerriere*."

"No kidding? Well, we can be confident the resemblance will end there."

Redding walked and looked around as he talked. "Every time I hear that name *Guerriere*, I think of *derriere*. Shows you where my head goes sometimes."

Redding's attention turned to a lone picture on a shelf of a woman in her mid-thirties and a boy about twelve. "Yours?"

Buckley nodded. "Daughter and grandson."

Still looking around the room, Redding tried to put Buckley at ease. "I wanted to make sure I didn't embarrass you the other night when I introduced you to those NATO officers."

"No, sir," Buckley responded uncomfortably. "I'm not used to it, but I survived."

"Nevertheless, I thought I'd get to see my first Medal of Honor, or at least that fistful of Purple Hearts I understand you've earned."

Buckley hesitated. "I don't keep them, sir." He pointed to the picture. "They have them."

"May I ask why not?"

Buckley was clearly uncomfortable. After a moment, he tried to answer, but Redding waved him off. "That's okay. I think I understand."

Redding changed the subject. "I've been curious. Why did you take this assignment?"

Buckley swallowed before he answered. "It's all they had for me."

Redding could hear the pain in his voice. An open book on the table offered an opportunity to change the subject yet again.

"*The Complete Works of Shakespeare*," said Redding as he flipped up the cover. "I'm impressed." Redding laid the cover down to the open page. "*Romeo and Juliet.* I played the part in high school—Romeo, I mean, not Juliet." Redding laughed at his own joke. His attempt at humor brought a slight smile from the stoic Buckley, and Redding settled for that.

Redding picked up the open book and scanned the page. "So, where are we here—Romeo's friend Mercutio is fighting Tybalt. Romeo tries to break it up, but in the process, creates an opening for Tybalt to stab Mercutio." He continued as though explaining the scene to a class, throwing his voice across the room and gesturing. "Romeo, enraged, kills Tybalt, his would-be future in-law. That'll mess things up at a Christmas get-together, huh?" Redding chuckled to himself, then glanced at Buckley for a reaction and got the same slender smile.

Redding pressed on, reading with a mock performance. "Romeo to Mercutio before he died: 'Courage, man, the hurt cannot be much.' Mercutio answers, 'No, 'tis...'tis not so deep as a well, nor so wide as a church door, but 'tis enough, 'twill serve. Ask for me tomorrow and you shall find me a grave man.' "

The men looked at each other for a moment, then Redding put the book on the table, still open as before, and made for the door. He stood in the half-opened door and turned to Buckley. "I think you will find this day very interesting."

Chapter Thirteen

The entire crew was on deck, standing in formation, but at ease as they spoke quietly among themselves, questioning each other and shrugging their shoulders. Miriam snapped pictures of the formation. The buzz of the crews' curiosity only increased when Redding emerged from below, wearing his period uniform and cocked hat. The uniform, as it turned out, *did* fit. Under his arm was the book from his cabin on the history of the ship in her wartime years.

"Ten-hut!" yelled James.

The crew gawked at Redding but snapped to attention. Miriam just stared with an open mouth.

Redding stood before James, waiting for him to collect himself.

"The crew is…assembled…as requested…sir," he muttered.

"Thank you, Mr. James." Redding walked slowly along the ranks, trying to read each crewman and officer. When he got to Buckley, he made sure everyone could hear him. "Master Gunnery Sergeant Buckley!"

"Sir," Buckley answered, staring straight ahead.

"The sailors and marines aboard this ship, are they combat ready?" Redding asked, throwing his voice across the assembly.

"Sir?" Buckley stole a glance at James.

"The big guns, boarding pikes, muskets, pistols, cutlasses. Are they trained in the defense of this vessel?" Redding asked emphatically.

James approached and interjected, "Sir, this goodwill tour involves education lectures, entertaining dignitaries, showing the flag, that sort of thing. The crew was mostly picked for that purpose."

Redding walked to the center position in front of the assembly. "*Constitution* is not only the oldest military ship in the world, she is the oldest ship still floating of *any* kind. More to the point, for our purposes, she also holds the distinction of being *still*...a commissioned US Navy warship." Holding up the book, he sneaked a look at Miriam. "It says in here the crews who served on her were the best of the best. For example, they could fire and reload the big guns in under three minutes. That's how you get a record of 33 and 0." He paused to read their faces. "We have a few days until we're due across the Med. We can watch the dolphins play in the bow wake or we can drill."

Redding caught sight of Miriam, her jaw still agape, and pressed his lips together to hide his smile.

"*We—will—drill*. Sergeant Buckley will lead those drills for marines *and* sailors. They will commence as soon as possible." He paused and scanned the faces of the crew and officers. "Officers, Mr. Buckley, you have your orders!"

"Aye, sir!" Buckley saluted with a glint in his eyes.

Redding forced a severe expression on his face, turned, and walked toward the quarterdeck, but James intercepted him and spoke in a hushed tone.

"Sir, we've only ever fired the salute guns. They were specially adapted for that purpose, and even then, just with powder, no shot."

James would be a problem, but Redding was determined to explain himself as little as possible. He pointed to the rack of cannonballs near them.

"Yes, sir, but those are just for show. And one more thing, sir. Technically, the marines don't operate the big guns—that's navy only."

Redding looked at James, then at Buckley who was already fielding questions from the contingent of marines and sailors.

"Yeah, Lieutenant, but my guess is he knows how to hit what he's aiming at."

With that, Redding walked to the quarterdeck, not wishing to invite any more questions. He didn't look at Miriam and didn't need to. He could hear her camera clicking away and took in the reactions from the crew from a distance.

Buckley faced the assembled crew. "I'll be coming up with a training schedule and will post it in the crew quarters." He looked at James and saluted. "That's all I have for now, sir."

Red-faced, James fanned his hand at the crew. "Dismissed." Then he walked to the gunwale, leaned over, and looked out to sea shaking his head.

The crew broke ranks but immediately huddled in groups. The buzz of conversation from them delighted Redding. When he turned his gaze to Miriam, she put her hands on her hips and cocked her head. He answered her with a shrug while mouthing the word *what?*

Buckley returned to the spar deck from a quick trip below, notepad in hand. He went methodically around the deck, counting cannonballs, examining the carronades' barrels for cracks and checking their undercarriage. Miriam snapped pictures of Buckley and the crew that followed him at a distance.

"Captain's right." Basker slapped Mac on the back. "This *is* going to beat watching dolphins and just sittin' round."

Mac answered Basker while watching Buckley. "Have you ever actually fired a gun? I mean, I know you've heard them going off in your neighborhood while you were sitting at the dinner table, but it's not the same thing."

The crew cracked up. Even Buckley couldn't contain himself. He looked over his shoulder at Mac and shook his head as if to shame him.

"Dude," Basker replied, pointing his finger at Mac's face. "I can throw a baseball a hundred miles an hour from over sixty feet away and hit a target no bigger than your fat grill. It's all hand-eye coordination. They don't teach you that in the Future Farmers of America."

Basker looked Mac in the eye as he pointed his thumb over his shoulder at the crew who laughed and applauded.

Mac pointed back at him. "Yeah, the FFA doesn't teach shooting, but every ranch hand knows how anyway. A bullet is the best rattlesnake antivenom there is, and hospitals are a long ride away on horseback."

Redding maintained his distance from the action on deck but leaned against the pinrail of the mizzenmast. Miriam used her camera lens as a gesture of contact with him, pointing it at him and zooming in, but he walked away to the quarterdeck and examined the spanker sail and its rigging. The concave surface of the sail caught, magnified, and reflected the morning sun onto Redding. He shielded his eyes from the glare as he gazed aloft at the sail and shook his head. The sound of a pigeon cooing caught his attention, and he looked for it in the rigging. A cock pigeon, neck feathers fluffed, strutted and cooed as he followed a hen the length of the spar on the mizzen topsail before she flew away in the direction of the Sicilian coast, leaving him perched alone.

"Been there, buddy," he said, nodding his head. "You're on the right ship."

The cock then flew off in the direction of the hen.

"What? Where's your pride? Well, good luck, pal."

Redding followed the flight of the birds toward Mt. Etna, off the starboard beam, its summit cloaked by a curtain of portentous smoke, warped by the winds aloft—from the south.

Chapter Fourteen

Open gun ports streamed the morning light across the gun deck as Buckley stood by a long gun with a class arrayed in an arc around it.

"The ceremonial saluting guns we've been using won't be of any use to us for this training, so it will all be new to you." He pointed to a rack of cannonballs. "The long guns fire the twenty-four-pound balls up to a mile, but with a lot more powder than we've been using for show—so there's going to be a lot more recoil. I'd better not see anyone standing behind one of these when a round goes off. Most of the guns are unusable, but we've got a couple of these long guns and couple of the carronades on the spar deck above to practice with."

Buckley pointed to the breach rope, a heavy rope connected to the hull at both ends and passing through an iron loop at the back end of the barrel. "The breach rope doesn't entirely protect you from the recoil. The gun is still going to jump back. The breach rope just keeps this starboard gun from becoming a port gun when it's fired, and it keeps anyone standing in back of it from becoming a smoothie on the inside of the opposite hull." He quickly scanned the faces of the class, then he pointed to Cooper, Bates, Kobach, and Gunderson, who were standing with the crew. "These will be co-ed classes, meaning the officers are going to be learning right along with the rest of you.

"Up to now, we've been just making noise." He walked to an open gun port and pointed out to sea. "The purpose of these drills is to find out what it takes to actually hit something."

Mac piped up. "No sweat, Gunny."

"You think not," Buckley replied. "Come over here and look down the barrel. All of you, pick a gun and look down the barrel."

The class gathered behind the guns and sighted down the barrels.

Buckley pointed through the gun port. "The ship is always moving, and there isn't a computer compensating for that. *You* are the computer."

Basker raised his hand. "If that means Tebic is gonna be our best gunner, we're screwed."

Basker and Mac pushed Tebic back and forth between them as the class laughed. "We'll see who's better at hitting the strike zone, Mr. ERA," joked Tebic.

"We're not really expected to hit anything with these, are we?" asked Guzman.

Mac turned to him. "Speak for yourself."

Buckley pointed to the back of the class. "Captain thinks differently, Mr. Guzman." The class whipped around to see Redding standing in the background observing the class, his arms folded behind him. Redding pulled one arm out and pointed the class back to Buckley.

Miriam took notes and snapped pictures but paid as much attention to Redding as to the class.

Guzman pointed to the open sea. "What do we use for a target?"

Buckley pointed to him. "You, if I find you're not paying attention."

Basker tapped the barrel of a long gun and looked at Guzman. "Yeah, I could picture you as a catcher's mitt."

Buckley clapped his hands. "Let's refocus here, people. This is nothing like firing the salute guns. They've been modified just for show." Buckley waited for calm, then held up a piece of paper with a handwritten numbered list. "These are the steps for reloading and firing. You will rehearse the steps on your own time until you remember them perfectly. I've put you in teams temporarily based on the number of people we have to work with."

He pointed to a block and tackle at the rear of the gun. "Step number *one*: haul back. The gun will kick back when it's fired but not far enough to get access to the muzzle. So, one man uses this block and tackle to pull it back farther."

He pointed to a pole with a twisted metal fixture on the end in a rack of tools overhead. "*Two*: worm it. The steel claws on the end of this wad worm clean out the barrel, removing scraps of canvas and cloth left in there from the powder charge and wadding. Those scraps will be smoldering, so you have to get them out of there before you reload.

"*Three*: sponge it." Pointing at another tool in the rack, Buckley continued. "You dip that tool with the sponge on the end in that bucket of water and ram it down the barrel to clean it and douse any particles that are still burning. If you were to skip that step and load the hot gun with a new pack of powder, half of you could end up as a red smear on the ocean out there. *Get it?*"

The sobering effect on the class was immediate.

"*Four*: ream it."

Classmates grinned and nudged each other.

Buckley held up a stiff wire rod and pointed to a small hole in the top of the gun barrel near the back end. "The gunner uses this reamer to clean out the vent hole here by the firing mechanism. It gets clogged when the gun is fired.

"*Five*: powder monkey—a good name for him considering this class." Buckley waited for the snickers to subside. "The next few steps are a two-man operation. Powder monkey puts a bag of powder in the barrel. His teammate, ram man, pushes it all the way down the barrel"—he pointed back to the rack of tools overhead—"with that wooden ram.

"*Six* is wad one." Buckley showed the class what looked like a miniature pillow. "The same monkey puts a packing wad in the barrel, then ram man shoves it home. The cannonball fits loosely in the barrel. Wadding fits tightly, so it creates a seal that delivers more of the explosive force to the ball.

"*Seven*: ball man. He's a separate guy, waiting with the twenty-four-pound ball. He puts it in the barrel. Ram man shoves it home.

"*Eight* is wad two, same procedure as wad one. Without the second packing wad, the ball would roll out if the angle on the barrel is downward.

"You've got to hustle and at the same time be damned careful. As soon as that team is done, *nine*: run it out. Both side tackle teams haul in their lines to run the gun out through the port. Jam the carriage right up against the hull."

As Buckley marched through the tutorial, Redding was increasingly impressed with his knowledge and command of the class.

"What's the next number?" Buckley yelled, testing the class.

"*Ten!*" came the loud response from the class.

"Right, *ten* is prime time. The man who was on the wad worm is now the primer." He held up a cow horn. "In this horn is a mixture of powder and wine." He looked at Redding. "Sorry, sir, I had to borrow some wine from the officer's mess."

"No problem, Sergeant," Redding replied with a wave of his hand. "Continue."

Buckley mimed the action of priming. "Mr. Prime Time pours primer into the vent hole that was reamed out earlier. Then he gets the hell out of the way.

"*Eleven*: aim it straight. The gunner is in charge of this step. He directs a guy on elevating the barrel." Buckley pulled down another long tool from the rack above the gun. "To lift the heavy barrel, he uses this tool, called a handspike, with this machete-like blade on the end. He jams the steel blade under the gun barrel and pries it up, like using a crowbar. Then he keeps the barrel at the right angle with this wooden wedge underneath the barrel in the back here, called a quoin. So, we'll call him the quoin man. The gunner also directs the block-and-tackle crews for side-to-side motion, but these guns weigh over two tons each, so that movement has to be limited—at most, a nudge one way or the other. That movement is also achieved by the handspike. In the old days, the blade would be jammed into the deck and the man would pry the gun one way or the other, but since that would chew up the deck, we won't be using it that way. Lastly, the gunner lets the ship help aim the gun. He's got to be aware of how she's moving—rolling starboard or port—as well as the pitch of the ship fore and aft." Buckley used his arms and hands to mimic the motion of the ship. "Sometimes you just have to wait for the target to move in line with the gun. In her fighting days, the captain would yell, 'Fire as your guns bear.' That's what it means. It means both the ship, and the target itself, are aiming the gun. Finally, there's the distance to the target and the rate of drop of the cannon ball over distance. There's a very complicated problem in algebra that governs that drop. I don't have time to teach it to you. We'll just have to learn from experience, and that will be good enough for our purposes."

Members of the class scratched their heads and looked at one another.

"That's right. It isn't easy," Buckley said. "You heard the captain say the original crews could do all this in less than three minutes, that's reloading, aiming, *and* firing. Considerably less time would be needed just to reload. That's our goal as well." He looked around the group, some of whom were shaking their heads. "When I say *goal*, people, I mean that as an order—and that's the *least* of it. You need to carry out the task without blowing yourselves up in the process." Pointing to Redding, Buckley added, "Captain doesn't want to have to write a letter to your folks saying you blew yourself up on this goodwill tour."

James came down from the spar deck in time for Buckley's admonition, crossed his arms, and leaned against the railing of the companionway with a look of contempt on his face.

Rachel Dover held a smile in James' direction but was nudged by Gunderson, who pointed to his eyes, then at Buckley.

Redding nodded his agreement with Buckley and wasn't surprised when James rolled his eyes at Miriam. Redding didn't expect to win him over. He wasn't going to make an issue of it, but neither would it deter him. He would use humor to keep the relationship on an even keel and to counter James' dour stiffness. James wouldn't cross him, and for now that was enough. His interest was in the response from the crew. Who among them would take the training seriously and would show signs of leadership? In that light, Cooper was already standing out. He observed her rapt attention to everything Buckley said.

"What's left?" Buckley looked around the class at mostly blank faces.

He pointed to Cooper, who had raised her hand. "We haven't fired the gun yet."

"Right," Buckley responded. "Glad someone's paying attention."

"Now comes the loud part," Buckley continued. "We'll call *twelve* Yankee—" He grabbed the lanyard connected to the firing mechanism. "—because the gunner cocks the flintlock mechanism, then *yanks* this lanyard. That trips the flintlock and fires the gun. Don't cock it until you're ready to fire to prevent any misfiring while the gun is being loaded and aimed. The gunner takes a hold of this lanyard. When he's—" Buckley caught himself and glanced at Cooper. "—or *she's* satisfied with the aim, he or she *stands...to...the...side* and gives it a yank. If he or she doesn't stand to the side, what's left of him or her gets knocked to the other side of the deck before it gets put under an American flag and dumped into the sea while

Captain reads from the Bible. Does everyone get that picture?"

Classmates looked at one another. Some covered their mouths as they looked at the opposite side of the gun deck.

"That was a real question, people!" Buckley insisted.

A chorus of "Aye" and "Yes, Sergeant" erupted from the class.

"How many steps was that, Mr. Basker?"

Basker grimaced, then counted with his fingers. "Uh, twelve, Sergeant."

"Right, the dirty dozen." Buckley pointed to the group. "Who can name them all?" Only a few hands went up. "Tomorrow, I want *everyone* to be able to answer that question. I'll post this sheet in your quarters. Now listen up while I name the first two gun crews."

Buckley called out the names of the two teams, then went on to pass out assignments for each of the jobs on his list.

"Okay, team one, get into position and grab your tools," Buckley said, then he pointed to Mac.

"All right, Mr. No Sweat, the gun is loaded; you're the gunner." Buckley peered through the gun port, scanning the sea ahead of the ship. "I see a chunk of driftwood about a hundred yards out and ten points off the starboard bow. That's your target. Let's see what you've got. I'll give the orders for now. In the future, that will be an officer. Nonparticipants will repeat the commands after me. I'll start my watch as soon as the shot is fired, and I'll just time the reloading process."

Buckley motioned for the rest of the class to back

away from the gun. Mac looked through the gun port and spotted the driftwood headed toward the line of fire. "Up a little," he called to the quoin man. Mac looked out to sea through the gun port. "A little more—that's it!" The quoin man jammed the wooden wedge in place and jumped to the side. Mac cocked the flintlock, held the lanyard, took a last look down the barrel, then stepped to the side and gave it a yank. The gun lurched backward as the powder ignited.

The crew grabbed their ears as the blast shook the deck and reverberated throughout the timbers of the hull.

"Oh my *God!*" Miriam yelled.

Redding muttered, "Now, *that's* what I'm talking about."

The class rushed to the gun port to see the cannonball splash into the sea about twenty feet from the target.

Buckley held a stopwatch in his hand. "Not bad, Seaman McAvoy. Clear out everyone, my watch is ticking. Here we go again. One, haul back." The team members jumped into action, but they were talking to one another. "No talking, just movement, people!" Buckley yelled. "Two, worm it." With Buckley shouting commands, the crew scrambled to obey, often bumping into each other from step to step until the gun was reloaded and they looked to Buckley for the time.

"Five minutes, people," Buckley announced, pointing to his watch. "That tells you how much work we have to do. Mr. Basker, you are now the gunner."

Basker strutted into position and gave a cocky wave to brush Mac aside.

"Is team two ready?" Buckley asked. "Show me

133

you can beat five minutes. Here we go."

"But the driftwood is gone, Sergeant," protested Basker. He continued looking out to sea and called to Buckley over his shoulder, "I see a patch of sea foam."

"Call it a batter and hit it, Mr. ERA!" yelled Buckley.

"Damn straight I'll hit it," Basker said, then looked out the gun port and called to the quoin man. "Down, dude, down!" The class chuckled as Basker pointed to one of the block-and-tackle crews. "You there. Pull it that way. The batter's crowding the plate!"

Basker took a last look at his aim, held the lanyard, went through a windup, and yanked the cord.

The rest of the class and Miriam plugged their ears against the thunderous report. Basker was the first to rush to the gun port to check his aim. The round splashed close enough to the sea foam to break it up, sending Basker into a strut as the class applauded.

"Move it, team!" yelled Buckley, looking at his watch. "One…"

The new crew was noticeably smoother than the first. Redding, James, Miriam, and the rest of the crew were looking at their watches.

When the cannon was reloaded, Buckley stopped his watch and looked up. "Better by roughly fifteen seconds. That's moving in the right direction. Now, while the steps are fresh in your minds, get into groups and rehearse them. I only have a half-dozen copies of the list." Buckley showed the copies to the junior officers. "Maybe one of the officers would like to take over and reassign the crew into gun teams for future practices," he said as he looked to Redding.

Before Redding could respond, Cooper jumped in.

"I've got that." She grabbed the copies, looked over the crew, and positioned them into groups, then called out assignments.

James pulled Redding's attention away. "I guess I'd better take inventory of the black powder if we're going to use it up at this rate—and, you know, those cannonballs are...well...collectible antiques."

"Yeah, well the Med is going to collect a few of them before we're done," Redding replied. "I'd sure like to be a fly on the wall at the ordinance depot back home when an order comes in for black powder and cannonballs." He laughed, then looked for James' reaction.

James responded flatly. "Yes, sir."

Miriam stood in the background within view of Redding and close enough to overhear the conversation. She looked back and forth between him and James with a quizzical look on her face.

Redding answered with an indifferent shrug.

Miriam shook it off and walked toward them while she reviewed the pictures she had just taken on the camera's LCD screen. "Got some great shots. Can't believe how much louder these guns are—and the smoke. Geez!"

"I'd better get back to my watch." James saluted and walked off.

"I'll join you," Miriam added. "The sun is just right for some good shots up top." She started off, stealing one last look at Redding.

He turned his cocked hat sideways, Napoleon style, and struck a pose with his hand in his blouse.

She held back a laugh, shook her head, and caught up to James at the companionway.

Redding motioned to Buckley, who had been touring the groups, listening to them practice the steps verbally. "What do you think?"

"Well, sir, it would take more powder, shot, and time than we have to get the sequence down to historic timing."

"Right. I know," Redding answered, as he admired Cooper at work.

"But I'm not going to tell them that," Buckley continued. "I presume that is in keeping with the captain's wishes."

"Right again, Sergeant." Then Redding turned to Buckley. "That reminds me—congratulations on your promotion."

"Sir?"

"You are now the ship's gunnery *officer*. See you at dinner." He turned and walked away from a stunned Buckley.

Chapter Fifteen

It had been the first good day since he took
command of *Constitution*. Redding still didn't
understand how the course of his own internal struggle
had tacked into a favorable wind, or where it was taking
him, but for once in his career, he found himself willing
to ride it out and let providence answer that question.

Redding pulled the ship's log off the shelf in his
cabin and opened it to the first blank page. He played
with a ballpoint pen in his hand while gathering his
thoughts, the mysterious experience of the previous
night still spinning in his mind, then stopped and
focused for a moment on the pen itself. He put down
the pen left with the log by Captain Lawrence and
picked up the feather quill placed on the desk as décor.
An antique inkwell sat next to it.

"What the hell," he said with a smile to himself,
dipped the pen, and wrote:

*June 29—This marks the first day of weapons
training. I placed Sergeant Buckley in charge and have
not been disappointed. Pending approval from Fleet, I
have given him the appointed rank of Gunnery Officer
under Section III, paragraph 3, and will make my case
for the permanency of that promotion at the
appropriate time.*

*Though the training has just begun, the response
from the crew is encouraging. Where they seemed to*

137

lack purpose and motivation upon my arrival, they have now shown a healthy competitive spirit and the desire to excel. I believe this will serve the navy well in whatever capacity these crew members serve for the duration of their enlistments. The same can be said for the junior officers. The training represents one of the few opportunities on board this vessel for them to learn leadership and demonstrate their potential for advancement. In that regard, a special note of recognition goes to Ensign Roberta Cooper, who has shown a welcoming attitude with respect to leadership responsibilities. I will so note in her personnel file.

Redding tapped the quill to his chin for a moment, then smiled to himself as he continued the log entry.

Radio malfunctioned last night—reason unknown. Also unknown if repairs can be affected on board. If not, will attempt repairs in Tripoli.

At dinner that evening, Redding was pleased with himself. He had everyone at the table, and most everyone on the ship for that matter, wondering what was to come next. Then "next" walked in.

Wearing a clean dress uniform, Buckley entered the wardroom and stood uncomfortably at the door.

Redding stood. The others looked at one another and rose as well.

"Ladies and gentlemen," Redding announced, "I give you Gunnery *Officer* Jack Buckley. Welcome, Mr. Buckley."

Buckley nodded nervously at everyone but avoided prolonged eye contact with anyone.

Miriam was the first to speak. "Congratulations, Mr. Buckley! Well deserved, I'm sure."

"Thank you, ma'am," Buckley replied quietly.

"It's Miriam," she insisted.

Buckley nodded. "Thank you, Miriam, ma'am."

"Congratulations, Mr. Buckley," offered Cooper.

"Thank you, Ensign Cooper," Buckley responded, shaking the hand Cooper offered.

"Welcome and congratulations, Mr. Buckley," offered Bates, extending his hand. "Well done today, by the way. Very impressive."

"That goes for me as well," Kobach chimed in. "Exciting stuff today. I learned a lot. Almost overwhelming, but I look forward to the challenge. I got that impression from most of the crew too."

"Yes...congratulations," said James, almost under his breath.

Buckley acknowledged the compliments. "Thank you all."

Redding looked around the table. "Well now, I'd say it's time for dinner. Sit down, everyone." He called into the adjoining room: "Seaman Guzman, if you please." Guzman entered with a tray of plates. "Seaman Guzman, there will be one more for dinner, as you can see. I've already told Seaman Tebic that will be the case from here on."

Guzman looked at Buckley. "Yes, sir."

The activities of the day might have dominated the talk at the table, but it seemed no one knew where to begin. Redding judged that his new uniform was one of the elephants in the room, which was fine with him. Even if he could have somehow explained his experience of the previous night, no way in hell would he have attempted it. Better, in any case, to keep them guessing and a little off balance.

James was the only one who couldn't seem to

139

come up with a question for Buckley regarding his knowledge of the guns, which the others had to pry out of him. His stock answer was that it interested him and that his assignment to the ship gave him plenty of time to read.

Redding looked at Miriam. "Looks like we have *another* history buff on board."

"Yes," she replied, looking at Redding. "It *does* look that way."

Redding indulged himself in the mischievous pleasure of knowing he had sufficiently stirred the pot, forcing Miriam to recalculate. During most of the meal, however, he ate quietly, pretending not to notice the questioning glances between Miriam and James and every nuanced expression from everyone at the table.

Cooper finished her dinner hurriedly. The ship's bell sounded 1900 hours. Lifting her plate for Guzman to take, Cooper had to hold it there for a moment while Guzman ignored her. She continued to hold it and cleared her throat loudly before Guzman took it from her.

Buckley observed the brief encounter.

Gunderson entered the dining room, stood behind Cooper, looked briefly surprised at the presence of Buckley, but gave him the "hi" sign and tapped Cooper on the shoulder. "Your watch, Coop."

She rose and addressed Redding. "May I be excused, sir?"

Redding nodded and Cooper rose to leave, but Guzman blocked her way. This time, she locked her eyes on him. In trying to avoid her, Guzman inadvertently caught Buckley's glare. He quickly stepped aside.

"Seaman Guzman," Miriam said, pointing to her dinner with her fork, "share my compliments with Seaman Tebic."

"Uh-huh," he replied.

Buckley dropped his flatware on his dish loudly enough to get Guzman's attention, who quickly adjusted his attitude.

"He'll be pleased to hear it, ma'am." Guzman glanced back at Buckley as if seeking approval, then carried the dishes into the next room.

Miriam glanced at Buckley, who had already resumed eating. Redding also observed the exchange but was more interested in Buckley's methods than in Guzman's moods.

"Mr. Gunderson," said Redding, "you were still on deck when I announced the presence of the ship's new gunnery officer, Mr. Buckley."

"That's great! Congratulations." Then he pointed to Buckley's plate as he took the chair vacated by Cooper. "But I hope that wasn't my dinner."

James kept eating during the exchanges but was noticeably silent as the laughter circled the table. When it subsided, Miriam caught his attention. "Changing the subject, Lieutenant James, why do you use a sextant to navigate? Why not a GPS?"

"Yeah," Redding chimed in. "You can have the one in my Buick if you're short."

"Just old-fashioned, I guess," replied James.

Redding put his plate aside and addressed Buckley. "Mr. Buckley, I was also impressed with your class today." Everyone at the table nodded in agreement, and Buckley shyly acknowledged them. "I sense the crew are taking this seriously. Do you agree?"

"Mostly, yes. The others will come around," Buckley answered confidently.

Miriam tilted her head and squinted. "Pardon me, Sergeant...excuse me, Mr. Buckley, but how do you know that?"

Buckley addressed Miriam directly. "It's 'Jack,' Dr. Hannah. Peer pressure, ma'am. Best training device ever invented—that and fear."

Buckley resumed eating. His laconic reply amused Redding, who glanced at James to read his reaction. James' stabbing at his meal answered his question.

The rest of the dinner conversation was marked by questions put to Buckley about the antique guns. Ensigns Koback, Bates, Gunderson, and Cooper peppered him about estimating ranges and calculating trajectories.

After dinner, Redding went topside to relax and reflect on the events of the last twenty-four hours. He didn't want company, but it showed up anyway.

James came up from his cabin carrying a book.

"Captain, may I have a word with you?"

Redding, seeing the book, replied, "My, *US Navy Regulations*. It must be serious."

"Well, sir," James answered in a somber tone, "I think so. Regarding your promotion of Sergeant Buckley..." He opened the book and flipping a few pages, then pointed to a page and read, "*Navy Regulations Section III—Appointments—paragraph 3: No officer other than the Commander-in-Chief of a fleet will give any acting appointment except as provided for above; nor will any such acting appointment be issued unless a permanent vacancy should occur in the established complement of a vessel which cannot be filled from supernumerary officers on board other vessels, and in which case the appointment must be in writing, and be subject to revocation by himself, his successor, or by the Secretary of the Navy.*"

Redding looked out to sea. "Uh-huh. Keep reading."

"Well, sir," James replied confidently, "if you're referring to the next sentence—*In the case of a vacancy by death on board any vessel absent from the United States, and acting singly, the Commanding Officer may issue a written order to supply the deficiency, which will continue in force until the vessel falls in with a Commander-in-Chief or arrives in the United States.*"

"That's the one," Redding answered. "We are decidedly absent from the United States."

"Yes, but...who died?" James responded with enough condescension to irritate Redding, but Redding paused to let it subside.

"Lieutenant William Sharp Bush, back in 1812," Redding answered casually. "Will that be all, Mr. James?"

James slammed his book shut and walked below.

Chapter Sixteen

When you're a man with more money than sense—
and you must use that money to attract women, or you
harbor insecurity over an uncertainty as to the public's
knowledge of just how wealthy and/or powerful you
are, or, lastly, you harbor a different insecurity
concerning a certain component of your anatomy—you
buy a cigarette boat. If you are the valedictorian in that
class, you buy the Ducati Edition: 2,200 horsepower,
120 miles per hour, $700,000. Then, you wear a pre-
distressed captain's hat to take on the appearance of a
blue water veteran and you pretend to know boats.
Oddly, that often works.

Three young beautiful women wearing designer
bikinis never meant to get wet adorned the bow seats of
a cigarette boat out of Malta. Its paunchy, balding
owner—in a swimsuit design that never should have
been offered in his size—was at the wheel, a view of
the Mediterranean and his aspirations, displayed in
varying provocative poses on the long foredeck in front
of him.

Using a hand to shield her eyes from the glare, one
of the women spotted *Constitution* on the horizon and
made her way aft to the cockpit. On a choppy sea, at
high speed, in four-inch stilettos, the walk wasn't easy.

"What's that?" she asked.

The owner lifted a pair of binoculars from the dash

and trained them on the horizon. "That's USS *Constitution*. You remember. We saw her in Messina."

"Go over there. We must invite her captain on board for champagne. I want to meet such a man," the woman insisted.

The bow of the cigarette boat rose as the throttles told the engines to make more horsepower. The distance to *Constitution* rapidly closed—until a boom from one of her deck guns and a column of water from the cannonball plowing into the sea caused the driver of the speeding boat to crank the wheel in the opposite direction and make his apologies. "Perhaps some other time."

****

On the spar deck, Buckley faced a large class of crewmen grouped into teams around the carronades. In the slack wind, the ship was nearly motionless so the target barrel floating a hundred yards off couldn't escape, but the crew was nevertheless discouraged and took to bickering among themselves.

"That's enough!" barked Buckley. "It takes everyone working together. The steps are the same as you learned on the long guns, just a bigger ball and a shorter barrel, so not as much range. That means the arc of the ball will be different, so the elevation of the barrel needs to be higher if you've got a distant target."

Redding approached, and Buckley snapped to attention. "Ten-hut!"

"Carry on, Mr. Buckley." Redding walked to the gunwale, looked out at the barrel, took a note out of his coat, taped it to the railing near the carronade, and withdrew to the rear of the class.

Buckley walked to the gunwale, read the note to

himself, smiled, and read it to the class. "Listen up. 'Four days liberty in Tripoli for the first crew to hit that enemy barrel.' "

The crew cheered as Buckley signaled his approval to Redding. The bragging and needling between teams started immediately. Redding stood off and enjoyed the scene.

Miriam was nearby with a pad, jotting down notes, her camera slung around her neck. She didn't notice Redding as he approached from behind and peeked over her shoulder until he cleared his throat to get her attention. She looked up, startled, then pulled her notepad away from his view.

"Just wondering if maybe you had any technical questions you needed answered," he asked with mock self-assurance.

As she walked backward, she pointed to Buckley and responded with a coy, "No, thanks. I've got professional help for anything like that."

Redding snapped his head to the side as if hit with a left jab, touched his mouth, then looked at his fingers while rubbing them together, as if checking for blood, then pursed his lips and shook his head.

Miriam turned away to hide her smile.

"All right," he said to himself. "It's on."

From his position near the helm, James observed the interplay between Redding and Miriam. He cast his eyes downward for a moment before turning his attention back to his duties.

In one of the few times Rachel Dover wasn't careful enough to look as though she was still at work, she stood gazing at James with a bucket full of seawater at her feet.

"That water is used to keep the deck timbers from shrinking and causing leaks to the deck below."

Rachel turned to see Gunderson standing over her.

"It's a lot more useful when it's spread on her deck, sailor," said Ensign Gunderson through a slight smile.

"Aye, sir," she answered, looking up at him.

Gunderson gave her a wink and a shrug. Looking aloft, he yelled up to the crewman on the upper platform of the mainmast. "You there. Do you see a wind line anywhere?"

"Aye, sir. Five points off the port stern, moving this way!"

Another blast from the carronade drew Redding's attention back to the class and brought jeers from the competing teams as the ball landed far beyond the barrel.

Buckley signaled with his hands. "All right, calm down. What did they do wrong? Who can tell me?"

He pointed to Mac, who had his hand raised. "They didn't time the shot to the rocking of the hull."

"Right, Seaman McAvoy."

Mac shot a superior look at Guzman, who looked away.

"Okay, team three, you're up next," Buckley shouted. "See if you can come any closer. That last reload was just over four minutes. Getting better."

The teams swapped places. Ensign Kobach, the gunner on the new team, studied the rocking of the ship, looked down the barrel, and counted to himself the seconds between the highest and lowest elevations.

James watched the class but kept his distance. Redding approached, but before he could say anything, the gun fired again. Both ran over to the gunwale and looked out to sea.

"Looks like the safest place in the Mediterranean might be sitting on that barrel," joked Redding.

"Who'd have thought there would be such a big difference between shooting blanks from a ceremonial cannon for show and actually trying to hit something?" James replied dryly.

Redding ignored James' sarcasm. "Well, it's good for the men." Then he glanced at Miriam and threw his voice in her direction. "Keeps those *traditions* alive!"

Miriam tried to hold back a grin while shaking her head at Redding, then looked at him and James, bumped her fists together, waved a flippant goodbye, and looked through her camera lens, as if searching for another subject.

James observed the exchange and replied in a muffled voice, "Yes, sir. Traditions."

"Actually, considering those guns were meant to hit a target the size of this ship, that last shot wasn't too bad." Getting nothing from James, he pushed on. "If nothing else, ya gotta love the sound and smell."

An uncomfortable pause prompted Redding to change the subject. "Lieutenant, it occurs to me that, even after reading your file, I don't know much about you. I didn't see any mention of a family navy connection."

"You wouldn't, sir. It was a long time ago," James replied.

"World War II?" Redding asked, honestly.

"No, sir, before that," James answered while he looked at the sails and the distant sky.

Redding waited, then pressed for the answer.

"And?"

"Around 1800."

"Wow, like when this ship was new!"

James nodded slowly and maintained eye contact with Redding, until Redding's eyes widened and he pointed to the deck.

James nodded. "Uh-huh."

"Huh, no kidding?" Redding said with amazement.

"One of my ancestors was a midshipman on this ship in these waters over two hundred years ago. No family in the navy since. Now, if you'll excuse me, sir, we're going to get some wind in a few minutes." James saluted and turned his attention to the men aloft.

Redding returned the salute, then caught sight of Miriam engaged in one of her solo martial arts exercises, this one using a ship's belaying pin as a weapon. She twirled it, spun it around her back and brought it to bear in front of her, poised as if confronting an adversary.

Redding stroked his chin. *She's probably imagining me.*

Chapter Seventeen

As night was about to overtake the last glimmer of dusk, the wind returned. Even under shortened sail, *Constitution* was making good time sailing in the arid Mediterranean breeze. She seemed to be sailing unreasonably fast for the wind, as though anxious to get to her next destination, the familiar waters of North Africa.

Miriam sat at a makeshift table and mirror setup in the quarters she shared with Cooper. For the first time since embarking on *Constitution*, she was applying makeup. She paused, looked into the mirror, and caught herself wondering why, but refused to reflect on it.

Cooper knocked on the door and opened it a crack. "Chow time, Dr. Hannah."

"Come in, Bobbi," Miriam responded. "I'll be done in a sec."

Cooper entered and stood behind Miriam as she applied her lipstick in the mirror.

"Want to try it?" asked Miriam as she held up the tube and looked at Cooper in the mirror. "It's not against regulations. Wait a sec, got 'em right here somewhere." She fished through a stack of books nearby. "Here it is, *Navy Uniform Regulations*." She thumbed through the pages and stopped at a dog-eared page. "*Section 2201—Personal Appearance*." She looked down the page and over to the next one.

"*Chapter Two, Section Four—Cosmetics*, and it's for women only. We can be sure this reg wasn't on board when this ship was new. Very thoughtful of the modern navy, don't you think?"

Cooper smiled slightly and approached cautiously. "I guess."

Miriam continued: "So here it is. *Cosmetics may be applied in good taste so that colors blend with natural skin tone and enhance natural features. Exaggerated or faddish cosmetic styles are not authorized with the uniform and shall not be worn.* Well, that's good advice anyway, don't you think?" Pleased to see Cooper smile, she continued. "Could have been written by one of those beauty experts for a woman's magazine. There's more. *Care should be taken to avoid an artificial appearance.*" She looked at Cooper and waved her hand. "That's not us anyway." She returned to the book. "Ah, the important part. *Lipstick colors shall be conservative and complement the individual. Long false eyelashes shall not be worn when in uniform.*" She studied Cooper's eyes. "You sure don't need false eyelashes. Perfectly good advice all the way around." She closed the book and returned it to the shelf.

Miriam gave up her chair for Cooper, who sat uneasily and looked at her image in the mirror. Miriam handed her the lipstick and stood over her while Cooper applied lipstick to a small part of her lower lip.

Miriam smiled at her in the mirror. "Looks like your shade—and definitely complimentary to the individual." Then she crossed in front of Cooper and knelt down in front of her. "Here, let me have some fun." She took the lipstick from her and applied it deftly to Cooper's lips. Miriam leaned back and examined her work, then stood away and pointed to the mirror. "What do you think?"

Cooper stared at her image as though she was seeing herself for the first time. She turned her head from side to side but kept her eyes locked on her lips.

Miriam nodded her approval. "*Now* it's chow time."

****

Redding discreetly glanced around the table between forkloads of a baked meat dish. Ensign Bates was on watch. Buckley was preoccupied with a notebook beside his plate, Gunderson and Kobach were oblivious, James was sulking, and Miriam kept looking anxiously at the door.

Redding paused for a moment, set his fork on his plate, and looked around the table. "Where's Ensign Cooper?"

"My fault," said Miriam. "I delayed her. She'll be along in a minute."

Redding displayed a bite-sized piece of food on his fork. "This tastes just like my mom's meatloaf. I'll have to tell Mom that Naval Intelligence hacked her recipe file. Boy, is she going to be sore."

"Good one, Captain," Gunderson said through a laugh.

Redding turned to Gunderson. "She'll probably make my sister put in a firewall on her computer."

Kobach joined in. "Maybe she'll write a letter to her congressman."

"That too," Redding added. "When it comes to tin-hat reactions, she's all in."

"That's Dad," offered Gunderson. "He's like the Energizer bunny when it comes to that stuff. He just keeps beating that drum."

Miriam chuckled at the interplay between Redding and the junior officers but had her eye on the dining room door when Cooper slipped in and sat down. She avoided eye contact with all but Miriam, who gave her a reassuring smile.

Redding was just about to take a bite when he noticed the change in Cooper. He looked at Miriam, who cocked her head toward Cooper. He took a moment to think, then shifted in his chair and gestured toward Cooper. "My, Ensign Cooper, don't you look nice this evening," Redding, said, then he glanced at Miriam for a reaction. She twisted her lips to the side. He bit his lower lip for a second, the straightened up and tried again. "You should be on a navy recruiting poster."

Cooper tilted her head up to reveal an embarrassed smile.

Miriam discreetly nodded her approval.

Redding pointed his fork at Gunderson. "Mr. Gunderson, you're a man of the world. What is your opinion on serving alongside women on a *combat* vessel?" Redding pushed the word "combat" while shooting a glance at James.

"Well, I don't know about 'man of the world,' " Gunderson answered, "but I'm a navy man, and I'm glad they made that change. Maybe it's different for my generation." He looked at Kobach who nodded in agreement. "That happened before my time. I never knew otherwise."

Buckley, who had not participated to that point, put down his pencil. "I have."

He scanned the table to the looks of surprise. "I

guess I'm the only one here who would."

"How's that, Mr. Buckley?" Redding asked.

"Well, let's see. That was back in, hmm, '93, the repeal of the combat exclusion rule. It was a big deal to rank-and-file gyrenes at the time. Most were against it." He nodded to Cooper. "Including me, sorry to say, but I've served with many women since then, taken orders from some of them, given orders to others, observed them, even in combat situations. I've found them to be dedicated, sometimes even more than the average guy. If anything, they seem to push themselves harder, I suppose to compete with men, maybe to overcome male prejudices." He pointed to Cooper and added, "I'd go into combat any day with Ensign Cooper, and that has nothing to do with her movie-star looks."

Buckley received a round of applause from everyone and an embarrassed grin from Cooper.

"Now you've done it, Mr. Buckley," Redding announced. "You've just unmasked your gift for eloquence and raised the bar in the process."

"No kidding!" Miriam added. "Where did that come from?"

Redding jumped in: "I've got this one. Mr. Buckley reads Shakespeare."

Buckley shrugged sheepishly.

"Really?" said Miriam. "That's great." With an eye on Redding, she added, "This passage is proving to be full of surprises."

Redding took satisfaction knowing the comment was meant for him but didn't let on. With the help of a couple glasses of wine, he was on a roll. "Speaking of which," he said, pointing to James, who had yet to join the conversation, "did anyone here know Mr. James is the descendant of an officer who walked these decks and sat at this table over two hundred years ago?"

Miriam dropped her fork. "What?"

Gunderson leaned forward. "Awesome!"

"No kidding?" asked Kobach.

Cooper joined in. "That's really something, sir!"

"That's right," Redding added, "an officer on this very vessel when it was fighting the pirates of the Caribbean."

"Mediterranean, sir," James interjected.

Redding laughed. "Just goofin' with you, Lieutenant—Mediterranean."

Even James managed a smile amid the chuckles from around the table.

"What about your family tree, Captain?" Miriam asked.

Redding sensed Miriam wasn't just making conversation. He stared straight at her. "I come from a long line of underachieving cavemen."

Everyone else at the table looked at one another, then at Redding and Miriam, who were locked eye to eye.

Redding sensed he had the momentum and wasn't going to give it up. "What's with all this martial arts stuff?" he asked Miriam as he made karate-like motions with his fork. "Where did you get your training?"

"Oh, here and there," Miriam answered as she looked up at him with her chin down.

"Does 'here and there' include a parade ground?" Redding grinned. "I thought I saw some majorette-type stuff in there."

Miriam paused a moment, then sheepishly nodded, twirling her finger in the air.

Redding had hit pay dirt. "No! Really? Yeah, come to think of it, I can see you in one of those short, pleated skirts, tassels on your high boots, leading the high school band at halftime."

Gunderson elbowed Miriam, leaned close and whispered in her ear. "Busted."

Miriam choked on a bite of food as she muffled a laugh. She shook her head and kept it down while she pushed her dinner around the plate.

"Okay, okay," Redding interjected. "If that wasn't enough, you also just happen to be an expert on Middle East history."

Miriam squinted at Redding warily.

Redding looked at the ceiling and tapped his chin. "In my opinion, Iran has been…trying to create other…midwifery…birth-of-nation Shia states."

Miriam rolled her eyes. "Hmm. Didn't know you were listening. What else do you remember from the speech?"

"Let's see," he answered thoughtfully while he stared at her. "History repeating itself, I'm with you there, but Iran wanting to be a *respected* world power?" He shook his head. "World power? Yes. Respected? No. Feared? Yes. Their version of respect is to be feared." He paused as he continued to think. "Let's see, what else. Oh, yeah, Iranian leadership is a puzzle?" He shook his head again. "No. I think their intentions are clear enough."

Miriam's mood turned to serious. "You think they're the enemy?"

Redding held his focus on Miriam and tapped the scar on his forehead. "When they're shooting at me, *yeah*!"

"We will see," she answered, locking her eyes on him as well.

Everyone seated around the table glanced at one another until Buckley interjected. "Sir, speaking of shooting, I've been doing some math. Our practice sessions have been going well, but at this rate we're going to run out of powder from the kegs."

"Those blank cartridges for the salute guns," Redding responded without taking his eyes off Miriam, "you have lots of them?"

"Aye, sir. Cases of them," Buckley answered.

Redding turned to Buckley. "Pry them open, dump out the powder, and keep on going, Gunnery Officer Buckley. As the saying goes, 'drill, baby, drill.' "

Chapter Eighteen

The blast from a blunderbuss Buckley fired from his hip shredded a bed-sheet-sized patch of canvas hanging from the end of a spar.

"Holy cow!" Tebic yelled.

"People, meet the blunderbuss," announced Buckley. "Crude but effective. Its name in Dutch means 'thunder gun'—good name for it. It's the predecessor of the shotgun, which you should take to mean it's a close-quarters weapon. You saw me fire it from my waist. You don't aim the blunderbuss like a musket; you brace it against your body. It kicks like a mule." From an open barrel, Buckley scooped up a handful of lead pellets. "This is what it likes to eat, but just about anything you can cram down its throat will do. In the old days, people used to use nails, rocks, just about anything."

Buckley passed the gun around the group. Each crewman judged the weight of it and simulated aiming it from their waists before handing the gun back to Buckley.

Tebic nudged Mac and whispered in his ear. A devious smile swept over Mac's face. He bent down to whisper in the ear of Thomas Thompson, a short pudgy seaman.

"No way," Thompson protested.

"Just do it," Mac insisted and elbowed Thompson

away from the group as Buckley handed the gun to Tebic.

"Me?" Tebic reacted meekly.

"*You*, sailor," Buckley said as the others nudged each other, pointed at Tebic, and chuckled. Then Buckley directed his comments to the class. "The loading procedure is just like all the other muzzle-loading weapons you've been learning about but with considerably more powder than the pistols or muskets. The effective range is no more than fifty to a hundred feet. At that range, the spread of the shot will be several feet."

Buckley supervised the loading of the gun by a trembling Tebic. Sailors in the rigging looked down on the action, while class members shook their heads and backed away.

Thompson returned from belowdecks with a small bundle wrapped in wax paper. He handed it to Mac, who pushed it back to him and whispered in his ear.

Thompson shook his head. "Uh-uh. Your idea. You do it."

Buckley positioned Tebic and pointed at the canvas target still hanging from the spar.

Sailors in the rigging waved their hands and shouted in panic. "No, Gunny, please! No!"

"All right, all right," Buckley conceded. He aimed Tebic out to sea and positioned the weapon on Tebic's hip.

"Grip it tightly and press it firmly to your hip," said Buckley as he positioned himself behind Tebic.

Tebic trembled as held his aim out to sea. Then he closed his eyes and fired.

The class on deck and the sailors aloft howled with

laughter as the recoil knocked Tebic on his butt.

James, Redding, and Miriam looked up at the action from the blunderbuss class, then back to a chart stretched on the bottom of the hull of the launch stowed upside down on the deck.

James pointed to the chart with a set of dividers. "We're here. Before we go to Tripoli, this is where we're supposed to take Dr. Hannah for a visit to the ruins about two hundred miles east of Tripoli."

Redding borrowed James' dividers, spanned the distance to the destination, then placed the dividers on the distance scale at the bottom of the chart.

"You know the wind is shifting?" Redding asked James. "We won't be able to hold this direct course."

"Yes, we'll be forced to tack pretty soon," James replied.

Miriam looked at James. "Tack?"

"Uh…zigzag," explained James, pantomiming the motion with his hands.

"What do you figure, arrival near those ruins tomorrow night sometime?" Redding continued, still examining the chart.

"That's as close a guess as we can make now—yes," answered James.

Looking up from the chart, Redding addressed Miriam. "It's my primary mission to get you to Tripoli and escort you back to Mitchell's party. What's so special about these ruins?"

Her posture straightened as she explained. "My hypothesis is that they served as a lesser base for the pirates—the corsairs—during the Barbary Coast Wars. Everyone thinks of Tripoli, but I believe that, once America decided to take military action, rather than pay tribute, the pirates spread their forces out more, rather than concentrating them where they could be attacked by powers such as the US with their superior ships. I think they dispersed their fleets to places like this so their enemies couldn't always tell where the pirates were coming from. It could be a significant finding. It could be the first example of guerilla warfare by sea." She added enthusiastically, "It could rewrite that chapter in history."

"What is the support for your hypothesis?" Redding asked.

"Old Berber texts—trading documents and a hand-drawn map I have that describes a fort beside a pirate port. The Berbers were mostly farmers and traders. The pirates were indiscriminate thieves. My theory is the Berbers had enough of their livestock and trading goods being stolen, so they had their own plans to take out the pirates, including, I think, at this particular site. It's conjecture, but they may even have been cooperating with the US Navy to supply them with that information."

"What do you do when we get—"

A blunderbuss blast interrupted Redding. The three looked in that direction.

"—when we get you there?" Redding continued.

"I'll attempt to confirm my theory."

"Can't you get pictures of the site from a tourist brochure or Google Earth?" asked Redding.

"No," she answered tersely. "This is off the beaten path, very remote. And it's not a tourist destination. It was never restored. It should be mostly buried in sand."

"So, these are supposedly the ruins of an ancient fort. Does it have a name?" asked Redding.

Miriam looked away, then back at Redding and James. "None that I know of. I call it Fort Hannah," she added sheepishly.

"Fort *Hannah*?" Redding chuckled. "You're lucky. Most people have to die before they get a fort named after them." He turned his attention back to the chart. "Very well. Mr. James, do we have a more detailed chart of that location?"

"I'm afraid not, sir."

Redding tapped the chart with the dividers. "Well, I don't like the idea of arriving there at night without a detailed chart."

James pointed at the site's location on the chart. "We know there's a small harbor on the west side of the promontory where the ruins are and a cove on the other side."

"Yes, but that's not San Diego harbor. It's damned small, and we have no knowledge of the depth." Turning to Miriam, Redding added. "The same natural forces that covered Fort Hannah with sand can just as easily have filled the harbor with sand. *Constitution* isn't a rowboat. She draws a lot of water, about twenty feet. There aren't going to be any harbor lights, and there's no moon for most of the night tomorrow. I do appreciate your goal, but this ship is my responsibility, and this is a rotten situation."

"Can't you just anchor offshore and wait for morning?" Miriam asked impatiently. "I can't see anything at night anyway."

"Doctor," Redding answered, "it is not only my mission to get you there, if possible, but to return this ship in one piece. Anchoring offshore is never a good idea. We prefer anchoring in sheltered—"

Another blunderbuss blast cut him off.

Their attention was drawn to the gun class across the deck as the class and the crew aloft howled with laughter. Basker, Tebic, Mac, and Thompson were shoving the gun at one another. Buckley stood to the side, his arms crossed.

A cloud of smoke, carrying with it a strange odor, drifted across the deck to Redding, James, and Miriam.

"What's that?" James asked. "Smells like barbecue."

All three sniffed the air and looked at each other. Redding answered, "Judging by the smell and the laughter, I'd say that was the meatloaf from last night."

Chapter Nineteen

General Husseini checked his watch and looked out the window of the two-story vehicle-maintenance building of the armory just outside of Cairo. A high cyclone fence topped with razor wire surrounded the facility.

As a black limousine pulled up to the guard post, the guard opened the gate, waved the limousine through, then stopped the vehicle and motioned for the window to be lowered. He leaned close to the limo, pointed the Amazonian Guard driver to the maintenance building across the compound. Husseini slung a satchel over his shoulder, picked up boxes from a table, and pushed a button on the wall to open the large garage door on his way out.

The limo drove into the building just as Husseini climbed down the stairs from the office. He pressed another button at the bottom of the stairs, and the garage door screeched shut. He motioned for the men in the garage to clear out. The rear passenger door of the limo cracked open from the inside as he approached. He opened it and entered.

Farzad moved over to make room for Husseini to sit next to him. Batul and the third guard sat across from them, a large duffel bag occupying the seat between them. Husseini handed the boxes to Batul. "These are the uniforms for the three of you," he said, then added with a smile, "I believe I have judged your sizes correctly."

Batul glared at Husseini momentarily, then placed the boxes next to her.

Husseini addressed Batul and pointed to the duffel bag. "Are your changes of clothing in there?"

"Yes, and the extra one you asked for."

"Very well. I will take them with me now. There will be provisions for you to clean up in the van. You will surely need to do so." Husseini pulled a map from his pocket, unfolded it, and showed it to Farzad. "This shows the route of your escape on foot. I have marked the important reference points in red. And this mark shows where the escape vehicle will be parked, a delivery-type van with no special markings on it. It has been modified as we planned. I don't envy you the trip, but it is necessarily long to get you away from the chaos you will create and the blockage of traffic the city police will impose."

Farzad examined the map. "That must be at least a half mile from the museum."

"Closer to a mile," Husseini responded. "You will need this." He pulled a small flashlight from his coat pocket and handed it to Farzad, who shone it on the map.

Husseini directed his attention to Batul. "There are more flashlights in the satchel. My people will be in charge of checking identification credentials of everyone there, but just in case any of Mitchell's secret service agents also check, identification cards for you are also in the satchel."

Turning back to Farzad, Husseini continued. "I will have a driver take you from your hotel in a truck marked as a catering service vehicle and give you access to the museum through a rear door. See that your people are in those uniforms before you exit the catering truck, but don't be seen in them at the hotel."

Husseini opened his satchel and pulled out a small electronic device with a switch and button. "The charges have been set where we discussed. This will send the detonating signal. The switch is off now. The range of the signal is considerable, so keep the switch off until the time comes."

Reaching into the satchel again, Husseini pulled out a Taser gun and addressed Batul, who leaned forward and smiled admiringly as she focused on the weapon. "You may find this very helpful in your efforts after the abduction." He put the Taser back in the satchel and handed it to Batul.

"Who will be at the airstrip when we get there?" asked Farzad.

"That will be Khalid Mustafa. Coded messages have been sent out to the network worldwide—no details, of course, but instructing all to stand by. What else? Oh, yes, the plane will return to Siwa for Mustafa, then to one of our bases, then back to your Libya location to pick you up the following day and take you to Iran."

Husseini looked at his watch. "Oh—we're missing it!" He turned on the radio in the passenger compartment of the limousine and tuned it until Virginia Mitchell's voice came through.

"I want to thank the NATO representatives I have been meeting with over the last several days for their input and guidance with respect to the upcoming talks that we all have faith will produce a result that will last,

hopefully, forever.

"Behind me is an example of one of man's great achievements: a jet-powered airplane capable of uniting people across the globe in a matter of hours. Generations to come from all countries of the world will look back on this time as a turning point in the relief of tensions that have prevailed since long before humans could even imagine such an achievement as that machine.

"Yet the power that airplane has to unite people of the world is nothing compared to the power of the understandings and agreements we seek in Cairo. Agreements that will allow people, especially of the Middle East, to live in peace and pursue happiness and prosperity without the threat of armed conflict.

"That plane is a symbol of how small the earth has become, which itself is emblematic of the necessity of our success. Thank you all."

"Oh my," scoffed Husseini, "so well said, Madam Vice President."

"This is Nigel Phillips of the BBC, once again bringing you this update on the preparations for the Cairo peace talks and, in particular, the role of US Vice President Virginia Mitchell in them. You can still hear the applause from the crowd in response to the message she delivered from a platform with Air Force Two behind her, including her description of the talks as a turning point. It was a message of—"

Husseini turned off the radio, but Farzad kept staring at it, glassy-eyed. "Turning point, indeed."

Chapter Twenty

"What's up with the chow, Trebek?" asked Basker.

"Captain's orders," Tebic answered as he laid out sandwiches and water bottles from boxes on a hatch cover near the foremast. "He said he didn't want to waste time, so this will be a grab-and-go lunch. More time for training, he said."

"That suits me fine," said Basker as crew members converged on the spread, grabbed up the sandwiches, and clustered in small groups nearby.

"Hey, Trebek," asked Basker with a mouthful of sandwich. "I seen you guys on those short-type cannons today." He looked around at the crew members nearby. "Me, I'm a *long-gun* man myself—know what I mean?"

Basker laughed as the crew groaned and gave him the thumbs down.

"In your dreams," Tebic replied. "Now, me and the carronades, that's another story. We're shorter but pack a *bigger load*. Know what *I* mean?"

Tebic bowed to the crew as they howled their approval.

Mac threw his dinner roll at Tebic. It bounced off him and landed near Basker, who picked it up and fondled it like a baseball.

"Oh, there he is," proclaimed Mac. "I can just imagine the Yankee pinstripes."

"Damn straight," Basker replied defiantly. "Pick a target."

Mac looked around the deck and pointed to Thompson eating alone about forty feet away. "Thompson's fat head," he said in a low voice.

The gathering had mixed reactions to the proposition. "No way." "Yeah, right." "Go for it." "Forget about it."

Ensign Kobach and Joshua Aarons stood nearby, enjoying the interplay.

Basker studied his target. Crew members pointed to him and laughed as he hunched over as if eyeing a signal from a catcher; then he went into a lengthy, contorted windup and flung the roll at Thompson.

"Hey!" yelled Thompson as the roll struck him square in the head. "What the hell?"

Basker threw his chest out and looked square at Mac. "Uh-huh."

Mac was quick to respond. "I suppose you have to do that big windup thing."

"Only way I can throw a strike," Basker replied, reluctantly.

"What about when there's a runner on base?" Mac pointed out. "He's going to steal on you."

Guzman jumped in from the sidelines. "Same answer. That's why he never made the majors."

Basker looked around at the laughing faces and walked off with his head down.

"Shake it off, ace," Mac said to Basker, patting him on the back. "None of those guys ever made a buck playing ball." Then he looked at Thompson, who was still holding the dinner roll and looking around. "And *that* was a *helluva* pitch."

****

The target barrel floated a hundred yards off to starboard when a carronade opened up on it, blowing it to bits.

Cooper stood at the smoking carronade still holding the lanyard with one hand, the other raised triumphantly. Her gun crew high-fived her and each other to the cheers and applause of the spectators on deck and the sailors aloft. Buckley shook her hand as Redding approached, pulled the note off the gunwale, and handed it to her. "Four days liberty for you and your crew when we make Tripoli. Congratulations."

A large cloud of smoke drifted along *Constitution*'s hull; the curve of her bow seemed to smile in contribution to the revelry on deck.

Basker followed Mac as he walked up to Guzman and pointed to his face. "Still think the captain's an asshole?"

Basker joined in from behind Mac. "Man, I'd pay to have this job."

Redding and James leaned over the starboard gunwale.

"What was I saying about the safety of floating on that barrel?" Redding quipped.

"Congratulations, men," Buckley yelled, "but no one's on liberty yet. Back to work. You're going to learn what these guns will do when they're loaded with grapeshot." He scooped up another handful of the lead balls. "They're like a blunderbuss on steroids. They're supposed to be loaded into the barrel in a canvas bag, so some of you are going to be tailors. We've got sailcloth below in storage. I want a half-dozen loads made up."

"I'll see to it," volunteered Ensign Bates.

"Thank you, Ensign." Buckley addressed the group. "We'll demonstrate that tomorrow. You need to see the spread of the shot over a distance. Take a break, then we'll see if you've improved any with your musket drills. Remember, my stopwatch still works."

****

That evening, Redding twisted the quill with his fingers while reading the log entry he had just written.

July 2—Nearing the end of our ability to conduct arms drills using the powder and shot available. Under Gunnery Officer Buckley, the crew has responded better than expected. The training has given the crew purpose and duties more demanding than they had previously and has filled time that would otherwise be idle. Team spirit and morale high as a result. Recommend citation for Buckley in that connection. Also recommend same regimen for future crews aboard Constitution. *Suggest it conveys additional benefit to the navy and the public from* Constitution *crews demonstrating said skills.*

Satisfied, he looked up to see the painting of Preble peering down on him, he turned the log to face the painting. "Yeah?" He smiled to himself, donned his cocked hat, and left the cabin, but the low door opening knocked the hat off his head.

Miriam entered the companionway from her quarters.

"Oops," she said, looking at the fallen hat.

"That happens to me every time," said Redding as he pointed to the doorway. "I don't know how they did it way back then."

"Maybe they were shorter," she suggested. "Or they learned when to duck."

171

They both leaned down to pick up the hat and knocked heads.

"Oh!"

"Ow!"

"Thanks, anyway," Redding said, picking up his hat. "I got it."

"Are you going up?" she asked, rubbing her forehead.

"Uh-huh. Say, later maybe we could get together to talk about your history book. I'd like to get—"

She stopped him with a "down, boy" hand gesture. "I think I know what you'd like to get. Are you really interested in this ship's history, or is all this just an elaborate pickup line?"

Redding shrugged innocently.

"You're the boxer," she said. "A boxer learns that if he can't outslug an opponent, he has to outpoint him. It takes longer, but he still wins. Well, it's not working with me. So, you can just go back to your corner and sit on your…stool."

The jab left Redding stunned. If this was a matter of footwork, he thought, he could deal with that, but the round wasn't over and he needed something to show for it.

"I get it," he called after her. "You're the opponent *and* the referee—convenient."

Miriam was already headed topside.

He called after her. "Can I at least know what round we're in? Who's ahead on points?"

She waved him off with her back turned.

"It couldn't be, could it, that you're just flattering yourself?" he asked as a parting shot.

Miriam answered without looking back. "Nope,

that's not it."

Women didn't fight fair. It was that karate stuff. They played by a different set of rules and with different weapons. Back in Messina, he laid his cards on the table. It wasn't easy for him to drop his guard. It wasn't his intention at the time, but he wasn't totally lacking in self-awareness. Feelings for her had prompted him to set her straight about that dark episode, to put the past in the past for a chance at a fresh start. Okay, his courtship skills sucked, but at least he put himself out there.

It was she who had used the boxing analogy, but he wasn't about to share where that part of his life originated. The effect on him of growing up without a dad had been profound. They didn't teach kids how to deal with that, and they didn't usually learn it from their mothers. They learned it on the street.

A sense of responsibility to be the father figure in the home—as a preteen—didn't leave a lot of time for the natural development of the social skills one normally acquired in those years. A boy could find himself in conflicts with other boys who, just as lacking in social awareness, turn ignorance into combat. With a younger sister to protect as his teen years progressed, it didn't get any easier for Redding. But he wasn't going to revisit that part of his past, even within himself.

As a boy, he had not learned how to channel negative emotions into positive ones, but may have picked it up instinctively. The result was a fiercely independent young man, self-made, for better or worse, awkward and lacking in social graces and programmed to deal with life in simple terms. When it's right, everyone should see it. When it's wrong, trust your instincts and go straight at it.

His instincts were proving to be a problem, as they often had to that point in his navy career, but he would attempt to employ them one last time. If the relationship with Miriam was going anywhere, she would have to make the next move. If not—maybe she just wasn't that into him.

****

For her part, Miriam was troubled by her own behavior and her feelings. Was playing hard to get and challenging this man on a psychological playing field her own way of not dealing honestly with her emotions, a way of keeping her guard up? Moses Redding certainly wasn't the kind of man she'd ever imagined herself with.

Maybe that was her problem. Maybe that pointed to a lack of imagination. Maybe growing up in the bubble of prep schools and the world of elite academia—where they only pretended life was hard—didn't prepare a person for life outside that bubble. Maybe the world wasn't flat. Maybe you didn't fall off the edge if you ventured beyond the horizon. Maybe intellectual pursuits could lift you in one sense but at the cost of *common* sense, even emotional maturity. Maybe the female trait of treating the mating game as a complex matrix of circular problem-solving was, well, bullshit. Maybe the battle of the sexes wasn't supposed to be such a battle. Maybe using an opponent's strength against him solved problems in karate but not in relationships.

She glanced over her shoulder at the sound of footsteps behind her. Her breathing was heavy, and her heart was pounding. Had she blown it with him?

They both arrived on the spar deck just in time to be greeted by another blast of muskets from Ensign Kobach and a row of sailors, producing a thick cloud of smoke enveloping and obscuring Redding and Miriam. The sailors reloaded as fast as they could while Redding fanned at the smoke for Miriam's benefit.

Miriam covered her mouth and ran away from the cloud.

Buckley glanced between his stopwatch and the class as he called out to Redding, "Sorry about that, sir! Didn't see you there."

"That's okay, Mr. Buckley. I'm not the EPA."

When the reload was completed, Buckley clicked the stop button on his watch and checked the time. "Not bad, but…" He pointed to Joshua Aarons and a group of marines with muskets nearby. "Corporal Aarons, let's see if you marines can do any better."

That set off a good-natured shouting match between sailors and marines. Buckley stepped away and let it roll.

"Did you know the Marine Corps is a department of the navy?"

"Yeah, the MEN's department."

"What do you call a marine with an IQ of 160?"

"A platoon."

"What do marines and sailors have in common?"

"They all set out to become marines."

"The marines are looking for a few good men, but the navy already has them."

Chapter Twenty-One

Constitution's personal accommodations were somewhat behind the times. She had undergone refits over the years, but with the limited space, the desire to keep her as original as possible, and not anticipating the current lengthy mission, separate gender accommodations never made it to the blueprint stage.

Thumbing commands to Super Mario pulled Tebic's attention away from guard duty at the shower door while Miriam was inside. Redding approached the shower in his bathrobe, looked down at Tebic, crouched against a bulkhead, his thumbs flying over the keypad of his smart phone. Redding smiled, shook his head, and entered the shower.

The combination of low lighting, a cool evening producing lots of shower steam, and Redding's mind looping through the problem of a relationship that was either in a state of paralysis or imaginary to begin with was enough for him to ignore the unsurprising presence of another occupant of the facility, which he presumed to be male.

Miriam's head, hair, and ears were getting a thorough washing while Redding, used to taking short water-saving navy showers, completed the task as trained. Finishing at the same time, both had their heads buried in towels.

But that didn't last nearly as long as the next

moment seemed to.

"Ahhh!" both yelled simultaneously—frozen, eyes forward for perhaps a moment too long before grabbing for their robes from hooks on the bulkhead.

Holding his robe in front of him, Redding could only offer the obvious explanation. "So, I take it Mr. Tebic was there…to…."

Miriam's head nodded like a sewing machine. "Yup."

"Then that's probably his forehead I hear pounding against the bulkhead."

"I suppose."

Redding looked toward the shower door. "You go ahead."

"Umm, you need to turn around so I can, umm," she said, looking down at her robe.

"Oh, yeah, sure, uh," he stuttered and wrapped himself so he could turn away. "On your way out, please tell Mr. Tebic I want to talk to him."

Miriam closed the shower door behind her. Tebic was leaning forward against the bulkhead of the shower, his hands grasping at his hair.

"The captain wants to…"

Tebic nodded his head, and Miriam slipped away.

****

The seaman on the *Constitution*'s fighting platform scanned the horizon for navigation lights on fast-moving freighters traversing the shipping lanes in the Mediterranean. Ensign Bates stood near the helmsman with an eye to the sky for any signs of a shift in the wind or change in weather. The course was as it had been since they left Messina—due south—and for *Constitution*, to waters, fragrances, and sights reminiscent of her youth.

Approaching the fourth of July, *Constitution* sailed as proudly as if she had been a part of the victory that gave meaning to the date. By way of her creaks and groans, she conveyed her feelings to all who were attuned to them.

****

Redding sat at his desk reading *A History of the USS* Constitution, trying to take his mind off the figure that had stood next to him in the shower. The wet, *naked* figure. The wet, naked, *stunning* figure. The wet, naked, stunning, *haunting* figure. He slapped his palm to his forehead.

Scanning the table of contents, he read aloud. "Oliver Wendell Holmes." He flipped to the pages of that chapter. "Sounds familiar. I think he was on a test question at the academy."

****

Sailors and marines swung in their hammocks with the rocking of the ship as Miriam sat on a stool in the crew's berth, still damp from her shower, a few beads of water, possibly sweat, on her brow, reading from an open book in her hands.

"Oliver Wendell Holmes Sr. was the father of one of the most famous Supreme Court justices, Oliver Wendell Holmes Jr., but he was a remarkable, multitalented man in his own right: a physician, professor, writer, inventor, and once the dean of Harvard University."

She looked up from the book at the young faces of the crew. "This ship owes much to the man, as does the navy and all Americans who can't imagine ever losing such a treasured national symbol, which is why I think you will appreciate this. It was a poem written by Holmes that saved the ship from the scrap heap she was headed for in 1830.

"Holmes was only twenty-one and living at home in Cambridge, Massachusetts. He came home from his studies at Harvard Law School—it was called Dane School at the time—and read a newspaper article about the pending demise of the ship. He wrote a poem about it *that day* and it appeared in the newspaper the following day. The poem generated such a response it was duplicated in papers across America, even distributed in leaflet form. The public outcry was such that the Secretary of the Navy canceled plans for the ship's destruction and, instead, ordered her refitted for duty. It says here that no one dared threaten her status thereafter.

"Holmes' poem used reverse psychology. Instead of pleading for the ship to be saved, he wrote what some called a sarcastic eulogy. The message was: Go ahead and destroy her. What difference does it make? She's only a heroic American icon!

"So, imagine that. It took a poem to save this ship. Here it is."

She found her place on the page and cleared her throat.

> Ay, tear her tattered ensign down!
> Long has it waved on high,
> And many an eye has danced to see
> That banner in the sky;
> Beneath it rung the battle shout,
> And burst the cannon's roar;—
> The meteor of the ocean air

Shall sweep the clouds no more!

Her deck, once red with heroes' blood
Where knelt the vanquished foe,
When winds were hurrying o'er the flood
And waves were white below,
No more shall feel the victor's tread,
Or know the conquered knee;—
The harpies of the shore shall pluck
The eagle of the sea!

O, better that her shattered hulk
Should sink beneath the wave;
Her thunders shook the mighty deep,
And there should be her grave;
Nail to the mast her holy flag,
Set every thread-bare sail,
And give her to the god of storms,—
The lightning and the gale!

****

Cooper loved to engage Miriam in conversation, which was usually fine with Miriam, but she was grateful that Cooper was on watch that night as she turned in her berth, unable to quiet her mind. If she needed conversation, it was with herself.

Not often confused, Miriam was now, and the reason was even more perplexing—a man. Even worse, a man who was a source of aggravation. She had him sized up immediately and had been confident in her assessment. Now, it was as if a mysterious warm wind had melted that image. She didn't like being confused, and she didn't like the gracelessness she had shown.

In a berth not far away lay a man she had unfairly

vilified. Captain Redding had a conscience that would not allow him to forget an experience unlike any she would ever have to endure. With an unanticipated complexity, he was a man for whom she had feelings that couldn't be denied. With so little time left to resolve the issues between them, would she look back on this voyage with regret?

****

Unable to sleep and with his eyes wide open, Redding stared up at the same planking that was above Miriam; it looked like a blank canvas with an uncertain future. She had suggested his interest in her was an attempt at a conquest. Was that evidence that men were from Mars and women were from Venus, with orbits millions of miles apart and not a damn thing you could do about it?

Intellectualizing the subject was not his talent. He resigned himself to focusing on his work, playing the hand he was dealt, and hoping for a better one. In reality, he reminded himself, Miriam's apparent lack of feelings for him was the least of his problems.

Chapter Twenty-Two

The Egyptian Museum in Cairo and the surrounding grounds were emptied of tourists and ringed with uniformed soldiers.

Built at the turn of the twentieth century, its marble floors had been polished to a high shine for the occasion of the visit of Vice President Mitchell, achieving an august appearance that belied its troubled history.

Established in 1835, the museum's collection had survived changes in location, damage from a Nile River flood, the transfer of its artifacts to Archduke Maximilian of Austria and a Vienna museum, and damage and theft at its current location during the riotous Egyptian revolution in 2011. It was no stranger to trauma.

Mitchell stood at a podium on a temporary platform in the grand foyer. In front of her was a small audience of invitees only with a crowd of reporters behind them. President Aziz and other dignitaries sat in a row of chairs behind her but visible to the audience. Nearby were Mitchell's aide Sandra Phillips, a woman in her early thirties, and four secret service agents. To the side stood General Husseini and Hamid Rahal, the president's Minister of Foreign Affairs.

At the conclusion of her remarks, Mitchell turned to President Aziz. "And we appreciate Egypt's hosting of the peace talks, where the cornerstone of a hopeful future for the Middle East will be laid." The audience applauded. "Thank you. And now, if you'll excuse me," Mitchell added and turned to Sandra Phillips, "my aide made me promise we would actually get to view the exhibits."

As Mitchell shook hands with dignitaries on the platform, Husseini nodded to a woman who had just emerged near the entrance to an adjacent hall. It was Batul in a docent's uniform who signaled Sandra Phillips.

"We're supposed to go that way." Sandra motioned to Mitchell and the secret service agents who bracketed Mitchell and Sandra as they followed Batul into the adjacent gallery where many artifacts, including an open sarcophagus with a mummy, were displayed. Once they were inside the gallery, Batul's two guards, also dressed as docents, closed and bolted its massive wooden doors, separating the room from the rest of the crowd in the foyer.

The secret service agents whipped around at the sound of the doors locking. Colonel Farzad entered from an adjacent hall. Mitchell immediately recognized him. "You! Where did you come from? What are you doing here?"

Two of Mitchell's four secret service agents bolted toward her. The other two charged Farzad, pulling their weapons on the run, but were gunned down by the two Amazonian Guards firing pistols drawn from their waistcoats before they turned their guns on the agents attempting to protect Mitchell.

Positioned nearest to Mitchell, Batul put the barrel of her pistol to Mitchell's head.

"Stop and drop your weapons," Farzad ordered the agents, "or your boss dies!"

The agents dropped their guns on the floor. Sandra picked them up, handed one to an Amazonian Guard and aimed the other at Mitchell.

Mitchell gasped. "Sandra! How could—"

"That will all be explained to you in good time, Madam Vice President," said Farzad. He, Sandra, and Batul guarded Mitchell and the agents while the two other guards, one with the satchel from Husseini slung over her shoulder, pulled plastic zip ties from their sleeves and bound the agents' wrists behind them. Pounding from outside the bolted doors echoed through the exhibit hall. Farzad pointed to an adjacent hallway where the captives were led at gunpoint to a chamber behind the protection of a thick stone wall. He pulled the electronic triggering device from his pocket and pressed the button.

The sarcophagus exploded, destroying the contents of the gallery, collapsing its ceiling, blowing out windows, and setting fire to the rubble.

The concussion knocked Mitchell to the floor. She looked up at Farzad.

"What is the meaning of this!" she cried, choking from the dust.

"Welcome to the peace talks, Madam Vice President," Farzad answered. "How do you think they're going so far?"

Sandra grabbed Mitchell's wrist, pulled off a watch-like device. "GPS locator," she said and threw it across the room.

Mitchell glared at Farzad. "You can't hope to get away with this. You are declaring war on the United

States of America."

"For starters, yes," answered Farzad. Then he pointed to his bodyguards and down a hallway. "Go!

"This war began long ago, and we are prepared to continue it," Farzad said to Mitchell as she was being half dragged across the floor. "Did you really think we would negotiate away our right to rule our own lands?"

****

When the shots rang out, President Aziz's security detail rushed him away from the platform and the screaming crowd. With a look of horror and pain on his face, Aziz clutched his chest. His knees buckled as he struggled to walk with two security agents supporting him. They had just escaped the museum when the bomb went off. The concussion knocked them off their feet, producing a cry of pain from Aziz. The last of the diplomatic reception attendees who were also fleeing the museum were knocked to the ground by the explosion.

Aziz's agents carried him to a bench in the parklike setting outside the museum, a safe distance from the destruction. His men formed a protective ring around him, and one called for an ambulance on a cell phone.

General Husseini and his men huddled nearby but away from Aziz's men.

It wasn't long before emergency vehicles and police sirens wailed in the distance. They arrived on the scene as smoke billowed out of the museum's shattered windows.

****

Farzad led the group down a hallway, away from the destroyed portion of the museum, as Batul held her gun at Mitchell's head. Sandra and the Amazonian

Guards trailed the agents, guns drawn.

They quickly wove through anterooms of the museum until they reached a utility room. Batul lifted a floor plate and climbed down ladder steps to the sewer below. The others stood guard over the hostages and listened for anyone approaching.

Farzad motioned to Mitchell. "You're next."

Mitchell choked on the stench as their group made their way down the ladder and into the sewer. The guards were stoic and silent throughout the trip through the ankle-deep filth, holding guns in one hand, aimed at the secret service agents, flashlights in the other.

Mitchell stumbled in her high heels as the guards pushed her over the uneven surface. Batul stopped them, pulled Mitchell's shoes off, and threw them in the muck they were wading through.

Each time the party passed near a drain from the street above, the sounds of the chaos they had created on the surface poured through the street grate. Farzad used his flashlight to check their positions with the map from Husseini. Nearly a mile from the museum, Farzad stopped the group at the light from a steel grate above. He examined the map, then motioned to Batul to climb the steel rails to the street above.

Batul removed the grate, then a panel on the floor of a van parked over the opening in an alley out of sight from the bustling traffic on nearby streets. She motioned for the rest to follow and climbed into the van. It was empty but for the duffel bag given to Husseini in the limousine. She sat crouched in the cargo bay with her gun aimed at the secret service agents as they assisted Mitchell up the steps and into the van. Farzad followed and waited for the two remaining guards and Sandra. One of the guards replaced the sewer system grate and the floor panel to the van; the other took the driver's seat. When Farzad tapped the back of the seat, the guard started the engine and put the van in gear but engaged the clutch too quickly, causing the vehicle to lurch as she drove off. Everyone in the cargo area grabbed for handholds to steady themselves. The secret service agents tried to pivot and make a move for the guns with their hands behind them, but Batul and the other guard steadied themselves and savaged the agents' foreheads with blows from their pistol barrels, knocking them unconscious.

"There now," Farzad said to Mitchell. "That's much better. Now we can all relax."

The inconspicuous van made its way through Cairo's nightmarish traffic as police, emergency, and military vehicles surged toward the museum and civilian traffic tried to escape the capital's center.

Farzad looked through the rear windows of the van. "Sorry you didn't get to see the exhibits, Mrs. Mitchell." Farzad smiled as the smoke rose from the museum. "I understand they are very impressive. Someday, perhaps we will build a museum to display the antiquities of the era before this day. I think an appropriate theme would be to feature relics of the decadent, unholy societies of the world." He grinned as he looked at her. "Maybe it will even feature you. Not just a wax statue, mind you, but *you.*"

Once free of Cairo's grip, the city and the Pyramids were obscured in a cloud of dust. The rural roads steadily deteriorated as the van traveled westward, hours from Cairo.

****

News crews arrived on the scene outside the museum and quickly surrounded Aziz's team as he was loaded into an ambulance. With Aziz barely conscious and no one in his party willing to speak to them, the media zeroed in on General Husseini, throwing at him a flurry of questions.

"General, what happened here?"

"What's the condition of President Aziz?"

"Who did this?"

"Where is Vice President Mitchell?"

"We have just survived the attack," said Husseini. "We have yet to make a full assessment, but"—he pointed at the destruction to the museum, now targeted by fire hoses from multiple engines—"the party of Vice President Mitchell was in that gallery where the bomb exploded. It is unlikely anyone survived, but of course we must wait and see. In the meantime, President Aziz is incapacitated. His exact condition is unknown, but knowing of his medical history, it is likely to be heart failure. I am assuming command under these emergency conditions. I will be mobilizing the army to maintain order, secure the capital, and the government, and actively seek out the malevolent forces responsible for this horrific attack."

A reporter shoved his microphone close to Husseini. "What will this do to the peace talks?"

"Clearly those plans are now in doubt," answered Husseini, "but that does not affect our current priorities, which I must now attend to." He started toward military vehicles parked nearby and signaled to his contingent to follow. They loaded into the vehicles and departed.

****

NAVCENT buzzed with activity like an ant farm

in panic mode. People ran between offices and workstations as television monitors in the communications center displayed the first transmissions from the attack on the Cairo museum. The BBC, Al Jazeera, and OAN were first on the scene, but none seemed to know more than any other.

Admiral Towne scanned one monitor after another, reading the chyron texts scrolling at the bottom of the screens. "This is all we have?" he barked at an aide. "I have to get my news from *television*! Who is in communication with President Aziz's office?"

"No one, sir," answered the aide. He pressed on his earpiece with one hand and held up the other for quiet while he listened. "General Husseini has declared martial law."

"Why would that kill the lines of communication?" Towne continued.

"We don't know that either, sir," said another aide. "The general's headquarters is giving us the runaround, telling us they are preoccupied with security issues and the like."

"What about the Cairo police?" asked Towne.

"And we've tried that too," the aide continued. "All we've learned is that they've cordoned off the area around the museum—that it's too dangerous to enter the museum and that the army has ordered all communications with the outside to be routed through them."

"They are too goddamned preoccupied to tell us what the *hell happened* to our vice president?" bellowed Towne. "Communications? What communications? Something stinks to high heaven. I never trusted that son of a bitch Husseini."

A technician raised his hand as he listened on his headset. "Admiral, sir…the State Department reports from the Secret Service that Mitchell's GPS locator is in the museum room that was destroyed."

"*Damn!*" Towne muttered and shook his head. He took a deep breath, held it, exhaled, and continued in a more measured tone. "Check with the other branches. See if they're getting the same response or know anything more."

"Yes, sir. Is that all?" an aide replied.

"No. Check with the Pentagon. I assume they're going to put together a joint branch teleconference. Find out when. And since I know they're going to ask, tell them we don't know a damn thing. I want all NAVCENT bases on alert and locked down. Cancel all leaves. And get the commanders of Marine Corps Force Reconnaissance and Navy SEALs on the line. I want to be able to tell the Pentagon we have teams ready to go. They are to gear up, be ready, and await further orders."

"Yes, sir," answered the aide, nervously scribbling notes.

"And get some cots in here," Towne said as he waved his hand over the entire headquarters area. "Enough for everyone. No one's going anywhere."

Chapter Twenty-Three

A melon sat atop the anchor capstan on the foredeck until a cutlass wielded by Buckley sliced it neatly in two at its equator. Buckley turned to face a class of sailors and marines arrayed around him, a few of them with cutlasses taken from the museum display.

"When this ship was new," said Buckley, "and for that matter, for many decades after that, this was an important weapon. You've learned how long it takes to get a second shot out of a musket. In a close-quarters battle, you don't always have that much time. That's why even today, with all our modern weaponry, marines are still taught hand-to-hand combat."

The contingent of marines didn't waste the opportunity to rib the sailors around them, who could only look the other way.

Redding stood near Miriam, who viewed the scene through her camera lens. James stood off at a greater distance but was glued to the demonstration.

"Two opponents," Buckley continued, "who both know what they're doing with one of these, can get into a duel that can last some time. You've all seen that in the movies. We won't be learning the weapon to that extent. We won't be learning to fence. That takes a lot of training. We will just learn to use it in its most brutal fashion." He held the cutlass with two hands. "It's very much like a baseball batting swing. Use two hands and treat the enemy like that melon."

Buckley surveyed the class. "The cutlass is not a weapon for the faint of heart." He surveyed the faces of the young crew members. "It is not dainty. It is brutal, vicious, and bloody. If you are face to face with your enemy, you must wield it without hesitation and without mercy. But in that sense, except for the proximity to your enemy, it's like any other weapon you've been trained to use, old or new. A real battle is not a computer game."

While the class looked at one another with sober expressions, Buckley pointed to a basket of melons near the capstan. "Okay. We're going to help Mr. Tebic prepare today's lunch. Line up along the gun'l. One at a time, grab a melon and put it on top of the capstan. I'm looking for one decisive swing of the blade, with speed, with power, and without hesitation. And—this is the important part—you must imagine the melon is someone's *neck*!"

Buckley's imagery produced audible reactions of disgust from some in the class. Miriam grimaced and turned to Redding, who gave her a dismissive shoulder shrug.

"The evidence of your success," Buckley continued, "that the blow was swift enough to kill instantly will be that the melon is cut all the way through. If you're really good, the two halves will stay on top of the capstan."

Buckley pointed to Aarons. "Corporal Aarons, show them how it's done."

Miriam quickly focused her lens, framed her shot, and waited for Aarons to deliver the blow.

Aarons replaced the remains of the melon Buckley

had sliced open with a new one. The class backed away from the capstan. In one continuous motion, Aarons pulled back the cutlass like a baseball batter and whipped it through the melon. The fruit rocked from the blow but remained on the capstan.

The class oohed and aahed as Buckley walked over and lifted up the top half of the melon. "That's what I'm talking about. Well done, Corporal."

Miriam pulled her camera away and smiled at the image on the LCD screen.

Redding applauded. "Way to go, Corporal."

Aarons searched out and found Ensign Kobach in the group. Kobach twisted his lips in response.

With the start of the drills, Joshua Aarons and Justin Kobach had added a rivalry to their friendship with no heed paid to Kobach's officer status versus Aaron's noncommissioned officer rank of corporal. Both hailed from the northwest, making the basis for a rivalry that much easier. Aarons was from Bremerton, Washington, and grew up within sight of the Puget Sound Naval Shipyard. So, growing up rooting for the University of Washington Huskies against Kobach's Oregon State Beavers came naturally to Aarons. For the both of them, Navy vs. Marine Corps had replaced Huskies vs. Beavers.

One by one the class attempted to duplicate Aarons' results, and yet another unofficial competition between sailors and marines commenced.

Buckley paid rapt attention to each participant. When the last of them had his turn, the deck was littered with sliced melons.

James worked his way through the class, past Redding and Miriam. He approached a sailor and held out his hand for his cutlass. The sailor presented the handle to James, who swung the weapon in the air and felt its balance.

"Gunnery Officer Buckley," James announced, holding out his sword, "en garde!"

The class looked at one another and stared at James and Buckley. They elbowed each other and crept back to form an opening around the two. Sailors who had been swabbing the deck put their mops in the buckets and moved closer.

"Certainly, sir," replied Buckley, presenting his sword.

The two started gently with James initiating contact that Buckley adroitly parried. It gradually grew in intensity, both men adding footwork to the mix of skills on display.

"Good, sir," Buckley commented. "Very good. You're no stranger to the blade."

"Correspondence course," James replied.

Redding and Miriam looked at one another with their mouths agape.

"Hmm," Redding whispered. "That was actually funny."

Miriam swatted him on the arm.

"Pay attention, class," Buckley said, looking around at the spectators. "When you're fighting with a sword, don't forget that you still have other weapons: elbows, fists, and feet. Combat fighting doesn't play by the rules in the Olympics." Both Buckley and James loosened their tunics and took a moment to stretch before reengaging. Buckley was stronger but less mobile. James was quicker but couldn't penetrate Buckley's defense. As they smiled through clenched jaws and sweat beading up on their brows, both men displayed a level of emotional intensity not previously witnessed by the crew.

When the combatants backed away to catch their breath, Redding approached Buckley.

"Mr. Buckley, may I cut in?"

"Of course, sir," Buckley answered with a surprised look on his face.

James' eyes flashed, and an eager smile creased his lips. He wiped his brow, stretched, and swiped the air with his sword. The audience of crew members grew even larger.

Miriam's eyes flashed between the two men. "Oh no," she mumbled under her breath.

Redding presented his sword to James. "Now, what do you call that last move?"

"Shall we stop at first blood?" James asked confidently.

Redding eyed James, then inspected James' uniform and the lone epaulet on his left shoulder, signifying the rank of lieutenant. On his own tunic, the epaulet was on the right shoulder, identifying him as a lieutenant commander.

"Bloodstains on these pretty uniforms might be a little hard to explain later," Redding answered, "but these epaulets make for nice trophies, don't you think?"

"Indeed," James answered with delight. "Epaulets it is."

Miriam shook her head apprehensively, let her camera hang from her neck and peeked through the fingers covering her eyes.

The engagement was tame at first as clashes from the tips of their swords clicked like the soles of tap dancers on the wooden deck. From the start, James was the aggressor and appeared to have the edge. Redding successfully parried James' thrusts but ignored opportunities to attack. Encouragement from the class showed it to be coalescing behind James.

Redding's expressions became increasingly insecure and his footwork appeared awkward, even stumbling, encouraging James to intensify his attacks and drive Redding back. When James finally pinned Redding against the capstan, Redding inexplicably dropped his guard for a split second, allowing James to slice the epaulet from his shoulder with a quick thrust and flick of his wrist, producing a round of applause.

Redding bowed to his opponent. "Touché, Mr. James."

Redding picked up the amputated epaulet from the deck, revealing a bloodstain on his shoulder. He presented the epaulet to James. "Your trophy, Mr. James. Congratulations." He raised James' free hand, faced the audience, and pointed to the victor.

"Thank you, sir," James replied proudly as he stole a glance toward Miriam.

Redding winced and twisted his head to look at his shoulder.

"You're bleeding. Sorry, sir, I thought I took it cleanly."

"Not a problem," Redding answered, "except that it will forever remind me of my second-place finish." He turned to Buckley and handed back his sword. "Carry on, Mr. Buckley."

"Chow time for everyone not on duty," Buckley announced, but it failed to move anyone. Crewmen pantomimed the swordplay they had just witnessed and took turns congratulating James.

Rachel Dover didn't wait her turn. She thrust her hand at James. "Congratulations, sir," she gushed. "That was very impressive." She beamed when he acknowledged her.

"Thank you, Seaman Dover."

Redding made his way belowdecks to his cabin, removed his tunic, and examined his wound through the hole in his blouse when a knock came at the door.

"Yes?" he called out.

Miriam entered and stood by the door holding a first-aid kit.

"You're getting in the habit of entering this cabin uninvited," Redding said with mock indignation while looking at her image in the mirror he faced.

"And you're getting in the habit of surprising me. Either the academy has a lousy fencing team, or you let him win."

Redding dabbed his wound with a rag. "The ship won. You saw the reaction from the crew. They gained an admiration for Lieutenant James they didn't have before. That's a good thing." He looked at her for a reaction. "Oh," he added, "and, at the academy, we were divisional champs three years in a row."

Miriam nodded the confirmation of her expectations. "This new version of you takes some getting used to," she said softly. "Here, let me help with that." She placed the first-aid kit on a table, opened it and removed a bottle of peroxide and a swab, then started to remove Redding's blouse.

"Gee, I don't know. This could be *really* embarrassing," he teased, still looking at her in the mirror while helping her remove his blouse.

"So," she said menacingly, "you can't get that shower scene out of your head, huh?"

She loaded up a swab with peroxide to the point of dripping and slapped it on his wound.

"Yyyesss! Thank you *sooo* much!" Redding cried out. "Now I know why you were so anxious to help."

Miriam barely contained her smile as she examined the wound. "This could really use some stitches. All I can do is tape it closed," she added, applying tape and gauze. "All done here, but try not to lift your right arm too high." She repacked the first-aid kit and made her way to the door.

"Thanks," he replied as he watched her leave through the mirror. "Sorry about that shower thing—NOT!"

Chapter Twenty-Four

Hours from Cairo, the van arrived at the remote airstrip near Siwa. The pilot repaired a leaky brake hose on the DC-3. The driver stopped the van near the hangar doors, got out, and scanned the sky and her surroundings. No one was in the area, and no dust could be seen in the distance on the road just traveled. When she opened the doors to the hangar, a pair of fruit bats flew out. She jumped back, then returned to the van and drove it inside.

Getting out and opening the rear doors, the driver drew her gun while Batul, the other guard, and Sandra forced the hostages from the van. The secret service agents were conscious but barely mobile. The blood on their scalps and faces was dry after so many hours of riding in the hot van.

With Farzad observing, the guards ordered the Americans to sit in a row of dirty airliner seats propped against the hangar wall. The two guards tied their arms and legs to the seats with plastic zip ties and gagged them as Sandra stood watch. Then one by one, Farzad, Batul, the Guards, and Sandra took turns going to a steel locker attached to the hangar wall, shielded from view inside the hangar by a free-standing partition, to change out of their filthy clothing. Farzad emerged in the full-dress uniform he had worn for the video denouncing the Gulf incident. Batul and the guards changed into their camouflage fatigues with red berets. Sandra wore the fatigues of the Egyptian army.

Inside the hangar, a large satellite dish was mounted on a rolling platform with cables leading to a makeshift enclosure in the hangar's corner. Its door opened, and a man emerged as Batul and her guards swung their weapons in his direction. The man crumpled to the ground, holding his hands up in front of his face.

"No!" Farzad shouted, holding up his palm. "He is with us. That is Mustafa."

Farzad waved off the guards. "Mustafa, show me what you have."

Shaking all over, Mustafa asked, "Who are they? They almost killed—"

"Shut up. We have work to do." Farzad could smell the urine Mustafa's fright had caused to soak a leg of his trousers and drip on the hangar floor.

"In here." Mustafa, still shaking, directed Farzad into the enclosure while looking over his shoulder at Batul, who smiled and pointed out the puddle to her team.

Inside, an array of electronic devices covered a shelf mounted against the wall. Their amber and green indicator lights flickered. A cable connected them to a notebook computer on a stool in the darkness under the shelf. "I was about to conduct the final test of the lines."

"And you are just *now* testing them?" Farzad replied with surprise.

"No, no, no," Mustafa said assuredly. "I am double-checking, *triple-checking*, so nothing goes wrong."

"And the satellite dish has been tested?" Farzad inquired.

"Yes, the upload was tested but not long enough to interrupt regular transmissions and call attention to it. We are using our own Egyptian Army's channel on the satellite, and we have Husseini's men at the control center to hide it until the time comes."

"And when the time *does* come, the Americans will be able to track the vice president to this location?"

"Certainly." Mustafa held his hand up. "There is no need for worry. That will be the easy part. It will work."

"And when we transmit, you will be here?"

Mustafa nodded nervously. "How long do I have to stay?"

"You will wait until dark, then pull out the satellite dish and aim it. You will stay until you know the transmission is completed. The pilot will be here by then to help you. Afterward, you will leave with him in the plane."

Leaving Mustafa to complete his work, Farzad returned to his captives. He pulled up a chair in front of Mitchell and the two secret service agents. Resting his gun on crossed legs, he looked Mitchell up and down and smiled. Her legs were covered with dried filth halfway to her knees and her feet were swollen and bloody, but she glared at him.

"You dare to challenge the might of the United States?" Mitchell said defiantly. "You are inviting the destruction of your country, your people, and not just by the US but our allies as well."

Farzad smiled. "Sure we are," he answered sarcastically. "Like the Vietnamese. More than two decades of war by France and the US got neither of you anywhere. You gave up. Nearly two decades of war in Afghanistan—you can't defeat your enemy and you withdraw. You stop short of total victory in the Gulf War, so you must return to Iraq, and then you stop short of a victory—*again*. You withdraw, but we do not. You come to fight us in Syria, and all you accomplish is to disperse us as refugees among you and your so-called allies, spreading our warriors to regions of the world faster than we could have dreamed."

Farzad put away his gun. Seeing the surprised look on Mitchell's face when she glimpsed the women in uniform, he smirked. "You recognize your captors, Madam Vice President? Forgive my indulgence. That's my own personal touch. You might say it's in my blood."

Mitchell ignored Farzad, addressing Batul and the guards directly. "You are Amazonian Guards with vows of loyalty to Muammar al-Qaddafi. He is dead. His heirs are scattered, imprisoned, or dead," she said, prompting smiles between Farzad and Batul. "Your country is free of that murdering monster! Don't you understand?"

Batul did not respond. Instead, she approached one of the secret service agents and, with the butt of her pistol, brutally struck him across the face. The second agent jumped in his chair, cursing through his gag.

"And the same will happen again," Farzad said to Mitchell, "if you dare to preach your warped version of history. Your Christian West doesn't learn. Since the Middle Ages, it hasn't learned. But you will pay the price for your arrogance and stupidity. And for that matter, don't be so sure who is really dead."

Farzad delighted in Mitchell's puzzled look.

"Bring her over there," Farzad ordered Batul, pointing to the hangar's opposite side.

The two guards picked up the rails of Mitchell's chair and carried her across the hangar. Sandra turned away as Mitchell glared at her. The guards set Mitchell down facing Farzad. Batul stood nearby, menacingly.

"Pardon the indignity, Madam Vice President. I just wanted us to be able to have a heart-to-heart in private. I've been looking forward to this."

"You underestimate us," Mitchell shot back. "Your actions will galvanize our people to action."

"World War II is ancient history, Madam," Farzad coolly replied. "Even 9/11 didn't *galvanize* the US. You haven't our will to win. You play by rules of engagement while we have but one rule: *win*." He rose and paced in front of Mitchell, his arms crossed.

"There is no *United* States. Your people are splintered and weak. Look in the mirror, Madam Vice President! The US has never been so divided since its civil war. You bicker among yourselves over meaningless causes, even ridiculous choices of words. No one is laughing at *us*. Our timing is *perfect*. *We* are the united ones. You cherish your lives and your wealth. We follow a higher calling. We are unafraid to die, and you haven't our patience. Your foreign policy changes with every administration. Ours has *never* changed."

Farzad pointed to Sandra. "How many years do you think it took us to get your Sandra Phillips into our cause and into such a high position, and do you think she is the *only* one?

"You want peace now, but we can live with discord and violence until we win—no matter how long it

203

takes." Farzad loomed over her to drive home his point. "When in your history have you ever had soldiers willing to strap on a bomb and kill *themselves* in order to kill just a handful of the enemy? We have thousands of such warriors. You threaten us with your military might? It is powerless when your enemy is among you and as determined as we are."

"You say you are united?" Mitchell questioned. "You cannot claim unity among dozens of independent splinter groups with their own leaders and purposes."

"Not *dozens*, Madam, *hundreds*," Farzad boasted. "You think we are splintered because we go by many names. You minimize our strength by referring to cells and lone wolves. That is fine with us. You think your people will be less frightened, allowing you to be less committed. You fail to see the design behind it. You do not want to see what would frighten you. We know your psychology better than you know ours. I see those lone wolves as a wolf pack. Your politicians and your military think conventionally. You do not do the simple math: all those many names we go by—worldwide—add up to the largest army in the world. It is already deployed, and thanks to the internet, we communicate quite well."

Farzad paced in front of Mitchell, waving his arms as his energy took hold but keeping his voice low enough so the secret service agents couldn't hear. "You think only in terms of conventional military forces. You do not understand anything else. Even one of your presidents was dismissive of our power and admonished your people not to fear us." He bore in on Mitchell, his face beaming with delight and laughing as he continued. "We shoot deserters. You traded yours for four of our generals held at Guantanamo. Those four are now in leadership positions in Afghanistan. From your *own* president, what more could we hope for? Fact is stranger than fiction."

Farzad pulled up an empty crate and sat on it in front of Mitchell. "Our massive army is merely awaiting a general and a mission—a singular event from which there will be no turning back. Japan had Pearl Harbor. You had the battles of Lexington and Concord. This will be ours."

"You can't possibly win an all-out war with the US," Mitchell said defiantly. "Japan and Germany learned that the hard way."

Farzad spread his arms before her. "But we are already winning. The Axis powers misunderstood America. They thought Americans were weak, lazy, interested only in a life of leisure—were isolationists—who would sue for peace after one devastating blow."

"And they were wrong!" Mitchell shouted.

"Only wrong by a few decades," Farzad responded. "And that was the last time your country showed the will to win a war completely. Since then: Korea, Vietnam, Iraq—twice—Syria—and your *crowning* achievement, Afghanistan. Twenty years of war ending in total victory for us—with a bonus, mind you. Eighty-five billion dollars of your weaponry and tens of millions more in *cash*. Why do we need your peace talks when we are victorious on the battlefield?"

Farzad rose, turned away to collect his thoughts, then turned back to Mitchell. "Your wealth has become your weakness. You think money is power. You rely on your economy for your strength. Yours is the short view. We build our numbers. We make more people.

We export them. They grow wherever we plant them. That, and our convictions, create power you cannot match. Money cannot buy that kind of power."

"Out of kindness, America and the West took in your people," Mitchell interjected.

"Yes," Farzad replied with delight, "thank you very much."

"You think those immigrants will turn on us now that they are enjoying a better way of life?" Mitchell added.

"You have seen what we are willing to do to those among us, even our own, who do not live by our values," Farzad answered and waved his finger admonishingly. "They are treated as enemies equal to you. So, they live in fear and are easily controlled."

"You seem to be forgetting the force that most effectively splinters you. The rift between Sunni and Shia goes back to the origins of your religion. The two are blood enemies. You slaughter each other."

Farzad smirked. "You must ask yourself the same question we have asked ourselves—'we' being the pan-Islamists. The question of who is our *real* enemy? The answer always comes up the same—*you*!"

" 'Pan-Islamism' is nothing but a political slogan," scoffed Mitchell.

"Whether for some it's a slogan to manipulate the masses, or for others an ingenuous statement of purpose—who cares? If it helps us defeat our enemy—again, *you*—we don't care. After you are defeated, we will deal with our own internal differences."

Farzad looked into Mitchell's eyes. "Could you have imagined we would hold positions of power in your cities and states, even in your Congress, and have enough influence in your media to make the subject taboo? We have people in elected positions in US swearing their oath of office on the Qur'an, even in your Congress. '*Some people did something.*' " Farzad broke out laughing. "We *are* winning. Isn't it amazing that laws are being contemplated that would make Islamophobia *illegal*! The West has people in positions of power who blame our acts on unemployment and global warming." Farzad laughed so hard he choked and had to catch his breath. "Even when we burn your churches, your leaders and your media don't call us out. We can kill hundreds of you without so much as a back-page story. You kill *one* of us and your nations' leaders call for new laws."

He enjoyed observing Mitchell struggle to counter his points and her discomfort at her inability to do so. "You are more concerned with images than reality. You trade a deserting sergeant for four of our generals for the sake of *image*! Your leaders have more fear of their image than of us! You have allowed us to have lobbyists in your country for our cause. We collect money from your country for our cause—your destruction! We *are* winning. Ask yourself, Madam Mitchell, in the last two decades, who has grown stronger worldwide: you or us? And to think, it has been right there in front of the world for centuries. The commands of our Qur'an and the hadith of Muhammad. Did you suppose they meant nothing to us? Did you suppose that those commands would have less meaning to us with the passage of time? Your own subordinate, Dr. Hannah, in her Naples speech, referred to your Thomas Jefferson's quote from the Tripoli ambassador to England two hundred years ago. He gave you our purpose and our calling. Did you think that has changed? Did you really suppose we would assimilate? It is against Islamic law for Muslims to assimilate into the culture of a non-Muslim country."

Mitchell raised her jaw in defiance. "It isn't just the US you will face."

"Ahh, you think your allies will stand with you?" Farzad replied contemptuously. "Their will is even weaker than yours. They wilt at the prospect of another failed crusade. They will abandon the US, especially after Afghanistan. They no longer trust you, or respect you, and they are too invested in manipulating their own people to *accept* our presence. They can't now admit the failure of those policies. I expect they will try to buy us off, keeping out of the fight, and claim their cowardice has a righteous purpose. They opened their doors to us, and now it's too late to close them. They are running scared. We have their leaders now saying we aren't *expected* to assimilate. Just watch—that will soon be America. We are already winning."

Mitchell began to wilt.

"We are among your so-called allies in even greater numbers than in the US. Perhaps, instead, they will become *our* allies. Hate speech against us is already a crime in Germany and England. And *we* have been the lexicographers! You think Russia and China will oppose us? If they hate us, they hate you even more. It will be in their self-interest to deal with us. They already have. We know we can't have the whole world, not *yet* anyway. So, we will gladly share it with Russia and China. You will be alone."

From defiance to apprehension to depression, Mitchell's expressions evolved as Farzad delivered his invective. She stared at the ground for a moment, then raised her head. Her eyes darted from side to side. Then she looked straight at him, eyes widening.

"Yes, Madam Mitchell," he added gleefully, "this is not a kidnapping for ransom. There would be absolutely no purpose in my telling you this if there were any possibility you would survive the event. However, you will have a seat of honor at our shot heard around the world." Farzad laughed as a look of horror transformed Mitchell's face.

"No matter," he said, bending down to face Mitchell, taunting her. "Your government will be as predictable as always. They will concoct a rescue mission that will fail." He pointed to the satellite dish. "We have seen to that. While publicly they will threaten us, privately they will attempt to buy us off. We will feign interest in those negotiations to buy the extra time needed to enact our operation's next phase. You see, we have learned from the West, much more than you have learned from us. Machiavelli was a great teacher. If you do attack us, you will give us our Alamo, or the sinking of the *Maine* or *Lusitania*, or even Pearl Harbor. We win no matter what."

He turned to Batul and bluntly ordered, "Now, gag her."

Chapter Twenty-Five

The sirocco winds kicked up from the south, fashioned swells on the sea, and forced *Constitution* to tack back and forth against it. It kept her crew busy aloft and on deck to trim her sails with each change in heading. She rose and fell with the waves, crashed through them with determination, and turned water into mist as she powered her way toward the horizon.

Buckley made sure the last day of weapons drills was as challenging as the first, but as had been the case virtually from the start, the crew embraced it with such enthusiasm and competitive spirit that it resembled a small-town Independence Day picnic, complete with competitive games.

Mac stood ready with a musket aimed at the sea beyond the ship's bow while Buckley stood by with his stopwatch. A line of sailors and marines examined their muskets and waited to take their turn after Mac.

"All right," said Buckley as he waved to get their attention, "remember, don't wait to reload after you shoot. Load on the run, and fire your second round to starboard, out to sea." He looked down the deck and pointed to a group of crewmen. "You down there. Give him some room." He looked back at Mac and raised his watch. "*Go!*"

Mac fired his musket, then—on the run—poured powder from his horn into the barrel, followed with a musket ball surrounded by a patch of cloth rammed down the barrel. He pulled off the spent caplock and applied a new one by the time he reached the hatch. A hundred and fifty feet from his starting point, he turned and fired the weapon into the sky over the starboard bow. The class cheered and clapped.

"Twenty-five seconds, Seaman McAvoy," announced Buckley. "Not bad at all. That's only a few seconds longer than trained soldiers took a couple hundred years ago."

Mac took a bow to a new round of applause.

"Who's next?" Buckley asked, looking forward at the crewmen awaiting their turn. Guzman raised his musket. "Seaman Guzman, signal when you're ready."

Guzman looked down the deck at Mac. The two made eye contact. Mac looked at his watch and tapped it while smiling at Guzman, who frowned and set himself. He signaled Buckley.

Buckley looked at his stopwatch. "*Go!*"

Guzman aimed and fired his musket over the bow and sped down the deck, reloading as he ran. When Guzman fired his second round, the audience turned to Buckley for the results.

"We have a new first place!" Buckley announced. "Twenty-two seconds. Well done, Guzman."

Guzman turned to Mac in the crowd, who pursed his lips and wobbled his head as the rest of the audience gave Guzman a round of applause.

"Okay," Buckley called out. "That gives the rest of you something to aim at. This is the last of our musket drills, so let's end the training on a high note. Who's next?"

Ensign Kobach and Corporal Aarons looked at

each other.

"What do you say, jarhead?" Kobach shouted across the deck at Aarons, then removed his officer's cocked hat. "No rank. You and me?"

"In that case, swabbie," Aarons answered, "I'm your Huckleberry!"

****

Emerging from the communications shack, Mustafa gave Farzad a thumbs-up.

Farzad turned to Batul. "Time to go."

Still gagged and bound, Mitchell tried futilely to signal her agents, but they just looked at one another, not understanding her and unable to speak.

Batul pointed to one of the Amazonian Guards, then to the van, and made a triggering motion with her finger. The guard went to the van and returned with the Taser. Pulling out the wires from the gun, she stuck the probes into the back of the jacket of one of the secret service agents. Standing back, she stretched out the electrical lines. With Batul holding her pistol on the agent, the second guard cut him loose from the chair.

Immediately reaching for the wires, he was knocked to the ground by the high-voltage surge from the gun, its trigger held down much longer than necessary.

"You can see that it is quite useless," Farzad said to the agent, standing over him as he groaned in pain on the ground. "Don't make your boss endure the same pain for your lack of cooperation." Addressing both agents, Farzad added, "Rest assured, you will be doing your job to protect Madam Mitchell by cooperating with our attempt at raising ransom money. This should all be over in a day or so."

Mitchell shook her head and uttered a muffled scream through her gag. He pointed to the guard holding the Taser. She pulled the trigger and held it down while the agent screamed through his gag as his body convulsed in reaction to the high voltage.

Farzad crossed the hangar and leaned down to Mitchell's ear. "Now, now, Madam Vice President, don't spoil the surprise. You will only make it worse for all of you." Mitchell slumped and sobbed.

When the agent regained his senses, Batul pointed to the airplane. The pilot put the tools away from his work on the brakes. Batul held her pistol on the agent. An Amazonian Guard led the agent to the steps of the plane still connected to the Taser wires. Once inside, the second guard bound him to a seat before removing the wires, then all went back to the hangar and returned with the second agent, using the same procedure.

The pilot started the plane's engines as Batul untied Mitchell. One of the guards and Sandra led her inside the plane. When the pilot taxied to the end of the runway, Mustafa shut the hangar doors from the inside, then leaned his head against them. The shakes had returned.

A cobra at the end of the runway coiled at the sound of the approaching DC-3. As the pilot revved the engines and took off, the snake was covered with a wave of gritty sand stirred up by the propellers but raised his head in fearless defiance of his huge adversary.

****

"We don't have a lot of these," Buckley told the assembled crewmen as he held up an antique hand grenade with a rope fuse protruding from a hole in its surface. "So, I'm only going to explain the method for using it," he said, as he looked around at the eager faces. "Don't think that because you've played baseball, you have the skill you need. Only the marines have trained with the modern version of this weapon. Sailors, listen up."

The marines in the group crossed their arms and looked arrogantly at the group of sailors. Basker and Mac waved them off.

"Yeah." Mac nudged the marine next to him. "This looks *real* technical. How could you *ever* learn something so complicated?"

"In the museum arsenal below," Buckley continued, "these grenades are all empty. To use one, you fill them with black powder and stick a fuse in the hole." He held up the grenade for everyone to see. "I made this fuse with rope soaked in the same primer solution we've been using for cannon drills. The longer the fuse, of course, the more seconds you have before it explodes. This length here will be about seven seconds, but they aren't precise, so you wouldn't want to cut it too close."

Buckley held the grenade at arm's length. "Here's the difference in the throwing technique. Don't throw it like a baseball. These antique grenades are too heavy. It would throw your arm out. Instead, heave it with a stiff arm, using your whole body like a catapult to get the distance, like so." He demonstrated the technique. "Anyone who's played basketball knows what a hook shot is. It's more like that."

"*Yes!*" exclaimed Rachel under her breath. "How far do you need to throw it?" she shouted to Buckley.

"With accuracy, if you're good and have a strong

arm, about a hundred and fifty feet or so. Even then, the shrapnel flies a lot farther than that," Buckley answered. "So, after you heave it, take cover. When it goes off, it doesn't just kill or disable the enemy. If they live through it, they're in the dirt, facedown. They're stunned. They're ducking for cover. That can be something to take advantage of."

****

On its way to the fort on the Libyan coast, the DC-3 hugged the terrain, flying in the canyons and below the peaks.

Inside the plane, the passengers shared cargo space with boxes of provisions for the garrison at the fort. Farzad and Batul observed the furtive looks between Mitchell and her secret service agents, the only communication they could effect with bindings and gags.

The plane passed near Tobruk on the Libyan coast, the site of a protracted battle between the British and Germans in World War II. An hour later, Benghazi could be seen off the starboard side.

"There is a view that might be of interest to you, Madam Mitchell," Farzad shouted over the din of the engine noise as he pointed out the window. "Benghazi, the sight of one of our significant triumphs and, with the complicity of your White House and State Department, your humiliating defeat. Be so kind as to add that fact to the others I pointed out to you in our earlier conversation."

Leaving Benghazi behind, the plane flew over the Gulf of Sidra on a southwest heading.

****

On board *Constitution*, training had ended for the

crew, but not their enjoyment of the experience. They clustered in groups around the spar deck, not wanting to part with their weapons, taking practice swings with cutlasses and drawing down on imaginary targets with muskets and pistols.

With potatoes swiped from Tebic's larder and a bucket for a target, a group of marines and sailors competed with each other in grenade-tossing accuracy. Rachel won a game of H-O-R-S-E, to the crew's surprise—until she proudly shared her experience as point guard on her league-champion high school squad.

Buckley strolled by and observed their behavior for a minute, then checked his watch. "I hate to break this up, but let's get the weapons back where they belong before chow."

The crew grumbled their reluctance but gathered themselves up, tallied the winners and losers, bragged or made excuses, and headed below.

The setting sun shot orange light through the portlights in Redding's cabin as he wrote an entry in the ship's log.

July 3—Final day of weapons training. Crew spirits high. Competitive spirit high. Cannon drills especially effective for building teamwork mentality. Gun crews have taken to naming their cannons and writing the name in chalk on the barrel, without knowing historic crews did likewise. Must be something to it.

He stopped after the last sentence, looked at it again, laughed aloud, and muttered to himself, "So I'm not a 'team' guy, huh?"

Effective character-building exercise, and for identifying leadership potential. Suggest cooperative arrangement with Coast Guard vis-à-vis tall ship training on USCGC Eagle *and subsequent joint* Constitution/Eagle *appearances on East Coast for recruiting purposes. Recommend* Constitution *crew to demonstrate weapons training as component of same. Will recommend leaders for those roles from current crew upon acceptance of recommendation.*

Wind shift and tacking created delay in arrival at Libyan coastal ruins. Chart of coast insufficiently detailed for night arrival. Harbor small and not marked with lights. Will sight land tonight but will continue under sail in circle route offshore to avoid hazards and time arrival for post-sunrise.

Tebic sat in a corner of the gun deck next to a long gun with the gun port open, his laptop computer, cell phone, and the pewter chamber pot from Redding's cabin connected in a tangled web of wires on a wooden bench before him. Spread out on the deck below his stool was the chart James used to plot the ship's position.

Tebic muttered to himself and took notes on a pad as he looked at the chart. "Okay, longitude is…latitude about…close enough." He punched up a table on his computer. "All right, Mr. UNISAT 6, where are you?" He typed longitude and latitude figures into search fields and waited. Reading the results on the screen, he wrote them in his notebook. "Altitude 97 degrees, azimuth 165 degrees, but with magnetic deviation—" He scratched his head and looked closer at the figures. "Uh-huh. UNISAT 6, you are *mine!*"

Using a handheld compass, he aimed the chamber pot out the gun port. He glanced back and forth between his computer screen and the chamber pot and adjusted the angles of the pot until the computer screen showed an anchorman at a TV news desk.

"Yeah! Gotcha!"

"Got what?" Rachel said over his shoulder, nearly knocking Tebic over with surprise.

"Geez!" he gasped and turned off the computer. "You scared the crap out of me!"

Rachel looked over his setup. "What in the world is all of this?"

Tebic composed himself. "I'm under orders to fix the ship's radio, only I *can't* fix it, so this is the next best thing—actually, better in a way. I can connect with the internet and make phone calls, text, whatever."

"Hey!" Rachel pointed to the chart on the floor. "That's Lieutenant James' chart. Does he know you have it?"

"No, and he's not going to know I have it or that it was ever gone," Tebic answered defiantly. "*Or* he's also going to know you call out his name in your sleep."

"I do *not*!" she said as she looked over her shoulder.

Tebic just nodded his head, smirking ear to ear. Then his expression changed and he regarded her seriously. "Look, this is for the captain's party. Don't mess it up."

Chapter Twenty-Six

President Jonathan Fairchild and the Joint Chiefs convened around a rectangular table in the "situation room" in the basement of the West Wing. Computer monitors lined the walls above wood paneling that hid sophisticated electronic equipment, providing secure communications with all branches of the military, including all of their bases worldwide. Secure communications are useful only when you have information worth securing. Such was not the case for those gathered there, or for Admiral Towne as he sat in his own situation room at NAVCENT with a monitor view of the high-powered assembly at the White House.

White House Chief of Staff Oliver Jenkins coordinated the discussion with National Security Adviser Bernard Nussman, CIA Director Mark Adamson, Army Chief of Staff Craig Hastings, and Secretary of the Navy Admiral William "Bucky" Buckholter.

"At least we know she's still alive," Buckholter offered the group. "Egyptian police confirmed her body wasn't found in the rubble, just the bodies of two secret service agents. Someone obviously knew what her GPS locator was and removed it."

Bernard Nussman interjected, "Before we go further, Secretary of State Olivia Leighton is on her way to Cairo to meet up with Vice President Mitchell.

She got the news in flight before her London stopover but took off for Cairo anyway. Any suggestions on that score?"

Towne's voice jumped out of a speaker in the center of the conference table. "*Keep Leighton the hell away from Cairo. Land her at the Naval Air Station at Sigonella, Sicily.*"

"Why Sicily, Admiral?" asked Nussman.

"Just a sec, Admiral. Your video isn't up," said Fairchild.

Oliver Jenkins moved to a control panel on the wall, punched a button, then turned to a wall monitor as Towne's image came into view.

"Okay, Admiral," said Jenkins. "Continue."

"*I don't think it's safe anywhere in the Middle East,*" Towne replied. "*I've got all of NAVCENT on lockdown. I suggest the same for all our bases abroad.*"

"Why is that, Admiral?" Nussman continued.

Towne took a deep breath. "*In my opinion, the boldness of this action suggests something other than a ransom-type abduction. We're looking at something much bigger, much broader.*"

White House Chief of Staff Jenkins looked doubtful. "Bigger and broader, Admiral? What leads you to believe that?"

"*Because I see it as an all-in play,*" Towne answered forcefully, "*like Pearl Harbor, a provocation that was meant to start a war and give the enemy a head start.*"

"You mean you think the Vice President will be assassinated?" President Fairchild asked. "They could have done that in the museum!"

"*Yes, Mr. President,*" Towne answered as he tried

to calm himself, "*but not if they wanted to use it to send a message, a rallying message—something dramatic. This could be the start of a recruiting campaign with a headline showing how powerful they are. Or something much bigger, a trigger signal to their operatives around the world. I expect we'll hear a message to that effect any time now.*"

Fairchild's frustration showed. He stood and walked away from the table but turned back to the camera to question Towne. "But *who*, Admiral, *who* would carry that out?"

"*Whoever conducted the kidnapping,*" answered Towne. "*Whoever set that bomb off but wasn't killed by it. Whoever has been conspicuously absent from the public eye recently, because he, or they, were preparing for this event.*"

"And?" Fairchild asked, still standing by his chair.

Towne paused and shifted in his chair, then gestured to the camera as he spoke. "*If I'm correct about the intent of this plot, then I think we have to consider that the key player behind this has to be someone of considerable rank and influence. I think we need to locate that Iranian, Colonel Farzad.*"

"*Really*, Admiral," interjected CIA Director Mark Adamson. "Farzad called you out in that video speech after the Persian Gulf affair, and now he's your chief suspect. Your objectivity may be in question. We have been looking into Farzad, but I don't expect we're going to find anything that would confirm that he is the mastermind behind any of this or, for that matter, that the plot is as thick as you suggest. We believe it's al-Qaeda in Egypt, and we're asking the Egyptian Army to let us in there so we can go to work."

"*With respect, sir,*" offered Towne, "*that sounds a little like rounding up the usual suspects.*"

Adamson bristled. "Based on what we have so far, it's a reasonable assumption!"

"*Uh-huh,*" Towne replied, "*and you're communicating with General Husseini in that regard?*"

Adamson hesitated. "We're working on it. There have been delays at their end because of the chaotic conditions."

"*You're damn right there have been delays,*" Towne came back, getting hotter. "*That's because Husseini is a snake. I think you must seriously consider that he may be in on it. Don't you think it's odd that he wasn't with Mitchell's party when the bomb went off? Then he assumes command of the government, declares martial law, and for the longest time no one can get through to him. I strongly suggest he's been buying time for the perpetrators to carry out their mission.*"

"But neither was Aziz with Mitchell's party when the bomb went off," Adamson answered sharply. "I suppose he's in on it too!"

"Let's all bring it down a notch, gentlemen," cautioned Fairchild.

"*Yes, sir,*" Towne answered. "*My fault, sir, but to Director Adamson's question, I doubt very much that Aziz is any more knowledgeable about this event than we are.*" Towne took a breath before continuing. "*Aziz, as you know, is weak. Nice enough guy, sincere, but weak, even to the point of being close to death. Has been for some time. If you are Husseini and want to take power, you don't need to kill Aziz with a bomb, and it's better if you don't. You just shove him aside, keep him under wraps. He's in the hospital. You have control over that. He may not survive, if you get my meaning."*

A courier entered the White House situation room and handed Adamson a document.

"Hold on, everyone," Adamson said. "This may be what I was waiting for." He read the document, then slammed it on the table.

"*Damn!* It's that Colonel Farzad. I told you we've been looking into him." He read to the group from the document. "He is the son of Muammar Gaddafi." He looked up sheepishly from the document and around the room, then continued reading. "An illegitimate son, born to a mistress. His birth was kept a secret. He was taken away as an infant to be raised by the mullahs in Iran. He went by various names to keep his identity secret until recently, when the Supreme Leader brought him out and made him a cabinet-level minister under his current name."

"Where did that intelligence come from?" asked Fairchild.

"Israeli intelligence, Mr. President," Adamson answered. "The Mossad."

"Why haven't they given us that intelligence before?"

"I think I can answer that, Mr. President," answered the Secretary of the Navy, "Bucky" Buckholter, looking from Fairchild to Adamson. "Because they don't entirely trust our ability to keep secret information secret. Compared to the Mossad's ship, ours leaks like a colander."

Adamson looked down at the table and shuffled his papers.

"That fits," offered President Fairchild. "The kid

was Gaddafi's insurance policy, someone to carry on if he didn't survive. Iran would be the logical place to hide him. Gaddafi promoted pan-Islamism. To a degree, so does Iran, and in any case, they would use that movement to gain power. This puts Iran square in the middle of this."

"But Gaddafi had lots of sons," insisted Army Chief of Staff Craig Hastings. "Why this one?"

"Yes," answered Fairchild, "and they're all either dead, in prison, or were given asylum somewhere and put under wraps. Maybe Gaddafi had a vision of the future. Turns out he was right."

Adamson answered while looking at the Mossad communication. "Apparently, this one is different. He was born while Gaddafi was married to his first wife. The mistress was Iranian and a present to Gaddafi from Iran." He briefly looked up from the page. "That would explain why almost no one would have known about him. And get this—he was born under the Comet West."

"Never heard of it," said Hastings.

"You never heard of it because it only showed up once, came too close to the sun, and blew up back in '76," answered Adamson, referring to the document. He looked around the table. "Now, Islam frowns on any beliefs in astrology in the sense of horoscopes and what not, but it's a gray area with them. Some of their teachings include the possibility that Allah, or his angels, indicate special powers have been bestowed on a person by signs from the heavens. Looks like Gaddafi may have thought Allah had something special in mind for this kid, and the mullahs agreed."

"In any case, his identity has been a complete lie to

this point," Nussman added. "That has to mean something. With the Cairo talks a day away, he's nowhere to be found. Even after his very public video broadside—and now the kidnapping. That has to mean something too."

Fairchild turned to Adamson. "Mark, this adds credence to Admiral Towne's take. We all have to consider that is a real possibility, so start putting together what-if scenarios as to what a more global approach by this band could mean. Now, what to do in the meantime?"

"In the meantime," Nussman offered, "we wait for the message that Admiral Towne suggests is imminent. If he's right about the purpose to all of this, he's right about that too."

"What capabilities do we have of knowing where a signal is coming from?" asked Fairchild.

"To get a message out across a vast region, or the world, you pretty much have to use a satellite uplink. With any such linkage we will be able to identify the location within a hundred yards or so," answered Adamson.

National Security Advisor Nussman leaned across the table to Adamson. "That's not going to help us much if the location is urban."

"True," Adamson responded, "but it probably wouldn't be. Too hard to hide an operation like that in a city. It would more likely be a remote location. Of course, that's assuming there will be any such transmission at all."

Fairchild continued his questions. "Where are we on forces we can deploy?"

"Making the assumption that, if we identify a

location within, say, a few hundred miles of Cairo, we currently don't have any ship-based assault teams within striking distance," said Navy Secretary Buckholter. "SEAL Team Three is aboard the *Boxer*. I've got it steaming at full speed from Diego Garcia, but they won't be close enough for at least a day. We'll have to rely on our land bases in the region." Buckholter looked at the camera in the situation room to address Towne. "Chester, jump in on this point. Where are you on prep?"

"All SEAL and Marine Force Recon teams under my command were ordered to gear up hours ago. They're waiting by their birds for an order. I recommend the same for Army Ranger units."

Army Chief of Staff Craig Hastings lifted his hand from the table. "Mr. President, that order has already been given."

"May I suggest," Towne interjected, *"that if this message comes in and it comes from somewhere in my territory—which I believe is likely—the people at your table buy my guys as much time as you can...if you can."*

"Right," President Fairchild answered. "We'll treat it as a hostage negotiation." Then he added somberly, "And hope that's *all* it is." Fairchild directed his attention to Towne. "Admiral Towne, I want to thank you for your analysis. You have painted a bleak picture, but it's one we cannot ignore." Looking straight at Adamson, who shifted in his seat, Fairchild added, "Perhaps it is one that's been hanging on our walls all along and we overlooked it."

Fairchild rose, walked to the wall, and leaned against it. "I repeat my previous order. I want everyone in this room to adopt the admiral's worst-case scenario. It shouldn't be the only scenario to consider, but it should be at the top of the list. We all hope he is wrong, but better to prepare for the worst than underestimate the enemy, which we've done far too much of in recent years."

Chapter Twenty-Seven

Egyptian Army soldiers, under the command of Captain Omar Naser, loaded explosives from a launch tied to a large steel fishing vessel at anchor in a cove below the ruins of the fort to the east. A man carrying a heavy crate stopped for a moment at the sound of airplane engines.

"They're coming!" He placed the crate next to several others on the deck of the fishing boat, ran to the high steel bulwark surrounding the vessel. He peered over it and down at the men in the launch.

"They're coming! Hurry!"

The DC-3's engines quieted as the pilot throttled back; then the propellers howled with the change of pitch for the landing.

Naser came out of the ship's cockpit and pointed to the bow of the vessel. "Stack those crates in the bow for now. We need to get over to the airstrip. When we get back, put the rest of those crates from the launch back in the truck for now. We'll finish this job later."

Naser rode in the passenger seat of the truck on the dirt road leading from the cove to the airstrip. Crewmen sat on boxes of explosives in the covered cargo area. When it stopped, they piled out to join soldiers from the fort garrison lined up in rank along the strip and covered their faces as the plane taxied to them in a cloud of dust.

The plane's propellers were still windmilling to a stop when its cargo door flew open. A soldier on the ground attached metal stairs handed to him by Batul, who was the first to exit, followed by Farzad. Naser directed some of his armed men to draw weapons and others to help with the disembarkation of the hostages.

Naser pointed to a vehicle near the plane. "Put them in there and taken them to the fort."

Soldiers wrestled with barrels of gasoline from a truck and rolled them to the plane where crewmen pumped it by hand into the DC-3's wing tanks. The pilot climbed out and yelled at the refueling crew.

"You there! Don't spill it on the surface! It will penetrate into the wings and create a fire hazard—and wipe that dirt off your fuel nozzle."

Farzad approached the pilot. "When you have finished, return immediately to the field at Siwa. Radio Mustafa when you are near. He will light the end of the runway with the headlights of the van."

"Then what?" the pilot asked.

"You will assist Mustafa in aiming the satellite. You and he will only stay through the broadcast, to make sure the signal is transmitted; then you will follow the orders of General Husseini and fly to the base as he told you until it's time to pick me up here tomorrow. Keep an eye on Mustafa," Farzad warned. "He is weak and panicky."

Farzad walked to the truck where Captain Naser was supervising the unloading of the fuel barrels. "Mustafa told me the test of the signal to the satellite from here was complete and successful."

"I can confirm that from this end as well. The technician is in the video room right now, making the final preparations."

"Fine. We have not eaten since early this morning." Farzad pointed to the Amazonian Guards. "Then we need to rest before tonight."

"That's been arranged," Naser replied. "You want your hostages to eat as well?"

"Their gags are not to be removed. Besides, why waste supplies?" Farzad said with a shrug and a wry smile. "For now, keep Mitchell in a separate room from her agents. She's not to get a word out to anyone under any circumstances."

Tapping his finger to his chin, Farzad walked away from Naser, then turned. "Is the ship ready?"

"It was being loaded as you arrived."

"The explosives are in the bow?" Farzad asked.

"Most of it, yes. You interrupted us. Too dangerous to install the detonating device now. We'll wait until the time comes."

"You have selected men for that mission?" asked Farzad.

Naser smiled. "When I told them it would make the attack on the USS *Cole* look like a door ding, I had no problem getting volunteers."

"Door ding," Farzad replied, amused. "I like that."

"Yes, and the men have painted a name on the vessel—*Maliyat Bialqua*."

"*Full of Power*. An appropriate name. I like their spirit. It means you have done well."

Chapter Twenty-Eight

From the fighting platform of the foremast, Redding could see the highest terrain on the rugged Libyan coast, close enough now for the desert breeze to carry the faint scent of wild thyme. The color of its red earth was enriched by the gilded hues of the setting sun. As *Constitution* bore down on the familiar landscape, its captain found himself talking to the ship.

"North Africa," he said as he gazed down at the deck. "Been a long time."

Miriam shielded her eyes from the glare of the setting sun off the water as she wandered the deck, looking in all directions.

Redding yelled down to her. "Did you lose something?"

She looked up to the mainmast.

"Over here!" Redding called from the foremast.

"Yes!" she shouted, and pointed to him. "You!"

"I'll come down!"

"*No!*" She craned her neck and yelled back. "I'm coming up!"

"I'll get someone to help you!"

"No, I can do it!" she answered as she started to climb the fifty feet of rope shrouds to the platform.

A sailor reached out to her, but she waved him off. Halfway up, she looked down at the deck. "Oh Lord."

"What was that?" Redding asked as he held on to a

shroud and leaned over the platform to look down at her.

"Nothing, I'm fine!" she answered unconvincingly.

Redding held on to the first of Miriam's arms that reached through the opening to the platform and helped her the rest of the way.

"I've never been up here," she said as she steadied herself from the movement of the ship. "Oh my! There's a lot more movement up here than on the deck. Thought I had my sea legs." She laughed nervously. "Guess not."

Redding chuckled. "You think this is bad, the next platform up is like a ride at Magic Mountain. Want to see?"

"Uh, maybe some other time." She looked down at the deck just as the ship swayed. Her knees buckled, and Redding wrapped her in his arms. "Oh my God. I guess looking down is not the thing to do from up here if you're not used to it." She looked at his arms still around her. "Umm, I think I'm okay now."

"Right. Sure," he replied as he loosened his hold. "Just hang on to the shroud."

"Yeah. Good idea." Miriam inched her way to the shroud leading to the platform above and grabbed on to it. "This feels better." She gazed at the horizon. "Wow, this is really something. Feels like you're halfway between the sea and heaven."

"Poetically put."

Miriam looked at him and smiled but didn't reply.

An awkward silence made both uneasy until Redding looked away and changed the subject. He pointed to the horizon. "There's your destination. I think it's that high spot you can just barely make out right there."

She sighted down his arm to the horizon, and he admired the glow her eyes took on as they picked up the setting sun.

"I see it," she said, a slight tremble in her voice.

Redding pulled away. "You know, maybe someone can tell me how a civilian gets a US Navy warship to alter course to some musty old ruins in the middle of nowhere."

"By having some pull with the vice president," Miriam responded with mock pride.

"Ooooh," Redding quipped just as the ship swayed.

Miriam tightened her grip on the shrouds and grabbed her stomach. "Yeah, ooooh."

"You feeling sick? Should I yell 'watch out below'?"

She waved him off.

"Sorry about that," he said, looking off toward the southern horizon.

"About what?" she asked.

"Well, that's a trait of mine. Not my favorite," Redding answered, thumping his forehead.

"Trait?" she asked, looking at him curiously.

Redding took a breath. "Making jokes to cover...uncomfortable moments. Changing the subject...things like that."

Miriam nodded to herself. "Now that you mention it."

"Yeah. Well...we won't have time to analyze that...will we?" he added, still focused on the horizon and avoiding eye contact.

Miriam paused. A somber expression swept over her face, and she looked away. "No, I guess not."

"Maybe you'd like to go below," he said, offering her a hand down to the shrouds.

"No," she responded quietly. She bit her lip, then shook her head and looked into his eyes. "You started this. It's my turn."

Redding backed off slightly as Miriam gathered her thoughts.

"Before we met...I had formed this impression of you—based, I guess, entirely on the problem I believed you created for me and my team—I told you about that."

When he did not respond, she continued, "Then I think I must have been looking for confirmation of that impression—the way people do...and..."

"And I obliged."

"I suppose." She searched the sky as if to find the right words. "But only because it fit the image I had created, not because the image was—accurate."

"I appreciate that."

Both were silent for a moment. Redding removed his cocked hat and ran his fingers over the gold braid. "So, what about the last few days?"

"Yes—the last few days," Miriam responded with hesitation. "I've had to come to grips with some realities—about you *and* myself. I haven't been entirely fair to you, which you may have noticed. That has everything to do with how I avoid dealing with my own issues." She looked at him. "A trait of mine that isn't *my* favorite."

"Well, now that you mention it," he said with a sheepish smile. "Oops, there I go again."

Miriam chuckled. "That trait of yours might be more of a gift than you think. Wish I had it."

"No, you've got plenty of gifts—" He stopped himself. His eyes widened as he looked at her. "Uhh…no…I mean…I didn't mean it that way. I…"

Miriam burst into a mixture of laughter and tears.

"Damn!" Redding exclaimed. "I suck at this." He waited until he was sure of his words and Miriam had quieted down. "Hell, I forgot what I meant to say, but"—his voice took on a more serious tone and he couldn't look at her—"for what it's worth, I regret we won't have more time." Then he turned back to her.

"I have the same regret." Their eyes locked for a moment.

"I don't relish the idea of living with regrets, Miriam, but I can't see past this one. You say you can connect dots." He pointed back and forth between the two of them. "How about these two?"

"That's the first time you've called me Miriam," she said softly as her eyes welled with tears.

"Captain Redding, sir! Dr. Hannah!" Cooper called from the deck.

"Up here!" Redding shouted down.

Cooper bent her head back and paused for a moment as she looked up at the platform. "Um, am I interrupting?"

Miriam wiped away her tears. "What is it, Bobbi?"

Cooper cupped her hands around her mouth. "Your presence is requested below—both of you!"

"Is there an emergency?" Redding called down to her.

"Well…kind of."

Redding turned to Miriam. "I guess we need to find out what 'kind of' means." He called down to Cooper, "On our way!"

Cooper walked across the deck, down a companionway, and out of sight.

Redding carefully helped Miriam down the shrouds, leading the way while making sure Miriam's feet above him made firm contact with the shrouds with each step. Once on deck, Redding led Miriam on the same path taken by Cooper. They descended the steps from the spar deck to the gun deck and looked around for her.

"Huh?" Redding muttered. "Where'd she go?"

They continued down the next flight of stairs to the berth deck. The off-duty crew chatted in conversation groups. Some swung in their hammocks.

"Why is it I feel like Alice chasing the March Hare?" Miriam joked.

"No kidding," responded Redding. Then he pointed in the direction of voices. "My cabin? I think the bunny went that way." As they continued toward the captain's cabin, the sounds grew louder.

Redding opened the door for Miriam and both entered the cabin to a loud "*Huzzah!*" from Cooper, Gunderson, Bates, Kobach, Buckley, Tebic, and James. The cake from Messina—somewhat the worse for wear and partially cut away—was on the table adorned with lighted sparklers made from cordage and gunpowder. Smoke from the sparklers filled the air.

"Hurry up and blow out the candles!" yelled James. "Before we all suffocate!"

Redding tried to blow out the sparklers but gave up. "No way these are going to blow out." He picked them off the cake one at a time and stomped them out on the deck.

"Happy birthday, Captain!" Gunderson called out,

followed by well wishes from the rest, except Tebic, who fussed with a hodgepodge collection of electronic equipment.

Fanning away the smoke, Redding looked around the room. "Who knew it was my birthday?"

Cooper pointed to Miriam, and Redding turned to her.

"Security clearance," Miriam answered, raising her hand.

"Mad Hatter, huh?" Redding said with a wry smile. "Nice acting job."

"It's one of my...*gifts*," Miriam said teasingly.

"Well, I don't know what to say—except thanks."

Miriam tried to hide the redness in her eyes, but James sighed almost imperceptibly, then approached Redding with his hand out. "Congratulations." As he spoke, he glanced at Miriam so that only Redding could see.

James prolonged his eye contact with Redding until Redding nodded.

"Thanks," Redding replied sincerely.

"It's a little stale," Cooper said, pointing to the cake.

"It looks great," Redding assured her. "I don't deserve it—but I'll eat it." He picked up a long knife lying next to the cake and handed it to James. "Lieutenant, you're handy with a blade. Please do the honors." Then he held up his hand. "Sorry, there won't be any blood this time."

As the group laughed, James took a fencing pose and pointed the knife at the cake. "En garde."

Miriam stopped James. "Not yet, Lieutenant. First the birthday surprise. Mr. Tebic?"

"I think I've got it!" yelled Tebic as he aimed the chamber pot out of the portlight while looking at his computer screen.

"Got what?" asked Redding. Then he pointed to the chamber pot. "Hey, isn't that my—"

"Shhhh!" came the reply from around the room.

A voice came from the speaker on the computer as Bates turned the screen so the group could see. Redding's mother and sister sat at a dinner table and waved. The video image was pixelated and froze occasionally, but it brought a broad smile to Redding's face.

"Happy birthday, Moses," they said in unison.

Redding's jaw dropped as he looked at Tebic. "How in the hell did you—?" Miriam and Cooper pulled at Redding's sleeves, edging him closer to the screen.

"Watch your language," Miriam whispered in Redding's ear.

"Can they see us?" Redding asked Bates.

"Yes, sir."

"Mom. Sis," Redding uttered in amazement, "this is too fantastic."

"Whoever Tebic is," his sister replied, "he's some kind of electronic genius."

Redding's mother jumped in. "I want you to give him a medal. He put this together. Don't ask me how he—"

Her voice disappeared and the picture went to static as Tebic, with a broad smile on his face, let his aim of the chamber pot slip while looking around the room.

"*Tebic!*" came shouts from everyone.

While Bates looked at the screen, Tebic re-aimed the chamber pot until the picture returned and Bates gave him a thumbs-up.

Redding waved at the computer. "There you are, Mom. We lost you for a few seconds." He looked at Tebic. "Yeah, I'll give Mr. Tebic something, all right," he said jokingly. "Don't you worry about that."

"We wish this was a happier occasion, Moses," his sister said sadly.

"Yes," added his mother. "Isn't it terrible? We just thank God you aren't involved."

The picture and sound went off again, and again it resulted in another chorus of "*Tebic!*"

"It's not my fault!" Tebic complained. "Aiming this thing out the window isn't as easy as I make it look, you know."

"What's terrible?" asked Redding, looking around the room. "What are they talking about? Tebic, can you get them back?"

"I don't know, Captain. Maybe up on deck I could get a better aim."

Redding pointed upward. "All hands on deck!"

Chapter Twenty-Nine

Inside the fort, Naser strapped Mitchell's secret service men to chairs, still bound and gagged, in a room that resembled the interior of an old airplane hangar. Rusty corrugated-steel paneling on the walls obscured the mud-brick structure of the ancient crumbling fortress. An aviation navigation sectional map was attached to the wall. They bound Mitchell to a chair between the two agents, all facing a video camera. Sandra tightened the gag in Mitchell's mouth. A technician looked through the view finder of the camera to frame the shot. Farzad checked his work, then he flipped through the pages of a notepad while the video technician turned on a set of bright television lights for a brief moment, then off again, leaving only the warm light of a few oil lamps for illumination. A second technician flipped the switches on a panel and read an array of indicators. Batul, the Amazonian guards, Sandra, and Naser stood by.

It was a moonless night. Armed men outside the fort talked and smoked while sitting on the running boards of a truck. One of Naser's sergeants emerged from the fort.

"Put out those cigarettes, you idiots!" he yelled. "You know what is in that truck!"

The sergeant waited with his hands on his hips as the men crushed out their smokes, but when he re-entered the fort, they laughed and lit up again.

There were no lights outside the compound. The sun had been down long enough to leave the stars as the only source of illumination. Only the men's voices and the glow of their cigarettes revealed a human presence. One by one, they made their way into the fort.

****

The breeze died down and with it the chop on the sea. *Constitution*'s black hull virtually disappeared against the sea and the night sky, leaving the faint image of her white stripe flying above the water like a free-floating ghostly apparition.

The glow from a few oil lamps was sufficient to light the portion of the spar deck where the birthday party group had recongregated around a hatch cover. They struck up conversations while Tebic and Bates attended to the video hookup. Tebic held a compass in one hand and the chamber pot in the other. Bates looked at the computer screen and turned it toward Tebic.

Corporal Aarons chatted with the navy helmsman.

"Corporal Aarons!" shouted Buckley. "Join us over here."

Redding stood at the bow holding on to a forestay.

Miriam approached from behind him. "Did you ever see such a black night?"

Redding turned to look at her, then looked up at the stars. "Yes, I have. It's common at sea. No moon and no lights from civilization. No dust in the air. It's the only place I've ever been where the stars go all the way to the horizon and the Milky Way looks like a bright cloud arcing across the sky. Next best thing to being an astronaut."

He looked toward the ruins in the distance and pointed to a dim light shining from the direction of the fort. "Looks like your secret ruins aren't so secret. Someone beat you to it."

Miriam looked at the light. Her face crinkled. "That doesn't make sense. There shouldn't be anyone there."

"*Here we go!*" Tebic shouted from his place atop a hatch.

Redding and Miriam walked back toward the gathering. She glanced behind her at the distant light from the ruins, then joined the group converging on the computer screen.

"Damn," said Tebic. "I thought I had it for a second, then I lost it. Sorry, everyone."

Tebic adjusted the chamber pot while looking at the screen. A new image flickered in and out of view.

"What was that?" James asked Tebic.

"I don't know." Tebic adjusted his pot while looking at his compass. "I think I picked up a different channel or a different satellite."

The image returned to the screen and held steady. It was Colonel Farzad, in the same uniform he wore for the video speech after the Gulf incident, standing behind Vice President Mitchell. The two secret service agents were tied to chairs and gagged. Batul and Sandra Phillips stood to the side of Farzad.

"What the hell?" Redding yelled. "That Iranian son of bitch—Farzad!"

"Oh my God!" Miriam gasped. "That's *Virginia*…and those are two of her secret service detail! And—what? That's *Sandra*!"

"Miriam." Redding motioned her closer to the

computer screen. "What's he saying?"

She leaned toward the screen. "Uh…'This is our moment to rise up…Allah is with us…We have the power to…fulfill our God-given decree to cleanse the earth of the infidels…They are powerless to stop us now…We are many, yet we are one.' "

Farzad pulled his pistol from its holster.

"He's got a gun!" shouted Bates.

Crewmen on duty began gathering around the group clustered near the computer.

Miriam waved her hand. "Shhh!" She continued interpreting. "He said, 'Behold the American vice president…The sword of Allah…will behead the devil and his minions.' "

A bright flash from the fort caught the attention of James and Buckley. On the computer screen seconds later, Farzad put the barrel of his pistol against the head of one of the agents and fired.

Gasps reverberated throughout the group on deck. The barely audible crack of a report from a firearm carried like an echo from the direction of the fort moments after the gunshot sounded on the computer speakers.

Redding and Cooper quickly turned toward the sound of the gunshot.

"Oh my *God*!" Miriam screamed.

Cooper held Miriam's shoulders.

"Son of a *bitch*!" Redding yelled.

"What the hell?" James mumbled, tapped Buckley, and pointed to the fort. Both looked back and forth from the computer screen to the horizon. Farzad aimed his pistol at the head of the second agent.

Redding looked at James and Buckley. "What?"

Miriam held her head in her hands. "I can't believe this! He's going to do it again! I can't watch!"

Miriam turned away from the screen. Cooper turned with her and looked back toward the fort.

Another flash appeared from the window of the fort. "Did you see that?" James asked Buckley, who was counting to himself under his breath.

The computer screen showed Farzad shoot the second agent. The gunshot sound again arrived at the boat moments after it came through the computer speaker.

"Those were gunshots," said Buckley. "About two miles away. I counted the seconds."

"That's the distance to that fort," Aarons added.

James pointed to the horizon. "Captain! There, on the horizon, at the ruins. Flashes and gunshots from there corresponded to the shots on the screen."

Redding straightened, looking to the horizon, then back at James.

"He's right, Captain," Buckley said. "The timing was the same but delayed."

"I saw them too, Captain," said Cooper. "And the light from the window is bright now. Before it was dim. Look at the computer screen. They're using bright lights."

Miriam pointed to the horizon. "But how could we hear it?"

"Sound travels far over water," Redding answered.

Tebic's eyes widened. He raised his hand as if in a classroom. "Sir," he said to Redding, "the satellite transmission would have a delay of a few seconds. That could account for the timing difference. The satellite signal would still get here before the sound from the shore."

Redding turned to Buckley. "What do you mean by the *same* timing?"

"Sir, identical," Buckley answered emphatically.

"He's right, Captain. It can't be a coincidence," James asserted.

"No," Redding said, paused to think, then held Miriam's shoulder and pointed to the computer screen as Farzad started speaking again. "Miriam, translate."

She refocused on the screen. "Umm...he said they have shown their power by taking the American vice president." When Farzad drew a sword from a scabbard on his side and held it near Mitchell's neck, Miriam gasped.

Redding pointed to the screen. "The words, Miriam!"

"Oh, God!" she said, tearfully, as Cooper tightened her hold on her shoulders. "He, uh...says...'For this symbol of Western decadence...and infidelity to Allah...we have a special ending that...will mark a new beginning.' " Miriam pounded her fist on the hatch but held her attention on the screen.

As Farzad's voice grew louder, the usual creaks and groans from *Constitution* hushed. Even her bow wake went silent.

Miriam wiped tears from her face as she struggled to continue the translation. " 'The dawn of America's day of independence...will see the sun rise...on our global jihad.' " Farzad pulled his sword away from Mitchell's neck and cocked his shoulders as if to strike.

Miriam clutched her hair but held her focus on the computer screen. Farzad's voice was at a fever pitch, but Miriam repeated it deadpan, choking back her own emotions.

" 'The death of this US leader will signal the birth of our worldwide caliphate…' "

Redding, James, Buckley, and Cooper glanced from the computer screen to the shore. A flurry of lights flashed from the fort. James and Buckley pointed to the fort. "There," they said in unison. Buckley again counted the seconds as Miriam continued translating.

" '… and will be your signal…to bring a rain of fire down on the throats of our enemies!' "

On the computer screen, cheers rang out from the men surrounding Farzad as they fired their weapons into the ceiling.

The sound from the volley of gunshots reached *Constitution* moments later. Redding checked with Buckley.

"Yes, Captain, same timing."

"That's it then." Redding pointed to Tebic's set up. "Tebic, can you use that stuff to get through to Fleet?"

"Uh, I don't know. I wouldn't know how to hack in." He paused for a moment. "No way with voice or video."

"*Any way at all!*" Redding shouted.

Redding's impatience made Tebic even more nervous, but he paused and lit up. "*Yes!*"

"What?" Redding replied.

"Holcomb!" Tebic said. "The admiral's aide. Maybe you saw him, sir."

"Big ears? Birth-control glasses?"

"That's him," Tebic answered. "He's a sort of friend of mine. I think I can use this to text him."

"Better than nothing." Redding looked again to the shore before turning to James. "Keep her offshore, no closer than we are now. Note the bearing to that light from the fort. Tebic, get going on that connection."

James jumped into action. He and Bates directed the crew into the rigging.

Redding turned to Cooper, Kobach, and Gunderson. "Douse all lights above and below decks, anything that could leak out the gunports. Start with my cabin."

"I don't understand," Miriam questioned Redding. "Why do you need to contact NAVCENT? They and the Pentagon and everyone in DC would have seen what we saw. They have technology to identify the source of the transmission. They're probably on their way right now."

"That's exactly what they're doing," Redding insisted, "and they've been fooled."

Miriam looked perplexed. "I don't get it?"

"Miriam, what did you see in that video?" Redding continued impatiently. "What did that look like to you?"

"Well, you saw it. They had Virginia there, and—"

"Not her," Redding interrupted, "the setting. What was that?"

"Just, some old barn...or something." Then Miriam paused and dropped her jaw.

Redding gestured to Miriam the layout of the scene. "Right, corrugated metal walls, with some kind of poster or something on the wall. Our picture was too fuzzy to make it out. How would that fit in with those ruins over there?"

Miriam stared toward the shore, then turned to Redding. "It wouldn't. I didn't think about it." She clasped her hands to her face. "All I could see was what was happening."

"It was a red herring," Redding responded. "A setup. That was like a backdrop for a TV show. Farzad doesn't want to die in a raid by US forces. He's on a mission and can't complete it if he's dead. He would know about our capabilities to locate the source of a signal. No way would he lead our military straight to him."

"But what about the transmission?" Miriam continued. "How could he hide that?"

Tebic waved his hand. "Hard wires, ma'am, sir," he said. "He could send the signal from point A but broadcast from point B."

"But our intelligence would know that too," Miriam insisted.

"They would know it's *possible*," Redding responded, "but they have to act on what they think they know for sure. They will only know of the deception after they act on it, and they don't have time to dig up wires to see where they lead." Turning to Tebic, he asked, "How long before you can make that connection?"

"A few minutes, sir, if I can have Mr. Bates' help." Tebic sputtered.

"Done," Bates interjected.

"Calm down and get it right, Tebic. We've got one shot at this."

"Well, now we know what your mom was talking about," Miriam said to Redding, her eyes welling with tears. "I can't imagine what's happening in America right now."

"I'm trying to imagine what's happening at Fleet Command right now," Redding answered, looking at the shore's distant light, "and I don't like what I'm coming up with."

"Helm, come right to 265 degrees," ordered James. *Constitution*'s bow stared ominously at the shoreline until the helm forced her to tack away.

Chapter Thirty

"Mark, what's your level of confidence in that location?" President Fairchild asked as he leaned toward CIA Director Adamson from his place at the head of the conference table in the situation room.

"Very high, Mr. President," Adamson responded, then turned his attention to the rest of the team at the table. "We were able to triangulate the source of the satellite uplink to within a hundred yards or so, as I said before. The area is remote, which fits with my earlier assessment—virtually nothing for miles around our target except for an old airfield, probably World War II vintage. It's near Siwa. That's an oasis settlement hell and gone from anything. Several hours' drive west from Cairo. Then, we have that aviation sectional in the video picture."

"Sectional?" asked President Fairchild.

"Sir, maps that only pilots use for navigation. We assume it's the sectional for that airspace, but the main thing is it confirms to us that it jibes with an airstrip location."

"*Excuse me, Director Adamson,*" Admiral Towne piped in from a monitor on the wall. "*I've got a problem with that last part, which makes me doubt the whole location finding.*"

"If you've got better intelligence, Admiral," said Adamson, "I'd sure like to hear it. According to

Farzad's message, we've only got until dawn, and it's about time we stop talking and start *doing*."

"No, Mark," the president interjected. "I want to hear this. After all, Chester was correct about the purpose behind the abduction."

"*Well, Mr. President—gentlemen,*" said Towne. "*For me, it's way too cute that Farzad left that aviation chart on the wall and the whole airplane hangar look. That would have been a damned stupid mistake, and let's face it, we're not dealing with a stupid man.*"

"The man is a maniac, a zealot," Adamson interjected. "That's a profile that makes mistakes."

"*No doubt he's a zealot,*" Towne countered, "*but his abduction plot worked. It was complex and well-coordinated. Plus, now that the scope of his operation is known, it's clear to me that he would have to have military people in his group, maybe even high up in the Egyptian army. Any high-ranking officer would know that we could pinpoint the source of such a transmission. Now, why would he do that?*"

"That still leaves the question as to whether or not we have any better intelligence, Admiral," Fairchild responded.

"*No, Mr. President. I'm afraid we don't. What I'm saying is, I'm concerned that we haven't any intelligence.*"

"*Mr. President!*" Adamson protested.

"Now, hold on a second. I'm sure the admiral simply meant he doesn't believe we know the truth yet."

"*That's correct, sir. Sorry about my choice of words.*"

Fairchild rose from his chair. He walked the length

of the room while the team looked at each other. He stood staring at the floor for a few seconds, then looked at his watch. "Gentlemen, I think I now know how General Eisenhower felt about giving the go order on D-Day." He turned to face the camera and Towne. "Admiral, you may be absolutely correct, but as I see it, we have no choice but to act on what we *think* we know."

"*I understand, sir,*" said Towne.

"Mr. President," Bernard Nussman interjected, "I do feel I have to go on the record with this. We are shortcutting our normal procedures. When we took out bin Laden, US Special Operations Command planned and coordinated every move."

"Yes," Fairchild responded, "and we had a hell of a lot more time to involve all those people and to plan every detail. That's what we *don't* have now." Fairchild directed his attention back to Towne. "The operation is in your theater, Admiral, and we don't have any army units close enough. That makes it your mission. What's your plan?"

"*Gentlemen,*" Towne began, "*we'll be operating out of Muwaffaq Salti Air Base in Jordan. SEAL Team Eight is already there and ready. They've been given the coordinates and the layout as best we could describe it.*"

"Admiral Towne," interjected Secretary of the Navy Buckholter, "your choppers are going to be heard for miles. If Farzad hears them coming, it's over."

"*Agreed, Admiral,*" Towne answered. "*That's why we're using the Osprey. They don't fly as fast as a C-130, but faster than choppers, and fast enough so the team will have more time to plan an attack once they arrive. They're quieter, but they land just like a chopper. We'll go in with just one bird; that's half a platoon."*

"That's not a lot of firepower, Chester," said Buckholter. "You could find yourself outmanned."

"True, Admiral," Towne responded with resignation, *"but the bigger issue is being discovered before we have a chance to complete the mission. This way we have a better chance of getting close without being detected. That's my view. Of course, you can override it if you see it differently."*

Buckholter paused, then directed his remarks to the others gathered in the room deep below the White House. "No, Chester, I see it your way. It's a gamble, but I think you're right."

"Thank you, Admiral," Towne continued. *"Even with greater stealth, the force will have to land miles away, because of the sound of the aircraft, and double-time it to the target area. I've seen the report from Mark's people that we've got decent terrain, pretty flat, consistent with an airfield. Thank God the moon doesn't come up until early in the morning. That's a break. It'll give them time in total darkness. They'll approach as close as they dare, send in eyes to survey the site, then plan the attack and go."*

"I want someone senior to lead the attack, Chester," Buckholter added.

"We're there, Admiral," Towne answered. *"That's Major Yamura. I'm putting him on the bird. Couldn't ask for better. Sharp tactician. If anyone can pull this off, it's him."*

Fairchild leaned forward. "You sound a little doubtful, Admiral."

"Candidly, sir, yes. The SEALs are great at going in and taking out the enemy. Rescuing a princess—that's another matter. If someone has a gun on Vice President Mitchell when we bust in, all they have to do is pull the trigger. I'm sure everyone in your room knows that."

Fairchild leaned back in his chair and replied glumly, "Yes, we do."

"Lastly, gentlemen," Towne added, *"in light of what I believe is the distinct possibility that, in connection with this plot, and General Husseini's behavior, a coup may be in effect in Egypt, I want permission to have fighter escorts for the Osprey as close to the target as they can get. I don't trust Husseini. I think we have enough evidence to justify that."*

There was a long pause in the situation room. Fairchild opened up the question to the group. "Gentlemen, what do you think? It's a bit like crossing the Rubicon."

Army Chief of Staff General Craig Hastings answered. "The Rubicon has already been crossed, Mr. President, and not by us."

"I agree with Craig," Buckholter added, "and with Admiral Towne. I'd rather be wrong and apologize later than risk the mission by the Egyptians interceding."

The group nodded their agreement.

"Done," said Fairchild.

"Then I take it, Mr. President, we won't be asking for approval to enter Egyptian airspace," Towne said.

"This will be a case of 'don't ask, don't tell,'" Fairchild responded. "Godspeed, Admiral."

"Yes, sir. Thank you, sir," Towne replied. *"One of*

254

my people has plotted a course over Israel, then east over the Med off the coast of Egypt. Mr. President, I'm asking you to get notification to Israel that we'll be coming."

"Done."

Towne continued. "*When they're well east of Alexandria, they'll angle southeast to Siwa. That's when they'll be in Egyptian airspace. The route is not as direct as a straight line from Salti, but it keeps our forces far away from Cairo and over Egypt for the least amount of time. The Hornets will jam Egyptian radar. Nevertheless, Mr. President, if they are threatened, I need approval to order the Hornets to shoot to kill if necessary.*"

Fairchild leaned against the table, his head down. Then he looked up and around all the faces. All heads nodded. "You have it, Admiral. Anything more to your plan?"

"*Only that my people will improvise as needed, which is always the case.*"

"We're on board with that, Admiral," said Fairchild.

"*In that case, gentlemen, I'm out.*"

Towne logged out of the meeting, which continued with the president addressing those in the situation room. "Domestically, gentlemen, we have questions on the table. I want to hear your thoughts on what our preparations should be."

National Security Advisor Bernard Nussman was the first to respond. "Mr. President, before and after the transmission by Farzad, we have seen significant internet and cell phone traffic from and between known terrorist suspects and organizations in the US."

"Domestic security is not our role," said Adamson, "but we can confirm similar results internationally. Lots of coded messages. They seemed to know something was coming."

"You previously asked us for what-if scenarios, Mr. President," said Hastings, who pointed to Nussman. "Based on Bernie's data, we must assume Farzad's transmission had the intended effect. We should even assume his intended audience had been prepped on this event in advance. I've already got our bases in the US and abroad on alert. All leaves have been canceled; everyone has been called in. Police forces across the country have been briefed to expect acts of terror. That means the leaks have probably already started. What I need from you is to invoke the code to federalize the National Guard. I need that and also an answer to the question of how much military presence you want on the streets of America."

"I'll invoke the code," answered Fairchild. "As to military presence on the streets…what would you say to staging forces near population areas—for fast deployment, if necessary—but not literally on the streets? I would prefer that our cities not look like Baghdad. With local police forces on the alert, that should be enough to handle most situations."

Hastings nodded. "We can do that. I'll move on that."

Nussman signaled the president. "There's another matter, sir, and it relates to Craig's work. You're going to need to address the nation. Tell them about our military preparedness and why they're going to see soldiers on the move. The public is also going to want to hear what we're doing about the situation with the vice president. Naturally, you can't tell them anything."

"My people are already working on an address," said President Fairchild, moving on to the next item on their agenda. "Based on Mark's outreach with our allies, they are going nuts. My phone is melting down. With the population shifts in some European countries, they've got a much bigger problem than even we do, and it appears they haven't a clue what to do about it. And—one last item. I'm going to get the FBI to tell me how the hell Sandra Phillips could have been radicalized and could have attained such a high position without them knowing it."

Chapter Thirty-One

Holcomb was out of the line of fire. He sat fidgeting at his desk amid the tension engulfing NAVCENT. All the action was taking place in the communications center down the hall.

His smartphone buzzed with an incoming call, a text message from Tebic.

—*We know where VP is. Tell Towne. No radio here. Text this # only.*—

"What the hell?" Holcomb said to himself. "Tebic texting me?"

Holcomb texted his response. —*We know too. Acting now.*—

Holcomb laid his phone on the desk and stood, staring at it as he backed away.

Moments later, the phone buzzed again. He grimaced and pulled at his hair as he leaned forward to look at the screen.

—*NEGATIVE! I have info. Tell Towne ASAP— Moses Redding.*—

"Oh, shit!" Holcomb frantically looked around the empty office, then stopped, cursed under his breath, picked up the phone, and headed for the door.

****

In the communications room, the tension was palpable. Towne was on a phone call and ignored Holcomb waving at him.

"Major Yamura, you're a go." Towne held his hand up flat to Holcomb, who waved frantically. "You'll have high cover from the F-18s once you're close to Egyptian airspace. You'll have darkness until 0300 hours; then the moon comes up and it will be full. Once you're on the ground, the Hornets will move back over the Med to international space and stay in a holding pattern until the Osprey pilot signals them that you are returning. They'll be jamming Egyptian radar, but if they *do* encounter a threat, they are to target the threat, warn them off, and if they don't heed the warning, they will shoot them down."

Holcomb grimaced and pointed to his phone.

"Not now, Holcomb, damn it!" Towne growled as he bit his cigar off at the tip and threw it on the floor and returned to his commands to Yamura. "Break radio silence only if the mission has failed and you need to be pulled out. One more thing, Major, and it probably goes without saying," he said solemnly. "Bring everyone back—regardless. Godspeed. Good luck."

Towne hung up and turned to Holcomb. "Now what the *hell* is it?"

"Admiral, sir, a message from Commander Redding. He says—"

"Redding?" he bellowed, "What the *hell* do I care about him right now?"

Holcomb swallowed and held out his phone. "It's about the vice president. He says he knows where she is."

Towne took a step in Holcomb's direction as the officers in the room began to converge on him as well. "How the hell would he know? And what's with the phone?"

"I don't know, but the text says they have no radio. Seaman Tebic aboard *Constitution* is a friend of mine. The text came from his phone, but I don't know how he did that. Look." He showed Towne the screen. "He thinks you're wrong about where they have the vice president."

"This is nuts! How would he know where she is? I don't have time for it. Send this message, in these words, all caps: Wyatt Earp, butt out and that goes for your xo too!" He pointed threateningly to Holcomb. "And don't bring me that bilge again!"

Holcomb nodded, left the room, and texted as he hurried down the hall to his office. He sat staring at his phone on his desk, then opened the desk drawer, brushed the phone in, and closed the drawer.

****

"*Butt out*?" Redding shouted as Tebic showed him his phone. Redding turned to the group still gathered on deck. "All right, listen up. This is the picture. The best information we have is that Fleet is on a mission to rescue the vice president. It's my belief they have been fooled as to her location. We know Farzad isn't bluffing. We know he's not seeking a ransom. If there is no rescue, Mitchell dies at dawn. We're the only force in a position to do anything, and we *are* a commissioned US warship. We've been ordered to stay out of it, but those orders were not based on the facts we know." He paused. "I've been in this kind of situation before—you haven't. I don't have the luxury of asking for volunteers. I need everyone, but you won't be held responsible for disobeying orders. That's on me. Anyone have a problem with that?"

Tebic looked skyward and rolled his eyes. "I'll take

'Holy Shit' for one thousand, Alex."

Redding looked the group over, then continued. "Officers, meet in the wardroom. Miriam, you too. Bring that drawing of the ruins you mentioned and all of your notes. Everyone left on deck, remember, no lights, not even a match. And no sound."

The crew and officers dispersed.

James approached Redding. "I'm on those orders from Admiral Towne too, Captain."

"That's right, Lieutenant," Redding replied, wondering how James would react. "And you know what disobeying orders has done for my illustrious career."

"It got you here, didn't it?" James said as a wry smile creased his lips. "So, what's the plan?"

Redding looked at James for a moment, then smiled. "Lieutenant, if we live through this, I'd be proud to serve with you in whatever doghouse they put us in."

Chapter Thirty-Two

President Fairchild sat at his desk in the Oval Office. Notes lay in front of him, but there was no teleprompter. A technician turned on the television lights. A video cameraman looked at him, counted down with his fingers—five, four, three, two, one—then pointed to the camera.

"To my fellow Americans at home and abroad, and to all peace-loving people of the world, I come before you at one of the gravest moments in history—not just for the United States, but for the world. By now, most of you have seen, or are aware of, the video message from a man, Colonel Farzad, who purports to be the leader of a worldwide jihadist uprising threatening many nations.

"His forces have captured our Vice President Virginia Mitchell and have assassinated her secret service agents to demonstrate the determination and power of his movement and as a symbol of the coalition of that power to wage war on the United States and many other nations from within. We have reason to believe his claims should be taken seriously—and we are doing so.

"In your cities and communities throughout America, you will soon see a significant military and law enforcement presence. These are not images we are accustomed to seeing in our country, but the threat from within our borders requires it. We would rather be overprepared than insufficiently ready to meet the threat.

"I call upon all Americans to be vigilant as to their surroundings and report any suspicious activities, but to stay home until we can better assess the effectiveness of the enemy's commands to its network.

"The threat itself is against all that America stands for and the American way of life—a way of life that was founded on the principles of individual liberty, including religious liberty, and the tolerance of diversity of religious philosophy. However, our tolerance has limits. It does not extend to acts of arson against our existence. Should the enemy act on the commands of this self-proclaimed leader, it will have made the mistake of enemies in our past, enemies that discovered the power of the will of the American people when compelled to act against evil in our self-defense. They will have, indeed, filled us with a great resolve.

"As for the crisis we face with respect to Vice President Mitchell, I send this message to Colonel Farzad and his followers. We will hunt you down and destroy you. We will not stop at our borders. Doing so would leave the seeds of violence abroad to grow, posing a future threat. You can *hope* your words will motivate your followers to violence," he said cautiously. Then he picked up the phone on his desk, stared directly into the camera lens, and said, threateningly, "My words into this device will bring the might of America down on you.

"Lastly, with respect again to our beloved vice president, I ask our nation to pray for her as she has always prayed for us." President Fairchild paused a moment, looked to the side, then back at the camera. "Make that, pray for a miracle."

Chapter Thirty-Three

The wardroom on *Constitution*'s berth deck had no portlights that could leak light to the outdoors. Illumination from oil lamps on the table in front of the officer corps cast shadows on the bulkheads around them. James, Buckley, Kobach, Bates, Bobbi, Miriam, and Gunderson stood silently as Redding studied the drawing of the fort from Miriam.

The group watched Redding as he paced the floor. He stopped occasionally to gesture in space, as if painting a picture of the battle to come. Then he froze with his eyes staring into the darkest corner of the room. He returned to the table and pointed to the map.

"Here's the promontory where the old fort is. We know by the light we saw that it's pretty high." He paused and scanned the room without focusing on the people.

He pointed to Buckley. "Mr. Buckley, get Corporal Aarons. I should have had him here to begin with."

As Buckley was leaving, Redding asked, "Mr. James, when does the moon come up?"

"About 0300 hours, sir."

"That helps," Redding replied quietly.

"And the sun rises at about six," James added.

"Won't matter," Redding mumbled, staring back and forth from the chart to the drawing. "It'll be over by then."

Redding's remark caused everyone in the wardroom to look at each other.

Redding motioned Miriam closer to the drawing and pointed to a spot just below the fort. "Miriam, what's this look like to you? One of your old Berber buddies drew a felucca in the harbor and a rowboat there that looks like it's headed into an opening of some sort."

"Yes, that was the key for me. It would be the most distinctive feature I was going to investigate that would confirm the drawing is of that particular location. It's described in the notes as a cave with a connection to the fort itself—an interior connection."

The group looked up as Buckley returned with Aarons. Redding interrupted his questioning of Miriam. "Corporal Aarons, you are here because you now have the temporary rank of sergeant and I need a younger version of Mr. Buckley. No offense, Jack."

"None taken, sir."

Aarons glanced at Buckley, who nodded and put his hand on the young marine's shoulder. Aarons looked at Redding and was about to say something, but Redding cut him off.

"Don't thank me. You're going to find out why over the next few minutes. We've been discussing this drawing of the location. You missed the discussion of the moon. Darkness until about 0300 hours, then full moon. Got that?"

"Aye, sir," Aarons responded.

Redding returned his attention to Miriam. "You mean a passageway all the way up into the fort itself?" he asked.

"Yes. That's common where there is a high wall

along the shore. Storm swells pound against the wall and can open up a cave. Then it grows when the earth collapses from inside." She sifted through her notes. "Building the fort on the promontory would have allowed the pirates to come and go directly from their ship to the fort within the protection of the cave."

Redding rubbed his chin while looking at the drawing. "So, it would be a natural cave that was pounded out by the surf and other elements. They built the fort on top of an opening in the rock formation at the top. That opening leads down to the floor of the cave, where they kept their launches in sheltered water. Makes sense. If they were attacked by land, they escaped to the cave, got in their launches, and went out to their ship. Or the other way around. They escaped into the fort from an attack by sea.

"And here," Redding said, pointing to the other side of the promontory, "on the east side of the promontory—it looks like there's another anchorage."

"There are essentially two harbors," said Miriam, "but just the first one you pointed out has direct access to the cave—that's the larger harbor of the two on the west side."

"Mr. Buckley, Mr. Aarons, and Mr. Kobach," Redding said, motioning to them, "take a look at this area here."

The men gathered closer as Miriam and the others made room for them.

"We know the fort is at an elevated point, probably the highest point on this drawing. What would you estimate, Mr. James, a hundred feet or more above the surf?"

James nodded. "From this distance, the light from

the window looked about that high."

Redding's eyes were still fixed on the map. "Miriam, look at your drawing here. These jagged lines look like maybe they're supposed to represent rock formations or something."

She scooted into position over the drawing. "Uh-huh. I agree."

Redding looked to Aarons and Kobach. "These rocky areas are scattered along the western side all the way down to the shoreline." He tilted the drawing up for them to see. "But not up here around the fort." He looked at Buckley. "The garrison up there right now had to get there and move in supplies. That would mean supply trucks up in this area near the fort."

"Right," Buckley added, "and they would post guards in that area."

"Agreed, Mr. Buckley, but the enemy believes that no one knows where they are. Otherwise, they wouldn't have tried to pull off this hoax, and they wouldn't have fired their guns in the air. I expect guarding their perimeter is not a priority."

Redding pointed again to the drawing. "From the shore to the fort right there, the rocks should help hide a force until they get pretty close." Redding looked at Buckley, who nodded his agreement. "And sandy soil would keep them quiet."

"I take it you are thinking of a two-pronged attack, Captain."

"Indeed, Mr. Buckley," Redding answered. "One from the western approach, attacking the fort. The other through the cave."

"The first attack should be from the exterior," Buckley said. "To draw the garrison out and away from the fort, so—"

"So, the second force can penetrate the fort, which is where Mitchell will be," Redding said, finishing Buckley's thought. "The second force will be waiting in the cave for their chance to get inside the fort."

"Permission to lead the western attack, Captain," Buckley said earnestly.

"I'd love to have you there, Mr. Buckley," Redding replied, looking him in the eye, "but there's going to be some running involved. And besides," he added, "you're going to see that I need you on the ship."

"Mr. James, you and Ensign Gunderson will stay on board to sail the ship," Redding said.

"I'm sure Ensign Gunderson can handle the sailing, Captain," James responded. "I'd like to take the cave squad."

Redding shook his head. "Thanks, Paul, but I can't put you there. The ship will need the best sail commander we've got, and that's you. You'll understand why in a minute."

Redding addressed Buckley. "I'm thinking they've got about four dozen men, give or take."

Buckley nodded slightly as he answered. "They'd just about have to be a guerrilla force…and that old fort couldn't quarter too many men. Sounds about right, fifty or so."

"Maybe a guerilla force, Mr. Buckley," said Redding, "but let's assumed they are well-armed. Mr. Bates, I'll lead the cave squad. You'll be with me."

"Aye, sir," replied Bates.

"Mr. Aarons and Mr. Kobach," Redding said, pointing to each.

"Sir!" came the simultaneous response from each.

"You will each lead a squad in a combined attack from the western approach to the fort. Ensign Kobach will be in overall command. Mr. Gunderson, the western squads will take the large launch. My force will be smaller. We'll take the captain's gig."

"Right, sir," replied Gunderson. "I'll make them ready."

"The enemy is going to outnumber you," James interjected. "If you made two trips, you could double your force."

"We can't count on outgunning the enemy, and that would take too long, doubling our chances of being detected. Besides, you're going to need every available man to maneuver the ship in those tight quarters and to escape when the time comes."

James nodded reluctantly.

"You can do this, gentlemen," Redding said to Aarons and Kobach. "I'm going to lay out the strategy. Keep your wits about you. Stay calm. Follow the battle plan, but also improvise as needed. Most of all: trust your instincts, be decisive, and..." Redding paused, looked down for a second, then set his jaw and looked back up. "*Don't hesitate.*"

Miriam looked him in the eye, but Redding pulled away.

"Mr. Buckley," Redding said, now pacing as he was thinking. "I want you to pick the squads based on your knowledge of individual performances during the drills. Load up the western force. They'll be doing most of the fighting."

"Aye, sir," Buckley responded. "I was just thinking of that."

Redding turned to James. "Mr. James will get each

force into boats offshore, as close as possible without our being detected," he added, pointing to the drawing. "The western force will land about here." Kobach and Aarons crowded in to get a better view. Redding stepped away from the table to give them room and talked over their shoulders. "Then work your way to this point at the bottom of the slope. Do you see what I'm talking about?"

"I see it," said Aarons.

"Do we wait there?" asked Kobach.

"No," Redding answered, "you get moving up the slope right away."

Redding went back to pacing. "The cave force will enter the cave and wait."

Miriam wrote furiously in her tablet.

"Miriam," said Redding, "you're taking *notes*?"

"Uh-huh," she said, still writing. Then she looked up. "For navy records, in case we make it out of this alive."

"Thanks for the vote of confidence," Redding said with a chuckle.

"What I mean is—" She started to explain.

"That's okay. I get it. Now what's this word in the space between those rows of jagged lines?" he asked as she examined the drawing.

"That's in Berber. It means path...pathway...trail. One of those."

"Good." Redding turned his attention back to Aarons and Kobach. "You will work your way up the slope, using the rock formations for cover. That reminds me," Redding added. "Everyone, lose the white britches and blouses of the uniforms. Go with jeans, dark shirts, and dark sneakers. That will be more important for the western squad than my cave team. Get as close as you can. Crawl if you have to. In the dark, you should be able to get pretty close. You'll need to take out the guards silently. Use a blade. Sergeant Aarons, that sounds like a job for a marine."

"That it does, sir."

"There shouldn't be too many guards. You'll have grenades with you. Look for something to blow up— something that will draw out the garrison and cause as much destruction as possible in the process. Getting as many of the enemy while they are grouped together is your best bet. Try to blow up something that will create a lot of light. Your eyes will be accustomed to the dark outside, but theirs will not. To keep your advantage, shield your eyes from the light of the explosion. The key to that blast is to pull them out, but they're going to come out shooting. They won't know what they're shooting at or where, so you should have an opportunity to get off a volley and cut down their numbers."

Miriam looked up from her note taking. She followed Redding's eyes as he alternately looked at the map and stared off, gesturing and narrating the battle scene in front of him.

"Mr. Buckley, issue all the pistols to the western squads. Everyone should have at least one. Save one for me."

"Right," answered Buckley, "we'll have just about enough." The gunnery officer turned his attention to Kobach and Aarons. "Remember to use them for close-range shots only."

Redding nodded his agreement. "Right, and I think we have enough cutlasses for all the officers and Aarons." He looked at the young faces around him. "It could come to your needing to use them."

The junior officers and Aarons signaled their understanding.

"The sound of your explosion will be my cue to advance into the fort's interior from the cave. I'll be assuming you have drawn their forces out, and there won't be any way for you to signal me otherwise."

"We'll get them out of there, Captain," Kobach said confidently.

"That's what I wanted to hear," Redding replied before turning to James. "That will also be your cue to move the ship into the harbor as close as you can without grounding her. Light from the explosion should give you a pretty good view of the harbor, but not the depth of the water. Take some soundings if you can."

Redding paced in front of the group. He held his chin in his hand, then spoke as he walked, occasionally looking up from the floor to make eye contact with the men and gesturing to make his points. "Use the enemy's weapons against them as much as possible. You kill a man who has a machine gun. If he's close enough to retrieve the weapon, grab it!"

He turned on them. "Fire in volleys if you can. You remember how much smoke a volley of musket fire creates. Use it. Fight a retreating battle back down the slope to your boat. Your job is to pull as much of their force away from the fort as you can, not necessarily to defeat them. Once they figure out you've only got muskets, they're going be very aggressive, but you will have a downhill pathway, so you can move quickly during your retreat and will have rock formations to duck behind. Don't try to run the full distance of the slope. They'll cut you down from behind. One squad covers the retreat of the other, leapfrogging each other down the pathway. Shoot, run, cover, shoot, run, cover. This is where you'll be thankful for Mr. Buckley's load-on-the-run drills." Redding paused for a moment and looked at Kobach and Aarons. "You're going to have to keep moving, fast. That means if a man falls, you can't try to take him with you. You won't have the firepower to hold off the enemy. You'd risk your entire squad. Make sure your people know that."

Kobach and Aarons looked at each other and nodded, then Kobach signaled to Redding that he had a question.

"Yes, Ensign?"

"What if we get pinned down, sir?" Kobach asked. "With their weapons, they'll be able to rush us."

"It's very likely you could be pinned down," Redding responded. "That's where the ship's crew comes in."

James leaned in.

"All officers in the shore parties will carry a flare gun," Redding said, then turned to James. "We have enough flare guns?"

James nodded his confirmation, and Redding continued with his attention on Kobach and Aarons. "Use the flare guns to mark the enemy's positions. Shoot the flares where you want supporting fire from the ship. Not up in the air, but right at the enemy." He turned to Buckley. "Now you see why you need to be on board."

"I get it," said Buckley.

"Use the fire from the big guns to make progress down the hill. The enemy will be ducking for cover. Chances are they've never had artillery of any kind fired at them. They duck, you run."

James interjected, "We don't have antipersonnel exploding rounds for the cannon."

"But we have rocks to hit," Buckley answered. "A cannonball hitting a rock will create shrapnel."

"Right," added Redding. "We have two operational guns on each deck, but not both on the same side." He looked at James. "That means to maximize our firepower, you'll have to get one gun on each deck moved to the other side. The question is, which side? That's your call, Paul."

James reached out to Miriam. "Let me see that drawing, Dr. Hannah." He studied it, positioning a hand at various angles on the page. "Based on our current position and the wind conditions, I'd say starboard."

"Starboard it is, then, and open all the gunports on the starboard side and run out the guns."

"But only two of them will be operational," replied James.

"The enemy won't know that. Mr. Buckley," Redding continued, "we can afford just two crews for the big guns. Who do you want to command that second crew?"

"Ensign Cooper," Buckley answered without hesitation.

Cooper smiled and looked at Buckley. "Thank you, Mr. Buckley."

"Dr. Hannah, if I may, what would this fort be made of?" Buckley asked Miriam, pointing to the drawing. "What material?"

"Almost all those old ruins are made with mud bricks," Miriam answered.

"Not stone?" Buckley replied.

"No, definitely not," she confirmed. "That's why most have weathered so badly. In fact, they were ancient even at the time they were used by the pirates in the early nineteenth century. Most likely built by a civilization long gone by that time. There are no nearby quarries, and these weren't built to worship the pharaohs or the gods, where expense wasn't an issue."

Redding addressed Aarons and Kobach. "Pass the instructions along to your squads as you prepare to disembark, but do it quietly. You'll also have a lot of rowing to do to get to shore, so you should have time to repeat these instructions to your squads in the boat, but again, do it quietly. Remember how easily sound travels over water. Pick replacement commanders in case you fall. I don't care about rank.

"Mr. Buckley, Ensign Cooper," Redding continued. "When the western squad has retreated to the bottom of the slope, use your guns to cover their escape to the launch and the ship. And remember, powder and shot are almost gone."

Buckley and Cooper nodded.

"The same goes for my squad," Redding added. "I'll fire a flare to let you know we're on our way back—hopefully with the vice president. If you see a green flare, we have her and she's alive. That means do everything you can to get her on board. If you see a red flare, we don't have her or she's dead." He directed his attention to James. Miriam covered her face with her hands. "A red flare from me means we failed and get the ship out of there *no matter what!*"

James started to speak, but Redding held up his hand. "That's an order." Redding held his hand and waited until James signaled his understanding.

Redding dropped his head, tugged his lower lip, and searched his mind for any detail he may have overlooked. He looked over at James and Buckley. "Gentlemen, do you have anything to add?"

"We haven't discussed the variable of the wind," said James. "We have no control over that."

"That's right. We'll leave that to providence. I know you'll get the most out of whatever wind conditions we'll have, but use the launch and gig crews to tow her out of the harbor if you must."

Buckley waved his hand. "There is one point I'd like to make, Captain."

Redding gestured to him to continue.

Buckley turned to Aarons and Kobach. "Show no mercy, men. You've never killed anyone and neither have your squads, but you're going to have to become killers for one night. Don't hesitate. Shoot them down. I'm going to consider that a necessary quality when I pick your squads—the ones I think can cut it—but you're going to lead them. You've got to bring that quality out in them."

Redding eyed Kobach and Aarons as Buckley delivered his sober directive. They looked at Buckley, then at Redding.

"We all saw their video, Captain," Kobach said.

Aarons added, "It won't be as hard as you might think."

Redding gave a satisfactory nod to them both. "Then everyone's got work to do and not much time to do it." He looked around the table and handed out the orders, starting with Buckley. "Get those squad assignments and raid the museum for weapons."

Buckley left, taking with him Aarons and Kobach.

"Ensign Cooper, take charge of getting the grenades loaded for the western assault squad. Then you and Mr. Buckley need to pick your gun crews from those who aren't going ashore."

"Aye, aye, sir," she replied with a salute.

As she was leaving, Redding called out to her. "And make sure the western force has some Zippo lighters."

Gunderson looked anxiously at Redding.

"Mr. Gunderson, have we got anything to wrap around the tips of the oars to keep them quiet?"

James raised a brow. "I guess the academy does teach history," he said with a smile.

"We'll use the crew's skivvies if we have to," replied Gunderson.

"Good. See to it. Then you will help Mr. James explain to the sailing crew what the battle plan is."

Gunderson left, and Redding turned to Bates. "Mr. Bates, see to the loading of all small arms *not* being taken by the squads: blunderbusses, extra muskets, et cetera."

Miriam waited for James and Bates to leave, then pulled on Redding's coat sleeve. "I feel so helpless. What can I do?"

Redding's answer was grave. "Keep writing. There won't be another moment like this in history, and you're the best person to record it."

"I don't know if I can write about it...depending on—"

Redding jumped in adamantly. "*Find* a way, Miriam. No matter what happens. Find a way to let our country know what we did."

"But I could help you," she pleaded. "I speak the

language…and I know the layout of the fort."

"Negative—subject closed," he said adamantly, stopping her before she could respond. "We're not going there to talk, Miriam, and this is not research. I don't know the language, but I have led men in a fight before, and I can't have you on my mind. Now, I've got work to do."

Redding squeezed her shoulder for a moment before leaving the wardroom.

She looked down at the table, then lifted her head. Her eyes widened with a look of determination. She clenched her fists and darted from the room.

Chapter Thirty-Four

The Osprey flew over the Mediterranean, well offshore, and approached its turning point east of Alexandria. F-18 Hornets flew over it from above, their onboard radar scanning the sky for Egyptian fighters that may have been flushed by the Osprey's approach.

Towne nervously awaited any word from the forces he had set in motion in the communications center at NAVCENT but did his best not to show his lack of confidence in the mission. Unable to sit and wait, he could only watch images on the array of monitors manned by specialists, monitors that tracked the progress of the Osprey and showed the Hornets' position. Monitors also showed each F-18's radar screens. On Towne's command, he could order them to fire on anything that posed a threat. Another monitor showed the gathering in the situation room at the White House. Towne could see the tension on the faces of the president and his advisors.

A technician turned in his swivel chair to face Towne, his head just below the signature layer of fog Towne had created with cigar smoke. "They're in Egyptian airspace now, Admiral. Nothing on their scopes."

With each passing minute, doubts about the likelihood of the mission's success weighed more heavily on Towne. His mind wandered to the text communication from Captain Redding and the orders he issued to him in his office many days ago after the Gulf battle. Orders he was compelled to issue by higher authorities. Orders that forced him to play-act the scolding he gave Redding. He had put down a man who may have responded exactly as he should with the knowledge he had, exactly as Towne would have done in the same circumstances. With his text message to Redding, had he now done the same thing again? Ironically, could it be that the orders he had issued Redding that day in his office put Redding in a position to know something the combined intelligence sources of the United States didn't know? It was too improbable, but given the events of the last twenty-four hours, perhaps probability factors should be tossed.

****

Under reduced sail, *Constitution* furtively stalked the light still glowing from the window of the fort. Attack squads assembled on her spar deck. In hushed tones, Kobach and Aarons schooled their men in the plan for the western force. Among them were McAvoy and Basker. Bates grouped the cave squad near them, including Guzman, and went over the rescue plan.

In the cabin she shared with Cooper, Miriam hurriedly wiped off all traces of makeup from her face. She pinned her hair up tightly on the top of her head and rifled through her closet and Cooper's. She stripped off her clothes, threw them across the room, and quickly donned a pair of jeans and a dark sweatshirt. As she pulled on the sweatshirt, she looked at her bosom and grimaced. She plowed through her closet and pulled out a large scarf, wrapped it around her chest, pulled it tight, tied it off, and rotated the knot in back of her. She grabbed Cooper's navy-blue watch cap from a hook on the wall and pulled it down as tightly over her hair and forehead as possible.

Cooper arrived on the upper deck with a sack of grenades and a duffle bag. Mac and Basker each took a grenade and stuffed them into their jackets. Aarons took the bag from Cooper.

Mac nudged Basker. "Remember what Buckley said. It's not a baseball."

"Don't you worry about me, farm boy," Basker answered.

"You guys got time to joke?" Guzman said, checking his musket.

"Just trying to stay loose," Mac answered casually. "Makes me a little nervous to go into battle with someone so uptight."

"Yeah," Guzman replied sarcastically, "like you've been in so many battles."

"Just sayin'," Mac responded. "Makes me think they might panic when the shit hits the fan, and you know what they say about that, *city boy*?"

Guzman ignored Mac and attached the bayonet to his musket.

Mac grinned. "They say, 'be standing next to a *country boy*.'"

Guzman stared back at Mac. "Like the man said, don't worry about me, *Farmer John*."

James climbed down the shrouds from the fighting platform of the mainmast and motioned to Kobach and Aarons to follow him. Buckley took over the prep of the western squad as Kobach and Aarons crossed the deck with James. The three approached Redding as he was discussing strategy with Bates.

"I've got good news and bad news, Captain," said James.

Redding paused for a second before answering. "I could use some good news. What have you got?"

James pointed to the shore. "There's a low fogbank developing along the shoreline. That'll give your squads cover as they row in and will muffle a lot of the sound."

"And the *bad* news?" added Redding.

"It could make it more difficult to maneuver the ship into the harbor. Can't tell how thick the fog is going to get, but"—James turned to Kobach and Aarons—"make sure that fire you start is a big one. I'm going to need all the light I can get.

"After you leave, I'm going to luff up. That'll keep us more or less in this spot until I get the signal and move in."

"Good thinking, Lieutenant." Redding turned back to Bates.

"Uh, there's more, Captain," James continued. "We'll have a problem with the ship, starting at about when the moon comes, around 0300 hours."

"What?" Redding asked. "She turns into a pumpkin?"

"Just as bad," James answered. "About that time the tide will start going out. We don't know how deep the harbor is, but if we get in close enough for accurate gunnery, we could end up without enough water under her keel."

"This just keeps getting better, doesn't it, Lieutenant." Redding shook his head. "Well, I told you what your priorities are." Redding turned to Kobach and Aarons. "We'll get our jobs done as fast as we can and get back to the ship."

Rachel and Thompson arrived on deck and approached the group. "Here are your flare guns, sirs," Rachel said, handing one each to Redding, Kobach, Bates, and Aarons.

"And your flares," Thompson continued, giving a handful each to Kobach and Aarons. "Captain, sir, one red and one green for you, I was told."

"Right," Redding said, stuffing the flare gun in his waistband next to his pistol. "Thanks."

"And Dr. Hannah suggested an oil lamp for you, Captain," Rachel added, handing him the lamp. "For inside the cave."

"Ahh, good idea." Redding handed the lamp to Bates, then looked around. "By the way, where *is* the good doctor?"

Rachel shrugged. "Don't know, sir."

"Hmm," Redding mumbled to himself. "Well, I want to take a minute with the crew. Lieutenant James, would you pull everyone together, please?"

James and the junior officers spread the word around quietly and the crew gathered around Redding in the center of the spar deck.

"The need for quiet means this can't be a loud pep talk," Redding began, standing at the pinrail around the mainmast. "You know what we're attempting to do, why it's essential, and why we're the only ones who can do it. The confidence I have in the mission comes from knowing how well you've all taken to the training and the individual character you've displayed. I'm sure this crew is as good as any that ever served on this ship." Redding, again, scanned the faces in the darkness for Miriam before he continued. "That's something to be proud of. This is where a commander would normally tell his people the importance of doing their jobs to the best of their ability. With this crew, I don't need to do that. Let's shove off. Good luck, everyone," he added, holding a salute.

All returned the salute and in turn replied, "Good luck, sir."

Aarons and Kobach signaled their squads to climb down the rope ladder on the ship's starboard side into the launch. Bates directed the smaller cave squad, grouped along the gunwale, to board the gig near *Constitution*'s bow.

James followed Redding to the gunwale. As Redding climbed over the gunwale and started down the rope ladder, James stopped him and pointed to his uniform. "You're going with the full Monty, even the hat?"

Redding looked up at his cocked hat, then back at James. "Didn't have time to change—and *hell*, yes." Pointing to the stern, Redding asked, "Do we have a bigger flag?"

"Uh, huh, the parade flag."

"Fly it!"

The crew in the gig was at their oars as Redding climbed down the rope ladder. He took a last look for Miriam, then he came face to face with the billethead of *Constitution*. Like sailors in a World War II submarine movie who patted a picture of Betty Grable on her butt before going into battle, he gave the ship a pat on her billethead and took his place at the bow of the gig. The rowers in both boats pushed their oars against the hull of *Constitution* to shove clear of her and began rowing toward the thickening fog.

Chapter Thirty-Five

The voice of the Osprey pilot crackled in Yamura's headset. *"Coming up on the target zone now."*

Major Yamura signaled his team, who prepared for the landing. The pilot reduced power, slowly tilting the aircraft's wings into a vertical landing position and setting down on a flat zone among the waves of sand on a barren ocean landscape. With the engines turned off but the props still spinning, the SEALs opened the doors, poured out, and deployed themselves in a defensive orientation around the aircraft. Yamura was the last to deplane and kept his headset on for directions from the pilot.

"Target is 273 degrees, three miles. Good luck," the pilot said over Yamura's headset.

Yamura pulled out his GPS device and gathered the team around him. He held up three fingers and pointed in the direction of the target. The team set off into the darkness.

****

The sound of the surf announced the proximity of the foggy shoreline to the crews rowing from *Constitution*, the dipping of their oars in the black water muffled by Gunderson's paddings.

When the launch holding Kobach's western attack squad scraped the sandy bottom, the crew shipped their oars, jumped into the water, and pulled the launch to the beach.

"That's far enough," Kobach said in a low voice. "The tide will be going out."

The squad reached into the launch and retrieved their weapons while Aarons advanced as far as he could down the beach to a path weaving up the hill through rock formations. He crept up the hill, crouched, and listened, then returned to the launch and Kobach.

"The path is there, just like on the drawing," he said to Kobach who waved at the squad and pointed down the beach.

The fog and the tall grass lining the shore hid the squad as they wove their way down the shoreline. On their ascent up the pathway, they ducked behind rock formations occasionally to listen for sounds on the plateau above.

****

Redding held up his hand to stop the rowers in the captain's gig. He leaned over the bow and cupped his hand to his ear. The lapping of the waves on the shore could be heard through the fog. He pointed to the east and the crew leaned into their oars. Moments later, the sea changed its tune as it crashed against stone and a hollow echo beckoned from the cave. As it came into view, Redding directed the rowers to the center of the cave opening, a jagged maw in the vertical rock face of the promontory that gulped the incoming waves. Once inside, he turned to his crew and put his finger to his lips, then climbed out of the gig, grabbed the bow line, and pulled them to the shallow water on the right side of the cave near an aluminum skiff with an outboard motor and an extra gas can.

He pointed to Guzman and to the gas can. Guzman

picked it up with his free hand and held his musket in the other.

Bates started to light the oil lamp, but Redding stopped him. He got the crew's attention with hand gestures, pointed to his eyes, then to the upper part of the cave, where a faint glow could be seen around a bend in the steep, upward-sloping cave interior. A narrow path curved in and out around jutting rock formations and extended up the right side of the cave. Redding quietly pulled his cutlass from its scabbard and hugged the rock wall as he inched his way up the path. Bates motioned to the crew for silence and led them to follow Redding.

****

Kobach led the exterior attack force eastward down the beach until the reeds along the shore gave way to the stone-lined pathway leading up the hill. Aarons took up a position behind the navy squad and at the lead of the marine contingent, but close enough to see Kobach in the darkness. As they advanced up the slope, Aarons reached under his dark outer shirt and tore out his white T-shirt. He ripped it into strips and jammed them into cracks in the rocks marking three locations along the path about two hundred feet apart.

Kobach raised his hand, then motioned the men to the ground. Aarons relayed the message to the men downslope. Kobach looked at Aarons, cupped his hand to his ear, and pointed upslope toward the fort. Aarons crept up to Kobach's position. They both crouched low and crawled up the path toward the sound of men's voices.

****

Yamura led the SEALs at a fast pace. His GPS

showed they were approaching the target. The terrain had been soft and rolling, and the team was tired. He motioned for them to rest where they were, then he crawled to the top of a rise. Peering over it with his telescopic infrared binoculars, he spotted the corrugated sheet-metal hangar and a smaller building near it. The image showed no signs of life outside.

He made his way down the slope to his men. "Two buildings about two hundred yards away. We'll move in groups of four. Let's go."

The first group scaled the slope and advanced toward the buildings, followed by the remaining groups. Yamura led the first group. He stopped periodically to check for signs of life through his binoculars, then waved them forward until they were within fifty yards of the large building. When the trailing groups reached the forward position, he pointed to two groups, drew a circular route with his hands in the air, and pointed to the hangar. He directed a third group of four to advance on the smaller building, then maintained surveillance of both buildings through his binoculars.

Reports from the groups crackled in Yamura's earpiece.

"Blue Two, in position."

"Blue One, in position."

"Blue Three, in position."

"Blue One. This appears to be an airstrip with a hangar. There's a satellite dish outside the hangar. Doors closed. No lights showing. Man door on our side."

"Blue Two. Man door on our side also. No lights."

"Blue Three. No lights. No signs of people in small

building."

Yamura spoke into his lapel mic. "All groups, move in close. Do not enter." He led his group toward the hangar as the other groups moved to the doorways. His group met up with Blue One at the man door.

He listened at the door, then spoke into his mic. "All groups go!"

The door easily swung open, and the group rushed in just as Blue Two entered the hangar from the opposite side.

The hangar was dark but for a glow of light through the seams around the door of an interior enclosure. Yamura pointed to the door, then stood back as one SEAL kicked the door open, followed by a second, who bolted into the room, sweeping it with his weapon.

Yamura entered the enclosure. Multi-colored indicator lights flickered from the transmission equipment inside.

The leader of Blue Three entered the hangar and approached Yamura. "Nothing in the small building, but there's been activity recently. We can smell oil on the ground outside."

"Right," replied Yamura. "Show's over here, if it ever *was* here."

He pressed on his lapel mic. "Blue leader to bird, move to the airstrip."

He took a last look in the equipment room. "Wait." He leaned down, took a penlight from his pocket, and shone it on a stool below the shelf. "What have we here?" He reached under the shelf holding the electronic equipment and stood back up, holding a notebook computer.

****

Redding leaned against the rock wall. Turns in the path around jutting rock blocked him and Bates from the view of the men speaking Arabic around the corner. He raised his cutlass, turned to the ensign, held his hand up for a moment, then thrust it forward. The two bolted around the corner to find two young men smoking and playing backgammon to the light of an oil lamp. Redding put his cutlass to the neck of one man, and Bates stuck the tip of his bayonet in the chest of the other. The rest of the crew rounded the rock formation and gathered around them.

Bates pointed to two AK-47s leaning against the rock wall. Guzman and another crewman grabbed them, slung their muskets on their shoulders, and used the enemy's weapons to guard the upslope direction.

"Evening, boys," Redding said quietly.

Cigarettes dropped from the mouths of the two sentries as they stared wide-eyed at Redding and gawked up and down at his uniform.

"Where is the American woman?" Redding asked the man as he slid the blade of his cutlass up and down the throat of the sentry. The sentry winced, and a trickle of blood oozed from around the blade.

When the sentry didn't answer, Redding motioned to Bates, who pushed harder on the tip of his bayonet.

The sentry cried out, "Ahh!" but was silenced when Bates moved the tip of the bayonet between the man's lips and into his mouth.

"Where is she?" he asked the second sentry, who spit at Redding's feet and muttered in Arabic.

"He suggests you do something with your goats, Captain," said a crew member.

Redding and Bates whirled in the direction of the voice to see Miriam. Bates turned to Redding, shrugged, and shook his head.

"*Goddamn* it, Miriam!" Redding said in as low a voice as he could.

"I'm no good on the ship." She pointed to the sentries. "But I can help here."

Redding pulled on his face. "You…I…*damn*!" he said through clenched teeth.

Miriam grimaced.

After staring at the ceiling of the cave for a moment, Redding exhaled and pointed to the sentries. "Ask them."

"In a sec." Miriam reached under her shirt, struggled with an undergarment, then pulled out a scarf and threw it away. "Ahhh, that feels better."

Speaking Arabic, Miriam asked the men where Mitchell was. One of them answered her defiantly.

"What?" Redding asked.

"More goat stuff," she replied, "this time with my involvement."

"You were saying something about *helping*?" Redding asked.

She studied the faces of the two men, then addressed her words to the older sentry, but pointed to the younger one and spoke in Arabic.

The older sentry squirmed. His eyes flashed between Miriam and the younger one. Miriam turned to Redding. "They're brothers."

Miriam pointed to the younger one. "Tie them up and gag that one."

"Use your belts," Bates said to two crew members.

Redding motioned a sailor to an iron door nearby

that led to the interior of the fort. "Listen at that door, but don't open it."

Miriam pointed to the gas can. "Give me that," she said to Guzman.

When the crew finished tying up the prisoners, Miriam waved them back. "Back off." She opened the can and thoroughly doused the younger man with gasoline. When she reached out her hand, Bates slapped his Zippo lighter in it like a nurse handing a surgeon the next instrument. Miriam leaned menacingly toward the older sentry, flicked on the Zippo and waved it close to his eyes as she spoke to him Arabic in a low, measured, deliberate tone.

As she spoke, sweat formed on the sentry's brow. His eyes widened, and he began to shake.

Redding looked at Bates and shrugged.

The younger sentry attempted to scream through his gag. The older brother trembled and pointed upward as he spoke to Miriam.

Miriam turned to Redding. "That room we saw from the ship. The only one with a window that looks north."

Redding, amazed, put his cutlass back in its scabbard, and addressed Miriam. "Damn, woman. I don't know what you said, but remind me never to piss you off. You're worse than me, but what the hell were you saying to him?"

Miriam replied dryly, "I asked him very sweetly if he would please tell us where Mitchell is." Then she smirked. "He also agreed that it was helpful for me to be here."

Redding choked back a smile, looked away, and shook his head, then motioned to Bates and pointed to the older sentry. "Get a gag on this one too." Turning to Miriam, he said, "You! Get to the back of the squad. I'll deal with you later."

Redding led the squad to the heavy iron door. The sailor listened at the door, then stepped aside. Redding slowly opened it and cringed when the rusty hinges screeched. He peeked through the narrow opening, then put his ear to it.

Guzman picked up one of the still-smoldering cigarettes, took a drag, and blew smoke in the older sentry's face, then held the glowing butt to the younger one and sniffed the gasoline he was soaked in. The sentry squirmed and arched his back away from the cigarette. Guzman backed off, flicked the butt at the older man, then turned his back to him and rejoined the squad.

Chapter Thirty-Six

"*Damn!*" Towne roared as he ignored Holcomb holding out a cup of coffee for him. "It *was* a setup!"

Yamura's voice came over the speaker. "*No doubt, Admiral. Someone even left you a message spray-painted on the wall.*"

"What?"

"*It says, 'Nice try, Admiral Towne.' *"

"That *son of a*—"

"*Yeah. But Admiral, it's not a total loss, sir. Somebody left in a hell of a hurry. Left behind a notebook computer. Could be useful...Admiral, do you copy?*"

"Yeah, go ahead, Major," Towne replied, still fuming.

"*Admiral, we still have the bird. Do you want us to evac?*"

Towne leaned against a desk and froze for a moment. "*Redding!*"

"*Sir?*" asked Yamura.

"No," Towne responded. "Stay put, but get ready to move out with new instructions. I'll send the Hornets back in for cover when that time comes."

"*Aye, sir. Blue Team out.*"

Towne turned to his communications technician. "Get the situation room back online. And find out where *Constitution* is."

295

Everyone in the room spun around. Holcomb dropped his coffee cup. The communications technician looked at Towne. "Sir? *Constitution*?"

"You heard me," Towne answered impatiently. "Get the ship's itinerary." He turned to Holcomb, who had started to creep back out of the room. "And you! Get that thing of yours to make a call, or whatever, to that guy you know on *Constitution*."

"Aye, sir," Holcomb replied timidly. "I'll—I'll try."

****

Aarons crawled back down the path to the squads and motioned them to follow him uphill. When they were near the top, he directed both squads to take up positions behind mounds of sand, then crawled to Kobach, who was hiding behind a rock closer to the fort.

About the size of a small country elementary school, the fort appeared to have been built in sections over a period of time. Cracks in the brick wall of the crude structure showed its age, some portions more weathered than others. The northernmost side rose precariously from the edge of the promontory. There were no windows on the west side wall facing the Americans. Just outside of the only door to the interior sat two Egyptian army vehicles, a newer open-top Jeep, and a Ukrainian-built double-axle cargo truck, both painted in desert tan.

Kobach pointed toward the fort and whispered in his ear. "Two sentries. That one smoking a cigarette and another one, but I think he left to take a dump or something. He's been gone awhile. There's that big truck and a Jeep parked closer to the fort. Too much open space between here and that sentry. We can't rush him from here."

Aarons looked in the direction of the sentry for a moment, then leaned in to Kobach. "Wait here."

Aarons crawled over to the navy squad and signaled Basker to follow him back to a position near Kobach.

Aarons picked up a rock and pointed to the sentry. He tapped the rock to his head. Basker grinned. He put his musket down and took the rock from Aarons. He studied the target and the weight of the rock. He tossed it aside and chose another one. Rising from the ground into a pitching stance, he started into his elaborate windup.

Aarons and Kobach frantically waved for Basker to stop, but Basker's focus never left the glow of the cigarette. The rock left his hand like an asteroid. The only sound came from the stone cracking the man's skull and his limp body hitting the sand with a thud.

Kobach and Aarons silenced the excited squad members with hand gestures. Basker stood in his pitching spot and smiled as he looked at the result of his handiwork. Aarons motioned him to get down.

Kobach scurried up to the fallen sentry and picked up his machine gun. He took a quick look inside the truck, then ran back to Aarons. Pointing to the truck, he whispered, "Captain wants something big. There it is. There are crates of something in the back and barrels. I smelled AV gas."

"Right," replied Aarons, "and the Jeep too."

Aarons pulled two grenades from the duffle bag.

He adjusted the length of the fuses on the grenades and waited for Kobach's signal. When Kobach gave him the "go" sign, he silently worked his way to the jeep. He kept an eye on the door to the fort while he lit the fuse on a grenade and tossed it in the Jeep, then ran to the truck, lit a much longer fuse on the second grenade, tossed it into the truck bed, and ran back to his squad of marines.

****

Inside the fort, Farzad and Captain Naser chatted as the soldiers in the crowded room played *dama* or squatted on the stone floor in conversation groups. Batul and her Amazonian guards kept to themselves away from the men who laughed and exchanged bets on the games—until a blast from outside shook the interior of the room and blew open the door.

Soldiers scrambled to take cover. Farzad bolted to the door and peeked outside. He pointed Naser. "We are under attack! Get your men out there!"

The men stumbled over themselves in the packed room as they collected their weapons. Batul and the other two guards looked at Farzad.

"Not you," he ordered. "Stay with me."

Naser gathered his soldiers near to him at the door. "*Go!*" he yelled, pointing his pistol outside.

The soldiers rushed out just as the Jeep fire ignited its gas tank. The secondary explosion sent a fireball twenty feet into the sky and the soldiers running for cover. The ones who had not yet made it out the door ducked back inside.

****

Redding heard the blast and the commotion through the partly opened iron door in the cave. He opened it farther and slipped through to a corridor lighted by oil lamps on the walls. The hall turned left toward the sea and right toward the clamor of the battle outside. He motioned for his crew to follow him in the opposite direction.

The sound of running bootsteps pounded the stone hallway from beyond a corner in the corridor. He waved his squad into an empty room they had just passed and stood behind the doorway, his cutlass drawn. A man armed with an AK-47 ran by and down the hall toward the noise from the opposite side of the fort's interior. When he was out of sight, Redding motioned his group back out into the hall.

"He came from the direction we're going. Might have been guarding Mitchell," Redding added as he signaled his group to follow him.

Bates, Guzman, and the second sailor with a machine gun covered the group from behind as Redding led them to the end of the hall and a half-opened door to a dimly lit room. He took a quick peek into the room.

Sandra Phillips held a pistol and leaned out of the window, facing the sounds of gunfire from the battle to the west that ricocheted off the corrugated sheet metal attached to a wall.

Virginia Mitchell sat bound, gagged, and slumped in a chair and didn't stir when the door slammed open.

"Drop it!" Redding shouted to Sandra as he and Bates rushed in. Sandra whirled around, fell backward, and dropped her pistol as her arms flailed, attempting to prevent her from falling out the window.

Guzman and the rest of the sailors guarded the hallway while Miriam rushed in. The bodies of the two secret service men were stacked against the wall. Miriam knelt beside Mitchell and held her face. There was no response. She felt her pulse. "She's alive," she said, then glared at Sandra as Bates removed Mitchell's gag and arm bindings and used them on Sandra while Redding held his gun on her.

When Mitchell slowly came to, Redding stood over her. Her eyes widened at the sight of his uniform.

"Madam Vice President," Redding said with formality, "Commander Moses Redding, USS *Constitution*."

"Huh?" Mitchell muttered weakly. Then she turned to Miriam kneeling in front of her and unbinding her feet. "Miriam?"

"Madam Vice President, I've moved up our appointment."

Shaken and trembling, Mitchell looked up at Redding. Her eyes widened as she examined his uniform. "You promise to explain this later?"

"Yes, ma'am, much later."

****

Several of the enemy soldiers outside dove under the truck and sprayed automatic weapons fire into the darkness just in time to become victims of the second grenade. It detonated the aviation gasoline and the crates of explosives, incinerating the truck and everyone around it, and formed a mushroom cloud of fire and smoke that grew high into the night sky. Soldiers who were kneeling nearby, firing in all directions, were blown away from the fire ball. The bright light turned the entire force into targets for the sailors and marines awaiting orders.

"Fire!" commanded Aarons and Kobach simultaneously. A volley of musket fire from the navy and marine squads created a cloud of black powder smoke in front them and cut down several enemy soldiers as they attempted to shield themselves from the blast of the truck.

"Retreat!" yelled Aarons. Both squads ran down the pathway and reloaded on the run as Kobach fired bursts at the enemy from his AK-47.

Aarons and his squad stopped at the first white cloth on the path down the slope. Aarons climbed on top of a rock to survey the scene upslope. An Egyptian officer ran outside and ducked behind the smoldering front half of the Jeep lying near the door. The officer surveyed the scene of corpses around him and waved the rest of his force out of the fort. They gathered near him.

Kobach tossed the AK-47 up to Aarons as he passed the marine line, then continued down the slope with his sailors to the second rag where they knelt in a line in the sand.

Enemy soldiers swept the lingering cloud of musket smoke with their machine guns, then charged through it.

Marines hugged the ground with muskets at their sides as enemy rounds passed over their heads. When the enemy burst through the smoke, they were backlit and silhouetted by the truck's still-raging fire. The marines rose up and unloaded a volley of musket fire that killed and wounded several of the enemy and created another thick cloud of smoke.

The surviving enemy scattered and fired wildly from behind rocks in the direction of the retreating marines. Aarons squeezed off a few rounds in the direction of the enemy, then climbed off the rock and led his marines farther down the slope. They passed the sailors who were ready for a volley of their own. Before they could make it past the navy squad, a marine was cut down by a burst of machine gun fire through the cloud of smoke.

Aarons knelt by the fallen marine and raked the rocks up the hill with a burst from his machine gun. He tossed it back to Kobach and continued down the slope to the marines.

Kobach raised his arm to ready his squad. He looked down the pathway to see the marines regrouping, then upslope, where the enemy was now charging through the smoke.

"Fire!" he shouted and dropped his arm in the direction of the enemy.

Musket balls thudded into the chests of enemy soldiers who screamed as they fell into the sand. The surviving enemy scattered into the rocks. "Retreat!" Kobach yelled to his squad.

The sailors reloaded as they ran down the slope. One was killed instantly by a round through his chest. Kobach returned fire with his AK-47, then checked his ammunition. An enemy soldier lay dead up the slope, his weapon at his side. Kobach fired a couple of short bursts at the rock formations and ran to retrieve the dead man's machine gun.

As he grabbed it, shots rang out from the enemy positions, hitting him in the side, above the waist. He hung onto the two machine guns as he struggled downslope to the marine squad who ducked behind the rocks with their muskets aimed toward the enemy. He tossed the AK-47 he had just picked up to Aarons and ducked behind a rock with the other, gripping his side. Aarons ran to him.

"You're hit!"

Kobach waved him off. "Get the men down the hill."

Enemy soldiers rushed through the smoke cloud from behind the rocks.

"*Marines!*" yelled Aarons. "*Fire!*"

****

Constitution burst through the fogbank. The harbor, now lit by the fire of the burning truck, illuminated her bright white stripe and the face of her billethead against the black of the night and water below.

Gunderson tapped James on the shoulder and pointed to the muzzle flashes from the battle onshore.

"Helm to port!" James yelled to the helmsman, then shouted to the sailors aloft. "Reef all sails except the jibs and the spanker!"

The momentum of the 2,000-ton vessel carried her into the harbor and through the turn, but *Constitution*'s forward motion slowed as sailors reefed the square sails on all three masts. Like monkeys in a forest canopy, they climbed through rigging, balancing precariously on the lines slung under the wooden spars as they gathered up the huge sails and tied them off. Only the spanker sail aft and the triangular jibs at the bow remained deployed.

"What's the lieutenant doing?" Tebic cried over his shoulder to Rachel Dover in back of him, as he inched his way along a spar high on the mizzenmast. "We don't have an engine. We'll never get out of here without these sails."

"I don't know, but he *does*," she yelled back at him. "So, *move* it!"

Chapter Thirty-Seven

Farzad surveyed the battle scene through the outside door to the fort. His jaw dropped at sight of *Constitution*, now slowing to a halt in the harbor. Batul and the Amazonian Guards stood nearby, joined by the guard from Mitchell's room.

"What are you doing here!" Farzad yelled to the guard.

"I heard gunfire…and I thought—"

"Get back to your post!"

The guard ran out of the room and down the hall. Farzad turned back to view the action outside but spun back around to the sound of gunfire from the interior of the fort.

He shouted through the outer door. "Naser! It's a trick! They are *inside*!"

Batul and the guards started toward the door to the corridor.

"No!" Farzad yelled. "Not you. We don't know how many of them are there. We will wait for help."

He crouched low and ran outside. The burning truck shielded him from fire by the Americans.

Naser ran toward Farzad, shielded his face from the heat of the fire with one hand, and pointed to *Constitution* with the other. "What's that?" he yelled.

"They are already inside!" Farzad shouted. "They're after Mitchell! I need men!"

Naser ran back into the darkness and dashed from rock to rock as he worked his way carefully down the slope. He yelled at his men who, one by one, ran back to the fort. A musket shot rang out from the darkness down slope. Naser staggered back toward Farzad in the dancing light of the blazing truck. He reached out to Farzad with one hand, the other clenched his throat as he fell face first into the sand in front of Farzad.

****

"Well, now they know we're here," said Redding as he stood over the dead body of the guard in the corridor. Smoke drifted from the barrel of Guzman's machine gun.

"Get going back to the cave door and guard that direction," Redding said to his squad as he pointed down the hall. "And grab that guy's weapon." Then he called back into the room, "We've got to move *now!*"

"Coming!" Miriam called back.

Bates stooped to pick up Sandra's pistol and jammed it into his belt. Then he and Miriam held Mitchell between them to help her walk. Guzman used the barrel of his gun to motion Sandra ahead of him and out the door.

The two sentries near the iron door were still tied up as Redding's squad re-entered the upper cave, still dimly lit by the oil lamp near the sentries. The gas can and the oil lamp brought from *Constitution* were next to them.

A sailor pushed the iron door closed. "This thing doesn't bolt from this side, Captain."

Redding looked around the cave, then pointed to the sentries. "Rip their clothes up and use the material to hog-tie these guys, then stack them against the door.

Miriam, can Mitchell make it with just your help?"

"I can," Mitchell answered. "I'm better. I can make it on my own."

Miriam shook her head at Redding. "No, but she and I can do it."

"Then light this lamp and carry it in your free hand," Redding said, handing Miriam the lamp they had brought.

Redding pointed to Guzman, Bates, and the other crewman who held enemy machine guns. "You three with the machine guns, protect Mitchell. Guzman, take that Sandra character with you. Bates, grab that gas can. Everyone, down the path!"

Redding and his squad hugged the cave walls as they inched their way downward around turns in the path.

Guzman nudged Sandra with his machine gun. "Any trouble from you and I crush your face with the butt of this gun."

****

With her starboard side aligned to the shore, *Constitution* was anxious to join in the fight. All sails were reefed except the spanker aft and jibs forward.

"Stand by the spanker and jib sheets," James yelled to the crews fore and aft, then tapped Gunderson on the arm and pointed toward the action on the western shore.

"Haul in the jibs!" James yelled to the crew at the bow. Then he turned his attention aft. "Let go the spanker sheet!"

The wind caught *Constitution*'s jibs, now drawn tight to the angle of the onshore breeze, and she obliged. She turned clockwise like a weathervane and brought the long guns of Buckley and Cooper to bear on the action.

James ran to a companionway and down the foot of the stairs to the gun deck. He yelled across the deck to Buckley and Cooper at their long guns. *"Prepare for fire on the western slope! Watch for flares!"*

"Right!" answered Buckley, then turned to Cooper. "Let's get our guns moving in that direction."

The block and tackle crews strained at their lines as the muzzles of the heavy guns reluctantly moved toward the fighting on the slope.

"To hell with the decks!" yelled Buckley. "Use the handspikes!"

Sailors on both gun crews pulled handspikes from the racks above them, stabbed them into the decks below the guns, and pried the guns in a clockwise direction.

****

Aarons scattered the sailors and marines behind the last of the rock outcroppings closest to the beach at the bottom of the slope, then looked around. "Kobach!"

"He's still up there!" yelled Mac as he ran down the path to Aarons. "A lot of them took off back to the fort. They must have detected Redding's squad." Mac grinned. "I got their officer, right in the throat."

"Mac, if I'm not back in twenty seconds, it means I'm not coming back. Then you're in command. Get everyone on the boat and out of here."

Mac looked up the pathway, then at Aarons. "Aye, sergeant."

Aarons weaved back and forth up the path and ducked behind boulders as he made his way up hill. He found Kobach slumped behind a rock, grimacing and bleeding from his abdomen. One hand was on his wound, the other holding the machine gun over the top of the rock.

"What are you doing?" Kobach asked as Aarons crouched next to him. He struggled to speak. "My orders were to keep going." Blood seeped through Kobach's fingers.

"Thought maybe you got lost," Aarons said as he looked at the rock formations up the hill. The enemy moved through the smoke and took cover behind the rocks as they worked their way down the slope. "Here they come!"

Both men opened up with their automatic weapons, ducking behind the boulder between short bursts. Aarons pulled a grenade from his clothing, lit it, and heaved it as far as he could toward the enemy. When it exploded, he fired another burst with his machine gun.

The enemy returned fire, hitting Aarons in the left shoulder, knocking him backward against a rock.

Aarons felt the wound and looked at the blood on his hand. He looked at Kobach and gasped, then smiled. "Hah! Aren't we a pair?" He looked at his gun. "I'm low."

"I'm out," responded Kobach weakly.

Aarons lifted himself to a crouched position and fired another short burst at the enemy with his good right arm. "They're moving in. Almost on top of us. What did you do? Tell them we were out of ammo?"

Kobach managed a weak smile.

A burst of fire from up the hill sent another round into Aarons' chest and out through his back.

Aarons coughed and struggled to breathe but pulled his flare gun from his waist as bullets from the enemy machine guns ricocheted off the rocks around them. He bent down low to Kobach. He coughed and choked as he spoke. "What do you say, swabbie? We've got 'em right where we want 'em—all around us. How about I call down the thunder?"

"You marines," Kobach gasped. "You would think of that." Barely breathing, Kobach nodded his agreement and handed Aarons his flare gun. "Semper fi, jarhead," he whispered with a smile and the last of his strength.

"Go Navy, swabbie," said Aarons, as Kobach's eyes closed and his last breath escaped him.

Aarons cocked both flare guns and aimed them at the rock formations nearest them and gathered his strength to yell back to McAvoy. "*Mac! Get out of here!*" He fired the flare guns.

Seconds later, thunder from two long guns on *Constitution* shook the air as their twenty-four-pound balls whirred and hissed through the air before they struck the rock formations upslope. The earth quaked violently from the impact that sprayed shards of rock and a cloud of dust into the air like a volcanic eruption.

Mac and the remains of the western squad picked themselves up from the sand. Mac took a last look up the slope, then turned to the men. "To the launch! On the double!"

Chapter Thirty-Eight

Banging on the iron door from inside the fort spun Redding around on the path down the cave wall.

"Take cover!" he said and waved his squad behind the jutting rock formations.

The hinges of the iron door screeched, and the bound bodies of the sentries toppled away from it as Farzad, Batul, the Amazonian Guards, and a dozen men pushed their way through to the top of the cave.

Bates opened up on the group with his machine gun, killing the first two enemy soldiers that entered the upper cave. The rest of Farzad's group dove for cover in the cave or retreated back behind the bullet-proof door.

"Open fire!" Farzad yelled from behind the partially closed door. "Stop them!"

A burst of machine gun fire from one of Farzad's men at the top of the cave forced Redding's party to duck for cover. Guzman popped back out and opened up on the enemy, killing two of them. Bates grabbed Miriam's lamp and threw it into the water. The lower cave went dark. Farzad and the rest of his force made their way through the iron door. Both sides exchanged fire, but the turns in the path around rock formations prevented either side from being exposed.

"Cut those men loose," Farzad said as he pointed to the bound sentries. "And open that door all the way."

Batul used her dagger to free the sentries. Soldiers provided cover fire while others pulled on the door. As it opened, light from the lamps on the corridor walls spilled into the cave.

Both Redding and Farzad peeked around the edge of the rock formations protecting them, then ducked back.

"Captain Redding!" Farzad yelled out in English with a laugh. "The great American hero! Nice hat!"

Farzad tried to take another look, but Redding was waiting for him and fired his pistol, ricocheting a round off the rock near Farzad's head.

"Very rude, Captain," Farzad scolded, then he aimed his gun around the corner of the rock and fired blindly at Redding.

The spray of bullets sent rock shards flying around Redding, slicing his forehead where he had been previously wounded. He wiped the blood off with his sleeve, then called back to Farzad. "Don't *make* me come up there!" He paused for a moment as he felt the breeze on his face blowing into the cave. He motioned to Bates. "Give me that gas can."

Bates hugged the rock wall with his back as he crept along the pathway and set the can near Redding. Guzman and the two other crewmen with machine guns kept the enemy ducking for cover, but a burst of fire from Farzad cut down one of Redding's men and tore through Guzman's shoulder. He looked at his wound, spat, and fired back, killing two of Farzad's men.

"You have your flare gun?" Redding asked Bates in a hushed tone.

Bates nodded.

"When I give the word," Redding continued, "get

Mitchell, Miriam, and the prisoner into that outboard skiff and head for the ship." He caught Guzman's attention. "Guzman! You and the women are going with Bates on my word."

Guzman waved.

Redding turned back to Bates. "Fire a green flare as soon as you're in the clear."

Redding stabbed holes in the gas can with his cutlass and threw it out on the water in the interior of the cave.

"I get it," Bates said, then motioned to Miriam, who had Mitchell propped up against the wall, protected by the rocks. "Get ready to run!"

Miriam looked at Mitchell's bloody feet. "Your feet."

"Never mind my damned feet! I can run," Mitchell responded with a wave of her hand.

Redding pulled out his flare gun, loaded it with the green flare, then checked with Bates and Guzman, who readied themselves. He fired the flare into the gasoline floating on the surface. A huge fireball erupted and quickly filled the cave with black smoke.

"*Go!*" Redding yelled.

The sailors staying behind with Redding opened up on the enemy above.

Bates and Guzman ran to the skiff. Guzman started the engine while Bates helped Miriam and Mitchell aboard.

"Get down and stay down!" Bates ordered Miriam and Mitchell.

Guzman opened the throttle and the skiff sped off toward *Constitution*. As soon as they were clear of the cave, Bates fired a green flare.

Batul fanned away the smoke. "Mitchell is in the boat!" she yelled to Farzad. The smoke from the gasoline engulfed the upper cave. "They're getting away!"

Farzad pointed to the rest of his soldiers. "Get to the roof! Fire down on them!"

****

Mac and the surviving western squad members rowed hard to *Constitution*. Enemy survivors of the artillery fire from Buckley and Cooper ran down to the beach and at long range opened up on the launch while its crew strained at their oars.

Basker pulled hard on his oar and looked at the sailor next to him. "Dude, did you see me throw that—"

Machine-gun fire from the shore ripped a line of splashes up to and through the boat. A round ripped through Basker's upper right arm. He grabbed it, slumped over, then straightened up and kept rowing with his left arm.

Mac called to the sailor next to Basker. "Wrap his arm with your shirt, stop the bleeding, then take his oar! The rest of you, row for your lives!"

The glow of the rising moon illuminated a cloud in the eastern sky when Farzad's men reached the roof of the fort. The fire from the exploding truck had died down. Near darkness had returned.

The skiff ran at full speed. Farzad's men fired down in the darkness at the sound of the outboard. The rounds splashed around the skiff. Miriam shielded Mitchell with her body.

Bates and Guzman raked the top of the short rampart shielding the enemy until their weapons were empty.

****

James yelled up to the men on the fighting platforms. "Fire on the top of the fort!"

Musket fire popped from the platforms at long range, but was effective only to get Farzad's men to duck behind the brick wall in front of them before they returned fire. Their random shots punched holes in the sails and forced sailors to take cover behind the heavy wooden gunwales of *Constitution*, but a sailor on a platform was hit and fell to his death on the deck.

James called to Gunderson, "Tell Buckley to target the top of the fort! I'll get the ship turned."

Gunderson ran below as James yelled out his commands to the sailing crew. James checked the wind blowing on the parade flag flying from the flag halyard over *Constitution*'s stern. "Let go the jibs! Haul in the spanker!"

Sailors on the quarterdeck heaved on the spanker sheets to haul the boom into a straight alignment with the deck, flattened to the wind blowing from seaward. On the foredeck, the jib sails flapped loosely when the crewmen released the tension on their sheets.

The wind slammed against the huge spanker and pushed *Constitution* in a counterclockwise pivot.

****

Buckley and Cooper peered through the gun ports as the barrels of their long guns slowly moved toward alignment with the fort.

"Maximum elevation!" Buckley called out to Cooper. "Knock the wedges out from under the barrel!"

The gun crews scrambled in response to orders from Cooper and Buckley. They removed the wedges that kept the barrels from achieving their maximum elevation. They heaved on the block and tackle rigging and jabbed the handspikes into the planking under the guns to pivot the guns counterclockwise.

Buckley sighted through his gun port at the fort, now outlined with back-lighting by the rising full moon. "Aim below the gunmen!" he shouted to Cooper. "Aim at the wall!"

"*What?*" Cooper shouted back.

"The mud—brick—wall!" Buckley shouted.

"Right!"

****

Redding and the remaining sailors used the cover of the gasoline fire and smoke to work their way down the path to the cave entrance. The sound of machine-gun fire from the skiff and from the enemy on top of the fort penetrated the cave.

The gasoline blaze subsided, but smoke still filled the cave. Redding and his men took off their jackets and covered their faces. A gust of wind blew into the cave. It cleared the air for Redding and his crew as it packed the upper cave with a toxic cloud.

Redding ran down the path to the gig and craned his neck to view the vertical face of the fort. Muzzles of the enemy machine guns flicked tongues of fire in the direction of *Constitution*. Redding loaded his flare gun with the red cartridge and fired it into the air, then ran back inside when the blasts from the long guns whistled toward the fort.

The rounds struck the wall of the fort just below the enemy gunmen, smashed through the mud-brick structure, and collapsed the wall. The bodies of the enemy soldiers fell with the debris into the sea in front of Redding.

"Way to go, Buckley and Cooper!" Redding shouted with his fist raised.

Farzad and his squad choked and coughed. "Out!" Farzad ordered. "Back inside the fort! Everyone to the ship! Gather everyone outside and send them to the ship at once!"

The screech of the iron door's hinges carried down to the mouth of the cave.

Redding yelled to his men. "Into the gig! We're outta here."

****

James ran to the forward gunwale as Bates tied the skiff to *Constitution*'s bow. Bates held the rope ladder for Miriam. "You first."

When Miriam reached the top, Bates held Mitchell close to him. "Madam Vice President, we're going to do this together."

Bates and Mitchell climbed the ladder and over the gunwale while Guzman untied Sandra's wrists. "You're next, you piece of shit," he said and pointed to the ladder.

"Tie her to the pin rail at the foremast," Bates ordered Guzman as he and Sandra reached the deck. Machine-gun rounds from the top of the fort whistled around them. Bates yelled at Miriam and Mitchell, "Get behind the gun'l and stay there!"

Mitchell furrowed her brow and looked at Miriam. "Gun what?"

Miriam grabbed Mitchell, pulled her to the gunwale, and tucked her in next to a carronade.

A red flare illuminated the sky off the bow of *Constitution*.

Bates turned James. "Sir, the captain has fired a red

flare."

The flare arced in the sky and floated down to the sea.

"We didn't see it—*right*?" James said to Bates.

"Right," Bates responded.

Mac's launch arrived at *Constitution*'s starboard side. He led his crew up the rope ladder where the crew on *Constitution* helped Mac's squad onto the deck.

Redding's gig was halfway to *Constitution*. James addressed the sailor nearest him. "Mr. Thompson, get in that outboard skiff and pick up the captain's party. Leave the gig adrift."

Buckley and Cooper reached the spar deck from below and approached James, who greeted them with a wide smile. "Ensign Cooper, Mr. Buckley—nicely done. Ensign, get Dr. Hannah and the vice president below. Use the captain's cabin." He spotted Gunderson and called out to him. "Mr. Gunderson, prepare to get her under way."

"Come with us, Virginia," Miriam said as she and Cooper helped Mitchell.

Gunderson yelled out across the deck. "All hands into the rigging! Prepare to make sail!"

James and Buckley ran to the foredeck as Redding climbed over the gunwale.

"Paul. Where is Mitchell?" Redding asked.

"In your cabin with Dr. Hannah and Ensign Cooper."

Mac approached the group. Redding, Buckley, and James looked past him, but Mac shook his head, and they stopped their search.

Mac struggled with his words. "We lost four, Captain," he said as his voice cracked, "including

Kobach and Aarons. I was put in command before it happened. With your permission, I'd like to write that report when the time comes."

"So you shall, Seaman McAvoy," Redding replied. "In the meantime, see to your wounded and tell them, well done."

Mac saluted, turned, and crossed the deck to the western attack squad, who attended to their wounded.

Buckley's head was down as Redding put a hand on his shoulder. "He was a good marine, Jack. You were right about that."

Buckley looked up. His expression warmed slightly.

"And without your training," Redding continued, "we wouldn't be standing here right now, and the vice president wouldn't be alive and here with us."

Buckley nodded his thanks. Still solemn, he saluted Redding weakly and left the group to stand at the starboard gunwale. He looked off toward the battlefield of the western attack force.

Redding turned to James. "You must have seen my red flare, Mr. James."

"Well, you know a lot of men have the same problem—color blindness. Wasn't that in my file?"

"How does it feel, disobeying orders?" Redding asked.

"Strangely liberating," James replied thoughtfully but with a mischievous smile.

"Uh-huh," Redding replied in disbelief. "Don't make a habit of it. You know where that can lead."

"You mean command of this ship?" James replied, smiling. Then, soberly, he added, "Speaking of which, the tide, sir; we've got to get her out of here."

"Right," Redding replied. "Pumpkin factor." Then Redding held his hand up for silence and listened. A second later he and James looked at each other and spoke as one.

"*Engines!*"

Chapter Thirty-Nine

"I found something, sir!" said a technician in NAVCENT's operation room. He pointed to his monitor that displayed a satellite image of the Libyan coast with what appeared to be a large ship at the entrance to a small harbor. Everyone in the room turned to look in the direction of the screen.

Admiral Towne jumped from his swivel chair at the nearby conference table, moved quickly to the technician's position and looked over his shoulder. "Can you zoom in any?"

"Yes, sir." The technician used his computer mouse to box an area around the ship, then tapped his keyboard. The boxed image expanded to full screen.

Towne could clearly see the outline of *Constitution*. "That's her. Where is that?"

"I need to zoom back out for that, sir," the technician answered. "Give me a second." An extended view of the Libyan coast popped into view in response to his typing. He pointed to the screen. "There, that's Tripoli, sir." He took a moment to calculate the distance to *Constitution*'s location. "Looks like they're about two hundred miles east of Tripoli."

"What are they doing way out there?" asked Towne, then turned to Holcomb as he entered the room pushing a cart of sandwiches. "Did you get through to that guy on *Constitution*?"

"No, sir. There doesn't seem to be a connection," Holcomb answered meekly.

Towne slammed his fist on the countertop. "*Damn!*"

"It's not surprising, sir," Holcomb added. "I don't know how he managed that connection in the first place."

The communications technician called out to Towne while he listened on his headset. "Sir, Mitchell's office on Air Force Two is responding to our questions about *Constitution*'s itinerary."

"Mitchell's office? What the hell would they know about it?"

"Hold on," the technician said into his boom mic to the party on the line, then answered Towne's question. "There's a Dr. Miriam Hannah aboard."

"Yeah, I know about her."

"It was a last-minute change to the ship's itinerary, sir. A side trip to some historic site at her request."

The technician pulled his boom mic away from his mouth as Towne questioned him. "Ask them what they know about that site."

"Did you hear that?" the communications technician asked into the mic. He held up a hand to Towne as he received the response through his headset. "Got it. NAVCENT out." He turned to Towne. "All they know is that it's the site of some ancient ruins that Dr. Hannah thought had some historic significance related to her research. They say Mitchell herself arranged it through the Pentagon."

Towne tapped the satellite technician on the shoulder. "Zoom back in to the tight image you had before. I saw something."

The technician repeated his previous procedure.

Towne pointed at the screen. "There! What's that? *Damn!* It's another vessel—and it's moving."

"Send those coordinates to Major Yamura and get him on the horn," said Towne to the communications technician. "Get me Captain Wilhite on the *Boxer*, and call the White House. You can put the White House on hold until I'm through with Wilhite." He pointed to a lieutenant on his staff. "Spin up an Osprey for me." Towne turned back to the communications tech. "I want to see those satellite images on the plane. Can do?"

"Can do, sir."

Towne called after the lieutenant, who was just about out the door. "And tell Captain Geertz to put as many marines on the bird as it will hold! You, Holcomb, you're coming with us and keep trying to make that connection."

Holcomb froze, his jaws clenched on a half-eaten sandwich.

"*Admiral Towne*," came Admiral Buckholter's voice on the speaker from the monitor of the situation room at the White House. "*What's the idea calling in and then putting us on hold?*"

"Yes, sir, sorry, sir. I have new information, and it's imperative that I act on it immediately."

President Fairchild jumped in. "*What information?*"

"Hard to explain, Mr. President, gentlemen, and it would take too much time. I have to move on it *now*!"

"*Damn it, Chester, do you realize who you're talking to?*" Buckholter protested.

"Yes, sir, very much, sir, but it doesn't change the facts. I have info on where Mitchell is."

"Admiral, this is Mark Adamson. The facts are that we are working on a second scenario, and you are ordered to stand by."

Towne paused for a brief moment, then shook his head. "Sorry, sirs, I can't do that. Gotta go. Logging out now." Towne looked at the communications technician, sliced his throat with his finger, then stared briefly at his finger before bolting for the door. Admiral Buckholter's shout slipped out of the speakers before the connection ended.

"Chester! What the—"

Chapter Forty

The throb of the fishing vessel's diesel engines pierced the night air. The full moon illuminated the ship's white hull in the distance.

The lookout in *Constitution*'s foremast yelled down to the deck, "Vessel—five points off the starboard bow! One half mile! Speed, about six knots!"

"*Damn!*" muttered Redding. "What is *with* that guy?"

Crew members froze in their tracks, then ran to the gunwale and looked in the direction of the approaching vessel. Buckley moved as fast as he could toward Redding from across the deck but had to grab a pinrail as the ship's motion came to a sudden stop. All on board were thrown off balance. Men in the rigging grabbed anything close to keep from tumbling to the deck. Redding and James were thrown against the pinrail around the mainmast.

Redding looked at James. "Pumpkin?"

"Yup."

Redding muttered to himself, "This just keeps getting better." He looked up at the sails, then sniffed the air. "That's thyme," he said quietly.

"What?" asked James.

"Sheet all the sails flat against an offshore wind," Redding ordered.

"*What* offshore wind?" James replied.

"The one we're about to get, Lieutenant."

"If we get a gust," James said as he looked at the rigging, "the masts could snap."

"Could be," Redding answered.

James shook his head, then shouted orders to the crew in the rigging as Miriam and Cooper reemerged on deck.

"What was that jolt?" Miriam asked.

"No time for that now," Redding replied as he pointed toward the enemy vessel. "We'll be under attack again in a matter of minutes. Take two men with you and guard Mitchell."

He turned to Bates and Buckley. "Get all hands on deck armed with whatever we have left. Mr. Buckley, put your sharpshooters on the platforms."

"We're almost out of powder, Captain," Buckley warned.

"Give them what we've got," ordered Redding. "If we lose this battle, it won't matter how much is left."

Redding scanned the deck and spotted Basker, his shoulder now wrapped, trying to load his musket with his one good arm. "Mr. Basker! Front and center!"

Redding turned to Buckley. "Basker replaces Cooper as the other gunner."

"Right," Buckley replied and motioned Basker to join him.

"Any ammo left for the long guns?" Redding asked Buckley.

"No sir, just what's in the carronades left over from our last drill—grapeshot."

"That'll have to do," said Redding. "Man those two carronades."

Mac and other sharpshooters climbed the rigging

with their muskets and took up positions on the fighting platforms. Mac called out to all the men.

"Hold your fire until they are close! Save your ammo!"

Farzad's remaining force of about thirty men lined the deck of the fishing vessel. They fired their automatic weapons at *Constitution* from behind the safety of the high steel gunwale at the ship's bow. Farzad kept Batul and the guards with him in the cockpit while crewmen on the foredeck loaded a rocket-propelled grenade launcher.

****

Cooper, Miriam, and two sailors armed with muskets entered the captain's cabin.

Vice President Mitchell pointed upward. "What's going on up there? Isn't it over?"

"No," Cooper said, then she turned to Miriam. "We need a better hiding place, and we need to move fast."

"Virginia, are you okay?" asked Miriam.

"Yes, but—"

"We're about to be attacked by sea," said Miriam. "We need to get you moved. Are you okay to move?"

Mitchell winced as she put weight on her blood-soaked bandaged feet.

Cooper called to the two sailors, "Help her." Then she pointed to an oil lamp. "Dr. Hannah, we'll need that. Light it. We're going below."

Cooper led the way down the stairs of the companionway, past the berth deck with the crew's hammocks still swaying from their hooks. They continued downward on the stairs past the orlop deck stacked with spare rope, lumber, and canvas, to the aft end of the hold, three levels below the spar deck. It was pitch black but for the glow from the oil lamp that revealed crates and barrels of supplies.

Cooper led them forward to the bow end of the hold, where another ladder connected the hold to the orlop deck above.

"Bring that lamp closer," Cooper told the sailor as she looked around the hold. "Let me have it." She took the lamp and gestured with one of her two pistols.

"Stack crates and roll some of those barrels over there near the stairs, then get behind them. Understand, if the enemy finds us, we know the ship in the darkness. They don't. If they find us, we can't win a shootout with them. We keep on the run, upward."

****

An RPG round fired from the enemy vessel a quarter mile away streaked across the night sky between the two ships, trailing a glowing smoke plume as it punched through one of *Constitution*'s topsails, set it on fire, and illuminated the men on the platforms aloft. Gunmen on the fishing vessel turned their aim on them. Two sailors were hit and fell to the ship's deck. Mac and the others ducked behind the heavy masts for protection. Crewmen on the spar deck used the thick planks of the gunwale as shelter from the machine gun fire that splintered the outside of the ship's hull.

A second RPG round blazed toward *Constitution*, struck her above the waterline at the berth deck, and punched a hole through the hull.

Constitution's keel was still jammed in the mud on the bottom of the harbor. The freshening sirocco offshore wind pressed against her sails. Her shrouds and masts groaned with the strain on her rigging, and her hull tilted at a steep angle. Buckley, Basker, and their carronade crews held on to the big guns as the deck tilted radically to port.

Suddenly, *Constitution*'s keel pulled free of the bottom. The deck began to level, but the sails trimmed flat to the wind didn't produce forward motion.

Buckley and Basker sighted down the barrels of their cannons, waiting for the angle of the deck to bring the guns to bear on the approaching enemy.

"On my command!" Buckley raised his hand and called out to Basker.

Constitution's billethead stared menacingly at the oncoming enemy as she answered the threat, obliging her crew by leveling her decks.

Another RPG round flashed just as the barrels of the carronades lined up with the approaching vessel. Buckley dropped his hand. "*Fire!*"

The two big guns lurched back with a deafening blast as they hurled over fifty pounds of golf-ball-size lead shot at the enemy. The grapeshot met the incoming RPG round in the gap between the two ships and detonated the rocket in midair. The lead of the grapeshot continued to the enemy vessel. It knocked out the RPG crew, blasted holes through the windows of the cockpit around Farzad, and ricocheted around the steel structure of the fishing vessel. Automatic weapons fire halted as the enemy dove for cover. The vessel veered off course momentarily, then turned back toward *Constitution*.

"Collision bearing!" James cried out to Redding as the enemy vessel bore down on *Constitution*.

"Prepare to repel boarders!" Redding shouted to the crew. "Take cover behind the gun'l!"

"Captain!" came Mac's call down from the fighting

platform. "They have explosives stacked at their bow!"

"It's a suicide ship!" Redding yelled to James. Both took cover behind masts.

"Seaman Dover!" Gunderson shouted from the gunwale. "Over here!"

Automatic weapons fire raked the starboard hull. Rachel ducked behind the gunwale and made her way to Gunderson's position. He pulled a grenade from his jacket. "What was your longest hook shot ever?" he asked.

"Half court," she answered.

Gunderson pointed to the enemy ship closing on *Constitution*. He handed her the grenade and pulled out his lighter. "There's a full-court shot for you. Go for it!"

Rachel peeked over the gunwale, then held the grenade out for Gunderson to light. "Dover—get it over their gun'l at the bow!" he said as he lit the fuse.

She judged the distance, extended her arm, and heaved the grenade with a grunt. It exploded in front of the oncoming vessel.

"Again," urged Gunderson as he handed her another grenade. "This is the *last* one."

He lit the grenade in her hand. She looked over the gunwale, clenched her teeth, and launched the grenade higher in the air.

****

Farzad's eyes grew wider as the grenade arced toward his vessel. Smoke and sparks trailed from the burning fuse as it spun through the air. He and his guards ducked behind the steel bulkhead of the cockpit. The enemy gunmen dove for cover as the grenade landed on the stack of crates in the bow. The explosion shook the vessel and blew the bow off just below the waterline, killing a half dozen of Farzad's men. Scraps of plate steel from the vessel's bow blasted toward *Constitution* and ricocheted off her hull.

Farzad, Batul, and the two Amazonian Guards picked themselves up off the deck of the cockpit. Farzad took the helm and aimed the vessel back at *Constitution*.

He yelled to his men through the broken glass of the cockpit. "We will ram them, board them, wipe them out, and recapture Mitchell!"

****

Gunderson slapped Rachel on the back. Cheers rang out from the crew but soon went silent as the momentum of the enemy vessel—now sinking slowly by the bow—pushed it toward them.

Buckley approached Tebic and Thompson, huddled behind the gunwale with four blunderbuss guns.

"Good man, Tebic. Thompson, give me two of those."

As the enemy ship drew nearer, the angle to *Constitution*'s fighting platforms increased. Mac on the mainmast platform and sharpshooters on the foremast and mizzenmast fired down on the enemy.

Constitution's bow bobbed in the black water as if beckoning the forces of nature to intervene. Redding looked aloft as the wind strangely reversed direction again and a cold, damp wind returned from seaward. The thick offshore fogbank moved back over *Constitution*, virtually cutting off visual contact between the forces.

"That's a break," Redding said to himself. "Where the hell did that come from?"

The enemy vessel struck and crushed the launch left by the western shore party. The collision slowed the momentum of the steel vessel until it rammed *Constitution*'s hull.

Buckley climbed on top of a carronade. Tebic and Thompson followed his lead. Enemy gunmen opened up with automatic weapons as they scrambled over the gutted bow of their ship and up *Constitution*'s hull.

"Now," Buckley ordered. He stood up with a blunderbuss under each arm. Tebic and Thompson braced their guns on their hips and aimed at the onrushing enemy.

"Fire!" Buckley yelled.

Lead, smoke, and a thunderous report issued from the antique weapons and four of the enemy gunmen were instantly cut down.

"Let's go!" yelled Redding to the men near him at the gunwale.

"Go!" shouted James on the opposite end of *Constitution*'s deck.

Farzad's remaining forces climbed over the gunwale in the fog and blunderbuss smoke. Redding and James quickly downed two of them with pistol shots, tossed the guns, and drew their cutlasses.

The burning topsail broke loose from its spar above and fell like a fiery cloud on some of the enemy soldiers trying to board *Constitution*, setting them on fire. The panicked men were easy targets for the sailors' muskets and the blades of James and Redding.

Smoke and fog prevented Mac and the sharpshooters above from distinguishing their targets. They hooked on to sail sheets and slid down to the deck.

Redding sliced through an enemy soldier who had made it to the deck, but he didn't see another taking aim at him until a split second before a heavy block on a rope from the rigging above swung down on the enemy soldier, crushing his forehead.

Redding looked aloft, mystified, then grabbed the enemy's machine gun and went to work on any targets he could distinguish in the fog. The balance of power was tipping in favor of *Constitution*.

Chapter Forty-One

Farzad surveyed the battle on the spar deck. He motioned to Batul and the guards. "Follow me."

They left the cockpit, crossed the steeply angled foredeck to the blown-out bow of the sinking vessel, crawled through the smoke to the hole created in *Constitution* by the RPG round, and scrambled onto her berth deck.

Farzad led Batul and the guards up to the gun deck and aft to the captain's cabin. When he opened the door, Batul and the guards rushed into the empty room with machine guns. Farzad grabbed an oil lantern. "Light this," he said, handing it to one of the guards.

From the light of the lantern, Farzad spotted bloody footprints leading out of the cabin. "She was here. They've moved her."

They opened every door and closet on the berth deck, then climbed downstairs to the orlop deck and searched through stacks of sailcloth, rope, and rigging parts.

"They aren't here," said Batul, then she pointed to the ladder leading downward at the aft end of the deck. "There's another level down."

****

A group of enemy soldiers gathered on the quarterdeck, but before they could attack, and with no indication of a wind shift, the spanker boom snapped from starboard to port, knocking some of them unconscious and slamming others against the gunwale.

"What the hell?" Redding asked.

On the foredeck, Mac swung his musket like a baseball bat into the face of an enemy soldier, cracked his skull, and sent him to the deck. Mac picked up the man's machine gun and fired a burst into another enemy soldier who was drawing down on Guzman as he was reloading his musket.

"Thanks, farm boy," Guzman said with a wave.

Mac picked up the gun from the fallen enemy and tossed it to Guzman. "Let's go!"

Rachel Dover found Tebic and Thomas Thompson hiding behind a mast, reloading their blunderbusses. Tebic rammed wadding down the barrel. He looked up at Rachel. "It's the only weapon I know."

"Give me that and load the other one," she said as she grabbed the gun and disappeared into the fog.

With his one good arm, Basker swung a belaying pin like a bat against an enemy soldier who held his machine gun the same way. Basker's form was better, and the man went down with a crushed face.

****

Cooper, Miriam, Mitchell, and the two sailors hid in the darkness and aimed their weapons at the sound of the enemy climbing down the ladder. The sailors cocked their muskets quietly and aimed through openings between crates and barrels. Cooper ducked down but held their shoulders.

When the light of the enemy's lamp began to illuminate their position, Cooper tapped the sailors on their shoulders, and they fired.

The lead guard went down. Her lamp went dark as

it crashed to the floor. The others ducked for cover.

Cooper shouted to Miriam, "Go!"

Miriam pushed Mitchell up the ladder to the orlop deck. Farzad and his guards fired their weapons randomly in the darkness. One sailor was hit and slumped to the bottom of the stairs. Cooper fired her pistol at their muzzle flashes from the rungs as she climbed the ladder behind the others.

Cooper's party reached the orlop deck. "Keep going!" she ordered. "Up to the berth deck!"

Farzad and his crew felt their way in the blackness back to the ladder they had used to get down to the hold. They crawled up the rungs to the orlop deck just in time to see Cooper, Miriam, Mitchell, and the remaining sailor disappear up the stairs at the opposite end of the deck.

The chase continued upward. When Farzad's party reached the berth deck, the crews' hammocks blocked the view of their prey. They held down the triggers on their guns and shredded the hammocks with bullets, raking back and forth across the cloud of canvas. The rounds cut the sailor's legs out from under him, and he fell to the deck.

Farzad, Batul, and the lone additional guard fought their way through the tangle of canvas hammocks to the stairs used by Cooper, Miriam, and Mitchell.

Cooper stayed back and fired her last pistol load at the oncoming enemy. The enemy took cover long enough for Miriam and Mitchell to make it up to the gun deck. Before Cooper could escape herself, a burst of fire from Batul sent a round through her side.

Cooper struggled to the gun deck with the enemy close behind. Bleeding heavily, she picked up a cannonball from a rack near a long gun, strained to hold it over her head, then launched it down the stairway opening, crushing the head of the Amazonian Guard leading the enemy party. Her body and the cannonball knocked Batul and Farzad down to the bottom of the stairs.

Farzad regained his feet and fired up the stairway. He threw the dead body of the guard aside, clearing the way for Batul to climb the steps. Farzad followed her.

****

The fog began to burn away as the sun rose on the harbor. On the spar deck, the fighting was hand to hand. Redding, James, Buckley, and Gunderson waded in with their blades. An enemy soldier picked up a musket with a bayonet attached from a fallen sailor and charged at James, who deftly swatted it away with his cutlass and ran the man through.

Redding searched the enemy bodies on deck for Farzad. He hoisted himself to the top of the gunwale and scanned the enemy vessel. Her keel now rested on the bottom of the bay. Nothing showed of the boat but the top of her wheelhouse. The hole in *Constitution*'s hull still smoldered from the explosion of the RPG round.

Redding jumped down from the gunwale, ran to the forward-most stairway, and yelled at Buckley. "Get below!"

Redding ran down the steps of the companionway and arrived on the gun deck, cutlass in hand, just in time to see Batul attempt to fire on Mitchell with an empty gun.

Cooper pulled her cutlass, held her wound with her left hand, and stumbled toward Batul, who drew her dagger and threw it into Cooper's chest, killing her instantly.

"*Bobbi!*" screamed Miriam from behind a cannon where she and Mitchell were hiding.

Farzad emerged from the deck below. He and Redding locked eyes. Farzad looked at Redding's cutlass, smiled, and raised his machine gun to shoot just as Buckley arrived from the stairs nearest Farzad and lunged at him with his cutlass.

"*Jack, no!*" Redding shouted as Farzad spun around and shot Buckley with the last rounds in his gun. Buckley clutched his stomach and slumped to the deck.

Farzad threw his machine gun aside and grabbed a handspike from a rack above a cannon. "Batul—the vice president!" he shouted as he tossed the spike to her.

Batul caught it in the air and charged Mitchell. Miriam pulled a wad worm from the rack, the nearest tool to her reach, and threatened Batul with the steel claws on its tip, but a swing of the handspike from Batul cut the staff of the wad worm in half.

In a rage, his cutlass raised, Redding charged Farzad.

Farzad picked up Buckley's cutlass and blocked Redding's blade.

"When your head is rolling on the deck, Captain Redding," Farzad said, pointing to Miriam, "hers is next."

Redding lunged at Farzad, who skillfully parried Redding's thrusts. He swung on the captain as Redding ducked.

The morning sun poured through the gun ports,

throwing shadows of the four combatants against the inner hull and across the deck.

Miriam and Batul squared off. Miriam kept herself between Batul and Mitchell. Holding the handspike, Batul smiled as she looked at the short wooden shaft held by Miriam.

Miriam breathed heavily. Her eyes widened as she spun the shaft like a baton, and motioned Batul to approach. "Batul, meaning self-denying virgin," Miriam said in Arabic. "Maybe that's your problem. You need to get—"

Batul screamed as she rushed at Miriam with her weapon, but Miriam twisted to the side like a matador and delivered a blow to Batul's ribs, knocking her back. Miriam started to charge in, but backed off and positioned herself in front of Mitchell.

The fight between Redding and Farzad raged around the gun deck. Farzad was skillful, but Redding had the edge and flashed a smile at Farzad to let him know it.

"You are beaten," Redding said. "Give it up and join your buddies at Gitmo."

"We define victories differently, Captain Redding—or hadn't you noticed?"

"Fine with me," Redding said through a smile. "I was hoping you'd refuse the offer."

Batul charged with her weapon cocked back, ready to swing. Miriam quickly closed the distance before Batul could unload and jump-kicked her in the chest.

Stunned and gasping for air, Batul dropped the handspike. Miriam pounced with blows from her wood shaft, but Batul backed up and blocked them with her forearms until she regained her breath. Batul delivered a punch of her own to Miriam's face. Blood spouted from her mouth as she fell backward and tripped over Cooper's body.

Miriam staggered away as she looked at her left hand, covered with Cooper's blood.

Farzad sliced through Redding's sleeve and drew blood. Redding sprang forward and drove him back. Redding glanced quickly at Miriam and shouted to her. *"Miriam, the sword!"*

Miriam looked at Cooper. Cooper's eyes were still open.

Batul picked up the handspike.

Miriam rose to her feet and picked up Cooper's cutlass.

Batul charged, her weapon aimed at Miriam like a lance.

James and Gunderson ran down the steps in time to see Miriam cut the blade off the wooden staff of the handspike with a swing of the cutlass. She advanced on Batul, chopped her wooden staff shorter with each stroke of her blade and shouted viciously at Batul in Arabic: "Her name was Bobbi—and she is the reason you are going to die!" Miriam pinned Batul helplessly against the barrel of a long gun and, without hesitation, ran the cutlass through her stomach until the point of the blade was stopped by the iron barrel.

Redding drove Farzad against the hull of the ship and swatted his cutlass to the deck. He was about to finish him off when James rushed in and held his arm. Gunderson followed with his cutlass and pinned Farzad to the hull as Redding held back his death stroke.

"Better alive," said James. "Don't you think?"

Redding backed off, lowered his blade, and hurried

to Buckley's side. He was face down on the deck, bleeding.

The captain turned him over. The old marine's torso was covered in blood, and his eyes were barely open.

"Hang in there, Jack," Redding urged. "We won. You don't want to miss the postgame celebration."

Buckley looked up at Redding and smiled weakly. "Ask for me in the morning…" he said with a fading voice as his eyes closed and his head slumped to the side.

Redding held up Buckley's head for another moment, then gently laid it down. He took off his tunic, draped it over Buckley, then walked slowly to James, looking back over his shoulder at Buckley.

"Casualties above?" Redding asked.

"Many," James quietly answered.

Farzad sneered.

"About face," he commanded James and Gunderson in a low, deliberate tone.

James and Gunderson looked at each other, shrugged, and turned away a split second before the crunch of cracking bones split the air like the snapping of dry wood.

James and Gunderson turned around. Farzad lay unconscious on the deck, his head bent sharply to his right. Redding grabbed the knuckles of his right hand.

"Take him to the spar deck and lash him to a carronade," Redding ordered.

James and Gunderson dragged the unconscious Farzad up the stairs.

Miriam knelt next to Cooper's body in the center of the gun deck and closed Cooper's eyes with her fingers.

Redding walked over to her and extended his hand.

Miriam looked up at him with eyes full of tears. "Give me a minute."

He backed off and approached Mitchell, crouched behind a long gun, trembling, but he stopped at Batul's body, still upright, but draped backward over the long gun with the cutlass protruding from her stomach. He glanced back at Miriam and said under his breath, "Damn, woman, you *are* worse than me."

Mitchell pulled herself up as Redding reached out to her. "Madam Vice President, do you still need that explanation?"

"No, Commander," Mitchell responded, nearly out of breath. "I think I get it. I don't understand how it happened that you and your ship came along, but I'm grateful you did."

"Let's get you back to my quarters." Redding wrapped an arm around her shoulder.

****

On the upper deck, *Constitution* crewmen administered aid to the wounded from both sides while others guarded the few enemy soldiers who had surrendered.

James and Gunderson emerged on the spar deck, still dragging Farzad. "I've got this, Lieutenant," Gunderson said and waved over a couple of nearby sailors. "Tie this one to that carronade and make sure he's not too comfortable."

James surveyed the bloodstained deck. Redding approached him. "Paul, get a crew to take that motor skiff out to pick up the gig that's adrift. Have the men use both boats to pick up our casualties ashore and bring them back to the ship—where they belong. Bring those secret service agents too."

Miriam came up from below with a horrified look on her face as she viewed the carnage. She made her way toward him stepping around bodies and pools of blood.

"Shall I have our dead taken below?" James asked, regaining Redding's attention.

Redding looked up into the rigging. The sun was shining on the sails and the parade flag aft. "No. Take them to the quarterdeck under the flag. Let them be in the sun a little longer. They'll be in darkness soon enough."

Chapter Forty-Two

Constitution relaxed in the morning sun and tugged gently at her anchor chain in response to the incoming tide. Her sails were reefed, but the parade flag, tattered and holed from automatic weapons fire, still waved from the halyard at the stern over the fallen crewmen who'd been laid out on the deck and covered with sailcloth.

Redding leaned over the gunwale in the direction of the fort.

With a damp rag in her hand, Miriam joined him.

Redding pointed to the fort. "The ruins of historic Fort Hannah got a little more ruined."

"But definitely more historic," Miriam answered as she dabbed blood from his forehead with the rag. "This spot on your forehead seems to be unlucky for you."

Redding didn't respond.

"If I may make an observation, you don't suck at *this*," she added.

"Poetically put," Redding said as he kept staring off in the distance.

Miriam examined the wound to his arm. "You said in the cave you'd deal with me later. Is this a good time?"

Redding paused for a second, then smiled with amusement. "Let's don't and say we did."

Miriam looked up from his arm and wrinkled her

brow. "Huh?"

"That was a pat response from a high school girlfriend of mine." Redding chuckled. "I've waited my *entire…adult…life* to use it on someone else."

"Well," she responded suspiciously, "that doesn't take a lot of analysis. I won't intrude on that memory—but I don't know how I'm going to deal with this one." Tears welled up in Miriam's eyes.

"I've given that some thought, and I'll tell you how I think this goes," Redding said as he turned back away from her and looked across the harbor. "You've studied military history and seen those documentaries on TV where they interviewed those old World War II vets, trying to get their stories recorded before they die. Most of them, even after all those decades, still had a hard time dealing with those memories of battles, violence, loss of friends. Just being asked to remember those experiences causes them to break down. It's heartbreaking to watch."

He turned to her, and she looked up at him. "That's now *us*. That's our future. I don't think we *ever* deal with it—and maybe we shouldn't be able to, completely, I mean. Maybe it's too important to be dealt with. Maybe we just bury it as best we can, and when we're old and somebody with a TV crew asks us what it was like, we react just like those old vets."

"Only we *won't* be old, Moses," Miriam added. "That's going to start tomorrow."

The distant sound of a propeller-driven plane got their attention. Redding pointed to the east. A moment later, a DC-3 came into view over the ruins of the fort, chased by the vapor trail of a missile that caught it and blew it up, strewing the flaming wreckage over the terrain that had been the scene of battle the night before.

"*What?*" Miriam shouted, covered her ears, and ducked behind the gunwale.

A flight of F-18 Hornets streaked overhead, followed by the thumping sound of heavy helicopters and an aircraft in the distance.

"Now what?" she asked with frightened look at Redding, who hadn't budged.

"That's the cavalry, arriving in the nick of time." He pulled her up and away from the gunwale and pointed to helicopters just visible on the eastern horizon, accompanied by an Osprey. "That would be your ride. Time to get Vice President Mitchell. We're going ashore."

Miriam grabbed Redding's sleeve. "First, I have a favor to ask." She started to choke up and looked down. "I assume you are going to write medal recommendations after this. I'd like to write the one for Bobbi."

Redding squeezed her shoulder and nodded. "I'll sign whatever you write."

The captain's gig arrived at the beach carrying Redding, Miriam, and Mitchell. Navy SEALs waded in to help Mitchell as another navy squad launched an inflatable boat and headed for *Constitution*. Mitchell turned to Redding before they led her off.

She offered him her hand. "If there's anything I can do for you, Commander, let me know."

"Well, ma'am," Redding said as he took her hand and looked back at the ship, "there *is* one thing."

"Name it," Mitchell insisted.

"If you have any influence over the people in

charge of Arlington Cemetery, I'd like a place set aside for my people—something special."

Mitchell looked back at the ship. "I do—and it will be my privilege."

The SEALs began to lead her off when Admiral Towne approached, followed by Holcomb. Mitchell pointed to Towne. "Now, I think here's someone else who will want to thank you."

Redding's brow furrowed. "One never knows with the admiral," he answered doubtfully, then added under his breath, "This should be interesting."

"I'll be going," Miriam said to Redding. "I guess this is goodbye."

Redding struggled to find the words, then gave up. "Uh…looks like we're back to the thing I suck at."

Miriam's smile made it okay.

"One more thing, ma'am," he called out to Mitchell, who stopped and turned. "Watch out for this one. She's trouble."

Mitchell glanced between the two of them and smiled.

Miriam felt Redding's hands firmly holding her waist as he unnecessarily helped her from the gig. She looked back at him and held his forearm for a moment before turning away to join Mitchell. He waited to see if she would take a last look back. She did not.

Holcomb spotted Tebic on the beach, still holding his blunderbuss, and ran over to him. Tebic puffed out his chest, cocked his head, and grinned ear to ear. Holcomb just shook his head, smiled, and gave Tebic a high five. Holcomb's smile widened as Tebic offered him his blunderbuss for inspection.

Admiral Towne greeted Mitchell and Miriam on

his way down the beach to the gig, followed by Major Yamura and the rest of SEAL Team Eight. "Madam Vice President—Dr. Hannah, I presume—I'm Vice Admiral Chester Towne of NAVCENT. I'll be with you shortly."

Towne surveyed the scene as he moved past them toward Redding, then sat next to him on the gig's bow.

Towne pulled up binoculars hanging from his neck and looked at *Constitution*. "Do you have any idea what a night battle between an 1800s frigate and a modern ship looks like on an infrared satellite feed?"

"Hmm," said Redding mockingly. Then answered flatly, "From a satellite feed? No, sir."

Towne hid his smile. "We'll take your casualties back with us and send a ship to tow her back to Italy. Your crew and the ship look pretty beat up."

"Sir, we're okay, and so is the ship. With permission, we'll take her back to Italy under short sail and make a few temporary repairs before we cross the pond. As far as the wounded, the ones who aren't critical, if you give us a medic or two who can patch them up while we're underway, I'd rather keep them with us, even if they can't work."

"Okay with me if it's okay with them." Towne gestured to Redding's bloody arm and forehead. "I assume that goes for you too."

Redding ignored him. "As for our dead," he continued, "I just talked to Mitchell about that, asked her for a favor. I think she'll come through on it. I'm asking you not to make any arrangements until you talk to her."

Towne nodded his agreement. "All right, but you're still short of crew."

Redding pointed to the SEAL Team standing on the beach nearby. "Who are all these guys?"

"Well," Towne answered, "that's SEAL Team Eight behind me. They're the ones that were sent on a wild-goose chase to someplace called Siwa. Those others are SEAL Team Three off the *Boxer*. Over there checking out the battle scene are marines from NAVCENT. They came with me. We didn't know what we'd find here, so we came prepared."

"Y-e-a-h," Redding replied, drawing out the word with a tone of sarcasm. He looked up at Towne and furrowed his brow. "About that goose chase…'butt out'?"

"Uh, yeah," Towne replied apologetically. "Sorry about that Wyatt Earp thing."

"No, that part I liked."

Towne hesitated, searching for the right words. "And—I think I speak for the top brass, myself included—sorry we were late."

"Well," said Redding, taking advantage of the opening, "look at the bright side. You got to shoot down that old airplane."

"All right. I guess you had that one coming."

"For the record, Lieutenant James followed my orders under protest."

Towne stood up. "You can skip the bull. I've got my own problems along those lines—with the Joint Chiefs no less."

Redding raised his brow as he looked at Towne. "*Ouch!*"

"Uh-huh. I think I caught something from you."

"Well," Redding quipped, a little too flippantly, "there's always *Constitution*."

"Don't push your luck, Wyatt," Towne warned. "But on that subject..." Towne looked away and kicked at the sand. "That business in the Gulf. I'll order a review, get Lt. Carter's testimony...Straighten all that out for you."

Redding nodded his thanks.

As Egyptian soldiers took Farzad toward their helicopter, he caught Redding's gaze and held it.

"There goes our buddy," said Redding as his eyes followed Farzad.

Towne held his hand over his brow and squinted his eyes against the glare of the morning sun as he stared at Farzad for a moment. "The left side of his face is purple."

"Uh-huh." Redding rubbed his right knuckles. "That's a good look for him, don't you think?"

Towne grinned. "How did *he* survive?"

Redding shook his head. "Wasn't *my* idea, but I suppose if you can squeeze some information out of him, it was worth it."

"I'd love to reprise waterboarding just this once," Towne remarked as he watched the soldiers escort Farzad away.

"Give him back to us for the crossing. I'm sure we could work something out." He looked at Towne, who chuckled.

"Just a thought," Redding said, then he pointed toward the helicopter. "What's with the Egyptians?"

"It's a long story. An attempted coup was part of this scheme. All across Egypt, they're still chasing people down."

"Speaking of which," Redding added, "what the hell happened? What's going on out there?"

Towne went on to explain what they had learned of Farzad's plot, the attempt to activate a worldwide terrorist network, and the outbreak of violence that was still going on around the globe. He gave Redding as many details as he knew about activities in the US.

A navy crew in an inflatable boat returned from *Constitution* with Sandra Phillips.

"How the hell did she ever get on Mitchell's staff?"

"I don't know," answered Towne, "but I'd hate to be the director of the FBI right about now."

Redding stared off in the distance. "You know it's not over—right?"

"We know," replied Towne, "but at least we also know a lot more about the level of the threat—how they work. That goose chase turned up a computer. Should be loaded with intel for us. For that matter, that Sandra Phillips woman should be a good source. Shouldn't be too hard to get it out of her. Glad you saved her for us."

"Back to the crew issue," Redding interjected. He pointed to the marine contingent that flew in with Towne. "How about those guys?"

"They're good marines, not tall ship sailors."

"We can fix that," Redding said, confidently.

Towne smiled and called to the leader of the marines. "Captain Geertz! Any of your IPT men want to help sail *Constitution* back to Italy, then on to Boston?"

Geertz turned to his men. Hands shot up from all of them.

Redding looked up at Towne. "IPT? Never heard of it."

"You wouldn't. It's what they call themselves. It's like a college fraternity with a Greek name."

"And IPT stands for…?"

"Get this, I Phelta Thigh."

Redding pointed to the marines. "They're *mine*."

"Okay. They're yours," said Towne to Redding. "Anything you want me to tell Admiral Buckholter?"

"Yes, sir. Tell him to get out his box of medals."

"Just write them up on your way home. I'll give Bucky a heads-up on that—even add my own two cents," Towne answered assuredly, then a puzzled look came over Redding's face.

"You remember a Master Gunnery Sergeant Jack Buckley?" Redding asked.

Towne shook his head. "Him too? Yeah. I'm the guy who approved his exemption to stay in the Corps. Now I regret it."

"Don't," Redding responded emphatically. "Over there is a vice president and out there what's left of the ship's complement—they owe their lives to Buckley and so do I."

Towne changed the subject. "What about her?" he asked, gesturing to *Constitution*. "Anything she needs?"

"Powder and shot," replied Redding, deadpan. He stood up. "With your permission, I need to get back to the ship."

"You surprise me, Commander. You're a different man than the one I met in my office."

"That's a long story too," said Redding thoughtfully. "Don't understand it myself."

Chapter Forty-Three

Redding sat at his cabin table, the ship's log in front of him and the feather quill poised in his hand.

July 4...

That's as far as Redding got with the most important log entry of his career, as *Constitution* sailed north from the Libyan coast on a course to Italy. He stared at the blank page, deep in thoughts, but unable to communicate them.

A knock on the cabin door turned him around.

"Captain, sir."

"What is it, Mr. Gunderson?" Redding answered, staring back at the log book.

"Your presence is requested in the wardroom."

Frustrated, Redding put the quill in its holder. "Very well. I'll be there in a moment." Redding rose, donned his cocked hat, and looked in the mirror.

He looked vacantly at the floor as he walked down the companionway and opened the door to the wardroom. It was brightly lit by oil lanterns and crowded with as many of the crew as it could hold. They were gathered around a table with the crumbling Messina cake in the center. The text on the frosting had been done over, and the text now read *Huzzah! Constitution—34 and 0.*

"Huzzah! Huzzah! Huzzah!" shouted the crew.

Redding stood, speechless, and stared first at the

352

cake, then around the table at the faces. There was James, Gunderson, Tebic, Basker, Guzman, Mac, Thompson, Bates, Rachel, and many others. He found himself also looking for familiar faces that were no longer there and had to pause for a moment. He bit his lip and turned away to collect himself.

"I already tested it," Tebic said sheepishly. "It's sort of edible, though the frosting tastes a little like gunpowder. But, you know, it's the thought that counts."

Redding turned back to the gathering. "I was just thinking of our shipmates. It's hard to feel happy right now, but I'm going to do my best to try, and I suggest you do the same. This helps, and I thank you for it. Let's make this a celebration of having served with the best *Constitution* crew ever—make that, the best *crew* ever—and under the worst circumstances."

James pulled out his cutlass. "I never did get to cut this thing. May I?"

"Cut me a big piece," came a voice from the back of the room.

James and the others laughed and smiled at the look on Redding's face as he searched the group.

"How did you get back on board?" Redding asked as the group parted to let Miriam through. Then he focused on James, who nodded.

"Yes, sir, that would be me, but she brought a note from the principal, that is, the vice president."

"Don't you have some big-time State Department stuff to do?"

"As it turns out, the peace talks have been somewhat delayed, so I'm sort of free for now—and who wants an airplane ride back to Italy when they can sail on *Constitution*?"

The room applauded.

Redding shook his head and pointed to the cake. "Save us some of that." He looked at Miriam. "Maybe I *will* deal with you now," he said as he pointed to the deck above.

Oooohs and uh-ohs issued from the crew as Redding and Miriam headed topside. Rachel Dover stared at James. Gunderson nudged her and whispered in her ear, "Your problem is Navy Regulation 1165. No personal relationships between officers and enlisted personnel. And he's a by-the-book guy."

Without hesitating or taking her eyes off James, Rachel whispered back to Gunderson, "Then I'll just have to become an officer."

Mac, Guzman, and Basker, his arm heavily wrapped and in a sling, ate their cake on the way to the gun deck. They leaned against a long gun and licked the last of the frosting from their fingers.

Guzman looked at Basker and pointed to his wound. "Too bad about your arm. Guess that leaves out baseball."

Basker and Mac shot looks of surprise at one another, then Basker replied, "No big. I'm diggin' where I am. My hitch is up in a couple months and I'm gonna re-up."

"Me too," said Guzman. "Maybe we'll ship together."

Basker offered Guzman his good left hand. "I'm cool with that—take some gettin' used to, though," he added with puzzled look on his face.

"Used to what?"

"You not bein' a asshole."

Mac and Basker kept laughing until Guzman joined in.

"Speaking of which," Mac jumped in, "and this goes for both of you anuses. It's 'rancher,' not 'farm boy.' Big difference where I come from."

"Yeah, sure," said Guzman. "*Big* difference. One pushes cows around, the other sits on a stool, reaches underneath them, and squeezes their tits."

Basker and Guzman high-fived each other, laughed, and pointed at Mac, who could only shake his head in defeat. Then their expressions changed, the laughter died, and all three went silent. They looked away for a moment before they focused back on each other, their faces blank.

****

Redding and Miriam stood on the quarterdeck. Redding was about to start the conversation when Tebic appeared from below deck with a printed message. "Uh, sorry, sir, but this just came in for you."

"How?" asked Redding, taking the message from Tebic.

Tebic beamed. "On our new radio. Admiral Towne had the spare in his Osprey yanked out, and he gave it to us. Um, Lieutenant James is mentioned on that too, so I told him about it."

"That's fine, Mr. Tebic, thank you."

The two saluted, and Tebic left as James approached.

"So, what's it say, if you don't mind my asking?" asked James as he walked toward them.

"Not at all. Don't know yet. Just got it. Hang on."

Redding read the note while Miriam and James looked at each other and shrugged. After a long pause,

Redding looked up.

"Says here I've been relieved of command, effective when we get the ship back to Boston," he said with a convincingly glum expression.

"I don't get it," stammered James.

"Oh, yeah." Redding traded the sullen look for a smile. "It also congratulates you on your promotion to commander and on being the new captain of *Constitution* at that time—and so do I," he added, extending his hand to James.

James looked stunned as they shook hands.

"Congratulations, Lieutenant Commander James," Miriam added.

"May I see that?" asked James.

Redding handed it to him. James smiled as he read the message, then pointed to the ending. "Says here, 'Big plans in the works for nationwide tour for *Constitution*—both coasts, president's orders,' " he added, grinning.

"Wow!" said Miriam with a coy look. "They act fast."

James looked up from the page. "It ends with 'Stand by for second message.' "

"Yeah. That's one I'm *really* looking forward to," said Redding apprehensively.

Redding caught a coquettish expression on Miriam's face as she looked away. "Something tells me you shouldn't worry too much about that," she said.

Redding squinted his eyes at Miriam.

"You'll miss the ship, I'm sure," James said as he walked to the gunwale and read the message again.

"Probably, but I have a hunch they'd never let me take her into battle again, so it's just as well. Besides, you belong with her. That's how these stories are supposed to end, right?" Redding pointed to James, then tapped the hull. "The boy gets the girl? God only knows what they have in store for me."

He took his hat off and examined it. "I *am* going to miss this hat, though." He played with the hat for a moment as Miriam and James smiled with amusement.

"Oh, one last thing, Paul. You'll find the log entry for July fourth is blank. I thought about it all day and couldn't find the words. It will be hard enough writing up the medal recommendations. They'll really tell the story, as far as I'm concerned."

"I couldn't have written it either," replied James. "Let's face it, that entry would be a book."

Redding and Miriam both nodded in agreement.

James saluted Redding. "Now, if you'll excuse me, we're shorthanded, so I have to take a watch and train some marines."

As James walked to the helm, Tebic returned to Redding with another message. "Thank you, Mr. Tebic."

Redding read the note and kept his focus on it while he glanced at Miriam who was chewing on her lip.

"Well, it seems I have a choice, and neither is the brig. Choices I never would have imagined."

"Strange events will do that." Then she grimaced slightly. "Sea duty?"

"No," he continued, "that's the weird part. These are strictly dry-land options."

Redding paused for several seconds studying the message.

She finally burst. "*And?*"

"One is teaching at the Naval Academy. Can you believe that? Me, a teacher? I was barely a student."

"That's not as weird as you might think," she replied. "Go on."

"The other is the Naval War College, doing God knows what."

"Well…" Miriam looked at the deck and paced as she replied, "At the academy, you would offer your perspective on topics that young officers need to get a grip on: decision making, evaluating odds, creating advantages, that sort of thing. They would look up to you as someone who isn't just teaching from a book. You would be in a position to evaluate the next generation of officers. Very important. The other is a think tank. You might give yourself a little more credit in that department. It's in Rhode Island. What do you know about that state?"

"It's small—it's cute. Keep going. This is useful."

"With the first you would be in Annapolis, near DC." She paused and looked at him. "Where I am now." She flashed a furtive glance at him.

Redding pretended to be deep in thought but peeked at her with his peripheral vision.

"With the second, you would be in my home state, where I…want to end up someday." She pulled back from him, grabbed his lapels, and looked him in the eye. "Fairchild and Mitchell's administration ends in a few months, so I will be making a decision as well."

Redding tried to control his surprise as Miriam waited for his response. "That sounds suspiciously like a proposal. Something tells me that on your walk with Mitchell you were doing all the talking."

Miriam shrugged, looked up, rolled her eyes, and

pursed her lips.

"Okay, it's official," he announced. "We're even. You suck at being coy. But as long as we're on the subject, how do you feel about adopting children?"

Miriam smiled broadly. "I'm *very* okay with it, especially since *I'm* one."

"Oh?"

"Why do you ask?"

He gazed out to sea with a look of satisfaction that surprised Miriam. "Because I have one in mind."

Miriam's brow rose as she stared at him. "Now *that* sounds suspiciously like a proposal—or at least a Moses Redding version of one."

Redding leaned away slightly and mimed a sword movement. "I can retreat, if you'd rather."

"Too late," she said as she threw her arms around him and kissed him in a way that erased any doubts he ever had. Then she leaned back and held his head in her hands.

He pulled her back in immediately and, gently holding the back of her head, kissed her until her knees buckled, then loosened his hold and pulled back slightly.

"Touché," she said. Out of breath and limp, she rested her face on his chest. "I guess those dots weren't so far apart after all."

He leaned her against the gunwale for support and put his arms around her to hold her there while he studied the ship, especially the spanker sail. Then he shook his head and turned back to her.

They leaned over the aft railing and gazed at a trail of phosphorescence revealed by the darkening sky and ignited by the wake of the ship leading away from the fire of the previous night.

Redding listened to the sounds of the young crew enjoying each other's company and perhaps the fact that they were still alive. The sounds continued to reverberate through the decks of *Constitution* as Redding and Miriam stood on the quarterdeck and gazed at the past under the boom of the spanker and the flapping parade sail.

The scars of the battle were evident everywhere as *Constitution*'s tattered sails filled with an offshore breeze that pushed her as best it could. With the return of her escorts and companions, the dolphins, she waved her ensign and showed her stern to the Libyan coast in the fading twilight of Independence Day.

Epilogue

The October day was unseasonably warm, but the leaves in Washington, DC, had already begun to adopt their fall colors. The previous weeks were jammed with events prompted by *Constitution*'s return home.

Crowds in patriotic colors and waving flags blanketed the shores of Boston harbor. It didn't matter that it was midday; fireworks greeted *Constitution* as she arrived. Air traffic from Logan International was delayed to allow the navy's Blue Angels to own the sky, streaking in formation overhead.

Humpback whales off Fort Strong on Long Island greeted the ship, breaching and spinning in the air before plunging into the water and dousing the ship's crew as they lined the gunwale.

Closer to *Constitution*'s berth, fireboats took over for the whales and spouted arcs of salutations. Where the channel narrowed and was nearly choked with pleasure boats, tugs escorted her to her berth at the museum site in Charlestown and a well-deserved rest.

As she came closer to her berth, her wounds were more visible to the onlookers, many of whom had camped for days to stake out their viewing spots and kept track on the internet of *Constitution*'s progress across the Atlantic. Fresh paint covered the temporary patch over the hole in her hull from the RPG round. Chips and gouges from the thousands of rounds of bullets that had struck her hull and masts were still raw and waiting to be repaired at home. They set the mouths of onlookers agape, and the clicking of camera shutters sounded like applause from a stadium filled with spectators.

The navy band greeted *Constitution* with "Anchors Aweigh," timed to the appearance of Navy Secretary Admiral Buckholter, Admiral Towne, and Vice President Mitchell from a VIP tent erected for the occasion, followed by the Marine Corps band trying to top the navy with their rendition of the "Marines' Hymn." Then both bands collaborated on "Hail to the Chief" as President Fairchild stepped from the tent, waved at the crowd, and made his way through the media corridor to the ship.

Indeed, Buckholter *had* brought his box of medals—a large box. The medal ceremony was lengthy, as were the speeches. Virginia Mitchell and Admiral Buckholter performed the honors when it came to the Navy Crosses, Navy Distinguished Service, and Silver Star medals, and the multitude of Purple Hearts, but Fairchild took over for the Medals of Honor for Redding and James and, posthumously, for Buckley, Cooper, Aarons, and Kobach—medals accepted by their family members—and the Medal of Freedom awarded to Miriam.

****

Moses Redding and Miriam Hannah sat together on a marble bench in Arlington Cemetery. Pushed into the background were the events of the infamous day and the weeks following *Constitution*'s return home.

Mitchell had wasted no time keeping her promise. She had personally taken charge of the site for the crew.

She found a prime, unused, and elevated location for the headstones and a commemorative marble wall. Carved into it were the names of the fallen and a poetic narrative of the event that would have made Oliver Wendell Holmes proud.

Flowers left by family members and the public still adorned the grave sites. The freshest flowers lay on Buckley's and Cooper's graves. Redding and Miriam sat beside them holding hands, as silent as their friends, knowing they owed them their future together.

A word about the author...

David Tunno is a WGA-affiliated screenwriter. *Intrepid Spirit* is based on one of his screenplays. Recently retired from a career as a trial consultant, he was a media commentator on such high-profile trials as O.J. Simpson, Rodney King, Michael Jackson, and the Unabomber. He was a commentator on KABC TV in Los Angeles, a guest on CBS's *Good Morning America*, MSNBC, and Court TV, and a source for *The New York Times* and the Canadian Broadcasting Corporation.

Visit www.tunno.com for more about his career and *Fixing the Engine of Justice: Diagnosis and Repair of Our Jury System*, his non-fiction book on the US jury system. He was a contributing author for the American Bar Association where he was also a lecturer, as he was with many bar associations across the US and UCLA's Anderson School of Business.

He holds a B.A. in theater and an M.A. in Communications. He was a professional actor with stage, film, and TV experience and is a member of the Screen Actors Guild. His background includes radio, film, and video production, radio news broadcasting, as a newspaper columnist and contributor to an online news site.

He is a sailor with cruising and racing experience and a pilot of a WWII era biplane and hot air balloons.

Learn more about David Tunno at his websites:

Tunno.com
Davidtunno.com

Thank you for purchasing
this publication of The Wild Rose Press, Inc.

For questions or more information
contact us at
info@thewildrosepress.com.

The Wild Rose Press, Inc.
www.thewildrosepress.com